What Happened

Books by Merle Miller

What Happened
On Being Different
Only You, Dick Daring (*with Evan Rhodes*)
A Secret Understanding
A Day in Late September
Reunion
A Gay and Melancholy Sound
The Judges and the Judged
The Sure Thing
That Winter
We Dropped the A-Bomb
Island 49

WHAT HAPPENED

A NOVEL BY

Merle Miller

HARPER & ROW, PUBLISHERS

NEW YORK, EVANSTON, SAN FRANCISCO, LONDON

1817

FIRST EDITION

STANDARD BOOK NUMBER: 06-012962-X

LIBRARY OF CONGRESS CATALOG CARD NUMBER: 70-96000

*This novel is dedicated to all the people
who tried to kill me along the way. And to David
I. Segal and David W. Elliott, who did not.*

What Happened

1 /

A Sacred Vow

Am I supposed to put in things you already know? Such as the fact that Christopher was here today? He thinks you're very attractive. Attractive anyway; I'm not sure about the very.

I have to admit I can't see it. Too much nose for my taste. I can't help wondering what Julius Streicher (wasn't that his name?) would have made of you in Germany in the thirties. They'd have cooked you up in a bake oven. No question of that. Me, too. Jews and fags. We went to the bake ovens together, often hand in hand.

I thought Christopher looked tired. Beautiful but tired. Did you and he light up? I notice he was wearing his rose-colored shades when he came out of your office.

I asked him what you talked about, and he said, "We talked about you, of course."

I wanted to know more but refused to ask. Christopher has to volunteer. He's like Charley in that. Charley always told you what he wanted you to know—and nothing else. It did no good to question him. He would simply say, "It's of no importance," that being a polite way of saying "Mind your own business." Charley was always courteous.

Christopher was doing his damndest not to look as triumphant as he surely cannot help feeling. The tour was an enormous success. No surprise to me. Some credit to me? Very little credit to me. I should think Christopher stopped learning anything from me at least a year and a half ago, and I doubt that he ever really needed me. A tape recording would have done as well.

I'm pleased with the success of the tour, though; at least I think I am, and I am certainly not surprised. Even the gentleman from the *Times,* long gone senile and born tone deaf, said that Christopher is ". . . the most promising talent of any pianist of his generation . . . not since young Van Cliburn ten years ago returned from his triumph in Moscow . . . a range . . . virtuosity . . . electrifying." Et cetera. You know how those people write.

Has it really been ten years since Van got back? The dark ages just ending, and I was being allowed to perform on some few platforms, and no one mentioned my personal appearances before The Committee or the magazine article all the ladies had read at their hairdressers', but I noticed that husbands no matter how decrepit, male students no matter how acned, and all Boy Scouts were kept out of reach. I saw a number of people looking at the scars on my wrists; my first appearance at Bellevue got quite a good notice in the *Daily News.*

The gentleman from the *Times* is right about Christopher. I think too conservative, though. I think that not since Schnabel . . . But then in addition to being in love with Christopher, I was his teacher.

He seems to be enjoying his success, not feeling guilty about it. That is one of the differences between us. I went on every stage as if I were on trial for my life and knew I'd be found guilty. I always wanted the adulation and always did everything possible to prevent it.

Oh, I have very high hopes for Christopher, provided he doesn't . . . The pitfalls come by the millions, and I have stumbled into all of them, often several times, and I have seldom been able to climb out. Why else am I here, for God's sake?

But Christopher is more resolute than I, more disciplined, more talented, certainly more beautiful, and he wants it, whatever *it* is.

And Christopher has not yet learned that life is a series of failures, that no triumph, however small, is complete, that nobody has it made, that there are no happy endings, that justice never triumphs, not for more than an hour or so at a time, that the only thing worse than today is tomorrow, that they never stop chipping away at you, and that one morning when you go in to shave there is no reflection in the mirror.

Christopher left his new publicity photograph, outlandishly autographed. God, I love him—such a soft-spoken boy, so polite; tough, too, though, determined, and all that incredible energy and chutzpah. Charm, too, great charm. Of course he has. Charm is required, along with gym and freshman English, in the Louisville public schools. Unless you're black.

Christopher is also smart enough to recognize the dangers of charm, and he relies on it only when it is necessary to get what he wants, which is everything that isn't nailed down.

Christopher's father disappeared in a bottle of bourbon shortly after Christopher was born, and his mother, a Louisville belle and a beauty as well as a charter Kentucky colonel, raised Christopher and a number of highly successful racehorses, among them two winners of the Derby. Christopher looks a good deal like her, although less militaristic. Beautiful, though. She absolutely insisted on that. Once she looked across the dinner battlement and pointed to a disturbance on his chin.

"Is that a pimple?" she asked.

Christopher confessed with shame that it was.

"Get rid of it," said the colonel, and since it was a direct order from his commanding officer, Christopher did.

Beautiful and nineteen. Myself, I cannot remember ever being nineteen and was certainly never beautiful. Baldness, for instance. It seems to me I have always been bald. Christopher's hair, shoulder length, is only a little blonder than God had in mind. His face has been described as Elizabethan, whatever that means. The Earl of Southampton or Shakespeare?

Christopher looks the way young pianists are supposed to look but almost never do. The first day I met him . . . he was sixteen, and the colonel said, "I know all about you, and you are a first-rate pianist, possibly more than that, and I am assured that you are also a good teacher. I read the article concerning you in *Confidential* magazine when I was at the beauty parlor some years back, and while I do not approve of such a publication and am glad that it is no longer with us, I notice that you did not sue, which I take it for granted means that the accusations are true. Now my son is a virgin, and I have every intention that he will remain that way."

I stood at attention, braced my chin, saluted, and said, "Sir, I assure you I have never raped anybody my whole life through."

"I count that as a sacred vow," said the colonel.

It turned out that Christopher was not quite a virgin; mothers, even when they are field-grade officers, are often mistaken about such matters.

For a young man six three in height, Christopher is possessed of extraordinary grace. He plays tennis, does various unseemly things on a surfboard, and is forever tanned, head to toe. He travels with four sun lamps and is often mistaken for a California boy.

When he walks on stage wearing the perfectly tailored tails, the white collar that resembles a ruff, and the smile, do you wonder that even before he seats himself at the piano, certain ladies in the audience feel a twitter in areas of their bodies they thought had long since gone dormant? And are you surprised at his popularity with the female grizzly bears who book all concerts?

Another thing. Christopher does not play the piano with his nose, as André Watts tends to and, on occasion, Van. You can forgive André. I can anyway, because he's so beautiful. Van, poor dear, has to get by on his talent.

❖

All right then. Assuming Christopher avoids some of the pitfalls, he ought to go straight to the top. Straight? I honestly don't think he has decided what sex he is. He has tried it with everything there is, including one small, nonpoisonous snake.

Straight to the top, and in the musical histories I will be a footnote: "Lionel, George, composer-pianist-conductor (1920–   ), teacher of Christopher Van der Zee, perhaps the foremost pianist of his day."

This afternoon Christopher said that he loved me, always would, he said, forever and a day.

I wonder where he will telephone from and will it be on the next tour or the one after that. . . . Maybe he won't telephone, which is the coward's way out. I always did. A coward, too? Alas, except in the war, I'm afraid so.

It's entirely possible that Christopher will perform the bloody deed in person, take my swollen hand in his, huge and brown—my God what fingers the boy has—look at me with those no-longer-quite-so-innocent blue eyes, and say that in Milwaukee (you can't drink beer all the time) or Kansas City (stay out of the railroad station; I've been busted there twice, both times by the same gay members of the vice squad) or San Francisco (I once fell in love four times on the way from the Mark Hopkins to the concert hall; the curtain rose a little late that night) he met . . . It could be a girl; I told you he hasn't made up his mind, and why should he have to, ever?

And through thinner, paler lips, he will say, "I'd give anything in the world not to. . . ."

Forever and a day? Never. Not during this waltz. Hogamus-higamus.

How do I know it will happen? I know because if Christopher doesn't say it, and soon, too, I will. I always do. I'm the leaver. Who was it who said, "You'll never forgive me for having sent me away, will you?"

I leave, sir, lest I be left. Strike lest I be struck. . . . Don't we all, always?

I know it will because I am officially forty-nine; the press releases
said so. I've only been officially forty-nine for a year or so. I was
thirty-nine for four years, five months, and two days.

I know it will happen because not long after Christopher and I
became lovers, about half an hour after the colonel left us alone for
the first time, he said, "You are the most intelligent person I have
ever met, and you are a fool."

And he was right.

So I am officially forty-nine, and Christopher is nineteen, just. My
God, the things they've got waiting for him. . . . I was eighteen the
year I met The Clarinet Player, played my first concert at Town
Hall, was wildly praised by the *Times*, went to London, and . . . I
was nineteen the year I wrote in the journal, "I believe that anything
is possible for me."

And meant it.

Christopher has a concert in Washington tomorrow night, and I
wished him all the best. I wish him all the best. When I'm with
him, I keep thinking of something my father once said: "I wish I
could do your suffering for you, but I'm afraid I can't."

I wish I could do Christopher's suffering for him; I wish I could
keep him from all harm.

Christ, he doesn't even know that the gods are jealous.

Forgive me. I cannot go on, not tonight. I keep thinking of the
first concert I played in Washington; Mrs. Roosevelt was there, and
afterward she came backstage, and . . . And two hours after that I
managed to get myself arrested in Lafayette Square.

My God, what talent I had then. A few days before I came here—
have I mentioned it?—I listened to a record I made that year. Beethoven's *Appassionata*. It was so good that . . . Put it this way. It was
better than Glenn Gould ever dreamed. . . . Artur Rubenstein
wouldn't even place. . . . Not as good as Christopher. Or Kapell.
Kapell was a pounder, but he was good.

Talent. How did I manage to dissipate it so completely? Why?
. . . No, I don't expect you to answer that one. I don't even expect

God to do that. . . . I'll tell you one thing, though. It would be helpful to believe in God at a time like this.

Before my mother made me sign up with the Presbyterians, I used to play organ in the First Methodist Episcopal. Five dollars a week and a quick grope from the Reverend Mr. . . . I never believed in God, though.

> Abide with me: fast falls the eventide;
> The darkness deepens: Lord, with me abide . . .

2 /

Conspiracy
and Circumcision

I didn't think it was much of a session. I guess I expect miracles. At these prices wouldn't you? . . . I know you never claimed . . . I am not accusing you. I am stating a simple fact. I am not one whit better than the day I came here, whenever that was. Forever ago. I was born here, wasn't I? I know I'm never leaving; you can count on that. Except feet first . . . One whit. Is a whit smaller or larger than an iota? A jot?

Such things used to worry me. I used to look things up. And I could memorize things, and I could hear.

Dear, fear, spear, queer.

The boy who used to be a ballet dancer followed me back here. He's a comely youth, but he's nutty as a fruitcake, and I said nothing doing. I said I'd given it up. I said I've sworn off. I said I eschew sex.

It was not always thus. Years used to go by when I thought about nothing but sex. I thought about sex, and I drank. And once in a while I'd play "Chopsticks" or run off a concerto for the left hand.

Why do you always accuse me of exaggerating? I almost never do. I almost never lie, either. . . . Hope to die.

Christopher is the same way. He thinks I exaggerate. He refuses to believe, for instance, that sometimes when I'm alone in a room

I burst into tears. For no apparent reason. Even if you or Christopher were to ask, I wouldn't be able to tell you the reason. Because there isn't any one reason. Everything and nothing is the reason.

A few months ago Christopher came into the studio, and there I sat, my head on the black keys, bawling my eyes out. Christopher said, "For God's sake, what's wrong?"

I said, "Nothing. I mean nothing special."

Christopher didn't believe me. He said, "At least whoever it was didn't beat you up."

I tried to tell him there hadn't been anybody, but he still didn't believe me. Would I have believed me when I was Christopher's age? Oh, I think so. I have always been melancholy, pessimistic, disappointed. Nothing has ever lived up to expectations. Believe me, nothing, ever.

I despise people who claim they had happy childhoods. They're all liars.

I was disenchanted the instant I leapt out of the womb, in full control of my faculties, like Minerva, which, not at all incidentally, was the name my mother had picked out for me. That and a crib lined in pink satin. She wouldn't let me out of that crib until I was sixteen or so. And I thought she would never let me graduate from breast feeding. I used to leave teeth marks all over the things. I was sure that the milk was laced with arsenic.

And after I reached the age of reason, about two months or so, I wouldn't touch a drop of the stuff. Sorry, Mums, I'm on the wagon. Nothing personal, dear heart. I'm just full up, and for once my eyes aren't bigger than my stomach.

I suppose you might say I've been making up for that early oral drought ever since. All of my habits are oral, the good ones (are there any?) and the bad, which are abundant and without exception illegal. . . . My God, they can't poison that, can they?

You can see what I mean about tits, though. Do you wonder that since Mums at last put them away, I haven't been near a pair. During the big-tit period in the movies, I tried not even to go within a block of a place where a tit picture was playing. Jayne Mansfield and Jane Russell haunted my dreams, not Boris Karloff. . . . Exaggerate? Who needs to?

   You are right about Rosenberg. He did have almost as great an influence on my life as either my father or mother. Or Charley. Or Lily . . . You Jews. As my mother so often said, "Jews are pushy; they like to crowd, and they take care of their own."

   Rosenberg. That was the way I thought of him at the time and still do. His given name was Murray, but it was so flagrantly inappropriate that I was incapable of calling him that or thinking of him as that.

   People like Rosenberg shouldn't have given names: Chaplin, Dietrich, Garbo, Rosenberg.

   I may tend to romanticize him, to make him larger and better than he was. I loved him, you see, not sexually, not remotely that. I loved him because he played the piano the way I wanted to, still want to, never will.

   I learned more about the piano from Rosenberg than from anybody else, including Lester Brockhurst, the teacher in New York who was said to be the greatest piano teacher of his time. I learned more from Rosenberg than from everybody else.

   The concert was on a night in February when nobody could remember the sun, and there were fifteen of us in the high school auditorium. When Lois Washington, the local librarian, introduced Rosenberg she said that she had already explained to our distinguished guest that due to the inclement weather—it was almost twenty below—scores of those she was sure had been looking forward to hearing him had simply been unable to get their driveways plowed or their cars started.

   That may have been true in a case or two, but even on the balmiest evenings there were never more than twenty-five or thirty people present. Not many people in town cared for music. Then, too, they were *her* concerts, *her* being Charley's mother, Sarah McCormick Payne. God, how they hated her.

"We drive to Des Moines when *we* want to hear some music. We just wouldn't give *her* the satisfaction." "Luveen and I never miss a Walter Damrosch concert on our Philco; we have the custom-built model; they don't even carry them at Smith's, not enough call at that price, and even at Yonker's in Des Moines the little clerk said they don't sell more than three or four a year. . . ." "I wouldn't put it past *her* to be getting a rake-off on those concerts, so called. . . ."

The man who walked on stage, without so much as a glance at the tiny audience, without a bow or a nod or a smile, was small-boned and short, no more than five three, and he was thin almost to the point of emaciation, the latter due to the fact that he never ate. In the nine years I studied with him, I never remember him eating, and I saw him almost every day.

Rosenberg's hair was thin, and even from where I sat, in the third row, I could see that his uneven shoulders were laden with dandruff. His eyes were large and wide and without hope; his mouth was thin and disapproving. His nose—ah, yes, doctor, his nose—was spectacular, as large, almost as large, as all the other features of his face combined. It was hooked, and it was speckled and as red and angry as a stoplight. One was tempted to ask if Rosenberg wanted tea or sugar with it. One thought of Cyrano.

His hands and wrists were large for the rest of him, and they were powerful. He was thirty years old, but that is only a statistic. Rosenberg had no age. His bloodshot, despairing eyes had seen everything and everybody and did not think much of anything or anybody. His voice was hoarse and harsh, from whiskey and cigarettes and disappointment. The tails he wore were not new. They looked as if they had never been new, and the suit had not been cleaned or pressed for some time. His tie was crooked, and his ruffled shirt was wrinkled, and as he played, it bunched up in front of his inadequate chest.

But then he placed those hands on the keys of the Steinway and began eight "Novelettes" by Schumann. After that everything else about him became inconsequential. I felt then the way I felt in London the first time I heard Emil Gilels. . . . Oh, yes; he's the best. No one else comes close. Not even Christopher. Sorry, love.

After the Schumann, Rosenberg played several of the Beethoven sonatas, ending with the *Appassionata*. . . . Ludwig wasn't what you'd call a reverential man. If he were around today, they'd have him up before more congressional committees than I appeared before. And my, what trouble Rosenberg would have if he were still around. He was a card-carrying member of. At least he said he was. And when he got drunk and disorderly, which was every night except, occasionally, on Sundays, he showed his card or what he claimed was his membership card to everybody. And to some people, like Chief of Police William H. Bender and Sheriff George B. Grossneck, he would say, "Come the revolution, I'm going to take care of you personally. Now how do you want to go—guillotine, hanging, deballing, or just plain shot?"

When the concert was over, all fifteen of us rose, and we applauded as long and as loud as we could; my hands were sore for days afterward.

Rosenberg rose, too, and still without a look at his audience walked offstage, and he did not return for an encore or a single bow.

Somehow—I wasn't sure how we got there, my mother always managed those things—we were backstage. Rosenberg, who was wet with sweat, was wiping his face with a damp towel. Sarah McCormick Payne was just behind me, as was Lois Washington. But as usual, my mother spoke first. She was holding my hand tight, and she said, "Sonny here plays the piano, too."

Rosenberg looked at me and said, "I'm sure of it."

"I thought perhaps if you had a minute, he might play for you. He does the Schumann."

"Madame," said Rosenberg, whose face was very white, "I would rather die than hear your son *do* the Schumann or anything else."

I didn't play, and Rosenberg didn't die, but he did something almost as spectacular. He fainted. He was taken to Mercy Hospital in an ambulance and was found to be suffering from, among other things, malnutrition and various ailments of the liver.

During the seven weeks Rosenberg was in the hospital I went every afternoon to ask about him, and the aging nun at the desk—she had the face of a saint betrayed—always said that he was coming along just fine. I never asked, but she also always said that Mr. Rosenberg was seeing no visitors.

By the third week I had saved up enough money from selling *Liberty* magazine to send him a dozen red roses, along with a card, unsigned, saying, "You are the greatest pianist I have ever heard, including Paderewski." I did not add that I had only heard Paderewski on the Victrola.

On the evening of the day Rosenberg was released from the hospital the personals column of the paper had a paragraph saying that he would remain in town for a while, to recuperate. He was in a weakened condition, suffering from . . . And he might possibly *consider* taking a few talented students of the piano, if he could find any who were qualified. *Consider* was in italics.

My father read the item aloud at supper. He said, "Do you want to take George or shall I?"

For my father to volunteer to do anything, to leave the house even, except to go to work, was unprecedented. He was the least aggressive, most inward man I have ever known; he was a man destined to lose, and he was the shyest man I have ever known. . . . I could never love anybody who wasn't shy.

My mother sighed loftily. "I'd rather take a licking. Rosenberg is a mean, pushy Hebrew, and I have never been so insulted in my born days as I was by what he said the night of the concert."

"He was sick," said my father.

"And he drinks like a fish. The paper practically comes right out and says so. How else would he have all that liver trouble? I don't want sonny to start drinking at his age, and you know how he picks things up from people."

"I doubt if there's much danger of that for a year or so."

"I just can't bring myself to do it, because the less you have to do with Jews in any way, shape, or form, the better off we all are, and he could try to get sonny into it."

"Into what?"

"They have this international conspiracy that Father Coughlin is forever warning us against. They even operate on them, and, Sonny, I don't care if I do say so, I do not want you circumcised. At your age you might catch blood poisoning, and while some people trust Rabbi Krantman, I would not want him, under the influence of Rosenberg, to . . . You know what I mean, Monte."

"I don't believe sonny has to worry about that."

"I know, Monte. You are inclined to scoff at Father Coughlin, and in the meantime, unbeknownst to any of us, the Jew communists on Wall Street—"

"I'll take him then," said my father.

"No, Monte, I'll take him. I would not want it said after I pass on that I have failed my duty."

It was March. It seems to me in those days it was always either March or October. Before dawn, the sky still gray, my mother, her only begotten in tow, was pounding on the front door of the peeling clapboard house on East Main where, the day before, Rosenberg had rented a room. I had a feeling it was the first place he stopped and, as it turned out, it was also the last, and that may have been the only luck in the whole of his luckless life.

The landlady, a member of a number of the same time-wasting organizations as my mother, was one Florence Canady, Mrs. Florence Canady; I don't know what happened to Mr. Canady.

My mother continued pounding until a voice from inside shouted something, and lights were flung on, and there was the sound of a wheezing, heavy body descending a staircase, I prayed not nude, and Our Lady of the Camellias opened the front door.

"Of all people, Mrs. Lionel," she said, "and at this hour."

Her sparse gray hair was in curlers; her body, largely gone to breast, was only partially concealed in a begrimed dressing gown that had once been crimson and, possibly, silk. It several times fell open all the way, and Florence Canady was wearing nothing else save the curlers and slippers and a little lipstick that she had hastily smeared just below her nose so as to conceal part of her mustache. I had never seen down there on a woman before. It didn't interest me much.

"I'm sorry to disturb you, Florence dear," said my mother, "but it's about sonny. He wants to take piano lessons. From the Jew."

Mrs. Canady gave me a gap-toothed, idiot smile. "I've heard you're a regular little wizard of the keyboard," she said. "Can you play any Irish airs?"

I believe I said that, unfortunately, my repertoire of Irish airs was limited.

"I could hum a few to show you," said Florence Canady.

"I'm sure that would be lovely," said my mother, "but the way time flies . . ."

"I wouldn't want to vouch for what might or might not happen in the lesson line," said Florence Canady. "Mrs. Dr. Jacobs was here yesterday with little Elaine, and you know how she can make a piano talk. Well, she started to play for the Jew, and I couldn't help but overhear. The language, the shouting, the names he called her. He said such an awful thing, Dora. He said they ought to cut off her hands rather than allow the little thing near a piano. Isn't that awful?"

"Awful," said my mother, but she said it without conviction, and she could not completely suppress a smile. I giggled. I was beginning to like Rosenberg as a person as well as a pianist.

"What kind of names did he call her?" I asked.

"Little pitchers have big ears," said my mother, throwing a conspiratorial glance in Florence Canady's direction.

"There was others trying to get him to learn them," said Elizabeth Barrett Browning. "They was all crying when they left. He wouldn't take any of them, and if you ask me, now that he's paid a week's rent in advance, the poor man don't have a red cent to his name."

My mother made a sound with her tongue, and I said, "I'd still like to know what names he called Elaine Jacobs, and I agree that it wouldn't be a bad idea to cut off her hands, but in the meantime, I'm freezing to death."

As I say, it was March, and the temperature was two above.

In the Canady kitchen, where the temperature must have been at least ninety, I gnawed at a debilitated doughnut and drank a glass of milk.

"The poor man was up all night," said the head of the House of Usher, "playing records. Mrs. Nose-in-the-Air—and you know who I mean by that, Dora—sent him a portable Victrola and some records when he was in the hospital. Sister Leonie told me that, but I haven't breathed it to a soul. *She* was after something. Had to be."

"Had to be," said my mother, using her bridge club voice.

"I'm glad for his sake," said Mrs. Canady. "He does like his music. Of course *maybe* what she had in mind was trying to jew him out of free lessons for that stuck-up son of theirs."

"I'm told he's not at all musically inclined," said my mother. "Is the Jew up there now?"

"He's asleep now. But like I said, he was up all night, ranting and raving, and some of the words in a foreign tongue. Drinking, too. He went down to . . . well, you know where he went, Dora, and he brought back three bottles of the stuff she sells. I'm referring to her bottled wares, though heaven alone knows what else . . . Anyway, I wouldn't put it past him to of drunk all three. Sister Leonie said he shouldn't be allowed a drop, but if they want a drink, how can you keep it from them is what I say."

"What time do you think sonny and I should come back?"

"Around one. I'll try and get some food in the poor man."

We were back at one.

I spent so many thousands of hours in that upstairs bedroom in the Canady house. Nine years, five days a week, three hours a day, sometimes more. Rosenberg could have been a rich man if he'd charged my dear mother at his regular rate, but he only charged for one lesson a week, one hour's worth. He insisted on that. "It keeps our relationship professional instead of personal," he said. "I insist on that." Do you wonder that I loved him?

The room was small, ten by twelve. The carelessly plastered ceiling and walls were painted a disconcerting shade of brown that grew darker and more menacing with each passing day. There was a scarred commode on top of which Rosenberg kept his unopened bottles. The empty bottles he put in the drawers and eventually someone, it must have been Florence Canady, threw them away.

An upright piano rented from SMITH'S MUSIC, CARDS FOR EVERY OCCASION, AND BOOKS was in the middle of the room, always in tune. For all I know, Rosenberg tuned it himself. Two adornments on the brown walls, one a print of a portrait of Beethoven—the demanding eyes, the wide, despairing mouth, the sorrowing chin: "Pity, pity—too late." The portrait was in a silver frame, the only evidence in the room that Rosenberg had known better days.

On the opposite wall, unframed, was the quotation from Herodotus that I then found so odd. "I know that the gods are jealous, for I cannot remember that I ever heard of a man who, having been constantly successful, did not at last utterly perish."

The narrow brass bed was covered with an apologetic throw, a chilling yellow. One did not have to test the mattress to know that it was lumpy. On the straight-back chair near the bed was the portable Victrola that Sarah McCormick Payne had given Rosenberg. And the records. Two dozen or so in the beginning; in the end, hundreds. I never knew what happened to the records.

That first afternoon Rosenberg was standing near the single window. It was open a few inches, the cold pouring in, making the room seem even more dismal. I knew he had been drinking, but I don't think my mother did. She said, "You may remember we have met."

"That is not the way I would describe our encounter," said Rosenberg, "but I have not forgotten you. Or *it*." *It* was me.

"I told you that sonny boy plays. He's been playing since he was a mere tot of less than four. We're a musical family. My mother played at the church. It was only a country church, of course, in Montour, but she played every Sunday and at Grange meetings— 'Humoresque,' Beethoven's Minuet in G, other classics. We're all of us musical. I sing. Christmas before last us Methodists did Handel's *Messiah,* and I . . . His father is an accomplished pianist as well, by ear; he can't read a note, but when he sits down—"

"Madame . . ."

"My dear mother has long since passed on, and she left us the piano in her will, and one day, as I say, sonny was only four years old, but when he got home from nursery—"

"Madame . . ."

"He'd heard it just once. Beethoven's . . . What was it called, Sonny?" No answer from sonny. After a look at Rosenberg's inflamed nose . . . "Well, to make a long story short, he's been playing ever since. His father drives him to Des Moines once a week, where he takes a lesson from a full professor of piano. At Drake University. Dr. Gordoni, Giuseppe Gordoni. You are no doubt familiar with him."

"I could not possibly be *familiar* with a full professor of piano, not under any imaginable circumstance."

"And twice a week sonny studies with the world-renowned Dolly Jackson, who has favored our community by settling down on West Maple, the old Vreeland manse. . . ."

My mother looked once more at Rosenberg's nose and perhaps realized that the renown of Dolly Jackson, befuddled by senility and bronchitis, had not reached him. She finished in a voice that was less than a whisper. "And sonny practices two hours every morning *before* he goes to school; he gets up at five, and in the afternoon, the minute he is dismissed from school, he rushes home. . . ."

Rosenberg scratched his nose. He closed his eyes, opened them, pointed to the piano, and said, "Play."

I played the Schumann Fantasy in C Major. I played it without error, all the right notes in the wrong way. When I had finished, Rosenberg was still looking out the window; he said nothing.

After a time, my mother said, "Didn't you think . . . ? What did you think?"

Still looking out the window, Rosenberg said, "What do you want me to say, madame? That in this desolate, windswept spate of ugliness I have listened to a great, even a good pianist? I have not. The boy is clearly a diligent worker, and considering the fact that he has ten thumbs, there were some few moments when the sounds I heard didn't cause me to shudder too violently. Beyond that, nothing."

He looked at me. "At least you didn't play a dainty little Chopin prelude."

"Will you take him on?" said my mother. "He is so eager to learn, and the night after your concert at the high school, he said . . . well, that he would like to study with you, and I have to admit his opinion of the good doctor at Drake and Dolly Jackson, world-renowned though she may be, is not favorable. He is not an easy little boy to please."

"I shall give it consideration," said Rosenberg.

My mother, not usually a shy woman where money was concerned, said, "I don't usually like to talk about . . . financial matters with an artist."

"How foolish of you. There is nothing artists enjoy talking about more. I charge the pupils I do take ten dollars an hour."

My mother made her famous clucking noise. She gave a noted imitation of a bantam hen. She said, "That is the most ridiculous thing I ever heard of. Dr. Gordoni—and he has played as far east as Davenport—only charges five dollars an hour, and Dolly Jackson only charges two."

"I believe in Miss Jackson's case—and I'm sure she's a miss—the two dollars should be left on the mantel."

"At ten dollars an hour we'd never be able to make ends meet."

"Madame, spare me the details of meeting your ends. I must tell you in advance that I see no evidence of real ability in your son. Of course I know *why* he wants to play the piano. All little sissies want to play the piano. Because it's so delicate. They don't have to get their pretty little hands dirty. They want to play because they're sissies, not because they have any real interest in or aptitude for music."

My mother said, "How dare . . . ?"

And in my mightiest voice I said, "Listen, you drunken Jewish sonofabitch, why don't you give me a chance?"

Rosenberg looked at me with what in someone else I might have thought was respect. "At least you're not held together with flour paste," he said. And to my mother, "Against my better judgment, I'll do it."

"Under the circumstances," said my mother, "perhaps we could make a more reasonable financial arrangement."

"Madame," said Rosenberg. "You seem to forget. *I* am the Jew."

3 /

Honoring My Father—
and Yes, I Suppose
My Mother, Too

I was very young, no more than six or seven, when my father read aloud to me: " 'Wishing to keep the prince ignorant of pain and of evil, the king had a heavy wall built around the palace, pierced by a single door with heavy bars.' "

I don't know where that's from; you'd think I'd have looked it up, but I never did. The things I never did. What did I do? When? . . . I was always busy, but I never got anything done. Not in the last ten years anyway, the last ten or twenty or thirty.

". . . George Lionel, the former child prodigy who is no longer a prodigy."

My father read that quotation for me, and he said, "I wish I could keep you ignorant of pain and of evil, but I'm not a king, and even he didn't make out too well in that."

If I could, I'd do that for Christopher. I would keep him ignorant of pain and of evil. I would protect him from all harm. If I knew how.

Of all my sons Christopher is the best, and I love him, am in love with him. I would gladly give my life, and all of that. . . . But I can do nothing more for him. I've taught him all I know. I've cherished him, now and again, when I remembered, when I wasn't too busy doing inconsequential things.

I've even been gentle with him. Sometimes. That's the hardest part. Being gentle takes a lot out of you.

When I was a child and was happy—and there were such times now and again, a moment here, a second there, I used to pray. No, I didn't believe in God. I told you that. You never listen. I didn't believe in God. But why take a chance? Why not cover all bets?

My prayer was always the same; it was: "Oh, God, keep it always now. Please."

He never did, though, not once. Like you, He was never listening. . . . But please, keep it always now for Christopher. Keep Christopher hopeful. Keep him beautiful. Keep him from being scarred by disappointment and defeat. From the loss of hair and teeth and talent. Keep it always now for Christopher.

> When other helpers fail, and comforts flee,
> Help of the helpless, O abide with me!

I had the most terrifying dream about Christopher last night. I dreamed that he had been . . . I almost telephoned to see if he was all right. I didn't, though. He needs his sleep, poor lamb. Tomorrow night he has a concert in San Francisco, and he's staying at the Mark Hopkins. But he won't be late for the concert, as I was. He won't search along the way for love, as I did. He doesn't need it the way I did, the way I do.

Love, love, love. It keeps being spoken of. By me. I cannot move without love, eat without it, breathe without it. It has motivated every conscious effort of my life. I have had always to make everybody love me.

But the minute it happens, he has to be punished for making the mistake of loving me.

And people who are dying to meet me have to be punished, too. The recreation director is dying to meet me. She wants me to take part in some *group* activities. She's heard me play, and she thinks . . . And you think it might not be a bad idea if I did it.

You know, every time I decide you're halfway intelligent, you come up with some imbecile nonsense like that.

I tell you. In my whole life I have never *ever* wanted to meet anybody who wanted to meet me. What kind of person would? Nobody nice. I'll tell you that.

It's the ones who don't want to meet me that I've always tried to captivate, transport, infatuate, enamor, ravish, enchant, bewitch.

How many times have we discussed it? Two hundred thousand dollars' worth of time, easily. And have you ever come up with anything remotely helpful? You have not. Nobody ever has. It's always that shit about how I ought to be fonder of myself. As if I didn't know. As if I hadn't tried.

But it has never worked. I am simply not my type. Sorry there, old boy. Now that you've stepped out of the shadows . . . Do excuse me. It was a case of mistaken identity. I thought I was somebody else, prayed I was somebody else. But I never will be, will I? Not this time around. And I don't want to come back as anything. Once is enough. Once is too much. I knew that the day I arrived.

Love, lovers. I take my lovers to distant lands, on expensive tours that bankrupt me; I buy them automobiles, town houses, country estates. I supply them with allowances fit for a king, present them with rubies and gold, frankincense and myrrh. Oh, I shower them with gifts, flood them, inundate them, but I am seldom kind to them.

Why is that, do you suppose? If you could answer that one, you might be worth the thousand dollars a minute you're charging me.

But about my father—and my mother. She once said, "Nothing ever satisfies you, does it? Nothing is ever good enough for you. I guess you get that from your father. Well, that's the only thing you'll ever get from him; so you'd better make the most of it."

And she sighed; she was a sigher. It's true about my father, though I'd have put it in a slightly different way. I'd say he was always dissatisfied with the state of things as they were, but then what I have never understood is how anybody nice could be satisfied. . . . And nothing gets better, you know; I've been around all these centuries, and not only have I not improved the planet. It deteriorates every second. With every breath I take. How could I have allowed it to happen?

My father. We were living on a twice-mortgaged, dust-blown farm just off the Lincoln Highway, and in the *Des Moines Register* that day was the news that Nicola Sacco and Bartolomeo Vanzetti had been executed. I doubt if anybody else in town had ever even heard of them, let alone mourned their passing.

But on that humid day in August my father, a majority of one, stood in a field of unharvested wheat, shook an angry fist at the sky, and wept.

Later he said, "I wonder if we will ever outgrow our need for human sacrifice." . . . He didn't? Baby, don't fuck around with my memory. It's all I've got left. Let it lie. Let it be kind. . . . "That last moment belongs to us—that agony is our triumph."

I remember when my father started to die.

I was twenty; I'd been in New York almost two years, the most perfect time of my life, or so it seems to me now. But maybe I was only young.

I was twenty and had just won the Leventritt, and while my name wasn't quite a Household Word, the way Van Cliburn's was almost twenty years later, in music circles I was just about the hottest thing around.

I never had a ticker tape parade, but my Rachmaninoff Concerto no. 3 was as good as Van's, in some ways better. The Philadelphia record is still in print, and only last year a critic for one of the stereo magazines compared it with Van's and André's. ". . . Of the three, Lionel's is by far the richest, the most sonorous. These days we are inclined to forget that young George Lionel had a pianistic technique that was reminiscent of the master of them all, Josef Lhevinne, and at his best Lionel . . ."

❖

I was on my way to a concert in Omaha. I walked in the front door of the tired green house on South Third Avenue, closed it behind me, and said, "Surprise, surprise."

My mother, who was on her knees waxing the floor in the hall, went white, stood up, and said, "You're in trouble. Bad trouble. I'm not surprised. I knew the minute that, despite my warning, you said you were going to New York . . ."

And there I was, a child again, naked and nine.

I guess you never outgrow that particular terror. Not if you live to be a hundred. Never. Once, I can't remember when, after I was grown, though, she said, "When you were just a little baby, not even a year old yet, I looked at you, and I don't know what came over me, but I thought, Sonny and I will never be close, and we never have been, have we? I blame myself, but those things are never anybody's fault, are they?"

I said, no, they aren't, and for all I know that's true, but I'd have done anything to get her approval. Oh, yes, anything. Hands and knees on broken glass, coast to coast . . . My father? He already approved of me. No need to work on that.

My mother kissed me, a beak's brush on the cheek, glanced at me, as usual found me wanting. "You're thin as a rail."

"As a matter of fact, I've gained eight pounds since the last time you saw me."

"You've lost weight. Now don't be afraid to tell your mother what's wrong. It's serious, isn't it?"

"Mom, I have never felt better in my life, especially since winning the prize."

"Yes, I've heard about that, but it's been my experience that a thing like that and a nickel will buy you a cup of coffee. You haven't had breakfast."

"I had breakfast on the train."

"The train—and what kind of breakfast is that at those prices?"

She led me, a drill sergeant with a platoon of one, to the kitchen and poured me a cup of coffee. The pot had been on the stove for hours. "The more it ages the better it gets; your Grandmother Winders was known for her coffee, and she used to keep it on the stove for days at a time. It was the talk of the community. I'm going to make you a little breakfast."

"Mom, I told you. I've had breakfast."

"Yes, of course, and that's why you're as thin as a pencil. You've had breakfast. In a pig's eye."

No change there, and it was going to be at least a side of bacon. And a dozen eggs. And baking powder biscuits. And the sausages. "Uncle George brought them after he butchered in the fall. They'll be good for you after all that Jew food you've been getting in Jew York." And the orange juice. And the jams. And the jellies. And the preserves.

"Now in the first place, whatever kind of trouble you're in, I'm glad to see you, and your father will be, too, although if you'd just taken my advice and . . . How many pancakes can you eat?"

"Some more coffee?"

"No, thanks. I've already had at least a dozen cups."

"Another drop or two won't hurt you. Have you got a girl? I'll bet you dollars to donuts you've met—"

"I haven't got a girl. I haven't got time."

I couldn't help wondering what she would have thought of The Clarinet Player. . . . Never had New York seemed so safely, sweetly far away.

"Well, if you're telling the truth, and I've told you time and again never to lie to your mother, that's probably just as well, at least for the time being. You'll marry and settle down and raise a family, but at this juncture getting saddled with a wife is just about the worst thing there is to hold a man back. Especially if you married beneath you. You do know how to take the proper precautions, don't you?"

"I do. How's Pop?"

"I want to talk to you about your father. You might just as well know. I've been worried."

She looked worried. She had dark eyes, and when she didn't

sleep, great purple circles appeared below them, as there were that morning.

"I worry about him," she said, "although I don't know why I should. If he were any kind of provider, he'd make money enough so that we both could go away someplace for the winter, and we wouldn't feel so run-down all the time."

"What's wrong with Pop?"

"It may just be my imagination, but I don't think he's been feeling up to snuff these last few weeks. Now why don't you run out and have a little talk, the two of you."

"I'll go out and say hello."

"And you're going to stay at least a week, at least, and I'm going to fatten you up, and there is no reason in the world for you to go back to New York. Ever. You could enroll at the university, second semester, and New York is a long way from home when you're down and out. And you will just never make out in a place like Jew York. . . ."

She said that and more, and before I was out the door, she was on the phone. "You could have knocked me over with a feather when he walked in looking like a million, new clothes, and he's put on weight, and . . . You read about his winning the Leventhal contest. Well, that is only one thing. To cap the climax, he . . ."

Not only had I been given the keys to Manhattan, been elected mayor, replaced Toscanini: ". . . and right at this very minute he's on his way to Omaha, Nebraska, to . . ."

Was, was, had, had, would, would. "It's no surprise to me. I always knew that sonny would go to the top in whatever line of work he was in. And Iowa is no place for a boy with his talents, his genius, if I do say so myself. And he has no interest in any way, shape, or form in being a big frog in . . ."

In those days a lot of backyards in that part of town had barns, built to accommodate the horses when people still drove horses, and cows; everybody used to keep a cow, even in my childhood. You milked your own cow, and if there was any milk left over, you either sold it to the neighbors or gave it away. My father always gave it away.

And pigs. Before anybody had heard of zoning laws, if you wanted to keep a few pigs, you did. And chickens. Nearly everybody had chickens and chicks, baby chicks. One of my earliest sorrows was coloring a chick blue for Easter. I must have squeezed it too hard because it stopped breathing. I cried for days.

Another early nightmare was of my mother decapitating a chicken by stepping on its head and of the headless thing jumping all over the backyard, spreading blood and terror on the grass.

"What do you mean you're not hungry? You know perfectly well there is nothing in the entire world that you like better than southern fried chicken, and I've saved you the gizzard. . . ."

Ours was a fine old barn, well built, with the kind of beams interior decorators get orgastic over.

Shortly after I started taking lessons from Rosenberg we bought a new Steinway "on time"; I don't know whether it ever got paid for, but we moved the old upright that had belonged to my grandmother into the barn, and I spent what I think were the happiest hours of my life at that upright—I never called it practicing—and composing.

Playing the piano never bothered me; it was the concerts that did me in. It was the people at the concerts, before the concerts, after the concerts. The people. I never liked them, not even when they were giving me a standing ovation.

Years before the time I'm remembering now my father had partitioned off a corner of the barn, put in a small oil burner, a rolltop desk, a chair, his favorite books—Bellamy's *Looking Backward*, William Morris's *News from Nowhere*, Schopenhauer's *The World as Will and Idea*.

The piano was beneath the haymow, and my father had put a great pane of glass in what had been the opening to the mow. The light was beautiful. I never found a studio where the light was that good. If I had I might have written *The Magic Flute*. I might have tried. I might have composed a perfect sonata.

Oh, probably not. Probably what I am is what I would have been, no matter what. That's what they say. They say you never change, can't change. They say you have to make do with what you are.

The day I'm talking about now my father was reading a collection of Shaw's plays. When he saw me, he looked up and smiled. Such a pleased smile.

He put down the book, and he said, "Oh, my, isn't this the nicest surprise ever." He had a deep voice. When he was in college, he'd sung in the glee club.

He said, "When I got up this morning I said to myself, 'Something pleasant is going to happen today.' I could feel it in my bones, but I couldn't possibly have imagined anything even half as pleasant as seeing you."

He hugged me, oh, not really a hug; men couldn't hug each other, not even fathers and sons; he touched my elbows lightly with his two hands. They were wonderful hands, long-fingered, well-shaped, almost delicate, chapped. They can't always have been chapped, but that is the way I remember them.

"I've got all the clippings about the Leventritt," he said. "I'm not sure I told you on the phone how proud I am. I'm not sure I ever could tell you. Were you scared?"

I wanted to say, "I was scared after I won, but not before." I didn't, though. I didn't think my father would understand. Now I'm sure he would have.

I wanted to tell him about The Clarinet Player, how beautiful he was, how sweet of nature, how always kind. I wanted to tell my father that The Clarinet Player and I loved each other, but I didn't do that either. I didn't realize how rare it was, and I thought it would last forever.

Christopher is perfectly right. I am a fool. An IQ of 168 means nothing.

My father stood a little away from me, looking proudly at me, and I looked at him, and I really saw him, maybe for the first time.

He had always been thin, but I could see that he had lost weight, not much, not yet, not as much as I've lost in the last month, but then his didn't come from not eating.

It was just the beginning of the illness, but his eyes were already too bright, too intense.

He was a small man. Five six, about that, spare, small-boned, dark brown hair, thick, his hair worn long for the time, rather bushy, long sideburns, and a thin brown mustache. A handsome man, not movie star handsome, good-looking, pleasant-looking.

You know what he reminded me of that afternoon? A Mathew Brady photograph I once saw, of a Confederate major after some awful defeat. Underneath the pleasure of my father seeing me there was that, the knowledge of defeat. That was always with him.

When I had finished telling him about all of my triumphs in New York—and in those days I didn't have to invent them—he said, "Oh, my, isn't that just fabulous?" Fabulous. It seemed an odd word for him to use, but I liked it.

I told him about the concert in Omaha, and he said, "Your mother and I are coming, of course. I mean we will if you want us to."

"I want you to."

I went to the piano then, and to my surprise it was still in perfect tune.

My father said, "Just in case you'd come home, as you have."

I played the Beethoven Sonata in A Major, as well as I had the day I won the Leventritt, and when I finished, my father was crying.

He said, "It's the most beautiful thing I ever heard."

And then we started talking. How was New York? Did I like it? Did it live up to expectations?

I forget what I said, but I must have made the city sound like Athens in the age of Pericles.

"Yes," said my father. "Yes, that's rather the way I thought it would be. From what I've read and what I've heard, that's what I thought."

He hesitated a moment, then, "When I was about your age, I thought I might join the Merchant Marine. See the world. There were so many places I had in mind seeing. Places I hope you'll see."

"Why didn't you join the Merchant Marine?"

"Oh, I don't know. I guess I just never got around to it."

"Well, it's not too late to see the world, for Pete's sake. I mean you're still a young man, and you don't have to support me and pay for my music lessons and all that, not any more."

"No, and to tell the truth, I'm sorry I don't."

I asked how he was feeling, and he said, "Fine, fine. You know I'm always feeling well. Why shouldn't I?"

That was about all. It doesn't seem like much, but we were closer to each other that afternoon than we ever had been before, ever would be again. Maybe that's as close as you're supposed to get.

Sometimes I would unexpectedly come into his study in the barn, and very often when he wasn't reading, he would be looking out the window at the small hills that stretched to the horizon and beyond, beyond to the cities he once dreamed of seeing and never would.

"Put some more sour cream on your pot roast, George. If you're going to play a concert in Omaha, Nebraska, they won't want you all skin and bones. And speaking of concerts, Monte, it behooves me to tell you that despite our permanently depleted financial condition, I am going to have to get a new dress for the concert. White satin, and I can wear it to Eastern Star after George's triumph in Omaha. And not only that . . ."

My father and I smiled at each other over the sour cream and the pot roast and the noodles sprinkled with caraway seeds. A resigned smile. My father and I were both back in jail; we were sharing the same cell.

We knew, too, that the jailer loved us. And that we loved her. Why, then, were we all so unhappy?

"Did your father tell you about Lois Washington?"

"Please, Dora, not at the table."

"He'll find out sooner or later, and he might just as well . . ."

"Now that you've brought it up, tell me."

"Dead. Hung herself. With her own silk stocking, in the bathroom at Mrs. Chandler's. You know that place on South Center where she stayed. She had that front room with the bay window, and for what she paid you'd have thought she ought to have the run of the house. But May Chandler drives a hard bargain. And of course, she always was funny, Lois Washington, I mean, long before she hung herself. Buying phonograph records in the middle of a depression, and asking us taxpayers to foot the bill. And painting lessons. No telling how much those painting classes at the library set us taxpayers back. Always putting on airs, too, and they say she was taking dope, and I'm not a bit surprised, the way she always was acting like she'd just been elected head of the whole shebang. So she hung herself, dead as a doornail the morning they found her. And now Mrs. Payne is getting funny. Mrs. Fearly says she started going downhill right after Lois Washington . . . Monte, why in the world are you . . . and when, may I ask, will you . . . ?"

My mother got upset, fidgety, if my father was out of the room for more than five minutes, and she got upset, fidgety, if he was in the room for five minutes. They spent all the years of their married life like that.

"Sonny, where in the world do you suppose your father is? Maybe he's had a bad accident. You know how he is. Just like you in more ways than I'd care to mention. The two of you are like two peas in a pod. Never look crossing streets. Do you think I should call the police? Maybe they've taken him to the hospital. I hope it's the Deaconess. I don't want him, hurt as he is, perhaps bleeding to death, in the hands of the mackerel snappers at Mercy. Not that some of those sisters aren't nice as can be, but being Catholic, they can't help . . ."

Or, "Monte, what in the *world* are you doing, just sitting there? Haven't you done the chores, milked Bessie, gathered the eggs, fed the chickens? I *thought* you hadn't. And help sonny bring in the wood for the cookstove. Nothing done and you just sitting there. That's your trouble, Monte, and it always has been. That's the reason you've never been a good provider. And don't light up that smelly old pipe until you get outside. And don't smoke while we're all trying to listen to 'Amos 'n' Andy,' getting the curtains all . . . And don't . . . And do . . ."

Herself, she was forever busy on matters of small importance, scrubbing, scraping, mopping, moping, cutting up parsnips and people, vacuuming, vocalizing, hoping, hating, wishing, wanting, festering, festooning, closing windows and minds, dusting.

I leaned forward for her very last words, through lips that had never been still. She said, "I didn't quite finish . . . scrubbing the kitchen floor."

Is there another world where she said the inevitable next "Now, Monte, don't track up my nice clean . . . Why is it that every time I finish scrubbing the kitchen floor, on my hands and knees, and with my arthritis, and I have this shooting pain in my left . . . No, a new one, lower down."

The night my father died, my mother, the surgeon, and I were sitting in the kitchen. The surgeon said, "Dora, do you feel you know him any better now than you did the day you married him?"

My mother sipped, sipped the black and bitter, sipped the bile, the regret, the lost and last years, and she said, "No, not one bit better, not one single bit."

It's late. All the lights are off, and it is quiet. I suppose that is one of the reasons you charge so much, the quiet. For me it is essential. Long before I knew I had a built-in tape recorder or that I could listen to ten different sounds at the same time and tell the pitch of each, I knew that my ears wounded more easily than any other part of me.

The moon is not quite full, and there is a sliver of snow at the edge of the sand. It is a little too far out for me to hear the surf, but I can see it. Comforting, I suppose. Eternal, I imagine.

Tomorrow I'll tell you what I remember about The Clarinet Player, who was the most beautiful man I have ever known, inside and out.

Now I'll take the single Seconal you allow me and sleep for four hours. That's how long they last, four hours, and then I wake up and wait for the dawn. Do you have any idea how long it can be, waiting to be dawned upon?

4 /

The Clarinet Player

The first thing I remember is an immaculate afternoon in the summer of 1938. We had gone to the Paramount to hear Benny Goodman, but almost immediately after Goodman started playing, I began hearing small, pained noises from the seat to my left. They got louder every second, and about halfway through whatever it was, The Clarinet Player said, "Man, if we don't get the hell out of here, they is going to have a mess of cleaning up to do."

So we got the hell out, and The Clarinet Player said, "That man don't give me *nothing*. I mean nothing *at all*. That man, all he putting in his work is spit."

"True, true. You are at least a million times better, but what did you think of Gene Krupa?"

"He is not no Chick Webb, but he is pretty."

"He is beautiful."

I don't remember how we met, maybe in one of the bars, although I'm not sure I had yet discovered the bars.

Maybe we were both in the same pit orchestra. From time to time during those first summers in the city I earned extra money by playing in a pit orchestra, usually when one of the regular musicians got sick or hung up on drugs or fell in love.

We met. That's all. I was eighteen, and he was eighteen and very tall and very black and, I've said, beautiful.

And nobody ever played the clarinet the way he did, and nobody ever will again. Artie Shaw? Benny Goodman? Not even close. On a Saturday night at the Savoy there were half a dozen men who played as well as or better than Shaw or Goodman. But these men, many of them still boys, were not rich or famous. Not the ones I knew. Their shirts were frayed at the collars and cuffs, and so were the cuffs of their trousers, and usually the seats of their trousers had been patched. Their shoes were always polished and always needed resoling.

There were four bands on the weekends, and two played at the same time and on the same platform. The wall behind the platform was painted blue, and spotlights pierced the clouds of smoke. It was hot and noisy, and I loved every sweet second of it. I was born knowing black is beautiful.

The clarinet players—naturally, I knew them best—would cadge cigarettes and liquor. You had to bring your own liquor. Wine was twenty cents a glass; beer was ten cents a glass.

The other clarinet players would listen to each other and comment on the sound, accurately and sometimes acrimoniously. But when The Clarinet Player was at work, nobody said anything except in a reverent whisper. "Shee-it, man; he *can't* be doing *that; nobody* can do *that*." Or, "Shut your big bazoo, man, and listen. Listen quiet. And you, too, woman; this ain't a time for talking."

A lot of the hostesses refused to dance when he was playing, and that cost them money. It was three dances for a quarter, and for a quarter you could buy a round-trip ticket to the moon.

"Not right now, mister, not while *he's* playing, thank you all the same."

"Listen to that, the way he blows it out all clean. That ain't something you learn. That is something you is born knowing how."

It was clean. It was something you are born knowing how. The Clarinet Player was as close as anybody can get to being a natural musician.

We both played in a jazz concert at Carnegie Hall, and the critic for the *Herald Tribune* said that The Clarinet Player was "a kind of genius." Fletcher Henderson thought so, too, and so did Cab Calloway, and so did Satchmo and The Duke, all of whom had good bands, and they all wanted The Clarinet Player to go on tour with them, but he wouldn't.

"Man, I start shivering and shaking and carrying on when I get below Ninety-fourth Street. I am just not the traveling kind."

"But don't you want to be rich and famous, a Household Word, your name on every lip?"

"One pair of lips is about all that interests me at any one time. I'm more your plantation-type nigger. You ever heard me play 'Old Black Joe'?"

I had many times, and it was never twice the same, and it was always perfect.

"No, I never took lessons; where I was born and raised, on 138th Street, there was never much going in the lesson line. But God took care of my learning the clarinet. You get in good with God, and you have got it made. And all us niggers is in good with God. That is why we is all so rich and happy.

"I was working for this Jew boy with three balls, hustling for nickels and dimes, lots of business in these parts for Jew boys with three balls. Still, there was times when I would just be setting around, watching, waiting, real patient, the way it says your good nigger has to be, and if you just be quiet enough and scrape and bow enough, maybe you earn yourself a fifteen-cent tip.

"There was only this one, no, two instruments in the Jew boy's store, a guitar and a clarinet, looking rusty and tired and beat. I never cottoned to a guitar sound, but one afternoon when the Jew boy was out, and I was minding the store, I took this clarinet down from where it was hanging and started tootling away. The two of us took to each other right off.

"When the Jew boy came back, I was sitting there on the counter, tootling away like I owned the place and maybe, too, the world. I could see how maybe he wanted to tell me to get my dirty black lips off his nice, clean clarinet, but he did not do it. He listens there a minute, and he looks at me, and he says, 'You want it?' I says, 'I could not afford to buy something like this. Never.' He says, 'I'm giving it to you. It's been laying around here, collecting dust and taking up space, since I can't remember when. Get it out of here.'

"And I do, and that's how it happens. You can see how come I'm such a big believer in God. God is a Jew boy, ain't he?"

"I presume so. The kid was."

"Well, there you are then. You can see why it is I'm always getting down on my knees, praying."

Later that same year, on a chill night in November, Gene Krupa showed up at the Savoy and we smoked a smoke, and then the three of us, The Clarinet Player, Krupa, and I, and, later, many others, were at it until noon the next day. After which I went downtown for a lesson, after which The Clarinet Player and I had dinner and made love, after which I practiced until four the following morning. After which I slept for two hours, and then started all over again.

God, what energy I had then, what optimism. Failure was what happened to other people.

Meeting Krupa wasn't as exciting as meeting Toscanini, which also happened that year, but Krupa must have been the handsomest drummer ever, and maybe the best. A very good drummer, a very decent man. I remember he asked The Clarinet Player if he could read music, and my love said, "Sure, I can read music, man. It's separating the notes that gives me trouble. And five flats always look like a bunch of grapes."

Was I happy during those years? Content with loving and being loved, with success, with adulation, with being a Household Name? . . . Is this an answer? What happened the morning after my first New York concert?

Oh, love, I was the talk of all of Gotham that morning. The gentleman from the *Herald Tribune* said, ". . . As was observed in this space earlier this year, George Lionel is a more than competent jazz pianist, but last night at Town Hall, Lionel demonstrated that as a classical pianist . . . At nineteen he has few if any peers. . . ."

And the gentleman on the *Times* raved—not the one who's in love with Christopher, an earlier one, and he sure as hell wasn't in love with me. I didn't have my imported hairpiece, hadn't yet had my nose fixed, hadn't . . .

I'll tell you this, though; he was tone deaf. The *Times* absolutely insists on that in its music critics. . . . Still, if they rave, who except me can complain about a little tone deafness?

". . . it is not too much to say that young Lionel . . . his range, his emotionality . . . virtuosity . . . tonality . . ."

Bullshit, all of it. You're not supposed to write about music anyway. You're supposed to listen to it. The only exceptions are George Bernard Shaw and E. M. Forster; they could write about it without making me sick to my stomach.

That morning there was a photograph of me in the *Times:* "Brilliant New York debut of . . ."

The phone never stopped ringing; people I'd never met claimed to be lifelong friends; my agent said he had booked enough concerts to last through three lifetimes, a million dollars or so a concert.

The world was my oyster that morning, and I took out my sword. I capered; I danced; I had eyes of youth; I spoke holiday; I smelled of April and May.

The Clarinet Player said, "You're gonna be rich and famous, man, and you'll forget about Old Black Joe here."

"I'm scared shitless."

"Why?"

"Something awful is about to happen; that's why."

"Something good has happened, and more good things are about to happen. Let's make some music, and then we'll make some love."

"Oh, go to hell."

I stomped out of the apartment, and in less than an hour I had arranged my punishment. On East Sixty-first Street between First and Second Avenues I met a red-haired brigand who, afterward, and it wasn't much, broke my glasses, blacked my right eye, stole the bridge that covered the place where I'd lost a tooth in an encounter with an earlier vagabond, and took all of my cash, three hundred dollars or so. Why did I have three hundred dollars in cash on me? So that somebody could steal it, of course, but what in the world did he do with an alien bridge?

What a museum they could start with the things stolen from me. I'd go myself.

Later, when I started to tell The Clarinet Player what I claimed had happened, he said, "Oh, man, don't *lie* to me, too." And he said, "I love you, but that isn't never going to be enough, is it?" And he said, "We'll get you patched up, and then we'll make some music, and then we'll make some love." And he said, "One person loving you isn't never going to be enough, and everybody loving you isn't never going to be enough." And he said, "Sometimes I look at you when nothing's happening even, and I feel like busting out in tears."

Not long after Pearl Harbor, The Clarinet Player and I, both a little smashed, wrote a parody on the "Praise the Lord and pass the ammunition" shit that was so popular at the time. We called it "God's the Referee for Our Side"—"He won't let the Hun/ Steal a single run—/ God's the referee for our side."

We used to play it and shout it at the Savoy, and everybody loved and understood it. The war had nothing to do with the people who played at the Savoy. Let the ofays kill each other off; all the fewer to be taken care of later.

A group of us used to hire ourselves out—a horn, maybe a guitar, some drums, me at the piano, and The Clarinet Player. We played at all kinds of fancy shindigs and met all kinds of unsettling people. I was usually the only pink one.

At one castle on Central Park West we played "God's the Referee," mocking the lyrics, expecting the customers to laugh the way they did at the Savoy.

But that wasn't what happened. Instead, some of the women burst into tears, and the men cleared their throats in a virile manner. I tell you. When there's a war on, you can get away with almost anything, except honesty.

A music publisher was among the guests and after he had dried his eyes, using only four or five Kleenexes (the munitions people aren't the only ones who clean up at such a time), he came over to the piano and asked who in the blessed name of Johann Sebastian Bach had written such a masterpiece?

It wasn't easy, but I confessed all, all except the fact that I had collaborated with The Clarinet Player. I hoped to spare him the thirty lashes I was sure to get.

But the music publisher cried an additional two Kleenexes' worth, and he said that he considered publishing "God's the Referee" to be his patriotic duty. Not only that, he said, he and I would be up to our ass in golden doubloons. And what's more, what the song would do for the morale of Our Fighting Men could not be estimated.

I figured that if golden doubloons and morale were involved, I'd better introduce The Clarinet Player and point out that the masterpiece was a collaboration.

The music publisher didn't seem any too happy with the news. He said he'd been thinking of having my photograph on the cover, in color. I suggested that a photograph of The Clarinet Player and me together would be even more colorful. The music publisher admitted that that was a possibility, but when the thing came out, there was a line drawing of a GI praying on the cover.

"God" was number one on "The Hit Parade" for sixteen weeks. It was said to be almost solely responsible for the fact that Our Boys held on to the Philippines however long it was. Our Boys hummed it as they pushed the Nips back into the Pacific. That's what the papers said anyway. And it was said in the circles in which I moved that General MacArthur was so excited that for days he forgot to put on his pancake. He used the light brown. Max Factor Number Four.

But most important, the music publisher got richer than he had been, and The Clarinet Player and I made what at the time seemed like all the money there was. We had a very good time with it, too, some of it anyway. We spent almost two months in Key West, which was very beautiful in those days. I don't know what it's like now. I couldn't go back alone and certainly not with anybody else.

Not long after we got back, my draft board started giving me a bad time.

It had never occurred to me that they'd take a sissy in the armed forces, but it seemed they would. They tapped you on the knee with a little silver hammer, and the psychiatrist asked how you felt about girls, and before you had a chance to say, you were off to Fort Bragg. A friend of mine opened the first gay bar down there.

I didn't have much interest in being an infantryman, although I had met a few. The Times Square area was loaded with them, all anxious, at least willing.

"Or, if you will, thrusting me beneath your clothing."

Either before it started or after it was over, most of the infantry-men told me what it was like being in the Infantry, told me to stay away. "They're murder on queers, murder. . . . But look, next time I'm in town—if there is a next time—I'll give you a buzz, and it certainly has been . . ."

I understandably decided against the Infantry.

"How you settled your head athwart my hips, and gently turned me over."

I had heard that as long as you spoke or could learn a foreign language, could pass certain memory tests, get through the physical, and jump out of a plane into a foreign country, the Office of Strategic Services didn't give a damn about your sex life. Or your politics. You could be both queer and a communist, and some were.

The whole thing terrified me, but then what didn't.

So I mentioned the OSS to Meg Taylor, who was then my land-lady in a brownstone in the Murray Hill district and who was a friend of the Roosevelts and, it turned out, The Colonel.

Margaret, Meg, Mrs. Paxton Taylor.

Paxton Taylor had been a famous crusading laywer, almost as famous as Clarence Darrow, and he had defended just as many unpopular causes and people. Those too good for any society and those not good enough.

He had been born in Dutchess County, New York, on a six-hundred-acre estate near Hyde Park. His family had more land and more money and was considered far more respectable and altogether tonier than the Roosevelts could ever dream of being. Paxton had been Franklin Roosevelt's best friend.

Meg Taylor said, "Paxton was even able to endure Franklin's mother for short periods of time. But when Franklin wanted him to be his attorney general, Paxton said no. He said, 'Frank, I don't believe in patching up the old system. I think we should tear it down and start all over.'"

Mrs. Taylor was a regal woman in her late sixties, and she was still beautiful, probably more beautiful than she had been as a young woman. She had the face of a patrician, and she walked like a queen on the way to her own coronation. She had white hair piled high on her head and the bluest eyes I've ever encountered.

I don't know why she rented the room to me. She certainly didn't need the money. What was it anyway? Ten dollars a week. She once said, "Paxton was a thoughtful man, and he left me more than adequately provided for."

Probably she was lonely. They had had no children.

I tell you. That was my lucky time. Nothing bad could happen. I was lucky, and Samuel Butler, that old auntie, was right; being lucky and in good health is the best there is; everything else ought to be against the law, punishable by death.

I was walking along the street one day and saw a small, discreet sign saying, ROOM TO LET; I rang the doorbell, and Meg Taylor came to the door. She looked at me, and I looked at her, and it was the kind of love they never make movies about.

She said, "I hope you'll like it." I said, "I'm sure I will," and I did.

Beautiful. When did things like that stop happening? Oh, shortly after they began. Or shortly before they began.

After I had settled my few things in the huge, airy bedroom, Mrs. Taylor asked me to join her for tea.

While we sipped the China tea and I ate three toasted crumpets, I told her a few things about myself. Even that first afternoon I felt that she knew more about me than I could possibly have told her, that she accepted people for what they wanted to be and in her presence sometimes became. She was not interested in making people better; she expected them to be better.

She liked The Clarinet Player, and he liked her, and the three of us went to a great many places together. I remember one evening we went to Town Hall to hear that peculiar lady columnist—her name is gone; sorry—and at one point she said in that peculiar voice, "Civilization as we know it is coming to an end."

And Mrs. Taylor, in a loud, clear voice, said, "I certainly hope so."

We started laughing and couldn't stop. An usher had to escort us out, and from the Town Hall stage the lady columnist said, "Fascist saboteurs follow me everywhere I go."

Forever after that sentence was good for a laugh. The Clarinet Player would say, "Man, no wonder I'm all fucked up. Not only am I black *and* queer, but fascist saboteurs follow me everywhere I go."

That first afternoon and many afternoons later Meg Taylor and I sat in the long, narrow living room with the Chippendale furniture, all slightly scarred, the worn Oriental rug, and the mantel on which were several photographs of Paxton Taylor, a good-looking man with a great mustache, a goatee, a long, firm mouth, and forgiving brown eyes.

He had been one of the great orators of his day, and once Mrs. Taylor played a recording of his voice made at a national convention of the Socialist party.

Paxton Taylor's voice had a certain New England harshness, and I remember only one thing he said, a paraphrase, I believe, from

Schopenhauer. "We are made for cooperation, like feet, like hands, like eyelids, like rows of the upper and lower teeth."

On the same mantel were two or three photographs of Mrs. Taylor, Paxton, and Franklin and Eleanor Roosevelt when they were young. I saw that the President had been quite a handsome young man, at least that many people would have thought so. Too much chin for my taste, too many teeth, and, always, that fatuous smile. The smile unnerved me. At least it did the two times I had dinner at the White House while he was in residence. I didn't like the smile, the lengthy talk about his stamp collection, or the fact that he didn't listen when I played. Or when anyone else talked. He was incapable of listening.

I remember several reproductions on the walls of Meg Taylor's brownstone, nothing very special, although in the living room was Michelangelo's *Night*. Plants in the large, rectangular windows that opened onto Thirty-fifth Street. Was there really araucaria? I get confused. It's mid-November now, and all those years have passed, and there are yesterday's commissions to atone for and tomorrow's omissions to worry about.

Sufficient unto the day has never worked for me. I've tried and tried.

It is mid-November, and there is a high wind and a chill rain, angry against the glass, and I am alone in this room, and I am also alone in the half-finished Payne house. And I am in an apartment on the East River in New York, telling someone I love (or was loved by; it's always hard for me to tell which) that it is over. Once it begins, it's over.

And I am in the brownstone on East Thirty-fifth with The Clarinet Player and Meg Taylor. He and I are playing for her. I can't hear what. Sad, though. An improvisation? Hundreds of those, thousands. Somebody once said that improvisation is the story of my life. "You certainly dissipated your talents, didn't you? Never really settled down to anything, did you? You could have been . . ."

As if I didn't know.

Let's say an improvisation. Were there tape recorders then? How beautiful it would be if I had tapes of all those hours we played together.

Of course I didn't need a tape recorder then; I told you. I had a built-in one, and I had close to total recall.

I didn't know how many things you have to forget.

VARIATIONS ON A THEME—Once, I believe in the spring of 1942, just before I went into the OSS, when I came home to the house on East Thirty-fifth Mrs. Taylor was having tea with an elegant-looking woman wearing a great string of pearls and a black dress that smelled of mothballs.

"Mrs. Phelps's late husband was with Franklin at Groton," said Mrs. Taylor.

Mrs. Phelps said, "He kicked a football like a ballet dancer; not that I'm implying he was effeminate."

"She means Franklin," said Mrs. Taylor. "Won't you have some tea, dear?"

I said that I wouldn't, thank you all the same.

"It was no surprise to Mr. Phelps that he turned out the way he did," said Mrs. Phelps. "We always knew that Franklin would be a failure."

I excused myself, and as I started up the stairs toward my room, I heard Mrs. Phelps say, "I want to explain to the young man, Meg. I wanted to make it clear to him that while some people said Eleanor was lucky to have married him, I have always felt that it was the other way around. And I am not speaking now of the propriety of cousins marrying. *That* is an entirely different matter."

I turned, and Mrs. Taylor winked at me and smiled.

"You know how it is with the Dutch," she said.

"If they really are Dutch," said Mrs. Phelps.

RONDO—Lester Brockhurst had given me the key to his studio, and I had played there nearly every night, often until dawn. One morning after I got back to the brownstone I went into the library, sat down at the piano, and played a phrase from Debussy's "Serenade for the Doll" that had been pestering me. Then I played the whole thing, as quietly as I could.

When I'd finished, Mrs. Taylor was standing in the doorway, and she said, "Thank you. It was beautiful, and please, after this play any time you want to and as loud as you want."

"I wouldn't want to keep you awake."

"I never really sleep at night. I read until about six, and then I sometimes drop off for a few hours. The old don't sleep. They don't need it, and I guess they're afraid of it."

Finally, a letter I got at the hospital in Paris.

You know how I feel about your being in this war. If I believed in God or gods, I would pray for your safety, but as it is, I can only fervently hope for it.

I do not believe in crusades. Blood-letting has never seemed to me to have bettered the world, no matter how worthy the cause. God, as the man said, is always on both sides.

But Franklin would have been very put out if he had been denied a war. In his secret heart he must even have been grateful for Hitler and that vicious little Italian and the Japanese. They made it possible for him.

As a boy he liked to play with toy ships and soldiers, and this is almost the same. I do not believe it can be said of Franklin that he is a man who can share another's anguish.

After the war, when I finally got back to New York, I went to the brownstone on East Thirty-fifth, but there was another name near the doorbell. I found later that Meg Taylor had died on the first of August, 1945, which was as well. I do not believe she would have liked what happened on the sixth. Or most of what has happened since.

She once said, "I'm a nineteenth-century woman; I regret that we have been forced to abandon the notion that progress is inevitable." And once, "You will never have an easy time of it, my dear, but try to endure. That is really all there ever is to do."

5 /

The Colonel

Meg Taylor had told me that he was president of a very old bank in Boston, that his family had been around as long as the Adamses, that he spoke God alone knew how many languages, that he had been graduated from Harvard with the highest average in its history up to then, that he was a bachelor.

She said, "I have to warn you, though. A great many people don't like him. He has a very sharp tongue."

The Colonel was thin; not too thin, properly thin, attractively thin. Not more than forty, I imagined, but with blue-white hair, and each feature, including the deep-blue eyes, seemed to me to be perfect. I detested him at once and loved him immediately.

He looked me over, and it was clear that everything he saw was unsatisfactory.

He said, "What in heaven's name are you standing at attention for? You're not *in* anything yet. Just looking at you braced like that makes me nervous."

He spoke in an accent that, if I hadn't known already, would have told me all I needed to know about where he was born and went to school and that he had never been hungry or cold except, maybe, when he lost his way on a ski slope somewhere.

I stood as at ease as I could manage, and The Colonel said, "That's somewhat better, but it's not much better. Now tell me why in the *world* you want to be in the OSS. We're not exactly filming an Errol Flynn movie around here, you know."

"I know that, sir."

"I admit it would brighten things up considerably if Errol were around. I have always found just looking at him a pleasure."

I longed to say that I had seen Flynn in *Robin Hood* nineteen times and could repeat every sentence of it from Fade In to Fade Out. I didn't, though. I said, "Sir, I want to be in the OSS because I don't want to be in the Infantry."

He laughed. Of course he had perfect teeth.

He said, "That's as good a reason as any."

Later, after I'd been interviewed by several more orthodox officials, I went back to The Colonel's office, and he said, "We'll *probably* be able to use you, although the decision isn't mine alone. I'll let you know."

I said, "Sir, it's rather embarrassing, but in case the subject hasn't come up, I think you ought to know that . . . Well, sir, the truth of the matter is, my whole life through I've been a sissy, and I think you ought to know it."

The Colonel sighed and said, "Please. I do not wish to be bored with the details of your sex life. I already know a great deal more about it than I care to know. It all seems quite routine to me, nothing whatever worthy of mention should they ever decide to bring Krafft-Ebing up to date.

"Just *try* to stay out of Lafayette Park. They put the most attractive members of the vice squad there, and you'd be *sure* to be picked up. After which I would have to make a *tedious* journey to the police station, go through an endless amount of red tape, and *pretend* to be cordial to an extraordinary number of *jealous* FBI agents, all of whom have memorized my dossier and are *furious* because Auntie Edgar *never* lets them have any fun.

"Besides, the whole thing is altogether rather tacky. I have found the group usually gathered in the men's bar at the Mayflower *much* more congenial. I never knew there were so many attractive blond ensigns in the world, every single one of them gay."

I followed The Colonel's advice about staying out of Lafayette Park, most of the time anyway, and I never got busted.

Besides, the area just behind the Lincoln Memorial was much more interesting, not to mention the vicinity of the Washington Monument.

I don't know what old Abe would have thought of the goings-on, but I always felt that George wouldn't have minded much. After all, he liked Alexander Hamilton much more than Martha Custis; Hamilton was prettier, for one thing.

When Hamilton married Elizabeth Schuyler, George pouted for days.

". . . their falling out could best be described as a 'lover's quarrel,' after which Hamilton demanded a field command at Yorktown."

If they'd had more things like that in the history books I studied in school, I might have been able to stay awake more.

One never had to bed down alone, though, not in Washington in those days, or these days.

In New York at that time my favorite rendezvous was always the Stage Door Canteen. Notorious, Brunhilde. Every time I got off the train I headed for the Canteen. You couldn't go out with the hostesses, but who wanted to? We went out with each other.

That first night The Colonel took me to dinner at the Metropolitan Club. I'm sure he was kind more because of Meg Taylor than because of me, although he was generally a forbearing man, and I thought and think that he was the wisest man I ever met, the wittiest, certainly the most intelligent. He was very important to me because he proved that you could be, I could be a sissy and not necessarily a freak.

Afterward as we stood in the dark street he said, "You're a very good musician, and you might become a great musician, which is far more important than jumping out of an airplane into the darkness.

Are you sure you don't want to tell your draft board you're queer?
You could get an immediate 4-F classification, and you could tell
people it was because of a heart murmur."

I said, "No, thank you very much, sir."

"Why?"

"I'm not sure if I know why. I just know that I have to go, and it
has more to do with me than the war. Does that make any sense?"

The Colonel sighed.

"Not much," he said, "but then sense and war seldom go hand in
hand. I'm sure I'm sending you off to certain death, but if that's the
way you want it . . ."

He started to shake my hand, but instead he kissed me on the lips,
and he said, "If you do get back, and the chances are ninety-nine
out of a hundred that you won't, you'll be a lot less tender, just to
start."

By the end of the second day of training in Alexandria I had decided either to kill myself or to go AWOL. But I did neither. I kept
on. I learned what I had to learn. I jumped out of a plane when the
time came. I shit my pants every single time, but I finished. They
said I was ready, and it was to be France.

I didn't see The Colonel at all during this period. I think he
didn't want to interfere. The night I left for England, he was in
California.

I loved him all through the war, though, and when I did what I
did, particularly the thing for which they later pinned a doodad on
me, I did it because I wanted The Colonel to be proud of me.

And if that sounds soupy, let it sound soupy.

Once after the war I asked The Colonel if he thought that Meg
Taylor had known we were sissies. He said, "People like Meg prefer
to ignore such things, the way the English ignore other languages."

During the years Harry Truman was President The Colonel was
either working in the White House or across the street in what was
then the State Department building. I asked him if he thought Mr.

Truman knew, and he said, "I once broached the subject to him sideways, and the President said, 'As long as people stay out of trouble, I don't give a good goddamn what they do after work.'"

Until he died I had dinner with The Colonel every time he came to New York and every time I was in Boston. It may not have been the last time I saw him, but I remember it that way. After dinner I walked with him back to the Harvard Club, and he said, "I was wrong when I said you'd come back from the war less tender. You didn't at all. You have never developed that necessary protective outer skin. That's why you're still just one great big open bleeding wound. And always will be."

He kissed me then and said, "Well, never mind. So am I. Tender people are much nicer really."

6 /

A Beautiful Time

You're right. I haven't said very much about The Clarinet Player's personal life. I never knew much about it. We never went through the autobiographical stage that has been part of every other love affair I've had.

In the beginning you tell it all, unexpurgated, and later they remember, and they say . . . Or I remember, and I say . . . Oh, you know what we say.

Besides, I wouldn't describe my relationship with The Clarinet Player as an *affair*. Dreadful word.

This. One Saturday morning or, more likely, Sunday morning as we were leaving the Savoy I said, "Don't you live around here?"

He said, "You might say that."

"Why don't you take me home and introduce me to your folks?"

"Man, let's get going. Let's go down to that White Tower on Forty-fifth and have us some eggs and bacon."

"Look, after all this time shouldn't I meet your mother at least?"

The Clarinet Player said, "My mother's away," making her absence sound as if she were at a spa in Belgium.

And I said, "Look, I don't care if you're poor. I mean if your folks are poor. I've always been poor. When I was a kid, we didn't even have—"

The Clarinet Player grabbed me by the collar and shook me; I never saw him so angry. He said, "There ain't no part of me here and never has been. I hate this place and always will. How much I hate this place you will never ever know."

He released me then and I smiled, the happy fool, and said, "I hate the place I was born and raised in, too. So I guess I understand what you're talking about."

"No, you don't," he said, his voice still fierce. "You don't know, and you never will."

"Why's that? I'm not exactly insensitive, you know."

He grabbed my right hand and held it out in front of me, and he put his black hand next to it. "This is why," he said.

He was right, of course; I've known a thousand black men, some of them hustlers, some of them people I met in a bar, some of them lovers, and although they have often tried to tell me, I am not at all sure it is possible to understand the special anguish of being black.

I don't remember when or how The Clarinet Player and I started going to meetings, and I certainly do not remember where we found the time. But in those years there were twenty-seven hours a day.

Later they wrote, ". . . Lionel's membership in allegedly pro-Negro organizations controlled by the communists . . ."

I did belong to a great many organizations that were supposed to help black people, no question of that, and some of them may have been controlled by communists.

As I've said, I never had any hangups about the color of somebody's skin. The first boy was black, and he said, "It's all right with me, but you wouldn't mind if I had a sandwich or something first, would you? I have not been eating with any great regularity of late."

My mother never taught me to hate black people because (a) there weren't many around; (b) it would never have occurred to her that it would ever occur to me to have anything to do with one ("and get a pound of nigger toes; you know how much you like nigger toes"); and (c) she was too busy worrying about the Jew conspiracy.

Anyway, a good half of the boys wandering through town on their way from somewhere and to somewhere, the Wild Boys of the Road, looking for a job or a meal or even a little affection, were black.

And so it really isn't so surprising that years later when I got to New York I belonged to committees and marched and signed petitions and ads and played at benefits for black people. I did all this almost thirty years before most people even started talking about civil rights. Certainly long before the Supreme Court decision in 1954.

My God, back in the late thirties at the Savoy you didn't have to be any too bright or black to figure out that there was something wrong somewhere. Any morning when you left, Lenox Avenue would be lined with people begging or selling their bodies, women and children, men. I'll do you for a quarter, mister. Want to do me for a dime?

If the only people who seemed to have an answer for what was wrong were communists, and they seemed to be, who asked questions?

I certainly did not.

And so The Clarinet Player and I listened to speeches about braver, newer worlds, and we were in Madison Square Garden one warm August night when a boy who had lost a leg in Spain said that it was better to die on your feet than live on your knees. He was a thin, intense young man with the beautiful look of someone who had seen a vision. He quoted a poem written by another boy who had died in Spain. I remember the last two lines:

> Comrades, the battle is bloody, and the war is long.
> Still let us climb the gray hills and charge the guns.

Then the boy in Madison Square Garden clenched his fist, and we all rose and clenched our fists, and we said, "Death to the fascists."

Maybe it was silly; it was useless, no question of that, but it had a kind of glory, and we were young.

In the 1950s people deprecated those days; they said they had been taken in; they said they had been dupes, and for the sake of the future of the republic they named the names of their one-time comrades and lovers.

I never deprecated. That would have been like deprecating the memory of The Clarinet Player, like deprecating my youth. No, I never did that, and I never named names.

I thought it was a beautiful time.

Oh, not all of it.

I remember in November of that first year The Clarinet Player and I were walking past the New York Public Library at Forty-second Street.

On the steps a hundred or so cops were using their billy clubs to beat the heads of fifty or so people, mostly young and scruffy-looking, as martyrs often are.

There were perhaps a dozen old people, too, and the cops were giving them an even worse time, one very old man in particular. Three cops with blackjacks were beating him on the head, the arms, the chest, the stomach. And a fourth was kicking him in the groin, and the old man was surrounded by a great pool of blood that grew larger every moment.

Several picket signs on the sidewalk said, "Protest the Munich Sell Out! Attend Rally at . . ."

After I was sick on the sidewalk, I said, "I didn't know such things happened."

The Clarinet Player touched me lightly on the shoulder.

"Baby," he said, "you are about two years old, if that, and that is one of the reasons I love you. Don't never change. What you don't understand is that about one thousand things like this happen every day in this town, and these here are white folks to boot. They usually don't hit white folks quite as hard as us niggers."

"But isn't there somebody to complain to?"

"Now who'd you have in mind complaining to, man? Mr. J. Edgar Hoover down in Washington maybe? Why, man, he *wants* cops to beat up people, the more the merrier. There ain't nobody to complain to, baby, not never. Let's go to a moom picture."

We did. It was *Camille,* with Garbo, and she died, as usual, and I cried, as usual.

On the way back to Meg Taylor's house, I bought the *Times,* and while there was nothing about the people being beaten up on the steps of the library, there was a photograph of a beautiful, terrified boy named Herschel Grynszpan, who was seventeen and a Polish Jew. Earlier that day he had shot but not killed a minor official of the Germany embassy in Paris.

In Grynszpan's room the gendarmes had found a letter from his father, a tailor in Hannover, written in August. ". . . Tonight it was announced that Polish Jews were being expelled from the cities. At nine o'clock the police arrived at our house and took our passports and took us to the police station. There we met many other Jews. They are going to expel us from Germany and make us go back to Poland. What shall we do there, son? And what will they do to us? Thank God you are safe in France."

After he was arrested, Herschel Grynszpan, who looked no more than fourteen, sobbed and said, "It is not a crime to be a Jew. I am not a dog. I have a right to live. The Jewish people have a right to some part of the earth. Wherever I have been, I have been treated like an animal."

I know he said it, because I put it in the journal I was keeping, and I've just looked it up. I've kept a journal most of my life; somebody once said that I've been more faithful to the journal than to any person ever, and that may be.

I remember that The Clarinet Player and I slept in each other's arms that night, in each other's tears.

It was still a golden time, though, those years before the war. Young and in love and famous. A standing ovation at the end of every concert. And once at Lewisohn Stadium they stood and applauded for almost half an hour, the longest and loudest ovation since George Gershwin's first concert there. . . . Did not my cup runneth over? Ah, no, alas, no. The daffodils of today meant nothing to me. I was forever looking forward to the roses of tomorrow.

And tomorrow came, but no roses. There was a war instead, and I met The Colonel, and I had to go to Alexandria for the training.

The Clarinet Player and I spent most of the final hours making love. I think perhaps it is like that only once in anybody's life. It has been only once in mine.

And then we walked to Penn Station, hand in hand. We wouldn't cry, and we wouldn't say good-bye because we didn't believe in good-byes and because it wasn't really good-bye. I'd have a leave after the training, and after that . . . It would be a short war; everybody said so.

On the platform we kissed; damn them all; we kissed, and we said, "See you," and then I got on the train, and he stood there for a moment, a tall, black knight in shining armor, and then he gave me half a smile and half a bow, and he ran up the stairs two at a time, turned at the top and waved, and that was the last I ever saw of him.

But it is still all there in my memory, the brightest memory of them all.

In the third week at Alexandria the letter came, as I had known it would. He had gone off to California with a group called The Chocolate Dandies. "You know how I always told you I started shivering and shaking when I got below Ninety-fourth Street. Well, that was before you left, man. With you gone, New York ain't no place at all to be, and I have got an awful feeling you ain't going to be back for a spell.

"I am not much for writing letters, but I'll see you around, huh? And don't worry about me. Uncle Sambo is not going to get yours truly. . . . I love you, whatever that's worth."

A little more than a year later the U.S. Navy decided that it was essential to our winning the war for The Clarinet Player to become a mess steward on an aircraft carrier. I didn't hear what happened until much later, but in May 1944 somewhere in the Pacific, the carrier was sunk, no known survivors, and in a very short time, what with the sharks and all, you couldn't tell a captain from a yeoman second class or a mess steward.

Bones are all white, like cum.

I have a record we made, "One O'Clock Jump"; it's in the cabinet over there, and sometimes when I am feeling particularly brave . . . I am able to listen to it clear through. But that hasn't happened in months. Or years.

The sound he made is still clean, though. Like no sound ever made, before or since.

7 /

Gunthers

This part is for me. I'm sure if I showed it to you, you'd find out what you've been looking for all this time, the essential clue that will answer all the questions. What you and the others haven't found. And never will. Because I always hold back. What I've written up to now is by no means all the truth, and it never will be.

Anyway, this is the secret part.

First, the way it has gone so far today:

This morning Bensy came knocking on the door at eight fifty-four, on the dot. Punctual Miss Benson . . . Yes, yes, I'm coming, Carmen, you with the cutlass in your hair. You don't have to pound the fucking door down, sweetums.

Good morning, Miss Benson. Yes, I'm ready. How's the doctor? Fine and dandy, is he? Isn't that fine and dandy?

And how is that beautiful laboratory assistant of his, Miss Benson? Would he like to be adopted? Yes, by me. What about Christopher? Nothing about Christopher, but I like a little variety now and again, quite a little. I can so have two sons at one time. I've had as many as six at one time. What you have to do if you have a big family is keep your sons from finding out about each other, because if they do, they are likely to get all spitty.

But if you keep your big mouth shut, you can have as many as six sons at one time, although it's tiring.

I believe in large families, though. Large families are the backbone of this country; they are what made this country great. Haven't you read, Miss Benson? You look like a *Reader's Digest* type to me, hon. You stink like one. No, nothing personal, sweetie. It's just that as your best friend . . .

Why the laboratory assistant? Well, in the first place, he is beautiful, and in the second place, he doesn't stink. . . . Yes, you do, Bensy dear. You stink like Buster Dean. Who is Buster Dean? He's a dentist, darl, and he stank. That's all you need to know.

You certainly do starch your uniforms, don't you, love? Don't they chafe you down there? Can't have that all chafed. You never know when you're going to need it. Yes, you do. I do. Never.

And as always, I thought, What in Christ's name will I say to you? I have nothing to talk to you about, you know.

I got back. I thought I'd never make it. Really I did. I thought I'd never find my way back. Those halls are long and dark and haunted, and Nurse Benson wouldn't bring me. She said I was rude to her. She thinks I'm crazy.

I don't know what Gunther thinks. Yes, his name is Gunther. It always is. . . . And he is stunning. Even more so close up. Stunning. Naturally, just when I meet him, he has got himself engaged. They always do. . . . I gather to a rich bitch. A debutante. Can you believe it? Those girls are still coming out.

Well, debutantes will be the first to go, especially debutantes who bamboozle Gunthers into an engagement.

It turns out he is Swiss, and we all know how trusting and guileless the Swiss are. I congratulated him, and he smiled. Perfect teeth. As perfect as The Colonel's were. If I ever meet his mother, I'll ask her what she fed him as a child. . . . He knows. They always know. His eyes are cobalt blue.

The first German boy was a Gunther. The arrangement for our rendezvous was precarious and dangerous, which made it all the better. . . . The danger is as necessary as the shame. . . . I'm a follower, but I haven't been beaten up too many times, not more than thirty or forty. Being beaten up isn't my thing. At least I don't think it is.

Following is, though, and it's the same no matter what part of the world it is. The skin is sometimes light and sometimes dark. Pink or brown or black. The color is unimportant. What the skin covers is. I like thin, graceful people. I could never love anybody with a fat ass, for instance, but I don't care how thin and graceful ballet dancers are, I could never . . . They are worse than actors, and as for ice skaters . . . Ballet dancers and ice skaters are always afraid, if you suggest anything even remotely interesting, that they're going to break something. "Now be *careful*. If I break my elbow, my whole career might be in jeopardy."

Eyes are important. I think I told you how I am about eyes. Black eyes, for instance. I've searched the world for a pair of black eyes but never found any. Once I thought I did, but with my luck, when he stepped out of the shadows the eyes would have been dark brown. And anyway, the price was outrageous.

But as I say, the pursuit is always the same. The heart beats faster, and there is a dry feeling in the mouth. The danger and, later, the shame.

They keep a very close watch on you in the OSS, and when I got back to Washington, The Colonel said, "You could have been court-martialed for that episode with the German boy. Now really, was it worth it?"

I said that it was, and The Colonel said, "Would that sort of thing constitute fraternization, do you suppose? I know you're not supposed to have sex with German girls."

Gunthers of the world, unite.

The second German boy was also named Gunther.

What I didn't tell you the other day when I was talking about noses was that I have had a bob job. That's why I'm so sensitive about noses.

Mine was large; not as large as yours, not as large as Rosenberg's, but too large for my face. Like Nikolai Gogol's nose. I read someplace that poor Nikolai's nose was "an enormous if not an unfaithful beast."

That's one thing I've always liked about Gogol's writing. He was concerned with noses, like me; queer, like me, and at the end crazy as a bedbug. . . . "Sell me some dead souls. . . . Are you interested in souls of the female sex?"

I went all the way to Germany to have the bob, shortly after the war, one of my better years. ". . . Lionel's return . . . an absolute triumph . . . his musicianship, control . . . in every way an event for which the entire musical world should cheer. . . ."

I met the second Gunther in Frankfurt, where the nose man did it. There are more beautiful male hustlers in Frankfurt than in any other city in the world, and they are almost as gentle as the boys who hang around the Colosseum in Rome. Blonder, though . . . Gunther was one of those. He was seventeen years old, and all of his family had been killed by one of our bombs, family-sized. I tried to explain how it was really their own fault.

I brought him back to New York, and when it was over we were still friends. He lives in San Francisco, and I get a Christmas card every year. All five of the children are boys and are blond and beautiful. He runs a bakery. There have been almost as many bakers in my life as Gunthers.

Bakers always smell of fresh bread; you can't seem to wash it off, and it isn't all that unpleasant. . . . Besides, if a pastry cook was good enough for Frederick the Great . . . Menshikov made Frederick a cherry tart, and Frederick made Menshikov ("Alashka") a general.

Things were simpler in those days. Frederick took only one bath in his entire life, but Menshikov bathed before baking every loaf of bread. All the bakers I've known have been scrupulously clean. Scrupulously.

Did I tell you Gunther is having a concert in New York tomorrow night, at Lincoln Center. They'll all be there, Lennie included, swinging and swaying.

I will not be there. I would not be there even if I were there. . . . No, I didn't tell you this. It's all over between Gunther and me. I've known that for some time. Loves me, my ass. I hope the bastard breaks a wrist just before he walks onstage tomorrow night. Let him suffer, too, the way I have. Nobody ever alleviated any pain of mine, and even Jesus had company when He left. I hope I do. Sure I'll settle for a thief. I've known a lot of thieves. Been on crosses with them, in bed with them. But when the pain starts, we're all on our own; it's every man for himself, women and children last.

. . . Poor Gunther with his broken list. What good is a piano player with a broken list? And those things never heal. They'll probably have to shoot him or something. . . . I wonder what happened to Christopher, not that I care much. He was getting on, losing his hair, his teeth falling out, and he never had any talent.

I did my best for that boy. But you can't make a pilk surse . . . Besides, he's only sixteen and a virgin, and sixteen-year-old virgins have never interested me much. I told you. I have never raped anybody, and I have never been to bed with a virgin. I wonder how it is the first time. There was never a first time for me. I was born unchaste.

I wonder how old Gunther is. He's not a virgin; I'll swear to that. He smiled at me. He has perfect teeth, and he knows. Why can't I adopt him? Beethoven would have adopted Dr. Wegeler if he could have. And protected him from all harm.

. . . the morning is now the most lovely part of the day—why not seize the moment, seeing that it flies so quickly.

I never seized a moment. I'm practically certain of that.

. . . what a humiliation, when anyone standing beside me could hear at a distance a flute that I could not hear, or anyone heard a shepherd singing and I could not distinguish a sound!

Do not show this to anybody. I am speaking to you now, George Lionel. Show this to no one. Burn it. . . . I've just read it, and there is no clue at all. To anything.

And I've never known anyone named Gunther.

Defeat at
Thermopylae

I have a history of the town in front of me now, and I see that the dials on the courthouse clock are described as "friendly." To me they were never that. I was menaced by the old men on the square discussing the price of corn and the cost of death. I was pursued by the linden and the larch on West Main. I was imperiled by the groves of beeches in the vacant lot near the school. And the poplar that made shadows on the window of my bedroom whispered messages of doom. The chimes of the courthouse clock, which I could hear on a summer night, said, "Run away and never come back. Run away and never come back."

I ran, not knowing you can never run far enough. A boy once said to me, "My mother is dead." I said, "Oh, no she's not." The boy laughed and said, "You're right. She's not."

It is like that with me and the town. I never really left. I cannot forget. Months of my life have been mislaid, years mismanaged and forgot, decades only half remembered. Was that on a *rua* in Brazil? This on a corner near the cathedral in Seville? An alley near Pigalle? A hotel lobby in Mayfair? Piccadilly underground? Broadway and Forty-third? Fifty-second and Lexington? . . . Got a light? Know what time it is? Where you headed? How much. *Bon soir. Buenas días.* Early morning? Late at night? . . . It's cheaper in the morning.

But I can remember every crack in every sidewalk of that town.

65

Every voice. The Esterhazy girls saying to my mother, "We wouldn't play with that little sis for one million dollars cash money."

Frances Esterhazy could have used a million dollars; she became the mother of six before her husband was electrocuted on a high-tension wire. It happened the week after he cashed in the last of his life insurance policy. Frances sued the electric company, but she lost. Now she takes in washing, a profession that the laundromat has made even more precarious. Marion Esterhazy moved to Gladbrook, where she had hoped to open a beauty parlor, but she was forever denied that worthy ambition when she failed the course in spit curl at a beauticians' college in Des Moines. She waits tables at the Kozy Koffee Kup.

I mention the Esterhazy girls because they lived next door to our house, and they lived half a world away. I mention them because they were plump and mean and stupid. I mention them because they are the kind of people I have always despised. I mention them because I wanted them to love me.

Oh, they have suffered, too, but where's the comfort in that? I told you I'm not Jesus. I cannot forgive sixty-six times six. Ever. And I'd have hated Paul; epileptics always frighten me. Suppose it happens during. Simon called Peter can't have smelled too good.

No, Judas is the one I'd have trusted. Jesus loved John.

Malraux's priest said that there is no such thing as a grown-up person. As if I didn't know. We are all little boys and girls inside these large, ill-fitting bodies. We get to be as tall as other people sometimes, and our voices change, and our balls drop, and our breasts develop, and years go on, and tears set in, and decades go out, but we are all still scared little kids fooling nobody but ourselves.

Can't you see that despite the silver threads in what's left of the gold, I'm really only twelve, going on thirteen.

Treat me like a child, please, an obedient child, an adorable, obedient child. That's what I've always wanted to be, an adorable, obedient, regular little man. I've sworn off sex. I'll eat my oatmeal and my spinach. I've given up smoking, and even before I got here I hardly ever had a drink before five o'clock in the afternoon.

. . . Oh, love me, cherish me, harbor me, foster me. Be my strong right arm. Be my rod and my staff. . . . That's what I've been looking for in the streets, on avenues, in parks on moonless nights, in inadequately lighted squares, near statues, in dank movies, in basements and attics, in barns and bars, bedrooms and beds. Someone to protect me from all harm.

I know what I want Santa to bring, in addition to a rocking horse and a doll that wets herself, yes, both an Erector set and a ribbon for my hair.

I'm eleven. I'm eight, going on nine.

Dear Santa:

About the defeat at Thermopylae.

In the town people were always either talking about baseball or playing it, always, all year round. Basketball was okay, but baseball . . .

It wasn't the game that interested them so much; it was the heady odor of possible loot. Billy Sunday came from just up the road, near Nevada, and he was said to have made millions in baseball before he went on to make more millions as an evangelist. And Bob Feller was born not far away. He, too, made a fortune playing the game, and they have his bust in the Baseball Hall of Fame.

I remember the day I first spoke to Charley about it. Toward the end of what turned out to be the last summer in town for either of us.

I said, "Do you realize I've got to go out for baseball this fall? Otherwise I'll never get a diploma, and while I don't think a diploma from this lunatic limbo has any value, I've still got to get one. So what in Christ's name am I going to do?"

We had been sitting on the edge of the small and sullen creek that crept through the meadow, just below the hill on which the new Payne house was being built, the one that was never finished. I remember the meadow as being all goldenrod, although here and there were, I believe, some few bedraggled dandelions and a forgotten daisy or so.

That final summer Charley and I had spent a good deal of time studying the mysteries of the indolent creek and watching the doomed house grow.

"So what in Christ's name am I going to do? I won't even be able to see the goddamn ball, let alone catch it, and when I'm at bat . . ."

"Oh, my God," said Charley, "the thought of you at bat. It boggles the mind. I've never known what that idiot phrase means, but now I do. My mind is totally boggled. As for catching the ball, you'll break your hands, or the ball will hit your glasses and break them, and the glass will get in your eyes, and you'll be blinded for life."

"All that or worse."

"Couldn't you get a letter from one of our local quacks saying that you're not physically fit for baseball? There isn't a doctor in town who, with the proper financial inducement, wouldn't pump air into somebody's veins, but when you come to something really basic, like baseball, they are incorruptible."

We got up. Charley skipped a rock in the creek, and we started up the hill toward the unfinished house.

"I'll think of something," said Charley. "So don't worry."

"Sure you'll think of something. You and Roosevelt and God."

That evening Charley and I went to the Casino to see what up to then was my favorite movie of all time, *Dead End*; I'd seen it four times. The Dead End Kids could not only play stickball, they could swim and talk dirty. So what if they were a little poor. Who wasn't? Even Toscanini hadn't eaten any red meat until he was twenty.

Half a block or so from the Casino Charley said, "You're going to volunteer."

"Volunteer for what?"

"When school starts, you're going right up to Coach Blabbermouth and tell him you can't wait to get out there and 'play ball.' "

"You bet. Sure."

"I'm serious, my boy. You are going to say that it's your duty to play ball and that you even know where you want to play, permanently. You tell him the place you can give your best to the team is far right field."

"I don't understand a word you're saying. I don't even know what far right field is."

"I do, and the chances of a ball ever making it out there is about one in a million. I've figured it all out mathematically. Baseball seasons will come and go, World Serieses will be won and lost, and a ball won't land in far right field. But *they* won't think of that."

"Are you sure?"

"Have I ever let you down? Of course I'm sure."

And for a while things turned out just the way Charley had predicted. The coach was delighted at my volunteering; he said, "You *might* turn into a regular boy after all."

Buster Dean said, "Sister Sue? I'll believe it when I see it."

So brief though it was, I became Our Man in Far Right Field, and even former enemies said, "You're doing all right out there."

The point, of course, is that I was doing nothing at all out there, nothing for the team, that is. But I did a good deal of conducting. "What's that you say? Maestro Toscanini is ill and he says the only person in the entire country he'd trust the N.B.C. Symphony with is me? You're sending first-class train fare? One way? I won't be coming back here, ever? But are you absolutely sure they're ready for me? Well, if the Maestro himself . . . All right, men. You may think I'm a little young, but I stand before you at the specific request of our beloved Arturo, and I am sure you men, being musicians, know that Mozart wasn't exactly aged when the Empress Maria Theresa . . . *Attention!* I am lifting my baton. . . ."

Then one oppressive day in October our team played Colo. Colo then had a population of 352, while we were what the *Times-Dispatch* called a thriving, ever-expanding metropolis of 25,000. Actually, 19,000 was more like it; that's what the census people said anyway. But our town was named after a justice of the United States Supreme Court; Colo was named after a *dog*.

We had never lost to Colo, either. The score was always about 999 to nothing, in our favor. But not the year Our Man was in Far Right Field.

Don't ask me what inning it was or who was at bat or the score; I could never keep track of things like that. I do know that I was in the middle of the second movement of the Brahms Third. I was, of course, conducting without a score, and I was, just as Rosenberg said I should, trying to keep in mind what Johannes Brahms might have had in mind when he wrote the music. I was also thinking that the world really could do without his Lullaby, although perhaps it isn't really the Lullaby so much as the frog-throated ladies who usually have at it. Johannes can't be blamed for them.

Then, suddenly, my thoughts and the second movement were interrupted. There was a great dissonance from everywhere. I looked up and realized that several thousand people were yelling at me and jumping up and down and groaning and pointing. It took me several seconds to see the thing, but there, sure enough, a little away from where the first cellist had been sitting, was the goddamn baseball, a slight rip on the surface mocking me with a grin.

I walked toward it, trembling, but by the time I stopped for it, my palms wet, the game was over. While I was endangering the future of the republic with Brahms, Colo had scored the winning four points. I don't *know* how.

A good deal of what happened after that I have forgotten or prefer not to remember. Most people in school, pupils and teachers, gave me the silent treatment for the rest of the year. I didn't mind that too much. In some ways I preferred it. Buster said, "Do you realize you lost us the fucking ball game, you four-eyed, cocksucking little sissy?"

And Coach Masterson, who had tears in his small, blank eyes, said, "Not that it meant anything to you, you little sis bastard, but this could mean my job. This is the first time since they crucified Christ that we've lost to Colo."

That afternoon I went home the long way around, but it's never long enough. My mother had already heard. Naturally. Everybody in town had already heard.

Mother, who was about as helpful as God when you needed her, said, "It's just one of those tragic things we'll have to live with. And of course Buster's mother. I can hear her now at the next bridge club meeting, lording it over me."

I said, "It's too bad you didn't have Buster as your son; he's more your type."

"No, I don't care a thing about Buster. He's a *mean* boy, and nobody has ever said that about you, that you were *mean*. However, in a town like this, being responsible for our losing to Colo will not soon be overlooked. It is one thing to play the piano, but baseball is the very backbone of America."

My father said, "For Christ's sweet sake, Dora. What difference does it make? It's only a silly little baseball game."

"If that had been Billy Sunday's attitude, he'd still be plowing the south forty in Nevada."

"This boy is going to be a much bigger man than Billy Sunday ever thought of being."

Charley had been in Des Moines with his mother. He called around seven and said, "I got the Stravinsky. The Cleveland Symphony. I'll bring it right over."

"I guess you haven't heard."

"I've heard. It's all my fault. I'm such a smart-ass. Just like everybody says. Mr. Know-It-All. I'm sorry but, friend, it doesn't mean a thing. Not a thing. I'll be right over."

I quietly hung up the receiver, and I made it to my room before I actually started sobbing.

By the time Charley got to the house, I had locked my door and was in bed, the covers pulled over my bloody and bowed head. I could not quite make out what my mother was saying to Charley, but her tone was that used in a house of death. Was there crepe on the door?

After a time Charley left, and my father tried the door of my room, but I wouldn't let him in. I wish now I had.

Eventually, because one does, because one must, I opened the door of my bedroom, came out, and went back to school.

But I was never again on a baseball diamond, any baseball diamond. I have never even looked at one.

When I got back to school Coach Masterson put me in the supply room, and when I mumbled my thanks he said, "Don't thank me. It was your buddy's idea, your so-called buddy. Mr. Snot-Nose. The smart-ass."

"Yes, sir, I know who you mean."

"If I had my way, I'd put every one of the sissies like you in a leaky boat, and out in the middle of the Atlantic I'd see to it that it sank. And don't try any of your funny stuff with me because if you do, glasses or not, I'll knock your goddamn sissy head off."

In my adolescence, when I was thirty or so, that last sentence would have made me roll on the floor with laughter, but on this particular day I did not laugh. I realized, and the knowledge startled and saddened me, that the coach hated me more than he hated Charley, more than he hated anybody, and he was a big hater. I was pretty sure I knew why he hated me most, but that didn't help much. It didn't help at all.

Coach Masterson was the kind of man to whom almost everybody in town felt superior. Thus he was popular and was forever being elected something. At one time or another he was president of all the service clubs, Rotary, Kiwanis, Lions, Optimists, for at least one term. He was everything you can be in the Elks Club, in the town, in the state, in the nation. He was a state legislator, after which he went to Washington as a congressman, after which he was governor of the state, after which the Senate. But he was not just any senator.

There was a time when his name appeared on the front page of the *Times, The New York Times,* almost as often as it had in the *Times-Dispatch.* And he was responsible for my name being on the front page of the *Times.* That was another time I tried to get out. I wonder how many there've been.

My feeling about *Dead End* was nothing compared to the coach's feeling about a movie with Pat O'Brien. It was about a football coach named Gore. Masterson had seen it twenty-eight times. He saw every single showing the first weekend it played the Casino, and he persuaded the manager, a fellow Elk, to hold it over for another three days. Then, aided and abetted by another outright crook, Superintendent of Schools Fred Storer, the coach called a high school assembly to announce that seeing the movie was *required* of anybody who expected to get a high school diploma.

He gave quite a lengthy talk about the film, but then he made the mistake of saying, "Are there any questions?"

Charley, who was, as usual, sitting in the back row of the auditorium, rose.

"All right, Payne. What is it?"

"Yes, sir. I wondered if I had heard you correctly. Did you say *required?*"

"That's what I said, and that's what I mean."

"That's interesting. *Required.* I'm sure you've checked that out with the board of education and, I am sure, with my father, who, as you know, is chairman. . . ."

"Okay, Payne. You win. All I'm saying is this picture is a picture every red-blooded boy and girl . . ."

The coach drove to Des Moines when the picture played there, to Waterloo, to Cedar Rapids, to Boone and Nevada; he even drove to Red Oak and Liscomb, and when it played in Chicago, Masterson took a week off to go to that fair city. As I say, twenty-eight times.

"Lots of nuances in that picture, aren't there, coach?" Charley would say.

"That's right. Nuances till you can't rest. I cry—I'm not ashamed to stand up like a man and admit it—I cry every time Pat O'Brien, he's the one that plays Coach Gore, makes that speech to the fellows. It's just before they play the Homecoming game, and Gore's boys are the underdogs. It's not only his boys O'Brien is talking to. He's also talking to God. You can tell that by the look on his face. He's talking to God because Gore knows that while this ain't no war or something like that where God gets *involved*, there's other times God has got to choose, and may the best team win, the cleanest team, the team where none of the boys is abusing themselves, and you boys know what I mean by that. God ain't got no use for a boy that abuses himself. That's what Gore is saying to God, and I'm not going to give anything away. I'm not going to spoil the picture for any of you boys that ain't seen the picture. I'm not going to let on I even know who wins the Homecoming game. But I will say this. You take one look at some of the boys on the other team, and you can tell, all drawn out and thin and all, you can tell that some of them has been practicing secret vices. And so can Pat O'Brien, the one that plays Gore. That O'Brien is a great actor, boys. One of the greatest. Did I ever tell you—?"

"That you wrote all the way to Hollywood, California, and that Pat O'Brien sent you a *personally* autographed picture of himself that hangs in a place of honor in your living room, just below the statue of Our Blessed Virgin? Yes," Charley would say, "I believe you have mentioned that a time or two, hasn't he, boys?"

"Let's play ball, boys. Let's play ball."

In the late 1940s and the early 1950s, when Masterson's voice was one of the two loudest and most feared in Washington, the newspapers and the news magazines did a lot of looking into the coach's past, but they didn't get it right. They never get it right.

When Charley and Lily and I were all in high school, the *Times-Dispatch* always referred to the coach as "Herbert Neil Masterson, famed director of athletics at . . ."

They did that almost daily because the coach was almost daily up to something that was of no importance whatsoever.

Physically he was an immense man, six three, and he must have weighed three hundred pounds, all blubber. Hair grew on him abundantly, black and coarse. It grew on the backs of his soft, forever perspiring hands; it grew on his oversized arms and legs, and it grew on his chest and neck, beyond his Adam's apple. But on the top of his head, his head being somewhat small for the rest of his body, there was no hair at all.

Not unexpectedly for a man who had been on the university football team the year it went to the Rose Bowl and who was almost All-American, Coach Masterson was volubly masculine. All of the time. To hear him tell it, and it was impossible not to hear him tell it if one was within a block of the childish voice, there were few women in town, young or old, ugly or beautiful, married or single, that he hadn't laid.

"Boys, except for a nip of Scotch whiskey now and again and working up a sweat in a competitive, manly sport, there is nothing that tests the mettle of a man more than a roll in the hay with a woman, and it don't matter a good goddamn what she looks like. You can always put a gunnysack over their head, and they all smell the same down there."

Have I said that the coach was a pillar of the Holy Name Society?

Except for Charley we all laughed at the coach's wit. And when he added, "That thing between your legs needs exercise just like the rest of your body," everybody, again excepting Charley, slapped his thighs. I did it with perhaps less conviction than the others.

Charley would say, "Now that you've proved how manly you are, coach, perhaps we can get on with the game."

At which point the coach would protrude his small and pink and girlish lower lip—I guess you would have to call it a pout—and he would say, "If I was you, Payne, I'd mind my *p*'s and *q*'s."

"I've never known what that expression means, minding your *p*'s and *q*'s. Perhaps you could explain it to me. You did take top honors in English lit when you were at the university, didn't you?"

"You know what it means, smart-ass, and you think just because your father owns this town you can get away with anything, don't you? And you think you're smarter than I am, don't you?"

"About the last there is no doubt at all. Are there other questions?"

"Let's play ball, boys. Let's play ball."

Charley didn't care much for baseball either, but since it was required, he played it during his junior year, and for the first time and, as far as I know, the last, our team won the state championship. The sports reporter for the *Des Moines Register* wrote that ". . . the teamwork was shoddy, not to say nonexistent, but due to the professional, close to big league pitching of young Charles Payne, the team managed to eke . . ."

The coach got into a real snit over that because if there was one thing he was big on, it was teamwork. "There are no individuals on my teams, boys; we're all for one and one for all. . . . You look as if you might have some comment on that, Payne. If so, don't be bashful. Speak up."

"No comment at all. I just want to remember the striking and original way you put it—one for all and all for one."

"Payne thinks he can get my goat, but I refuse to let that happen. When I see other people fly off the handle, I just sit back and smile. I've steeled myself against losing my temper. It wasn't easy, but that's what separates the men from the boys." The coach had a very high-pitched voice, but that did not prevent him from making a great deal of money by giving speeches all over the state, particularly at commencement time.

Although the coach pouted for days over what the sports reporter for the *Register* had written about the lack of teamwork among our boys, he was eventually able to dismiss the whole thing as a communist plot.

"I *used* to look up to the *Register*. Why, when I was a kid, even younger than most of you boys, I'd get up every morning at six, and sometimes it was way below zero and then some, but I wasn't ashamed of good, hard work. Good, hard work never hurt nobody,

boys; it's only your sissies"—a sidelong glance in my direction—
"your sissies and your commies that are afraid of work, and the commies start by subverting the sports pages of our newspapers.

"That's what happened in this case, boys, because if there is anything we are, it's a team, but the reds, the commies, the sissies . . .
And they aren't all Hebrews, I don't say that, although I notice the
man that signed this piece of sissy perversion calls himself Rosen.
And you don't see an awful lot of people named *Rosen* in the *Christian* churches on a Sunday." (Laughter.)

In those days people in Iowa didn't talk much about the communists, but the coach saw reds everywhere—in schools, churches, the
government, everywhere—and should anybody try to challenge him
(very few ever did), he would silence every tongue but Charley's
by saying, "You don't know what you're talking about, and I do,
because I've *read*. . . . They haven't all got bushy beards and stuff
like that, although most of them ain't any too anxious to bathe. And
like I say, they ain't all of them of the Hebrew persuasion. Some of
them, boys, may be just as white as you and me; they may even be
living in this very town, teaching in our schools, preaching in our
churches. . . . Yes, Payne, what is it this time?"

"Coach, has the school board switched your job around?"

"What's that supposed to mean, Payne?"

"I thought I saw Mr. Thornton in the cafeteria at lunch, but
maybe that was somebody else."

"I'm sure your point when you get to it is going to be a lot of
laughs for all of us, Payne."

"I simply mean that to my great surprise, and you are in no way
equipped for it, you have, apparently, taken over Mr. Thornton's
classes in political science."

"No, Mr. Smart-Aleck Payne, I am simply trying to teach these
boys a few facts that as Americans they have a right—"

"Coach, you are an incompetent director of physical education,
but that is what you are paid for and all you are paid for. Not your
asinine views on politics."

"I have every right—"

"No, you haven't. You have no right at all. To the contrary, while you are in the physical plant of the high school—"

"The boys in the American Legion pay good money for me to explain—"

"The boys in the American Legion—and I'm glad you used the word *boys*—are cretins."

"All I'm saying, boys, and this has nothing to do with you, Payne, or with your friend Sister Sue there, I'm saying if you boys want to learn, and I know what I'm talking about because I've read, the commie . . ."

Charley looked at his wristwatch, and the coach said, "Anybody that wants to talk to me *after* school, I'll be here. . . . Let's play ball, boys. Let's play ball."

"We'll play ball in good time, coach, but first I believe you have an apology to make."

9 /

Model Citizens

I'd swear I told you. I gave up reading the *Times* two, maybe three months ago. One morning I cried five times before I got to page six, and I always skip page one. So I just stopped reading it. You can't cry all the time. Mustn't, shouldn't, won't. . . . Crying, criers. A woman in Indianapolis once said, "I couldn't possibly love a man who cried."

I wanted to say that I couldn't possibly love a man who didn't. I didn't say a word, though.

I got busted anyway and spent the night in a cell with a black drag queen dressed in early Joan Crawford. Shiny high-heeled shoes with red tassels, carrying that large purse that Joan carried before she got rich in *Mildred Pierce*. The queen's name was Guinevere, and I asked her how she picked out such a name, and she said, "I was in love with a boy named Lancelot. And he wrote this poem, 'To love one maiden only, cleave to her,/ And worship her by years of golden deeds.'"

I didn't laugh, couldn't laugh. I said that that was nice. I'll tell you this, though. Stay out of the bus stations in Indianapolis. Especially Trailways. The place is loaded with members of the vice squad, some of them, I admit, quite attractive. But they arrest you afterward. The law, sir, is a ass.

❖

Yesterday, I think it was yesterday, Miss Benson came twice and rattled the door. I told her to go fuck herself, and presumably she did because she hasn't come back. That I know of. If she does, I'll put Buster Dean to work on her wisdom teeth.

Last night Gunther came. I didn't open the door. He said that he wanted to talk to me, personally, he said, about a personal matter, and he said he had a bottle of vodka, and we could have a little fun, he said. . . . Liquor is strictly forbidden, and sex with members of the staff is not looked upon favorably. So, since I do not believe in breaking the rules, I told Gunther I'd had a little fun with too many young men; I told him to go marry his debutante; I told him I'd bedded down with many a groom the night before the nuptials, "one last fling before I resort to closet queenery." I told Gunther there had been too many bottles of vodka in my life. I told him I was tired. I asked him to bring me a single-edge razor, newly sharpened. I said I'd begin by cutting it off; then I'd start on my wrists, again.

In answer to your other question. I think I always *knew*, but I don't think I was very sexy as a kid. I didn't have much sex, either. There were the transient boys down by the railroad station. Some were beautiful, and some were white, and some were black, and they all had stories to tell. The stories were always sad, and the black boys' stories were sadder. That was the only difference.

Oh, a loathsome boy cousin caused me to do certain things when he was fourteen and I was nine, and when I was twelve there was a man in the men's room at the Casino, but then in every boy's life there is a man in the men's room of a movie theater somewhere, and it either means something or it doesn't. . . . The English say the age of consent is thirteen, which I think is high.

As far as boys in school were concerned, I tried not even to think about sex. I didn't have too much success with the not-thinking part, but with the not-doing, yes. Nothing to do with morality. As is usually the case, it had to do with cowardice and the fact that there weren't many boys around who interested me much. God had not been kind to most boys in the town.

But then, I believe early in 1934, a CCC camp was opened west of town. The Civilian Conservation Corps was, you may remember, one of Franklin Roosevelt's earliest inspirations. Boys in their late teens and early twenties were taken from the grimy, vice-ridden city streets and placed in camps in the healthful out-of-doors where they planted trees and picked up sticks and piled cordwood and raked. As I recall, they earned thirty dollars a month, and they wore khaki uniforms.

This noble effort not only helped with the unemployment problem. It got the boys ready for the army.

The boys in the camp were from places like Des Moines and Davenport and Sioux City, and they were from poor families, many of them Irish and Polish and Swedish, and genetics being what they are, it is, they were often extraordinarily good-looking. One night in The Magic Lantern a Polish boy named Ned, whose father was an out-of-work plumber's assistant, told me about some of the very odd goings-on in the camp. Then we left The Magic Lantern, and in the dark, deserted high school football field, Ned taught me a few of those things, most of which I'd known about all along anyway. I remember I said, "Is there much of this sort of thing going on out at the camp?" Ned said, "We aren't sure about the commandant, but otherwise . . ."

Later I met other boys from the camp, and they said that Ned exaggerated but not much, and they told me about other CCC camps, same story. I always wondered if Franklin Roosevelt knew, and the time during his third term when I had dinner at the White House and played for the assembled guests, I was afraid I'd blurt out the question. As a result, I didn't say a word the entire evening. The Secretary of Labor was there and she did most of the talking. As I said, Mr. Roosevelt did not know how to listen.

There were two boys in school I couldn't help thinking about, though, almost incessantly. One was Eldon Rickets, who was an usher at the Casino and who in his uniform proved that D. H. Lawrence was right in saying that men would be more emancipated and prouder if a universal law was passed making it mandatory for them to wear coats that did not conceal their buttocks. Eldon was certainly handsome in the uniform that met Lawrence's qualification, but I never discussed *Lady Chatterley* with him. I had not yet read it. Neither, I am sure, had Eldon, and we never had sex anyway.

He said, "No, thank you very much, but I'm saving it."

Eldon was very polite.

The man looked down in silence at his tense phallus, that did not change.

Nicky Pondorus was the handsomest boy in town, almost any town. He had blue-black hair worn long, very long for those days, and a great dark shaft of it would, I expect at will, fall over his eyes, which were also beautiful. I was sure that he had practiced the throw of his head that hurled his hair back into place. But who cared? He was Greek, wasn't he? Nicky had full red lips and a smile that was as professional as the gesture with his hair. He was lazy and a liar and a thief, and I used to follow him everywhere. I never thought he noticed, but one night when the moon was full and there was snow on the ground, he turned and said, "What do you want from me, kid, following me around all the time?"

I couldn't have answered if I'd had the voice for it, but Nicky, whose father ran The Magic Lantern, said, "I know what you want, kid. How much money you got on you?"

I said, "Fifty cents," and Nicky said, "I've been known to get up to five bucks a throw. You must be kidding."

I said, "I haven't got much money, ever; I take music lessons; but I could help you with your plane geometry. I mean I've heard you have trouble with math."

"That's a deal," said Nicky, "but next time try for a dollar at least."

❖

A few months later Nicky was caught holding up the Rock Island railroad station. He had not quite finished tying up the stationmaster, Mr. Durrell, when the town police, for once on the alert, burst in.

Armed robbery, even when you are sixteen years old, as Nicky was, can result in quite a long stay in the pokey, but Judge Holt, noted for his harshness, was in this instance notably lenient. The sentence to Eldora was no more than a slap on the wrist, six months, with time off for good behavior.

After Nicky's day in court Mrs. Judge Holt was heard to say, several times, "I thought perhaps the judge was going to invite young Pondorus to the house for dinner or even the night before he was sent off for a summer vacation at Eldora, at the taxpayers' expense."

"I don't care what you say, Amelia," said the judge. "All that boy needs to become a model citizen is a helping hand."

"I guess we all know whose helping hand you have in mind," said Amelia Holt.

Everybody in town predicted that Nicky Pondorus would end up either in the state penitentiary for life or in the electric chair, but that is not quite what happened. I last saw him in 1946. I was living and studying in Rome and had gone to one of the Greek islands for a week's rest. Nicky stopped off for dinner at a famous restaurant on the island.

We met at dinner, and afterward Nicky, his benefactor, and I sat drinking on a terrace over a bay where the yacht was moored. The yacht looked as if J. P. Morgan might have hesitated before spending the money. Nicky's benefactor, a Spanish Falangist who was minister of something or other in the Franco government, had given the yacht to Nicky, whom he referred to as his nephew.

At one point Nicky stretched, and he said to me, "We're a long way from home, kid, and if my father could see me now, he wouldn't believe it."

Later (we sat up until dawn) Nicky said, "I've never done a day's work in my life, and I know I should be ashamed of myself.

But sometimes I ask myself, if I'd gone to work like I should have and tromped around in them tomatoes at the canning factory and saved my money and married some dumb broad whose idea of a good time is a weekly roll in the hay and shelling out a kid every nine months or so, how many yachts would I have now?"

Nicky's uncle, whose knowledge of English was minimal, patted his nephew on the knee and smiled, and Nicky looked down at the yacht and smiled.

I suppose someday Nicky will get his just deserts; my mother always said that everybody does, always. I'm not so sure, though, assuming I know what just deserts are.

I once asked Nicky if it bothered him, taking money from men.

He said, "One business is as good as another."

To which I had no answer. Is there one? You people made the rules. And I tried to live up to them. I tried being what you said I ought to be, but I couldn't. I can't. . . . I'll tell you one thing, though. I will not go to the crematorium quietly.

10 /

Vows
of Chastity

As to our new home, my wife has done everything possible to please me. The apartment is comfortable and nicely arranged; everything is clean, new, and attractive. And yet I look upon it all with hatred and resentment. . . .

Your unchanging and deeply devoted
friend,
P.T.

I was thirty years old, and on sunny days it seemed to me I had never known disappointment or defeat. My career had never been more lustrous. I was fortunate in not being in love. . . . I was the man who had everything. And what do you give to the man who has everything?

You give him a wife.

She was a pretty girl, a pretty woman, I suppose, twenty-five years old; a dark, impish face; large, trusting eyes; small, small-boned, a magnificent figure. Everybody said, boy, are you lucky. Is Dede ever built?

I suppose they were right. The female figure is a subject I really have not studied up on.

Smart, too. She was music critic for a newspaper on Long Island, and she had studied piano almost as long and as hard as I had,

". . . but I knew fairly early on that I'd never be anything but a bystander."

On the other hand she had written, ". . . in every generation there is one pianist whose talent is supreme, and for his generation, George Lionel has demonstrated that he is without a peer . . . not only excels as a technician but . . ."

When we met she said, "I hope you won't mind if I just sit at your feet and worship you."

I ran and hid in the bathroom, locking the door behind me.

She said through the door, "It will do you no good to hide from me."

I opened the door and came out, and she said, "The only real question is *when* we get married."

She said afterward, "I courted George for almost six months before he broke down and agreed to marry me."

Actually it was closer to a year, but I was away most of the time.

She said, "When George is on tour, he lays them in the aisles."

Not true, except for an occasional very short affair with a pretty young usher. Aisles are uncomfortable. And the boys always say, "I guess you might call this the fall of the house of usher." I do not know why they always say it. I only know that they do.

One day when Dede's courtship was particularly ardent I said, I think without a sigh, "Well, I guess we might as well get it over with."

She said, "How romantic you are."

I'm not at all sure I can answer the question you asked yesterday. About the marriage. Why? Why did I of all people get married? To a pretty woman, an intelligent (IQ 152) woman, a nice woman? Why did she marry me?

The latter is easier to understand. Other people's motives usually are.

In the first place, they all think they can make you go straight. I have yet to meet a woman who doesn't. . . . How *could* you like boys when there are girls around? The trouble with you is you've never known a really good girl; you've never known me. And once you do, and let's hop into bed and talk it over, you'll shun boys forevermore. The mere thought will make you sick. Prove I'm wrong.

So Dede was going to see to it that I went straight.

Others had tried that before; others have since. Only last week one of the more palatable nurses right here in this very institute . . . Never mind.

Dede was sharp enough to recognize certain small, what you might call self-destructive tendencies in me, but she believed, so help me God, that she could cure them.

I told her that the inside of my head had been had at by more than a few trained personnel, all of whom had given up in despair.

Nonsense, said Dede. What you need is love. It makes the world go round, and it will make all the difference in your case. You have been warped. I will unwarp you. In your childhood you were denied the tender-loving-kindness that we are all guaranteed in the Constitution, and I am more than willing and able to provide it. Late perhaps, but better late than . . .

Dede was a great doer of good, a partaker in worthy causes, and she was sure that, although I was not tax deductible, she could keep me from skinning my knee or, if I did, she could kiss it and make it well again. . . . And don't cry just because that bully boy bloodied your nose and took away your week's allowance. What were you doing on Forty-second Street anyway? All those tough-looking boys in tight pants. Why do they wear such tight pants? And a lot of them are really quite good-looking, aren't they? But what are they standing there for, smiling those vacant smiles?

Never mind. Mummy will fix it. And here's another quarter. Run down to the candy store and get yourself another ice cream cone with sprinkles. That's a good boy.

And you have to practice, and Mummy is going to get you all dressed up in your little velvet Buster Brown suit, and Mummy will hold your hand all the way to Carnegie Hall.

Mummy is going to be so proud.

It was a noble effort. Dede was and is a noble woman, and the only trouble with nobility is that it tends to get a little monotonous now and again.

Dede kept saying, I don't care if you have sex with other people, even with, well, you know, boys. I don't think sex is all that important. It's certainly not the most important thing in our relationship. All I really ask is that you don't pause tell me pause about it unquote.
And she said, As long as we're all right together, that's what counts and all that counts. And she said, We do love each other don't we question unquote.

And I kept thinking, At last a chance to be like all the other little boys. I may not be able to play baseball, but I can take me a wife. "Sorry, fellows, I won't have time for another; the little woman is . . ."
I wanted so much to conform. I always despised the average man, and yet I always wanted to be like him. Explain it? Lucille, it's been years since I've even wondered why. That's one of the troubles with you people. You think if you can explain something, it doesn't hurt any more. And you think if you *label* something, it's cured. . . . Sorry, chickie, wrong in both cases.

You know something? There were a few times, enough to prove I shouldn't be allowed out, when I thought the marriage might work.
But in my more sober moments, and there were a few, I knew perfectly well that you can't straighten out a drunk or a sissy, and I'm both. Always have been. Always will be.
So we went ahead and did it, and instead of getting arrested, we got hundreds of telegrams of congratulation and were written up all over.
I was sober enough during the nuptials, and in fact the whole thing led to that part of my "Love and Kindred Ailments" where

the wedding march and the funeral march get all mixed up, the part that leads to the bassoon solo with the flute obbligato.

I started drinking rather more than usual after the final "I do," and I didn't stop until after the Tijuana divorce.

I was faithful, though, for more than seventy-two hours. It was not until the early afternoon of the third day of the honeymoon that Maximinho, who was surely the most beautiful Brazilian bar boy anywhere, and I drove off in the hot January sunset of Rio.

Dede didn't ask where I'd been; she never did. She was too smart for that.

After that there was always another boy on every corner and sometimes as many as two or three in the middle of the block. Believe me, I did my best. I wore dark glasses with lenses so thick it was impossible to tell what sex anybody was, let alone what he looked like.

I stayed out of the bars. I didn't even walk on a street where there was a Turkish bath. I put triple locks on the door of the apartment and of the studio. Did it work? Did anything work? Answer: no, nothing.

There were only 112 giant steps between our front door and the nearest Gristede's. I know how many there were because I counted them almost daily. But even that short distance . . . We lived in a posh apartment house in what was otherwise a shabby Italian neighborhood, and in that particular Gristede's there were an extraordinary number of handsome Italian boys who knew the score, knew the score, knew the score. And they all wanted to deliver. "I'll bring this stuff up personally in about half an hour. Okeydokey? Your wife, I mean the missus, won't be there, will she?" There were two friendly neighborhood boys, of Sicilian descent, Mafia pledges, in our friendly neighborhood liquor store. They were so anxious to deliver and so often did that at times I gave up drinking for a day or so.

For further protection, deliver me from all evil, I stayed out of subways and buses; I didn't set foot in Grand Central. I took taxis between the apartment and the studio. . . . For all the rest of my

life New York taxi drivers have been elderly, garrulous men of un-
redeemed ugliness. Not during The Marriage. It was impossible to
find a driver who was not young, handsome, and agreeable. It seems
to me that without exception they volunteered to come up to the
studio and listen to my latest mazurka.

Even the window washer. I had the windows of my studio washed
four times a week, free of charge. They were the talk of West Fifty-
seventh . . . Let us not speak of the delicatessens, of the corners near
Carnegie, of the shadows in cinemas, of the bookstores, drugstores,
Chinese restaurants, Greek restaurants. Of.

Look, comparatively it was as if as a bachelor I had taken vows
of chastity.

At first Dede tried to overlook my present by concentrating on
my past. We were living in an apartment I'd lived in for three years
before the marriage, sharing it with various lovers. Dede redeco-
rated the apartment half a dozen times. She scrubbed; she fumi-
gated; she burned candles and incense and charcoal and sulphur
and spruce. She recovered and rebuilt all the furniture. She burned
the old linen and bought new. She joined several churches and
took up astrology and Zen, and when she had, or thought she had,
exorcised the spirits of all those who had shared the apartment
with me, she collapsed into an easy chair, drank most of a fifth of
gin, and accused me of being queer and promiscuous.

I denied the latter. I had lived up to my side of the bargain. I
had never told her about any of it, and I had never brought anybody
to the apartment while she was there. Except once, and that was a
mistake. The boy, a chimney sweep as I recall, carried the whole
thing off rather well.

I said, and at the moment I'd have sworn I was telling the truth,
"Dede, it's contemptible to make such an accusation. I have never—"

She said, "It's my fault. It was my idea."

I said, "Do you want to get the divorce or should I?"

She said, "I will. I need a vacation, and I've never been to Mexico."

And that is the way it ended. Dede and I still see each other now and again. She has never remarried. I, too, have remained single. You don't find two Miss Rights in one lifetime.

It's been a long time since I wrote that last sentence. I don't know how long. There are no clocks and watches in this room and won't be, not while I'm here. Clocks and watches are as lethal as Hammond organs. I once tore the cuckoo out of one of those clocks and jumped up and down on it maybe a hundred times, killing it dead.

The thing belonged to my fancy Aunt Leta, and do you know what she did? She cried, and she said, "I loved that little cuckoo."

I tell you. Except for my father and grandfather everybody in the Lionel family was a damn fool.

I have torn up the cadenza. A couple of days ago I thought it wasn't too bad, but now I know better. It was composed by a man who has long since lost whatever talent he may have had, a cocksucker at that.

This is the season of losing. The wild crab apple tree has lost all its blossoms, and it's raining, and everywhere there is the sound of thunder. At first the room only vibrated a little, but now it is trembling.

I think maybe lightning struck the administration building. I certainly hope so. . . . Something is burning. I hope all of them burn to death, including Gunther, especially Gunther. He's the one who led me astray. I hate blonds, especially German blonds. My ass he's Swiss. Germanness sticks out all over him.

You know who he looks like? He looks like the German lieutenant who told them to start in on my hands. . . . Is *that* what a crematorium looks like? I thought it was bread they were baking. Hot cross buns. Wiener schnitzel. . . . The kikes are going like hot cakes, and they are all circumcised, every man-child of them. No one is immortal, though, and the next time around we'll all go.

. . . someone is poisoning me. . . . One of my enemies has succeeded in giving me poison and has already calculated the exact time of my death.

11 /

Some Kind
of Mistake

The last time I saw my Grandfather Lionel was the Sunday before he died.

We had had the usual Sunday dinner at high noon—pot roast with sour cream, pork roast in home-brewed beer, fried chicken, roast turkey with sausage stuffing, ham, potato pancakes, mashed potatoes, boiled potatoes, noodles with caraway seeds. And Waldorf salad, a slice of canned pineapple, with cottage cheese *and* whipped cream *and* a cherry *and* a walnut. Three or four kinds of pies. And angel food and chocolate and yellow cake. And homemade ice cream, vanilla and strawberry and chocolate.

If I was very, very good, I sometimes got to lick the paddle of the freezer and once in a rare while got to turn the crank.

That was the meal, served at high noon and sprinkled with acrimony.

After the meal was over, my grandfather, who was a light eater, always went to the living room, put the rotogravure section of the *Des Moines Register* over his face, and went to sleep.

But that Sunday he didn't. After a few minutes he said from under the paper, "I used to think they weren't really mine."

He was speaking of eleven of his sons and daughters, who were in the sun parlor. My father was not among them. He was never among them. He was the youngest, the twelfth, and he was to have succeeded my grandfather in the bank. He was the only one who went away to college. He went to the university in Iowa City to study banking.

Of course all the others hated my father. "He's the one got sent to college." When one reminded them that all of the others—there were eight brothers, four sisters—had been offered the chance to go to college but had turned it down, knowing they weren't up to it, they said, "I could of run that bank with one hand tied behind me and without no college degree neither. What's that but a piece of paper? . . . Monte was always showing off, getting good grades in school and all. Grades never meant nothing to me. I knowed more when I was born than is in any of them books."

They were arguing. They could not be in a room for more than five minutes without raising their voices in anger. Is whooping cough more of a threat to life and limb than shingles? Is the Ford a greater work of art than the Chevy? Does it take more get-up-and-go to farm than to run a creamery? Is it nobler to be an Elk or a Moose? A Lion or an Odd Fellow? Is the airplane here to stay? If God had intended us to fly, he wouldn't have equipped us with wheels.

They spoke of goiter, of cancer, of artery hardening, of thrombosis, of adultery, never having heard the word except in some dimly lighted, half-remembered Sunday school. Thou shalt not . . . They all did, with the sheep in the meadow, the cows in the corn, with the hired man, with the traveling salesman peeing his name in the snow. They despoiled and demeaned. The word *love* never crossed their lips, their minds, or their hearts.

"The doctors can't have made a mistake eleven different times," said my grandfather. He removed the rotogravure and sat up. He listened to the loud, flat, angry voices. He said, "When you have children, you have no choice in the matter. You have to take what you get and make the most of it. Judging by what I got, except for your father, God must have a grudge against me."

He always talked that way to me. As if I were grown up. He did not speak at all to the other grandchildren, of whom there were, unbelievably, fifty-nine, including two lackluster girls with cleft palates.

Everybody hated everybody, me the most, going and coming. I thought at the time I was the only sissy among them, but later a walleyed cousin who was an all-round athlete and a complete shit took up light housekeeping with an interior decorator named Sadie, once Sam. Bernadette is now in his fifties, but his mother, Auntie Vivian, still insists that Benjamin is waiting for Miss Right to come along. Mr. Right? And what's wrong with Miss Sadie? Bernadette and Sadie make an annual pilgrimage to Lourdes. So far not a single miracle, but they've picked up a lot of lovely antiques that they sell in the old schoolhouse they've remodeled. You take an old country schoolhouse and two dykes and you've got an antique shop, around here anyway. *A is for apple.*

"Your father's the only one that's worth a hill of beans," said my grandfather. "You ought to be proud of him."

I said that I was, and my grandfather patted me on the head. He was a mild-mannered man; he wore a black mustache, and he had an abundance of black hair, parted in the middle. He spoke softly, and he never quite lost the Boston accent, although he had not been there since he was fourteen. He was always talking about going back. " 'Out of the darkness, flee from the jungle. Return to civilization.' "

He was an admirer of Sydney Smith, the English cleric, and was forever quoting him. " 'Never give way to melancholy. Resist it steadily, for the habit will encroach.' " " 'I have gout, asthma, and seven other maladies, but am otherwise very well.' "

On that last Sunday he smiled up at me from under the mustache, and he said, "I have every reason to think that you can be just as remarkable a man as you are a boy. Try to be. They'll hate you for it, but they'll hate you anyway. So try to be of some significance. Try not to fritter yourself away."

I walked with him to the door of the back parlor; he used it as a study; he hid in it; he cursed God in it and prayed in it; he did all his living in it; he spoke to the walls in it, but outside the walls he hardly ever spoke at all, never to his wife, not once. What would he have said? She had the temperament and the intelligence of a discontented Guernsey.

My grandfather leaned over and kissed me. He said, "Be good to your father. He is a very tender man." He smiled at me, a tender smile. He said, " 'What pain a man suffers when he is forever surrounded by fools.' "

He said good-bye, and then he closed the door behind him.

He died the following Thursday, just before or just after his Packard rammed into a weeping willow that was a few hundred feet south of the dusty farm on which Matthew Payne had recently foreclosed the mortgage.

The farm was my grandfather's last possession, and when he foreclosed, Matthew Payne said, "The world is not kind to those who lose, Amos."

The doctor said that my grandfather had died of a coronary. I have always thought it was a broken heart.

The only thing resembling a suicide note on his body was written on a piece of tablet paper that was folded into his wallet. One line: "Human life must be some kind of mistake."

12 /

Buster Deans

You've met him, seen him anyway. Of course you have. The Buster Deans of the world are running things, everything, everywhere.

At the time I'm talking about now Buster was eighteen and a senior in high school. Everybody got to be a senior, and everybody was graduated. All you had to do was sit there and wait.

Buster was thick-wristed, stump-bodied, fat-assed; they always have fat asses, always. If a thought had ever started across the wide prairie of Buster's head, which was covered with spikes of carrot-colored hair, the thought had not completed the journey.

It was November, and there was the threat of snow in the air and the promise of a winter that would be colder and longer and more depressing than the winter of the year before. It was dark. The lights in the show windows of the stores on East Main were all turned on, but in winter when weren't they? It was on such a day that I talked to Lily for the first time.

Charley and I were on the way to the library, and Buster was coming in the opposite direction. He had a disconcerting lurch when he walked. I was never sure whether one leg was shorter than the other or Buster had just never learned how to walk.

I was always afraid he'd fall on me, and in addition to the physical damage I was sure would be done, there was the matter of

Buster's pimples. His face was perpetually ablaze with them. You had only to glance at him, which you couldn't always avoid, and one or more of the pimples would burst, like bombs in midair.

And Buster's odor. I cannot describe it. I have no intention of trying. It was Buster's own, perhaps the only unique thing about him, and Buster was as aware of it as Lady Macbeth was aware of the blood on her hands.

He tried just as hard to get rid of it, too, with as little success, because despite showers and scrubbings without end, the smell remained.

Poor Buster, unskilled in walking, his face aburst with pimples, possessed of a smell. Do I feel no sympathy for him?

No, none, not then, not now.

On the November day I'm talking about here Buster stopped directly in front of Charley and me, but, fortunately, he didn't fall. He leaned toward Charley at something of a tilt, and every pore of his body was open and at work. In November, mind you, with the temperature in the low teens and falling.

He did something with his right eye that I believe was supposed to suggest a wink, and he said, "Payne, there's been something I've wanted to ask you. The coach and me's been talking."

"I'm sure of that," said Charley, "but there is nothing you could say or any question you could ask that would interest me in the least."

Charley stepped around Buster and started away.

Buster said, "The coach and me was wondering about you and the sis here. We figured either you was a sis, too, or she's blowing you. Which is it?"

Charley turned around and hit Buster twice, once on the chin, breaking a host of pimples but nothing else, then in the stomach area, and Buster fell to the sidewalk.

Charley and I walked on.

I said, "Jesus, I didn't know you could do that."

"Frankly, neither did I."

"Weren't you scared?"

"Of course," said Charley.

I didn't know it at the time, but the next day after swimming class Charley went up to the coach, who was clad only in a stopwatch. Due to the coach's modesty and his fear of rape, I was spared that sight.

"Yah, Payne. What's on your mind?"

"I understand you and Buster Dean have been having a few conversations if you can call them that about me and George Lionel. Is that true?"

"Yes, Mr. Smart-Aleck Payne, we've had a few about you and the sis and whether he's doing you and if so you must be half sis yourself, which I wouldn't for a minute doubt. We've had a few and we'll have a lot more. You got any more questions, smart-ass?"

"No more questions, just a little advice. I don't want you here next year. I want you out of this town by next September at the latest."

Using the voice of a fraudulent street-corner Santa, Masterson said, "Ho, ho, ho. That is rich. That is very rich. You ain't exactly running things around this town for a while yet, and it's a free country, and Buster Dean and I . . ." Have I mentioned that the coach had the voice of a twelve-year-old girl?

"By September at the latest," said Charley.

"That'll be the day," said the coach.

The following summer the *Times-Dispatch* announced that Coach Herbert Neil Masterson had, reluctantly, submitted his resignation to the school board, which had, reluctantly, accepted it. By going to Traer, the paper said, the coach was bettering himself, and to stand in the way of a man's journey upward . . . Meantime, we were lucky indeed to be able to secure the services of . . .

Traer. Well, it wasn't quite as bad as Colo. At the time the coach went there to better himself it had a population of 1,417, and the Traer school board managed to persuade the coach, in addition to his athletic duties, to teach two courses in English literature and one in manual training.

I don't know much about Traer, but I do know that a woman born there in 1882 wrote, after escaping, a simple, heartwarming novel about the place. Naturally, it won a Pulitzer Prize in the 1920's. An uncle of mine once had the Ford agency there; he said the best thing about Traer is that it isn't too far from Cedar Rapids.

There is this. For days before the coach got on the train to go to Traer, a distance of forty-two miles, the sports editor of the *Times-Dispatch* suggested, no, demanded that the local citizenry show up at the railroad station to demonstrate its appreciation for what the coach had done for the town. Chief of Police William H. Bender, the noblest Elk of them all and himself a one-time captain of our baseball team, sent a bevy of the town's finest to keep the crowds in check. Twenty-three people appeared, including Buster Dean.

But by that time I was in New York, and Charley was in New Haven. My mother sent me the clippings, and when I showed them to Charley, he said, "I wish there was somebody we could call to warn them about what they're getting. But there never is anybody, is there? And they'll probably love him in Traer."

The people of Traer started Coach Masterson on his giddy political journey.

That same summer Buster Dean got an athletic scholarship, whatever that may be, to a dental collage in I believe Ottumwa. It was on the front page of the *Times-Dispatch,* along with a heavily retouched photograph of Buster that helped with but did not solve the pimple problem.

I'm not sure Buster graduated from that college, but since such places seldom fail anybody capable of passing Basic Eraser Cleaner, I'm reasonably sure he did. One of my recurrent nightmares is of being forcced to go to Buster Dean to have him work on a wisdom tooth.

I'll send Bensy.

I'm pretty sure of this. If I'd known when I was seventeen that fifteen years later in Washington I'd encounter Coach Masterson again, and had even a suspicion of what would happen when I did, I think I'd have checked out then.

When I was in high school, nobody but a few moldy American Legionnaires and some indefinite old ladies with uncombed hair and wildness in their eyes paid much attention.

But in Washington, when Masterson spoke, the world listened, and some people, including a President, trembled. A few laughed, privately, first being sure the windows were closed and the shades pulled.

Some people killed themselves over Masterson's actions and passions. Some were killed by them. . . . I tried. That was the first time, but, as usual, I botched the job.

In my whole death have I ever done anything right?

13 /

Lily, Lily

You are perfectly right. You are probably always right; otherwise I'd be sitting there behind granny glasses, taking notes on *your* perversities.

I'm sure it would be "good for me" if I returned Lily's call or agreed to see her, but I can't. I won't. Later maybe, maybe never, but not right now.

Yes, I like her. I like her as much as I've ever liked anybody, but I still can't see or talk to her.

The first time I talked to Lily she was standing in front of Herman's department store, looking at the yellow bathing suits in the window. It was cold, but then all the days of winter were cold, and it began in mid-September. Once there was a foot of snow on Labor Day.

Of course I'd seen Lily before, many times, seen her on the street, in the library, seen her picture in the paper when she was on the school honor roll, which was almost every semester, but *noticing* is something else again. Dede claimed that in all the time we were together, I never really noticed her, and that may be true, since I was blind drunk most of the time.

I was on my way to the library. The green net shopping bag was filled with 78 rpm record albums. Ours was the first public library in the state to buy and lend records. Sarah McCormick Payne and Lois Washington were responsible for that.

I was allowed to take out as many as six albums at a time, which is the reason my right shoulder is so much lower than the left.

Herman's was the best department store in town. They had Hart Schaffner & Marx suits, and one of my minor ambitions in life was to have one, single-breasted and charcoal gray. All of my suits were double-breasted on the theory that the double breast prevented chest colds, and blue serge on the theory that "You can go to your own funeral in a blue serge suit and you'll be well-dressed."

Years later in Rome a tailor who looked like a kindly Borgia made twelve charcoal gray suits for me, single-breasted, but before I had a chance to wear them I met Bernardo, the boy-man for whom the "Lament for a Defeated Soldier" was written.

No, it was written for me and dedicated to him.

I immediately started gaining weight, all that pasta and lovemaking. I always put on weight when I'm in love. Lack of exercise for one thing.

Eventually not one of the suits would fit me, by which time the love had drifted away, faded; ennui set in. It's almost never anger with me; it's lassitude; it's boredom.

Anyway, I never wore the suits.

One reason I noticed Lily that day was that the streets were nearly deserted. It was below zero, too cold to be standing anywhere. A gale wind was blowing down East Main, whipping angrily at the secondhand snow.

But despite the wind and the cold, here was this girl looking in Herman's window. She was wearing a bright red coat that looked like a hand-me-down. I could tell she didn't like it and that it wasn't warm enough. She had on a blue beret, blue earmuffs, and a dark blue scarf that was knotted again and again around her neck. Her nose was pink, and the rest of her skin was very pale; she wore no makeup.

People have said that Lily has great style, and I guess that has always been true.

I've told you I often mislay entire decades, but I do remember that when Kennedy was in the White House, she and Bruno Hyerly were often there. They were there the night Casals played.

I remember that because I was in Savannah, Georgia, that night. I was in great trouble. If there is anything they hate worse than a nigger in Savannah, it's a fag. Especially the cops. . . . I didn't die, but I wanted to. You asked me where that half-moon scar on my left cheek came from. I forget what lie I told, but it came from a Savannah cop who first knocked me down and then stepped on my face. He was wearing heel clips.

Anyway, while I was in the hospital, I read in the *Times* about the Casals concert and that Lily and Bruno Hyerly were there. And I thought, Lily has it made; Lily has the handle; she has solved The Problem; she knows The Secret. I remember the story said, "Mrs. Hyerly was wearing . . . displaying her great sense of style, as usual."

Lily was never really beautiful, but she became very handsome, and she always knew how to walk and always had a good figure.

When she walked down the street in the town, a lot of boys turned and looked at her, but despite what they might have heard about her mother or feel about Lily, nobody ever whistled. And nobody ever made snide jokes about her.

That first day when Lily saw me she smiled and said, "I was looking at that yellow bathing suit, and I was thinking that when I grow up, I'm going to spend practically all my time in a bathing suit."

Herman's window was filled with bathing suits, both men's and women's. "For your winter and/or summer vacation. The latest styles from Chicago. Buy now and save."

At that time I don't think anybody in the town went on winter vacations. And even in summer people seldom ventured farther away than the Black Hills of South Dakota or Hot Springs, Arkansas. Nobody had been to Europe.

Lily said, "When I grow up, I'm going to live someplace like southern France, where it never gets cold."

I said, "Who isn't?"

"My brothers for two. They can't wait to start jumping up and down in the tomato vats at the canning factory. They actually enjoy being peasants."

"Are you sure of that? I mean have you ever asked them? If you did, you might find out that they have something else in mind. It's been my experience that people come up with a lot of surprises if you ask them, and if they tell the truth. The latter is very rare, of course."

Lily laughed. "I've heard you were smart as a whip in addition to being a genius at the piano, and I guess they're right because when you say something like that, I have to reexamine all my theories about people. Especially my brothers."

"That is the price we all have to pay if we want to learn, isn't it?" I said, and we both laughed.

She said, "I'm Lily Farrell, but I guess you already know that. Are you going to the library? I hear you've listened to every record they've got."

I said, "I've not only listened to them; I've memorized the orchestrations for most of them." In those days I was never modest.

Lily said, "I've got a collection of my own records, not very many, and I'm sure all the obvious choices. But you could help me, assuming we get to be friends."

"I've got a feeling we're going to be friends."

"Well, I'm not exactly one of your prize packages as far as this town is concerned. People call me things like a pushy peasant and all. But I'm learning about music, and I'm learning about painting. I've got a book with all the famous paintings in it. I bought it for my mother. And I buy her two records a year, one for her birthday and the other for Christmas. I say to her, 'Ma, what do you want for a present?' And she says, 'Lily, this time, just for a change, how about a record? You know what I like.' She thinks it's a big joke. What she likes is Wayne King and the 'Lady Esther Serenade,' and instead I buy Mozart. But my mother's all right. She's a good egg. And I'm *talking* too much."

"No, you're not; I like it."

"Well, you see, I don't usually talk to most people, but I feel I can tell you everything. I don't know why."

I said, "Lily, it was written in the stars that you tell me everything."

"I hope you're right. It was written in the stars. I'll tell you another thing that was written in the stars: that is that nothing around here has anything to do with what I really am. Does that make any sense? I mean do you ever feel that way?"

"All day and all night every day and every night."

Lily laughed again and said, "Can I walk to the library with you?"

"You may."

"I know *may*, damn it. *Can* is able. You have to tell me. Every mistake I make, you have to correct me. Don't spare my feelings."

"I will, but I have to warn you, being seen with me won't do your popularity much good."

"Who cares about that?" said Lily, and she took my hand, and we walked to the library together.

At one point Lily said, "What do you know about Aaron Burr? I have to write this goofy term paper about him. Other people get George Washington or Thomas Jefferson. I get Aaron Burr, who was a crackpot and a traitor. And the reason I do is Miss Quigley, the bearded lady, who, incidentally, could use about a ton of Burma-Shave, hates my guts."

I said, "There seems to be some doubt that Burr actually was a traitor. If you could write a term paper suggesting that he was framed, which a great many reputable historians believe . . ."

"That's a brilliant idea," said Lily. "Brilliant, and it's just the kind of thing Quig the Pig will go for. Thanks a million."

At the library I said, "Good luck with your term paper."

Lily's blue lips touched mine, the first time a girl had ever kissed me.

"I've never trusted to luck," said Lily. "It doesn't pay. What you have to do is run faster than anybody else and in the right direction."

And she started running, against the wind but in the right direction.

May. Lily was sitting in the bright sunshine on top of the library steps. She was wearing a white dress, very simple, not all frills and fluffs and flounces. I said that it was pretty, and Lily said, thanks, she'd made it herself. Copied, she said, from a photograph in *Vogue*.

That all by itself impressed me. Most girls in town, if they sewed at all, got patterns from *Delineator,* and the dresses they wore were always awful. And when they were paid an undeserved compliment, they invariably said, "Oh, this old thing. It's as old as the hills." Invariably.

Lily said, "Can I buy you a Coke or something?"

"I wouldn't mind having a Coke, but aren't you mixed up? Isn't the boy supposed to do the asking?"

"If I waited for you to ask me anything, I'd die an old maid."

"Okay. Cherry."

As soon as she finished her chocolate soda, Lily said, "Thanks to your advice, my term paper on Aaron Burr was the talk of the seventh grade for at least an hour or so. I got an A minus and a nice little pat on the ass from the guerrilla girl. . . ."

"Would you like another chocolate soda? This time on me?"

"No, thanks. Look, I suppose you hate dancing."

"You suppose right. I don't know how, but if I did, I'd hate it."

"All right already. But would you even consider taking me to the seventh grade dance at Anson a week from Friday? I don't really want to go, but I'm class president, and it's expected of me."

"Thanks, Lily. Almost anything else you'd ask me, I'd say yes, but not this."

Lily was not going to cry, but she was close to it, and she said, "Okay. I won't urge you. Let's go."

"Stick around for a minute, Lil. Why me, for God's sake?"

"You're the only one I've got the guts to ask."

"Lil, I really don't dance, and anyway, considering my reputation, they might make fun of both of us."

"Not while I'm around. They won't dare."

"How come you're class president anyway? Are you all that popular?"

"They hate my guts, but they know damn good and well that I'm the only one around who can get things done, and, just for instance, when they needed to raise money for the basketball team's new uniforms, it was Lily who did it."

I said, "Okay, if it'll help I'll do it, but it's against my better judgment."

Lily's thin, white hand touched mine, and she said, "I'll never forget, never."

Lily wouldn't let me pick her up at the house on South Center, which I regretted, because her two brothers would probably have been there, and I liked looking at them. Thin, blond boys, prettier than Lily but not as pretty as Eldon Rickets.

We met just outside the gymnasium at Anson School. Inside, the teachers stood grim and gray-faced against the brick walls, their expressions forbidding anybody to have a good time.

Lily and I stumbled through several dances. At least she didn't try to lead, and she was certainly the prettiest girl there and the best dressed. And the youngest. I don't mean in years, but I could see from the faces of the others that they had already given up expecting any surprises. At twelve. That's one of the hells of it. "Pardon's the word to all."

Everybody tried to ignore Lily, but they couldn't. You could see that they hated her, the girls anyway.

Several tall, graceless boys who must have been members of the basketball team carried Lily around the floor with them and told her how many baskets they had made that year, how many home runs, how many times they'd swum across the "Y" pool. And wouldn't she like to play a game of checkers, dominoes, take a ride to the Green Gables, where you could dine and dance and diddle? Catch anyone?

One of the boys wasn't bad, Les Carver, a guard on the team. We had met briefly one afternoon, just after Les had been swimming in the pool at Riverview Park. He was still damp. . . . We didn't speak at the dance that night.

Another boy, Don Albertson, a brooding, hood-eyed sixteen-year-old—he'd failed third grade twice—was largely knees and Adam's apple, and he asked Lily to marry him. She declined with thanks. Ten years later Don Albertson, who took seven years to get through high school, was scalded to death in a vat of boiling tomatoes. The entire vat had to be thrown away. The widow sued for a million dollars, and the canning factory settled for $75,000, of which Lawyer Druker took only a little more than half.

Once late in the evening, around nine-thirty, a teacher whose name I don't remember, if I ever knew it, came up to Lily and said, "Don't you think that dress is a little . . . much for a school party?"

Lily's dress was pale yellow, cut straight up and down, sleeveless, without an adornment of any kind except for the amber beads that belonged to her mother; the dress came to a little below Lily's knees.

"What do you mean, *much?*" said Lily.

"If you don't know, dear, I'm afraid I can't tell you," said the teacher, who was wearing a black lace crepe de chine with tiny rosebuds more or less in the place one assumed her nipples were.

"Why did you mention it then?" said Lily.

"You always have been too big for your britches," said the teacher, and I, ever helpful, said, "Are you wearing britches, Lily? Why didn't you tell me?"

The teacher looked at me and said, "If I were *you*, I'd watch my step. This isn't even your school, although I must say it's no surprise seeing you two together. Birds of a feather."

"Have you turned in the grades yet?" said Lily.

"I have."

"And did I pass?"

The teacher said, "If I am anything, I am fair. You are by no means my favorite pupil, but I did pass you. I gave you a C."

"Then why don't you fuck off?" said Lily, and to me she said, "Let's get out of here."

When we got outside, Lily sat on the curb and cried for quite a long time. She said, "Wasn't that cheap of me?"

"She deserved it."

"That's not the point. I got just as cheap as she was, and if my mother heard about it, she'd absolutely die of shame."

I thought, The notorious Eileen Farrell, who puts out eats and booze and herself for every . . . I said, "I doubt that she'll hear about it, Lil. I wouldn't worry."

"I'll know, though, and that's what really worries me."

I don't remember what I said to that. I do remember that it was a soft night and everything was green. The night air even seemed to smell of green, which is my favorite color. I once wrote a tone poem called "Three Moods in Green," and I played it in Paris and Denver and Syracuse and Santa Barbara and never again.

That was either in 1963 or '64 or '65; it was the year the killing began again, and the newspapers started printing pictures of dead soldiers, and every dead black soldier had The Clarinet Player's face. All. That boy died every morning in every newspaper, no matter where I was, sometimes several times every morning.

Of course I knew that he was already dead, but I couldn't prove it. They never let you prove a thing like that.

One morning in Toledo, Ohio, after looking at what was easily the hundredth picture of the dead Clarinet Player, I hanged myself in the bathroom; I used a silk rope I'd bought the day before.

I kicked away the chair, but I didn't hang there long enough. I don't know how long it was; it just wasn't long enough.

The bellboy, who had arrived with my breakfast, cut me down with a steak knife. You must have read about it.

They took me to the hospital, and while I was there a psychologist interviewed me, although he did all the talking. He kept saying, "You wanted to be found, didn't you? That's why you ordered breakfast, isn't it? You wanted to be found."

I didn't say anything. What would you say? Maybe he was right, and suppose he was? What would it prove?

But that is another reason I no longer read newspapers. I can't bear to see another picture of the dead Clarinet Player, and they are dying everywhere these days. Soon there won't be any clarinet players left. Anywhere.

Wouldn't you think dying once was enough? Even Jesus only had to go through it twice.

After I left the hospital, I checked in here. That was the third time. The doctor, your predecessor, who fancied himself a wit, said, "Oh, dear. The bad penny's back again."

Lily let me walk her halfway home, as far as the north side of the M. and St. L. tracks. She said, "Maybe it is an awful dress."

"It's not, and you know it's not."

"Why do they hate us so much, do you suppose?"

"I don't know. Maybe because we're different."

"Different and poor," said Lily. "If you're rich and different, nobody says a word. Which is one of the reasons I'm going to be very, very rich."

I said, "That doesn't seem any too easy these days."

"Don't worry," said Lily. "I've got everything figured out."

Lily had most of it figured out, and things went pretty much according to plan—except in the important areas, the ones where you break your heart. . . .

I think it was the first year we were in high school, and Lily said, "I'm going to get a job at Kresge's this summer."

"That doesn't sound like much fun."

"Fun isn't the idea. The idea is money. M-o-n-e-y. I've got to start saving up for college. And anyway, in addition to the loot I'll be learning something, and before long I'll be running the place."

Lily got the job. She was thirteen, but she told the manager she was seventeen. I'm sure he didn't believe her, but she came cheap. She started behind the notions counter, trinkets you could not imagine anyone wanting, combs, earrings, buttons, hairpins, fake cameo brooches, special this week only fifteen cents, and *genuine* pearl necklaces, three for a dollar.

I was familiar with the notions counter because I had stolen things there. I kept what I stole locked up in a steamer trunk in the barn, along with my diary. I used to doll up in some of those notions, and I had a red sateen dress that I'd stolen from the ladies' ready-to-wear at Britnall's. It had a little style, and I certainly liked it better than any of the double-breasted suits my mother bought me at Penney's. Better than the knickers. . . . I pretended my name was Georgette. And that was years before I'd heard about Proust and all the boys he gave girls' names. And who'd ever heard the word *drag?*

Lily worked behind the notions counter all summer. "And a very valuable summer it was, too. Among other things I learned that there are a great many people in the world who, given a choice between gold and dross, prefer dross."

When the summer was over, Lily started working in the office, helping keep the books, typing, shorthand (she taught herself), buying, hiring, firing. By the time she was a senior in high school, she was assistant manager of the store.

All this, and she only worked after school and on Saturdays.

Oh, Lily was ambitious all right, and she was hard-working, too. In school she got straight A's, not only in subjects like English and civics and French—even so indifferent a scholar as myself could do that—but, unforgivably, in chemistry and physics and solid geometry. I've never really known what solid geometry is.

Lily was also editor of the school paper and, in her senior year, of the yearbook. She played the lead in the senior class play, Abby in *The Late Christopher Bean.* I was in it, too. A no-good named Tallant . . . Isn't it odd? I can remember most of the lines. The things that stay with us and the things that don't.

Lily sang in the glee club, lead soprano, was a student counselor in the YWCA, and played triangle in the school orchestra.

The latter, admittedly, is an activity for which keeping awake is the main requirement, but the others took energy and determinad, in some cases, even intelligence. No wonder they all said she was a pushy little peasant.

"I've got a scholarship at the university; so, natch, that's where I'll go. It would not be my choice. Howsoever.

"I'm going to study design, not that I expect to learn much, and I'm going to be Phi Bete and pledge Kappa Kappa Gamma, which has the silliest and richest and snobbiest girls, fools every one of them, and they'll hate my guts, but they'll ask me to pledge because they'll need my grades to keep up the house average.

"I expect, among other honors, all richly deserved, that I'll be honorary cadet colonel. Big deal. That means that you get to go to the Military Ball with the cadet colonel, who'll be a dummy being honored because he didn't drop his rifle too often in ROTC.

"And after I graduate, laden with honors, I'm going to Chicago, first stop, and then on to New York. I'm going to be this very famous dress designer. Any questions?"

"One. What if something happens along the way?"

"Nothing will. I won't allow it."

"And another thing. Why are you going to join Kappa Kappa Gamma if the girls are all fools?"

"To prove that I can, I suppose. I know that isn't a very good answer, but I'm stuck with it."

"And what are you going to do after you get to be this big designer?"

"*Then* I'm going to fall in love and be fallen in love with, marry somebody rich and handsome and noble, and we're going to have gobs of children and live happily ever after."

Lily's career worked out pretty much the way she had in mind. But when it came to love and marriage . . .

If only we didn't need to be loved. I have probably said, "I love you" more times than any other living American, and every time I said it, what I really meant was, *You* love *me*, don't you? Say so then, say it over and over and over.

14 /

What a Pity

I know I haven't said much about Sarah McCormick Payne. Can't you see it hurts too much to talk about her? Yes, yes, I know. It has to hurt so that I can get better.

Tell me the truth now, doctor. Do you honestly think I'll ever get any better? And if I don't, what's the point of hanging around? Breathing in and breathing out has never been all that important to me. Picking them up and laying them down again.

Beethoven didn't want to live after he lost his hearing. I know I'm no Beethoven. I don't need you and Rosenberg to tell me that. My mediocrity makes my going all the more urgent. What am I doing anyway? Adding to the clutter is what I'm doing. Taking up space.

Sarah McCormick Payne.

When I was eleven years old, my mother decided that I should become a Presbyterian. "It's high time you stopped associating with the hoi polloi. Besides, the Paynes are devout Presbyterians, and you will no doubt develop a friendship with them, particularly with young Master Charles."

I said, "But when I was baptized, Reverend Goosens said I'd always be a Methodist."

"Reverend Goosens is a good enough man, but he is a fool."

"But you told me I could learn a lot from him."

"In foolishness, yes, I did."

So the following Sunday I became a Presbyterian, but I continued to play the organ at the Methodist church for Sunday vespers, Wednesday evening prayer meetings, and the Christmas play. I still got five dollars and a grope for each appearance.

Matthew Payne had built the First Presbyterian Church; at least he had made the first and by far the largest contribution. He had chosen the architect, too, a Chicago man who later designed the house that was never finished. I believe he had been a student of Louis Sullivan.

The brick of the church was a soft pink, and the church was really very beautiful, everything on one floor, sliding teak walls that could separate the building into eight different rooms or it could be a single large auditorium. The pulpit was made of cherry wood and shone in the sun, and there was a single small blue window above that mirrored the sky.

Nobody in town liked the church except, presumably, Matthew Payne, Sarah McCormick Payne, Charles, my father, and me. Maybe Horton Payne. It was hard to tell what he liked and what he didn't. Maybe Lois Washington.

The minister was one Maitland Wilkinson, of whom my mother said, after our first meeting, an encounter that lasted perhaps ten minutes, "Padre Wilkinson is a quality person; that was obvious at first glance, and I am told his sermons are inspired."

Actually, Wilkinson was a curiously inarticulate man; he had a slight lisp, and even the least sibilant words came out as if he had a mouthful of hot mashed potatoes.

He was not more than thirty, a moist-palmed, dandruffy man whose silver-blond hair was already in rapid retreat and whose pale blue eyes were as watery as the end of his nose.

My father was against my going to church, any church, but that was one of the things he didn't believe was worth worrying about. "Taken in small doses, I doubt that religion has ever done anybody a great deal of harm. As long as you don't take it seriously. And as minor prophets go, except that He was ashamed of His mother and never too sure about the identity of His father, Jesus was all right. Paul, on the other hand . . . if he were living in Chicago at this time, he'd be a leading member of the Capone gang, maybe the head."

That first Sunday the Paynes were, as always, fifteen minutes late, but neither the Reverend Wilkinson nor anybody else would have dreamed of starting the service before they arrived. It would never have occurred to anybody to grouse about it, either. The Paynes' late arrival was as much in the order of things as the divine right of kings.

Naturally, they occupied the first pew to the right of the pulpit.

Charley's mother came in first, looking just the way she'd looked two years earlier, on a humid day in August. I remember it was about the time I started reading the Beethoven *Conversation Books,* probably at the suggestion of Lois Washington.

I recognized at once that whatever other differences there were between us, Beethoven and I had in common a feeling of perpetual melancholy, as well as problems with the weather:

I am being punished by the weather, and the sonata goes badly, largely because of the kitchen maid. . . . She made an ugly face when asked to carry up wood, but I hope she will remember that Our Saviour carried His Cross to Golgotha.

The August afternoon I first saw Sarah McCormick Payne she was wearing a plain white linen dress, with no adornments. I remember thinking that with all that money she surely could have afforded a charm bracelet or a string of cultured pearls.

She was wearing white shoes, too, and they were spotless, so clean that I wondered if maybe she didn't throw each pair away after one wearing.

She had a long face, too long for real beauty, too long even to be considered handsome. It was a face El Greco might have painted, although from what I've heard El Greco would have preferred to paint Nicky Pondorus. Nicky might have posed for that green nude in *Vision of the Apocalypse*. Though why anybody would paint Nicky's body green I cannot imagine.

Sarah McCormick Payne was dark. Charley inherited her complexion. Her eyes were large and round and sad. Her brown hair was worn long and loosely gathered at the nape of her neck. She was nearly as tall as Charley when he was full grown; he was six one.

She was long-legged, small-breasted, slender. Like Lily she took the trouble to walk well.

I doubt that Sarah McCormick Payne noticed me that first afternoon. I was such an easy boy to overlook. I remember she spent some time in the library, talking to Lois Washington, those two lost souls. I hid under the granite steps outside, also lost.

After she came out of the library, I followed Mrs. Payne home, half a block behind, loitering in the angular shadows of the spiteful trees that lined the vengeful sidewalk.

At the door of the house on West Main that had once belonged to my grandfather, Sarah McCormick Payne turned, and she seemed to be looking at where I was standing, but I don't know whether she saw the slight distension on the larch that was me. I always meant to ask.

"What a pity," Sarah McCormick Payne once said.

I don't remember what we were talking about. It could have been about anything, any of us.

Yes, I'm coming, just as soon as I adjust my hairpiece. Do you think mauve hair becomes me?

I've been meaning to ask. Do you realize that this was the hour I usually had my first drink? Is that the reason you chose it?

Oh, I never thought you were stupid. Now that you've asked, what I do think is that you are square. Yes, square, a sweet square with a big nose.

When was it, yesterday or the day before, when you asked me if I thought Whitman and Peter Doyle had had "relations." How delicately you put it.

I'm sure they did, lover. One does not discuss poetic imagery with horsecar conductors. At least I never have.

I put my hand on his knees. . . . We understood.

I shall dote on myself. There is that lot of me and all so luscious.

15 /

The Portrait
of a Lady

I believe I was talking about Sarah McCormick Payne and the afternoon I followed her back here. Wasn't I? And it was either yesterday or last August.

I know I should make carbons and then I could check. I don't, though, and I won't. I told you. I never needed carbons. I never needed a score when I conducted. I could always remember everything. They used to call me "Miss Total Recall." No, I never married, and no matter what they say, I am still a virgin. Thomas Carlyle's wife died a virgin, you know, but they were only married for twenty-five years. He was shy, and besides, he had a case on the Reverend Edward Irving.

O poor mortals, how ye make this earth bitter for each other.

Sarah McCormick Payne. Another afternoon, not the one I followed her. . . . Of course I'm skipping around. I not only can't remember; I can't keep track or order. You can do that when you get ready to publish these—what? Meanderings, reports. The case history of . . . Why don't you call it *The Diary of a Madman?*

Save me, take me away. Give me a troika and horses swift as a whirlwind!

One afternoon Sarah McCormick Payne said, "I should have been born with a tattoo saying, 'Do Not Transplant in Iowa!'"

It was an afternoon in late July, not a leaf moving, not a blade of grass. Two huge orange butterflies performing a ritual dance near where we sat, in the Shakespeare garden, not far from the slender row of rosemary. July 1938. The summer Charley and Lily and I were graduated from high school; escape time.

Charley was East—everything on the other side of the Mississippi was East—looking over the colleges, letting the colleges look him over.

The longest summer ever because I still didn't know whether Lester Brockhurst would take me as a pupil. Rosenberg, an old friend of Brockhurst, had written saying . . . oh, all kinds of lies about how talented I was, how promising, how disciplined. . . .

At the time Brockhurst hadn't yet answered the letter, and of course, if he didn't, if he didn't accept me, if I didn't get to New York by September at the latest, I would surely die. . . . It's odd how even back then I felt so mortal.

Anyway, in the meantime I was working very hard on a fugue. . . . Rosenberg thought it wasn't bad, and I wanted to finish it before I died. No matter what happened to me, the fugue would live forever.

I did finish it. I finished things in those days, and some summers later it was done at Tanglewood, and that was the end of that.

I blamed the failure on the conductor, me.

Late July then, and Mrs. Payne and I were having iced tea. I had said something to make her laugh, and I liked to see her laugh. Such a quick laugh, transient but fine while it lasted. Even her eyes took part.

She was wearing a very light blue dress. I remember that, and she was quite tan. I guess she was tan from sitting in the sun. Previous summers she and Lois Washington had gone for long walks in the country. But not that summer. Lois wasn't feeling well that summer, and nobody knew what was wrong. At least nobody was saying what was wrong. About half the time she didn't even show up at the library, and people on the library board were saying that they'd probably have to replace her. Valuable as she was.

No matter. This was one of Mrs. Payne's good days. She talked about her childhood, more, I think, than ever before or ever again. I think I knew more about Sarah McCormick Payne than anybody else in town, maybe even more than Charley, probably more than the man she married.

I never told anybody what we talked about. . . .

"Mostly we just talk about music."

"That seems very difficult to believe. All that time and all you talk about is music. What do you say?"

"Oh, Mom, for heaven's sake."

"Now, George, I'm going to ask you a question, man to man so to speak and shame the devil. You know. I told you about men and women."

Unsaid but thought: Yes, you did, but the way things are going, it doesn't look as if that particular information is going to be of much use to me. I said, "And the birds and the bees. Yes, you told me."

"Now keep this under your hat, but as you know, I wouldn't put anything past that woman, nice as she seems to be with you, whatever her reasons. Do you think she might be carrying on with the Jew Rosenberg? That's what I heard at Star the other night. Nobody knew for a fact, but Carrie Geoghegan claims she saw the two of them going into the Royal Kandy Kitchen last Friday, late in the afternoon. They looked like they'd *been* someplace, together, and Carrie couldn't help putting two and two together. Now what's your considered opinion?"

I couldn't say anything to that one; I was laughing too hard.

And later, "George, I might just as well come right out in the open. She hasn't tried anything funny with you, has she? I mean she hasn't . . ."

"No, Mom, she hasn't."

"I'm not one of the reaper McCormicks or the Chicago *Tribune* McCormicks. Everybody around here thinks that, and I used to try to tell them they're wrong, but if there's anything most people don't want to hear, it's the truth.

"My father often said that we were the intelligent branch of the family, meaning the poor branch. If in fact we were related at all. I've never cared enough to find out."

Her father was president of a small denominational college in one of the less resplendent suburbs of Chicago. He was considered something of an expert on the work of Ralph Waldo Emerson and was working on what was to be the definitive biography of that monolith.

Nothing can bring you peace but yourself. Nothing can bring you peace but the triumph of principles.

Sarah's father kept saying that he would have finished the biography twenty years earlier if additional and essential facts hadn't kept cropping up, cropping up.

It was not until after his death that the manuscript on which he had been working for so many years was found in an old trunk. It contained fewer than thirty manuscript pages and fifty or so six-by-nine file cards on which had been jotted a few often illegible notes.

Of course, he who has put forth his total strength in fit action has the richest return of wisdom.

The good doctor's wife was Irish, and before their marriage she had been his housekeeper. She was a superb cook, and it was said that the floors of the house were so clean you could eat off of them.

Glenna McCormick never spoke when Dr. McCormick was in the room. It wasn't allowed. But when he was not in the room, she was never silent.

"I wouldn't trust Fred Johnson as far as I could throw him. M.D. my eye, and the thought of undressing in front of a man that's drunk half the time. If you're ever ailing, Jenny, and God forbid, that young Dr. Ludwig is the best chiropractor ever to hit this town. He's studied osteopathy, too, not to mention that he's just as pretty as a picture. And when you're not feeling up to snuff, you just lay there, and he rubs and rubs, and before you can say Jack Robinson, you're your old self."

And, "When I married Dr. McCormick I'd been a Catholic up to then my whole life through, but after all, this is a Lutheran college, and so, to make a long story short, before our nuptials were said, I left the Mother Church, and ever since have been a very, very happy member of . . ."

And, "What I always say is old friends are best friends, and on bingo nights at Saint Cecilia's, I see the girls I used to play jacks with when we were just starting out in life. That was at the *old* Saint Mary's. Where that big meat market is now. It breaks my heart every time. They've got all those plucked chickens where the altar used to be. And I'll bet Father Corrigan is turning in his grave, knowing the sacrilege that is everywhere among us now. I'll have a double butter on my popcorn, Yetta."

Sarah had never heard her mother speak a word of ill against the great doctor, and she would have supposed that her mother even loved the man.

She came all the way from Iowa for her father's funeral, one of the few events in which he was ever involved in which she found any pleasure.

After the lies had been told and the dust returneth, Sarah said to the place her mother was standing, "You must have loved Pop, in the beginning anyway."

Her mother looked up from the stove where she had hidden most of her life and said, "I never even liked him. The first time we met I never even liked him. And after we were married, I used to pray every night that he'd die, and that was when we still talked a little, before you was born. And Tuesday when he finally passed on, I got down on my knees and thanked God."

Sarah was just able to say, "Why on earth did you marry him then?"

"Who else did you think was gonna ask me?" said her mother.

It should never be forgotten that misfortune, be it great or small, is the element in which we live.

In the third year of his marriage Dr. George Kendall McCormick ordered his wife to have a baby. A boy baby. Was that clear?

His wife, Glenna, said that it was, and she tried, and she cried, and she prayed, but the baby was Sarah.

Some of the nurses at the hospital thought Dr. McCormick was going to strike his wife when he found out that she had disobeyed him.

A blue vein on the left side of his forehead pounded more angrily than usual for a moment. Then he took off his pince-nez, polished it with the large red silk handkerchief he always carried in the breast pocket of his suit, and said to his wife, "I shall never forgive you for this, Glenna, and I shall never again address you either in public or in private for the rest of your life."

How did Sarah know that?

Her father told her, of course; he always told her that on her birthday and sometimes on Christmas and Saint Swithin's day, after which it rained for forty days and forty nights.

But that wasn't always Sarah's only birthday present from her father. On her twelfth birthday he gave her a photograph of himself on which he had written, "For my daughter in the hope that she will not always be a total disappointment to her father."

Dr. George Kendall McCormick, M.A., Ph.D., never again spoke to his wife, though, and he seldom spoke to his daughter. When he did, he told her that she was a plain girl, that she had less than a plain mind, that she was insubstantial, incomplete, less than satisfactory, disappointing.

He often said, "Silence in a woman is her greatest ornament and many times her only ornament. The latter has never been more true than in your case, daughter."

Is it surprising that Sarah was a quiet girl? Quiet as a mouse, people said. They said still water runs deep.

She was forever practicing the piano, "Dum-de-de-dum-dum, dum-dee . . ." Forever crayoning, watercoloring, painting.

"But what in the world *is* it, Sarah? What is it *supposed* to be? Did you mean it to look like something? Somebody?"

"Color the pictures in the book like the other little girls, Sarah."

And she read all the books she found in the glassed-in cases in her father's study. The usual, books he had collected but never read. Dickens and Thackeray and Tolstoy and Balzac.

"No, Sarah, I have not read it. I have been too busy doing things that are, perhaps, of more import, and haven't I told you not to interrupt me with trivial and stupid questions?"

How could he have read those books? When was there time? He was always either working on the Emerson book or addressing multitudes. One person was a multitude.

And there were the novels of Henry James. There was in particular *The Portrait of a Lady.* Sarah lost count of how many times she had read that: scores, hundreds.

And there was never any doubt in Sarah's mind that she was Isabel Archer and that she had been born for afternoon tea.

Under certain circumstances there are few hours in life more agreeable than the hour dedicated to the ceremony known as afternoon tea. There are circumstances in which, whether you partake of the tea or not—some people of course never do—the situation is in itself delightful.

Sarah was sure that sometime in her life there would be at least one such afternoon. But maybe there would be a thousand. Maybe every afternoon would be like that. It could happen, couldn't it? Had happened, hadn't it?

. . . her head was erect, her eye lighted, her flexible figure turned itself easily this way and that, in sympathy with the alertness with which she evidently caught impressions. Her impressions were numerous, and they were all reflected in a clear, still smile.

What a perfect description of herself, Sarah thought. To the letter, to the life. Wasn't she always smiling, clearly, stilly?

Wasn't she always waiting for her father to say, "But you're very beautiful yourself, Sarah-Isabel. I hadn't noticed, but you have become a very beautiful girl."

He never did, though; Sarah kept pitching pennies in the wishing well, and it was years before she realized that it was bottomless.

Finally, and these things take forever, it got to be the spring Sarah was a senior in high school.

Yes, we've gone full circle. This is where we came in. Escape weather. Again? Again. Always.

What in the world do they mean, a generation gap? Generation gap. It's one of those things people keep saying over and over and over again, without really thinking about it. What happens is that we (me, I, Miss Officially Forty-Nine Here, lover of Christopher, who is nineteen) sometimes forget how much it hurt then because it hurts so much now.

Pretend to forget, want to forget, have to forget.

Why do we always have to be black and blue, inside and out? Can't they make a salve or something? A cerate? What do they do in all those laboratories all the time?

Spring. The spring before Sarah was transferred from San Quentin to Devil's Island. That's all you ever get, a transfer. She wrote letters of application to dozens of colleges on both coasts, anywhere but the Middle West.

She wrote the letters, sealed them, stamped them, then walked to the post office and mailed them. Then she waited, and she waited. Waited. Weeks passed, months, and there was not one reply to a single letter. Dum, de, de, dum, dum.

Then one afternoon when she was dusting her father's study, and she was allergic to dust and to tears, she found crumpled in his wastebasket the envelope of a letter addressed to her. The envelope was from a college on the West Coast and was addressed to her. Its contents were gone.

That evening when Sarah set the table for dinner, she put the envelope on her father's plate. He saw it as he sat down, put it in the breast pocket of the Brooks suit, and continued smiling.

He smiled a good deal of the time, displaying what appeared to be an unusually large number of square, white teeth. Somebody years before had mistakenly told him that he resembled Theodore

Roosevelt, which was the reason not only for the smile but for the push-ups and the deep-knee bends and the deep breathing in front of every available open window. It was the reason for his depressingly good health.

The guest at dinner that evening—there was always a guest at dinner; it was impossible to imagine Dr. George Kendall McCormick and his wife dining alone, and Sarah didn't count—was one Geoffrey Comstock, a giddy man of sixty with hair the color of puce. He was head of the philosophy department, and having been disappointed in love at twenty or thereabouts, he had never married. He never went anywhere without a copy of Shakespeare's sonnets in the pocket of his tweedy jacket. "One never knows when one will meet up with a boy ignorant of the beautiful things in life but hungry for them. And to me the Bard was never more eloquent than when he penned the sonnets. 'My glass shall not persuade me I am old/ So long as youth and thou are of one date.'"

Dr. Comstock always had a male undergraduate as his house-keeper; he preferred a boy majoring in home economics.

The dinner that night was like thousands of others, in the past, in the future. The Eminent Educator at home, a friendly dinner, beloved wife, adored daughter, distinguished guest.

There were many quotations. "As the great Emerson said, 'Books are the best of things.' . . . 'This world belongs to the energetical.' . . . 'I find that Americans have no passions. They have appetites.'"

And on and endlessly on. And his wife Glenna chattering away about nothing. It was the only chance the poor thing got a chance to talk, when there was a guest in the house, and there were all those words bottled up inside her, all that wisdom. "I'm so glad to see you enjoy your food, Dr. Comstock. As I have so often told Sarah, though she never listens, those who masticate their food properly never suffer from nervous stomach or hardening of the arteries. . . . Life is what we make it, which is the reason I always have a smile on my face, although my heart is sometimes heavy. Don't you agree, Dr. Comstock? Haven't you found, as I have, that the important things in life are the simple things in life? . . . And what do you think I should take to the covered-dish supper in the basement of . . . And I have started hemming the living room drapes, after which I think I will dye them. Blue? To match the overstuffed . . ."

And Dr. Comstock, a banquet of one: "Mrs. McCormick, I should simply adore passing your recipe for potatoes *Duchesse* along to Russell, the dear boy who is keeping house for me this year, and in exchange I'll give you his recipe for filet of sole with sour cream and chopped almonds."

And Dr. George Kendall McCormick: "If you'll excuse me for a moment, Geoffrey. Sarah, I will see you in the study in ten minutes sharp, and without an argument. Are there any questions?"

"One or two, but they can wait," said Sarah.

"I'll assist Mrs. McCormick with the dishes," said philosopher Comstock. "It'll be such a nice change. Russell, dear boy, won't let me lift a pinkie at home."

Sarah was in her father's study in ten minutes sharp.

Dr. George Kendall McCormick was seated in a black leather armchair that was a relic of his days at Amherst. Nobody else was ever allowed to sit there.

"I wonder if you'd mind sitting over there. That particular chair happens to be a favorite of mine. I picked it up at an old curiosity shop in Northampton, and it is said to have accommodated the be-hinds—at different times, of course—of Emily Dickinson and Noah Webster."

He was sitting very straight in the chair, and his left hand could be heard fingering the envelope. A lock of his thin yellow hair had fallen on his forehead; a student who should have been knighted had once described him as looking like a wilted chrysanthemum.

He stared at his daughter the way she had seen him stare at a half-crazy boy who had set fire to the chemistry building. And in the voice he used when he assured graduates that they would be the leaders of tomorrow, he said, "I am not proud of having opened your mail and having burned the contents. However, circumstances alter cases, and I want you to know that this odd caprice of yours about going to college on some other campus is a personal affront to me, and I have no intention of permitting it.

"If I had had a son I would naturally have seen to it that he attended one of the Ivy League colleges, perhaps my own alma mater, where he would, like his father, graduate with the highest honors. And afterward, it would have been my fondest wish that he spend at least a year at Oxford. But you are not a son, and I believe that you will find it quite taxing enough on your intellect to get a degree right here, on a campus on which I am not without influence."

Sarah said, "I knew you wouldn't agree, Father, but I'm going away to college even if I have to earn my way by waiting on tables."

"Perhaps waiting on tables is the profession for which God intended you. As you may know, it has long been my considered opinion that allowing women to learn to read was a major error, and allowing them to vote has been a disaster. And both have certainly never been more true—"

". . . than in my case. Yes, I've heard you say that now and again through the years, but I do not plan to hear it many times again. When I leave here, I have no intention of ever coming back. Among many other things, I do not ever again want to hear the sound of your voice uttering endless clichés."

Dr. George Kendall McCormick leaned toward his daughter and struck her with his right hand. His fingernail scratched her cheek, drawing blood, and he said, "You will leave when I give you permission to leave, and in the future you will speak when I give you permission to speak, and when you do, it will be respectfully."

Sarah felt two drops of blood fall from her cheek to her neck, but she did not wipe them away, and she did not cry. She said, "And after I finish college, I am going to Paris and London to study painting and the piano, and I am going to be a very famous pianist and an equally famous painter, and I am going to spend every spare moment for the rest of my life despising you."

The next afternoon when Sarah got home from school her father had put all of her paintings and drawings and watercolors and all of her music in the furnace and lighted the fire. It burned all through the evening, filling the house with a faintly acrid smell, and it being a particularly warm evening in early June, the house was really too hot for comfort.

The dread of man and the love of man shall be a wall of defense and a wreath of joy all around.

Sarah left the white clapboard house shortly after sunup, white clapboard, blue shutters, colonial, quite a beautiful house really. By then the sacrificial smell was gone, but on the green front lawn, broad and green and neatly kept, a magazine-cover lawn, were some few black ashes.

She walked out of the house, quietly, not even slamming the door; she crossed the lawn, gently kicking aside an errant ash. She looked up at the morning sky, which came in an infinite number of promising blues, not a cloud anywhere; clouds were obsolete, and the newly scrubbed street was as immaculate as the sky, and straight, no need to turn, to swerve, to detour, to stop. The street led to the ends of the earth and beyond, and everywhere the sky would be blue and promising and without clouds.

Oh, God, keep it always now.

Sarah's first stop, only temporary, was in Chicago, where she took a temporary job at Carson Pirie Scott. Temporary. She was seventeen. In the evening she studied painting at the Art Institute, and she studied piano with a very good teacher. And she read all the classics she hadn't yet read, and she taught herself French, and she went to all of the concerts and all of the lectures and all of the plays and parties, and somewhere she met Horton Payne. . . . "Horton was . . . I'd never known many boys; my father frightened them away, I guess, or maybe I did, but Horton was . . . oh, so much fun; we used to laugh. *Everything* struck us funny. Horton was so . . . different then, totally different. . . . It wasn't until we got back here . . ."

Horton Payne was studying banking at the University of Chicago, and he, like Sarah, was embarked on an odyssey of which Chicago was only the first stop. Paris would be next, and the journey would never end; really it wouldn't. It was 1919, a year when anything was possible. "We'll go to Paris, and you can study the piano and painting, oh, for years and years, as long as you want, and then we'll live in Rome. And in Florence. You said you wanted to live in Florence. I'll work for one of those banks that have branches all over the world, and they transfer you every two years, and then when they're ready to make me president, we'll come to New York and have a family, and . . . Wouldn't you like to live like that?"

Sarah McCormick Payne looked at the oppressive July afternoon, at the sky that was now orange, with many black clouds, threatening clouds, looked at the rueful, remembering rosemary, and she said, "Naturally, I told Horton that was exactly what I had in mind, had always had in mind. I said that I wouldn't dream of living any other way, and I had no doubt at all that that was the way it would be. But then neither did Horton. I'm sure he didn't. I have to keep reminding myself of that. When we came back here, he kept saying, 'We'll only be here for a week or so, darling, a month or two at most, and we can stand anything for a month or two. With a future like ours we can.' "

But that came later. What came earlier was that they told each other that they loved each other. That's always the way. I told you. I could have told them if I'd been around at the time, told them they were mistaking panic for love, loneliness for love, pity for love, the fact that they were suffering from the same disease for love. . . . How can you tell what love is if you're seventeen (Sarah) or nineteen (Horton) and never known any, never seen any. . . . I mentioned Bartlett's. They can fill you in on war and death, those poets and philosophers, but about love, nothing. Do *you* know what it is? Have you ever met anybody who does? . . . Siggie hasn't got anything useful to say on the subject. He never was, loved or loving, giving or receiving, never.
. . . No, you're mistaken. I know nothing of love. It wasn't I who raised my hand. No answers from me, ever. I did all my homework,

too, years of it, decades of it, and I do not know, did not know.

Even Shakespeare failed on that one. Why else did he take up with the Earl of Southampton? "In vowing new hate after new love bearing."

And so Sarah and Horton got married, the two adventurers, world travelers, fellow aliens. They got married, and the minute the fraudulent words had been said and agreed to, there was a moment of alarm. The alarm always comes afterward. The groom, after kissing the bride, said, "I'll bet Father will be furious." Sarah, knowing something of fathers, said, "Will it make any difference if he is?" And the groom said, "It'll be the first time in my life that I've ever done anything without . . . well, without telling him, getting his permission. . . . Oh, he'll be furious all right."

There was a moment of alarm, and then the bride thought, I mustn't make the mistake of thinking everybody has my problems. What Horton has is a nice, close relationship with his father, a mutual understanding; they talk things over. It's one of those relationships straight out of Louisa May Alcott. It's *Little Men.*

Sarah McCormick Payne said, "Poor Horton. He did his best; we all do our best, and it's never good enough. . . . Not long after we got here I knew it wasn't for a month or so; it was forever."

Mrs. Fearly swept into the garden then, looked down her awesome nose at us, and said, "You done?"

"We're quite finished, Mrs. Fearly," said Charley's mother.

When we were alone again she said, "After Horton and I were married, there was an item about it in one of the Chicago papers, and I got a note from my father, the last word from him ever. 'If I may quote from the immortal bard, "Sell when you can. You are not for all markets." I am glad to see that you sold, I should think to the first bidder.'"

Sarah McCormick Payne said, "You can't keep on pretending to be something you're not, not when you're grown up you can't. I see a psychiatrist in Des Moines, and he keeps telling me it's very dangerous to keep . . . pretending. I am not Isabel Archer and never have been, and it is not the perfect middle of a perfect summer afternoon and never has been and never will be."

She touched my hand, and the touch was as furtive as her smile. She said, "Don't worry, dear. I'm not going to cry. I gave that up some time ago. It might be a good thing if I could still cry, but I can't. And so I get up in the morning, and I play a game called getting through until Tuesday. And I try to forgive myself and Horton and my father and Horton's father, none of which is easy, but then it isn't supposed to be, is it?"

"I guess not."

"I hope you never find out for sure," she said. "If I were half as bright as I like to think I am, I'd control conditions instead of letting them control me. That's what the doctor says, and I'm sure he's quite right."

She took my hand again, this time held it very tight, and said, "Try not to let them hurt you too much. They'll try. They never stop trying, and you are especially vulnerable, I think. Promise."

I said I promised.

She said, "I've talked to you as if you were an adult, but then you are an adult. Some people are born grown up and knowing about suffering. These days, if you're at all sensitive, you either suffer or you have a frontal lobotomy."

I said I had to be going, and she said, "I know. I've talked too much. Be kind to Charles. That arrogant manner of his. Underneath he's very vulnerable, too, and he's fond of you and respects you."

She kissed me, a suggestion of a kiss really, and I was aware of her scent. Soft, not insistent, as transient as her smile. She said, "We tell ourselves that when we have children we won't make the same mistakes our parents made, and sometimes we don't, not quite the same, but we make others that are probably just as bad. But I have very high hopes for Charles. In my more exuberant moments I think he could be something very special. I have very high hopes for Charles, and for you."

16 /

The Most
Sincere People

The ballet dancer followed me again, after I left your office, whispering obscenities. He molested several children we encountered along the way. They're all child molesters. Look, I know; I've been forced in my work to spend a lot of time around fairies, and they disgust me. They all ought to be put in a leaky boat out in the middle of the Atlantic and sunk. That's what they did in the Middle Ages. All undesirables went. All. It's cheap, too; burning costs money. And with drowning, if they start asking questions later, you can deny it. Where's the evidence, you say? Where are the corpses delicti? There's not a bone as far as the eye can see. And no cum. No cum anywhere.

I don't know why ballet fags are always making passes at me, sniggering disgusting things in the foul air. I suppose it's because of Cecily Broadmoor. Yes, I mean *the* Cecily Broadmoor. The famous one. Infamous one. The entrepreneur of the ballet. I do.

Eventually, some things being inevitable, I'll tell you about her. . . . She killed Charley, of course, murdered him in cold blood, and when they take her to the gas chamber, I'm first in line to turn on the gas, and I've never believed in capital punishment.
◆

I don't know how much later it is. I took my Seconal right after
lunch, and now it's either four or four hundred hours later. It's night
time, hell time, too late for redemption now. . . . Breathe in the
poisoned air, boys and girls, and straighten up that line or I'll give
you a slap in the mouth that will knock you from here to next
Thursday. . . . Onward, Christian soldiers. Marching off to war.
With the Cross of Jesus . . .

I think I said that Charley's mother came in first the Sunday I
became a Presbyterian, and then came Horton Payne, carrying
apologies suitable for any occasion, and finally and clearly against
his will, Charley, who did not look as if he would ever apologize to
anybody for anything.

Charles McCormick Payne was tall for ten, and he was not especially sturdy, but he was graceful. That impressed me because I
was never sure which was my right hand, which my left foot, and
I was nothing but hands and feet.

Charley's hair was thick and black. He was darker than his
mother, had a high, wide forehead, and eyes that were larger than
his mother's and less sad. He had his grandfather's stern mouth and
sharp chin, and since Charley's chin was not encumbered by a Van-
dyke or other ornaments, it looked as if it could have been used to
sharpen knives.

Charley held his head high; he looked at no one, spoke to no one.
He marched down the aisle at attention and seated himself in the
pew next to his father, his back ramrod straight. His manner was
that of someone who knew he was going to be profoundly bored,
but he wasn't. He slept during the entire sermon, still sitting at attention.

When the hymns were sung, Charley did not open a hymnal or
his mouth. I opened both but didn't make a sound. What a fraud I
was, am.

During the prayer Charley didn't bow his head; he just yawned
several times, and when the collection plate was passed, Charley
handed it to his father without even glancing at it.

After the service, when Reverend Wilkinson stood at the door of the church, shaking hands, Charley kept his right hand in the pocket of his jacket.

Wilkinson, looking embarrassed, cleared his throat of a lifetime's accumulation of phlegm, then said, "Well, young Master Payne, did you enjoy the sermon?"

Charley said, "I was asleep, but even if I'd been awake, I doubt that I would have."

Then he walked out.

Everything Charley did that morning I wanted to do, would have done if I'd had the guts—and the imagination.

And God how I hated Charley, envied him, loved him. Yes, I loved him—but when the time came, what did it matter? What could I do? Can you ever do anything? Except be sorry.

I once said to Charley of somebody, "But he's sincere."

And Charley said, "It's the most sincere people who cause most of the trouble in the world. I'll take a charming charlatan every time."

17 /

Streets to 42

Are all fags—sorry, all homosexuals—promiscuous? I don't know, hon, but we come in all sizes, shapes, and colors, and the question makes about as much sense as asking if all kikes—sorry, Jews—are skinflints. All black boys big-donged.

Lamb, I've been to bed with numberless Jewish boys, and some were niggardly and some were not, and black boys, big-donged and small, and I never did get around to asking them if they were typical.

Some were tasters, and some were lovers, and it was always over before it ended.

Promiscuous. It's true that I went to Forty-second Street the very first night I was in New York. One of your predecessors said, "You went there like a homing pigeon, didn't you?"

He was wrong. You people are often wrong. I went to Forty-second Street expecting to find Ruby Keeler and Warner Baxter there, the way they had been at the Casino back home. Instead I met a good-looking boy from the hills of Tennessee who hated his father, hominy grits, and, like Nicky Pondorus, any kind of manual labor. He went back to the hotel with me, and Keith—I always remember their names—told me the story of his life. I even remember a good deal of what he said.

"I had a choice between becoming a tenant farmer like my old man or my five brothers and hustling, and I didn't have a trade or nothing; so I decided, what the hell, hustling is better than pickin' cotton. And it is, ain't it?"

I said that it undeniably was.

Keith said, "Sometimes when I don't get picked up, about four in the morning I go to Grand Central, and I cry."

And he looked in a mirror and said, "I'm almost twenty-one, and some of them say I'm losing my looks. What do you think?"

The next morning Keith was gone, and so were three J. C. Penney shirts, a pair of slacks, and the fifty dollars I had hidden in my left shoe. . . . Never hide anything in your shoes. That's the first place they look.

Ned Rorem claims in one of the diaries that some bandleader once said that Ned's trouble and the bandleader's was that they both want to be loved by everybody in the world and they can't meet everybody in the world.

Myself, I *have* met everybody in the world. I have bedded down, always at a price, with every Tom and every Dick and every Harry. Every Boris, every Jean, every Mario, every Carlos. There have been regiments of Carloses in my life, and whatever their countries, whatever their names, they all had a story to tell. "It must be interesting. It happened to *me.*"

Streets. The Street. If you are born a Georgia cracker and get fed up with corn pone and are beautiful, you end up either heading your local chapter of the Klan or on The Street. A Street. There is very little white supremacy on any of The Streets, and if you've been to bed with one black man . . . In the dark all tricks look pretty much alike anyway, and the pay is about the same as you get picking oranges.

Not to mention all the tricks, color be damned, willing to listen to the story of your life. The autobiography is always more interesting than the sex.

❖

Yes, I am promiscuous, was promiscuous. I tried to stop. Truly I did. Time after time, decade after decade, and I've given up drinking and greenies and barbiturates. Lifetime after lifetime.

Once after finding myself hung over in a male bordello in Tangier on the morning of my thirtieth birthday, and to make matters worse it was Sunday and April, I looked around, vomited, then got a plane and flew back to New York.

I went directly to the apartment, locked the door, and didn't come out for four months. They left the food on the welcome mat.

Then I did unlock the door and go out, and it happened six times before noon.

And just after the war I had a blackboard in the studio, and every morning when I got there I'd write, "Sex is ridiculous." And every evening after a couple of drinks I'd erase it.

Laurel is green for a season, and love is sweet for a day . . .

See the fag. The fag sleeps around. The fag is, all together now, p-r-o-m-i-s-c-u-o-u-s. Bag the fag. Buy a beer for a queer. Don't boot a fruit. Don't throw beans at queens. . . . Give the fag a basket. A tisket, a tasket. A brown and yellow basket. . . . See the fag run. Run, fag, run. Bye, bye, baby in the treetop. When the wind blows, the cradle will drop. Bye, baby bunting. Daddy's gone a-hunting.

And a boy named McKennon said, "Who needs girls? We've got the sissy here."

See the fag run.

Run, fag, run.

Catch the fag.

"I'm first. I thought of it."

18 /

Those Who Can

I guess that is the answer, isn't it? You say, "Things happen to people," and you've said it all. No rhyme to anything, no reason; it's all accident, and some people are lucky, and some are not and life is not just.

"Things happen to people."

Begin there and end there. But if that's the case, who needs philosophers?

Of course in my more paranoid moments, and some have been more paranoid than others, I used to think they went for the shiny ones; the brighter you were, the more they wanted to dull you, diminish you, cut you down to size. The more they hated you.

Charley and Lily and I were always the brightest in any of our classes. I really think that's true, and it always seemed to me and I believe to Lily and Charley that most of the teachers gave us a harder time than the dummies. Maybe not.

Anyway, I will never know what it is with teachers. Never. Grace Challey, for instance. She was my third grade teacher in Arnold School, which everybody said was a better school than Anson, where Lily went. They didn't mean you could learn more at Arnold. They meant it was tonier. There must have been a dozen or so spades at Anson, but at Arnold we had only this one pickaninny, a toothy, terrified little girl name Juanita, who wore her hair in pigtails and spent most recesses hiding in the girls'. When they were being kind they called her Topsy.

I never talked to her. We stayed in our separate cocoons. I spent most recesses in the basement, near the furnace, even in the spring and early fall.

Everybody at Arnold School was poor, too, but most of us were Depression poor. Our poverty was not a permanent thing, the way it was with most of the kids at Anson.

And Arnold was far enough away from the canning factory so that except on the hottest days in August, when we weren't in school anyway, there was hardly any smell.

Grace Challey was new to the town; only the year before she had graduated from what was then the state teachers' college at Cedar Falls. She was all blond and pink and dewy-eyed, and even in winter she wore the sheerest dresses, organdies and crepe de chines, under which were sensible slips of white linen.

How I know that last is a mystery I cannot explain. I certainly never looked very closely. And how do I know that her sizable breasts were locked in brassieres made of steel and always one size too small? Somebody must have told me. Nicky?

Grace Challey was described as being pretty as a picture, and her voice was a little girl's voice, to me unbearably high-pitched. . . . I don't think there's anything sexual in the fact that I prefer voices in the lower registers. Baritones rather than tenors. Although having anything at all to do with a singer is a mistake. They are always spraying their throats and humming.

I remember Miss Challey blew a whistle to get everybody lined up before marching us into class. She insisted on very straight lines and was forever shoving those who were even a little bit out of line. She was a slapper, too, and a grabber, lots of black and blue marks among the third graders, especially the boys, especially in the pubic area.

One day she shoved me and was about to grab me, and I said, "I do not wish you to touch me again under any circumstances, Miss Challey. Is that understood?"

I was terrified; I always seem to have talked big when I was terrified.

"Look here, you little sis," said Miss Challey, and she raised her hand to slap me but didn't. I guess she thought the "sis" was punishment enough.

What I've just described happened in October, and nothing much else happened between us until just before Christmas vacation. We were again lined up in front of the classroom, like a platoon of Pershing Rifles being readied for another war—against Russia, against Ethiopia, Liechtenstein, against Heidi, against Shakespeare's sonnets, against thought, nine times nine, who or whom, and diagram a sentence and spell *potato*.

As usual, Miss Challey cautioned against whispering, "and I do mean you, Darlene Sanders. Your tongue never stops wagging, does it, and that had better not be gum you're chewing, Estelle Joiner; perhaps it's your cud. Cows have cuds and, like you, are overweight. And if you are jiggling, Rose Poindexter, I will give you a slap in the mouth that will knock you from here to next Thursday."

Miss Challey did not like girls, but she more than made up for that by the way she felt about boys.

"And, Lilian Zalinsky, you know perfectly well that I told you if you came to class one more time wearing earrings—"

In midsentence Miss Challey looked down at me, pointed to my right hand, and, her voice even shriller than usual, said, "I wonder if you would be kind enough to tell me what *that* is."

I said, "I should think anybody would know what it is, Miss Challey, but since you don't seem to, I'll tell you. It's a music roll, and inside the music roll are some sheets of m-u-s-i-c that I am planning to study."

"In other words, while I am trying to pound a little sense into your sissy head, you are planning to study music. Is that it? Well, not in my class you're not."

She reached for the music roll, and I said, "I've warned you before about touching me. Take your hand off the music roll at once."

Miss Challey took her hand off the music roll and slapped me as hard as I've ever been slapped. My cheek smarted, but I refused to cry. I looked straight at her and said, "Do not ever touch me again. Do not ever call me a name and do not grab. Is that clear?"

Miss Challey, her voice almost inaudible, said, "Let's straighten up this line now."

She never again called me a name, and she never called on me in class, but she did give me straight A's, which I had earned.

I don't know where I found the courage to talk back to Miss Challey, but I do remember that at recess a girl named Nancy said, "You got a lot of guts for a sis." I forget Nancy's last name. I remember that she had reddish hair and freckles and that she kept wanting to show me what she looked like down there and wanted me to do the same. "I want to see if a sissy has got a thing like the rest of the boys." I never did, but Nancy continued to pull her skirt up every time she saw me. She wore pink bloomers. . . . God, I'm old.

Miss Challey made her own end, as people usually do. In the spring, just before the school year ended, she was found in our local lovers' lane in her Model T runabout. There were four boys with her, two of them thirteen, one fifteen, and one just turned twelve. That was Nicky Pondorus.

The night Nicky and I were on the Greek island admiring his yacht I asked him about the incident with Miss Challey, and he said, "She promised each of us five dollars, and if the cops hadn't of interfered, I think she'd of come across. But for a teacher, she sure had a lot to learn about blowing."

He turned to his benefactor and said, "You must understand that my price was considerably lower in those days."

Some time later, near dawn, I said, of course I did, one always does, "Nicky, what did you think of me in those days?"

Nicky said, "I thought you was the spunkiest little bastard on wheels. You wouldn't take any of their crap."

"I don't believe it."

"I wouldn't kid you about a thing like that," said Nicky. "All I've ever been is a pretty face. Besides, if it hadn't been for you helping me with my math, I'd never have got me that high school diploma, and in my line of work you've got to have a high school education."

Teachers. Miss Alma Hartnell was a local girl, and she was paid to teach French in the high school. Her father was a brakeman on the M. and St. L. Her mother was a maid at various places on West Main. So was Alma Hartnell when she was in high school, and during the four years she was at teachers' college in Cedar Falls she worked as a waitress.

I don't know what alien ambitions tore at her when she got her teacher's certificate, but returning to Our Town was certainly not among them. But that is what she did. Maybe our school board was the only one that made her an offer.

Do you wonder that she was filled with hatred? Hatred of things, of people, of places, of the town. Hatred of herself in particular, of course.

Not to mention Miss Nellie Bosley, who was mistress of Latin and was said to read some Greek. Miss Bosley had been born in New York City, was a graduate of Wellesley, a member of the DAR, said she had a private income, and drove a Cadillac.

"I certainly don't *need* the pittance they pay me here, but to turn it back would create *such* bookkeeping problems."

And, "Anybody can learn and teach a modern language. All you have to do is *listen,* and in my humble opinion, students, such trifles as French, Spanish, particularly French, should not clutter the groves of academe. Such subjects could, perhaps, be endured as extracurricular activities, like tatting. On the other hand, *any* respectable education begins with the classical languages."

And Miss Hartnell, after mispronouncing *tante;* "The language

I am teaching you is *living, spoken,* not laid out, embalmed, ready for burial, like some, and I am sure you boys and girls are smart enough to know what I'm getting at."

Yet on certain subjects Miss Hartnell and Miss Bosley were in complete agreement.

One April afternoon when I was a sophomore I was sitting at a small desk in a dark corner of the downstairs hallway. I was hall monitor, a job of no distinction. A monitor's main business was to carry messages from one classroom to another, but there were never any messages.

This particular afternoon a wisp of a man came up the broad stone steps to my left and stood before me for a long moment. He wore coveralls that were stained and not new. He smelled of the need of a bath. An uncombed fringe of yellow hair fell over his narrow forehead, and he had no teeth.

He asked to see Miss Hartnell, and in my best monitor's voice I said, "And who shall I say is calling, sir?"

"Say her father," said the old man, "say her father here."

I did, and Miss Hartnell, her cheeks aflame, marched out of the classroom ahead of me. She shouted at the old man, "I told you never to come here. I told you I'd kill you if you ever came here." Then, remembering me, "And you get back to study hall."

"But I'm the monitor."

"You get back to study hall or I'll kill you, too," said Miss Hartnell, and her voice meant it.

Miss Hartnell did not have to kill her father; he conveniently died a few months later, and I will never know what urgent message caused him to risk his life and mine by coming to the school.

But if you think Miss Hartnell hated me before . . .

In early June of that same year, when I was once again hall monitor, I heard Miss Hartnell say to Miss Bosley, "Keep your voice down. You never know what that little sis will pick up, even when we're in the girlies'. Of course what they really ought to do, they ought to make him use the girls' room. He sure is more of a girl than a boy. . . ." How they giggled.

A moment. Then Miss Hartnell: "I've had to give Lily Farrell an A. I'd rather take a licking, but I had to do it. For my money she's pushy and always will be, but, I suppose, what could you expect with a mother like that, putting out for every Tom, Dick, and Harry that comes down the turnpike."

"I couldn't agree more. I don't for the life of me see why we don't have more pupils like little Elaine Jacobs. She's a quiet little thing, and the Jacobses are quality people from way back. I can always tell breeding, can't you, Alma?"

"From a mile off. Breeding, if you've got it, sticks out all over, but Lily Farrell doesn't even know the meaning of the word."

"And the sissy there is even worse. If there is one thing I cannot stand, it's a sissy, although he never opens his yap when he's in my class. He knows better. And he gets straight hundreds in every quiz I give him, except the surprise, and he got a ninety-eight in that."

"You think maybe he cheats?"

"That four-eyed little sis? Too big a coward. No, what else has he got to do, pounding away on that piano and studying? That's all he ever does, while the real boys are out playing baseball. But I don't think he cheats. If I ever caught him so much as thinking about cheating while I'm around . . ."

"That's one of the troubles with sissies," said Miss Bosley. "You can never tell what they're thinking behind those four eyes: Now with a regular boy . . ."

"A truer word was never said," said Miss Alma Hartnell. "The two of them, the sis and Lily Farrell. I think they're in cahoots, the two of them."

"Do you mean . . . is Lily Farrell peculiar?"

"So far as I know, not in that way. I mean she likes boys and all, but nothing but trash will so much as wipe their feet on her and her mother. They're putting out, the two of them."

"You mean her and the sis?"

"What he does in that line I wouldn't even like to think. That's one subject I never discuss with my pupils. No, I mean Lily Farrell and her mother. Like mother, like daughter, as the feller said."

"Speaking of the sis. Did I ever tell you, Alma? A few weeks back the sis was sitting there in class, his mind a million miles away, and I said, 'Mr. Lionel doesn't seem to be with us today, boys and girls. Where are you today, Mr. Lionel, if you're not here in class with the rest of us?' And you know what he said? You know that funny voice of his, sounds like a little old woman. He said, 'If you must know, I was listening to the second movement of Beethoven's Ninth.' Did you ever hear the like, ever in your whole life?"

They started laughing.

19 /

Morning
of the Day

Look, I'll admit my father never made what you'd call money, and he was out of work for months and months, years and years. I think in some ways part of his life ended the day Matthew Payne came into the bank and said to my father, "My son Horton is returning from Chicago tomorrow. He will be taking over your job. You can stay until three if you'd like, but there are certain changes in the office that I'd like to have made. So if you'd like to clean out your desk now . . ."

That was in 1920, and my father was twenty-five years old and impatient. The whole of the world had to be remade, and if God had taken six days . . . not that he believed in God.

Years after the March morning I'm talking about here, I met several men who had been my father's fraternity brothers at the university, and one of them used the word *romantic* to describe him; the others nodded. "Romantic." Yes, that described Monte to a T.

The same man said, "Your father was a man who believed in things."

That evening I played a concert at the Memorial Union, and I cried like a baby all through Mozart's Sonata in A Major, because my father had never heard me play it and had loved it, because I was playing it well, because I still thought anything was possible for me, because I wondered if he ever had thought that about himself.

Maybe he did, in the days before the morning Matthew Payne came into the bank and said what he said, also saying, "I now own the majority of the stock and I intend owning all of it."

Matthew Payne was not a subtle man, but then he was rich, and if you are rich, you can not only be different, as Lily said, you can be an absolute bastard and get away with it.

After that last day in the bank, everything went wrong for my father. He borrowed money to open yet another miniature golf course just at the time everybody stopped playing miniature golf; he bought land in Florida during the boom of 1926, and the land he bought turned out to be half under water, but by that time the bubble had burst anyway.

Go to Florida . . .

Where the whispering breeze springs fresh from the lap of the Caribbean and woos with elusive cadence like unto a mother's lullaby . . .

Where the silver sickle is heaven's lavaliere, and the full orbit its glorious pendant.

My father got a job in the office at the canning company, but when they started laying people off, he was one of the first to go.

And then one morning he put on coveralls and came downstairs and said to my mother, "I've got a job at the canning factory, canning corn."

My mother said, "Not as a common day laborer."

He said, "Yes, as a common day laborer."

I think it was then that he started reading all those books.

And then he lost the job as a common day laborer; nobody worked in those years, except my mother.

❖

Yes, she made all the money. There wouldn't have been money for the music lessons or even for my clothes if it hadn't been for what she made at J. C. Penney. The clothes were bought at a discount, and I always hated them, but at least I didn't freeze my ass off.

My father was impractical. I grant you that, too. And he was weak. The morning I'm talking about now was in March, and it was Monday. I know it was Monday because my mother had got up at four and done the laundry. She did it in a washtub near the potbellied stove. The washing machine had been repossessed.

After the laundry was done, she made breakfast, and then she packed my school lunch. We couldn't afford anything except a half pint of milk at the school cafeteria. "And don't share your lunch with a soul now, George. You are inclined to be generous to a fault, a characteristic you have inherited from your father, among other weaknesses. As I keep reminding him—and if I've reminded him once—the Lord helps those that help themselves."

And then she made lunch for my father and put it on the back of the stove, and she packed a lunch for herself and went to work and was on her feet and out in the public all day at Penney's. "I can personally recommend this particular pair of bloomers because I personally . . . And why people trade in Jew stores when you can buy American and cheap at half the price, and we don't know where the money we spend with them goes."

And then she came home and made supper, and we listened, first, to a detailed account of her day out in the public, and then we listened to "Amos 'n' Andy," and then she started talking again. ". . . and here you were at home sitting on your ass, Monte. I sometimes think you're not worth the powder and shot it would take to blow you up." And she would at the same time be redding up the kitchen and cleaning the rest of the house, the latter always noisily near the chair where my father was trying to read Thorstein Veblen on *The Theory of the Leisure Class*.

"Nobody ever got rich by having his nose stuck in a book, Monte, and if I've reminded you once . . ."

But the day I want to tell you about was nothing like that. I want you to understand that day. Assuming it is possible for anybody ever to understand another's day, share another's sorrow, joy. Even a man like you, a compassionate man, a loving man, a man trained for and with experience in looking into the heads of other people.

Look, that day was as important as any in my life, and if you don't understand it, you'll never understand me.

My father was silent all during breakfast, and that was unusual. Most mornings he'd come downstairs, and the *Register* would be there, leaning against his egg cup, and he'd say, "Well, let's take a look at the funnies."

He didn't mean "Maggie and Jiggs" or "The Gumps." He didn't have time for those. He meant what was on all the other pages of the paper, and he'd search out every indignity, never having far to look. My father was a caring man; they used to say I took after him.

Sometimes my father would read the indignity aloud, and sometimes my mother, who would be doing six other things at the same time, would listen.

My father would say, "Franklin Roosevelt is an empty-headed charlatan. There's only one man who could have saved us from our folly, and that's Norman Thomas. However, our electorate prefers the fifth-rate, always has, always will. A *holiday*. What a word to use to describe closing the banks. Dancing in the streets. Let them eat cake. A *holiday* isn't going to save the American banking system. Socialization would."

Or, "This editorial is written by a fool. It says that Hitler is going to be a *stabilizing* influence in Germany. What's happened in Germany is a victory of the lumpen proletariat, and Marx specifically warns us against them—the dissatisfied ignorant, the envious ciphers, the swellers of the crowd. . . . Shaw says those who can't do anything else *teach*. I say that those who aren't up to teaching write editorials for the capitalist press."

Or, "There's a new law in Hungary. All the girls have to wear chastity belts until they get married, and their fathers keep the keys. I wonder how that kind of thing would work out here. I hope Roosevelt doesn't hear about it, because if he does . . . Have you got any of your old chastity belts about, Dora?"

And my mother: "Your heart is as big as all of the out-of-doors, Monte, but we have personal problems of our own, and it is time to face the facts and no two ways about it, especially with a new administration in the White House. If Grandfather Lionel, and a fine man he was, none better, had been a little more like Matthew Payne, we would today be living in the house on West Main, and you'd be sitting where Horton Payne is today, and you know more about banking in your little finger than he—"

"Dora, there are times when I realize it is impossible to make you understand what I am getting at, and I fear it always will be."

That's the way it was most mornings, but on this one, not one indignity. Even my mother was subdued, although once, frying an egg, doing her hair, washing a cup, she said, "What's the matter, Monte? Cat got your tongue?"

"My esteemed wife," said my father, "I am going to ask you something I never have before."

"What's that?"

"To shut the hell up."

At a few minutes before eight he rose from the table, dabbed at his mouth with the linen napkin—have I said that he was a fastidious man?—and said to himself more than to my mother or me, "I keep asking myself what I did wrong, but the real question is what I ever did right."

My mother said, "As President Roosevelt himself has told us, 'The only thing we have to fear is fear itself.' "

"Oh, God. I told you he was a charlatan. He even stole that from Montaigne, but who has exposed him? Who has read Montaigne? I have. I have read Montaigne, said the Little Red Hen, and a hell of a lot of good it has done me. Well. I might as well get dressed.

Under the circumstances a shroud might be just the thing. Did you launder mine, Dora?"

"I ironed a nice white shirt for you," said my mother, "the broadcloth one I got you at Gildner's two Christmases ago, and wear the red polka dot tie Aunt Karlene got you in Chicago, the one from Carson Pirie Scott, not the one from Rosenblatt's. Quality tells, and I don't want you in a Jew tie when you see Horton Payne."

My father sighed and said, "Dora, you are one of God's originals, no question about that, and my only problem is I don't believe in God."

"That's neither here nor there," said my mother, "and bring down the clothes brush."

My father walked to the door of the stairway, his back straight, his chin braced like that of a West Point cadet; he always carried himself like that when he was in trouble, bad trouble, as most troubles were in those days. That walk was the only military thing about him, though. He despised soldiers, sailors, cops, athletes, and newspapermen, especially those who wrote about sports. "Never trust a man who makes his living describing children at play."

When he got upstairs—I heard his measured pace on the wide, separated oak floorboards—I said to my mother, "I suppose it's none of my business, but—"

"It's none of your business," said my mother, "and I don't want a word out of you. I want you to eat your oatmeal and drink your milk in silence, and I neither need nor want your opinions on either. I am quite familiar with your feelings in the matter."

"Which is no doubt the reason I have to eat what I hate more than anything else in the wide and shining world morning after morning after morning."

"The reason you have oatmeal every morning, and oatmeal sprinkled *luxuriously* with raisins and brown sugar, I might add, is that it's cheap and filling. Not only that, the little boy down the street would be tickled to death to have what you leave on your plate. Not to mention the starving Armenians."

"If you're not going to mention the goddamn starving Armenians, then why the hell are you always goddamnitohell doing it?"

We weren't talking to each other, you see, not really; we were shaking our fists at the thunder, like Beethoven gone deaf and fearing for his sight; we were baying at the moon like a lonely and bewildered dog; we were accepting our fate with a sure knowledge of what was to come. I had yet to read the Greeks, but certain things are automatic. One is, one always was, everyone I mean, born with the knowledge that he is an uncrowned king and, thus, a figure of tragedy. Even the most inarticulate among us know that. Only fools make a melodrama of it; they try to cheat the inevitable by all kinds of tricks, by grabbing power, demanding acclaim, piling up money. But Herodotus had it right. It always ends the same way. We are food for the worms, who dine slowly, or the flames.

That morning I saw that my mother was close to tears, which surprised me. She never cried in real life. Not when the only brother she liked, even loved, died lengthily and in great pain from cancer of the prostate, not when she realized that the man she had married would never appear in *American* magazine as "another personification of the dream that has made this country . . ."

My mother cried at movies; she cried while reading certain stories in *True Story* magazine; she cried when reading *Photoplay:* "Why Clark Gable Will Never Be the Same Now That Carole Lombard Has Passed On"; she cried all during certain radio programs: "Young Widder Brown," "Backstage Wife," "Mary Marlin," "Ma Perkins." But, as I say, almost never in real life.

"I'm sorry I talked back."

"It's too late now; you should have thought of that before you said what you said."

And there we were, right back where we started, where we ended.

About half an hour later my father came downstairs again. His hair was neatly brushed, except for the clump in back that would never stay down. He had on the double-breasted blue serge suit, the one he wore to his funeral, and it was neatly brushed and not quite as shiny as his shoes. He had on the red polka dot *goyim* tie, and his face was pale.

He put on his Tyrolean hat with the green feathers; the hat was jaunty; that's really the only word to describe it, and he certainly was not jaunty. Somehow, the hat made him look even sadder than he was. I can't explain why he wore it.

He said, "Wish me luck. I'll need it."

I said, "You look like a million dollars." Until the day he died I never called him anything, I mean anything like *Pop* or *Dad* or *Father*, certainly never *Monte*. Monte was Monte Blue, a star of the silent screen, and I loved him almost as much as I later loved Errol Flynn. I wrote to Errol, and whoever it was sent me his autographed picture with his shirt unbuttoned way down. I hid the picture under my mattress, but my mother, that immaculate housekeeper, found it and destroyed it, and neither of us ever mentioned it. Just as we never mentioned the letter to Eldon Rickets that I hadn't sent. It said, "Dear Eldon, Although we have never met, I have long worshiped you from afar. . . ." She destroyed that, too.

No, I never called my father anything. I just looked at him and spoke, not always kindly, I'm afraid.

I never told him that I loved him, either, which may be the reason I've told so many people since. I always begin with that. "My name is . . . and I love you."

With an introduction like that, at least you know where you stand, for a few minutes anyway.

My mother gave his shoulders a single, nervous brush with her hand. He'd forgot the clothes brush. She said, "Be sure there's no dandruff on your shoulders when you go in because that's one of the first things a man like Horton Payne will notice. He gets a haircut and a shampoo every Thursday at the Tallcorn, and Lucille Patton, who's my Electra in the Star and does him, says he has hands that are softer than most women's. I wish you took better care of your hands. If Grandfather Lionel hadn't . . . but then he did and it's over and done with and more's the pity. Your hands are all chapped, but that *may* be an advantage. They are hands that have known honest labor."

"He'll either say yes or he'll say no," said my father, "and my hands and dandruff won't have anything to do with it."

"Horton Payne is not the man his father was and never will be," said my mother, a pronouncement that nearly everybody in town felt called upon to make at one time or another.

"And don't try to show off. About what's wrong with the capitalistic system and so on. If there are barricades to be mounted, Horton Payne will be on the other side, and so will that son of his. Not to mention Mrs. Nose-in-the-Air."

I said, "Good luck," and he kissed me on the forehead.

He said, "I'll tell you all about it tonight. I'm trying to get a second mortgage on the house, and if I don't . . ."

"For heaven's sake, Monte," said my mother. "Don't upset sonny before he goes to school. Miss Pratt says that he is smart enough for any good purpose but very highly strung and likely to fly off the handle at any given occasion, and while she is consistently urging him to take part in sports, sonny is often the last to be called when they are choosing up sides."

"Many damn fools are called," said my father, "but it's the birdbrains who are chosen."

He went out the door, slamming it hard.

I said, "I'm not going to school today." And then, aware of the gathering storm on my mother's face, added, "I'm too nervous. In fact, I'm a nervous wreck and very highly strung. But where are the strings on which I am strung so highly? Does Miss Pratt her ass is fat have the answer to that?"

"If that is intended as a humorous remark, it has fallen flatter than a pancake," said my mother, "but I leave the matter of your going to school to you. Go ahead and be a failure like your father for all I care."

I said, "Anyway, Rosenberg's got two free hours this morning, and while I will regret missing the wisdom of Lola Pratt, I believe I'll go see him."

My mother, who couldn't stand the idea of passing up anything free, said, "Perhaps just this once, but don't get into the habit. It's rare enough getting anything free out of a Jew."

I laughed and said, "You are one of God's originals all right," and for the first time in, say, years, I kissed her.

"We're a family," she said, "and wild horses couldn't pull us apart."

I didn't go to school that morning, and I didn't take a lesson from Rosenberg, either. What I did do was go to the M. and St. L. depot, but there was nothing new written on the walls of the men's room, and the only Wild Boy of the Road was about forty and needed a shave and a haircut and, I was sure, a bath. I wanted to humiliate myself that day, be humiliated, humiliating—but not with him. I was sure there'd be other opportunities. When were there not?

Old Mr. Durrell, the stationmaster, and he also ran the newsstand, said hello and how was I, and I bought a *Register* from him. I always bought a *Register* from him so that he wouldn't think anything funny.

I walked up the steps of the viaduct and stood there for a while, looking down at the railroad tracks, wondering if I would have the guts to jump when the time came. I was very scared. If Horton Payne did not give my father the second mortgage, we would be out in the streets before you knew it, and I had seen enough foreclosures to realize what that meant. Two people in town that I knew by sight had killed themselves when it happened. A man had shot off his head with a .45 and a woman, the mother of six, had put her head in an oven. They took the kids to an orphanage near Ames.

Other people I knew just left town or went on relief, and when that happened, they kept their faces turned away when you passed them on the street.

The woman in charge of relief was named Mabel Evans, and if you were white, Miss Evans always started out by saying, "I can understand when it's niggers, but with white people . . . My forebears founded this town and don't ever forget it. They never asked for free handouts; they'd have died first, and if you are *com-*

plaining about a little perfectly healthy mold in the bread, you can cut that away with a knife, spelled k-n-i-f-e. You do know what a knife is, don't you? You can cut your wrists with one, too."

I'd heard her say that.

No, death would be better than going on relief. What was so bad about death?

The nine-sixteen train to Chicago stopped for water, and I thought of all the people on that train who were eating big, hearty breakfasts and not worrying about being foreclosed or going on relief. Such people would never have to worry about things like that.

And I thought of running down the steps of the viaduct and jumping on the train. I would tell them I was the Lost Dauphin. I was the Lost Dauphin, wasn't I? I pretended that to myself all the time. But I knew that nobody else in the entire world would believe me, and so I stayed on the viaduct, and after a while the train left, and it started sleeting.

A little later Lydell Griswald stopped his truck near where I was standing.

He said, "Want a lift, kid?" And he winked at me.

I said, "Okay. That will be fine," and I hopped in.

Lydell was a tenant farmer on an eighty-acre farm south of town. The farm had been foreclosed and belonged to the bank. I had noticed Lydell before, quite often as a matter of fact, usually on Saturday night when he came to town. And he had noticed me. I knew that. He was young and for a farmer really very handsome. His skin, the skin on his face and neck—nobody ever worked with his shirt off in those days—was brown and not all dried out the way most farmers' skins were. He had bluish green eyes, very nice, and, like most other farmers, he shaved and took a bath on Saturday. I myself took a bath on Saturday and, sometimes, if I was playing the piano someplace, on week nights as well. As I say, this was Monday; so both Lydell and I were relatively clean.

"Where you headed, kid?"

"Noplace special, I guess, not right away anyway."

"Want to take a little ride, down to the Indian reservation? I got to pick up some stuff down there. I'll bring you back."

"Okay." By that time we both knew what was up; you always know that. You don't even have to speak the language.

Lydell said, "You're not going to school?"

"Not this morning."

"That's good. We'll take a little ride and have us some fun."

We went to the Indian reservation first, and we came back by way of the limestone quarry at Le Grand. Never anybody around the quarry in March, especially when it's sleeting.

Afterward, Lydell told me that he was twenty-three years old and that he had married his wife, Mabel, because she was already four months knocked up and claimed it was his, only everybody around Montour had been banging her, and he'd only done it once. He was never sure the kid was his, and after they got married, all she ever did in bed was groan and say, "You about done, Lydell?"

They had three boys, all of whom took after Mabel.

I said that that was certainly a pity, and Lydell said, "Don't never get married, kid. Don't never let them talk you into it."

I said that I'd keep that in mind, and Lydell said, "Now you won't say anything about . . . well, you know, about this monkey business, will you?"

I shook my head, wondering, as always, who in the world I would tell.

Lydell drove me back to the place on the viaduct where he'd picked me up, and when I got out of the pickup he said he'd be seeing me around, and we did see each other, usually on Saturday night, but we never spoke or smiled or anything, and he never gave me another lift, and the day I was on the farm with Charley . . . You'll see.

I hadn't humiliated myself, though. What I had done was much worse, in the long run very much worse, and I have done it over and over and over. I had wasted my time.

❖

We will end on a cheerful note. I laughed the other day, the day you asked me at what age when I was a boy I would like to have known myself. I suppose that's one of your standard questions, one of *the* standard questions, but Jesus, I came back here and double-locked the door and laughed. I couldn't stop.

I forget what lie I told. You'll remember. You never forget any-thing you want to use against me, do you? You sonofabitch. I think you're working for them. That's why all that note-taking, and you claim you're not taking notes.

I think the room is bugged, too, and so is this one, although what good that does I can't imagine. There's been nobody here except Christopher and Gunther, and sometimes you can't tell them apart. I can't anyway, except Gunther is German. All Gunthers are Ger-man, and they are all orphans, and they are all beautiful and lonely and lonesome or dead. . . .

But about your question. Let's settle this once and for all. There has never been a day in my life, not an hour, when I would not have gone to any lengths to avoid meeting me.

I'd rather die than meet me, rather die, rather die.

My soul to take.

I've never picked the right lovers, either. If I was going to take up with Germans, why couldn't it have been somebody like Ludwig II? Wagner did. It was love at first sight. That and the fact that Ludwig paid off all his debts, gave him a house, a yearly income of eight thousand gulden, and promised to build him an opera house. "One look at his dear picture helps me again."

I wish you'd turn off the machine. I scream in my sleep, and it's always same dream. There's a lake, and I don't know how to swim, and somebody says, "Okay, kid. It's either that or this. This or that." And another: "I'm first. I thought of it."

The lake is pine, and green is my favorite color.

Beauty Is

I'll tell you one thing in my favor. At least I think it's in my favor. I never seduced anybody, not that I'm quite sure what that word means. It's been my not inconsiderable experience that very few passes have ever been made unless the passee was receptive, usually anxious. Not necessarily willing. A great many people like to say no, but everybody wants to be wanted, everybody. . . . Testing, testing.

I always thought I was the ugliest little boy who ever lived. It never occurred to me that I could have love without paying for it. Everybody has to pay for it in one way or another, and money is the least expensive way.

Yes, I'm getting to it.

The night I went to the Payne house for the first time was probably the most important night of my life up to then, and I had never felt uglier or more incomplete.

At home we had dinner at the usual time, five-thirty, and there was the usual silence. My father read the *Times-Dispatch* at supper, but there was nothing to read aloud. The *Times-Dispatch* was largely concerned with who had spent the day shopping in Cedar Rapids and whose daughter-in-law was visiting for the week from Ottumwa.

The usual silence except that three times my mother said to me, "Have another pork chop and some applesauce."

When I three times refused, she said, "You've got to keep up your strength."

I said, "You sound as if I was going to have a baby," which made my father laugh.

"They may ask you to play," said my mother. "You'd better plan to take some music with you."

"It may surprise you to learn that I have memorized one or two things, besides which I have no intention of entertaining the Paynes. I am not an entertainer."

"*Moonlight* Sonata is nice. Maybe if you're off your feed I ought to make you a little milktoast."

"For God's sake, can't you understand anything? I am not hungry."

"I understand that you've got a big evening ahead of you. That I do understand, and you and your father, apparently, do not."

"I am going to spend an hour or so at the Horton Paynes'. What's the big deal about that?"

"The big deal is that you have a chance to become friends with the most important people in this town, and I for one want to see you take advantage of it."

"Dora," said my father, "let George alone. If he doesn't want to go, he doesn't have to."

"I'll go. I don't mind, really. What the hell, I might even learn something."

"You might learn how not to be a failure like your father," said my mother, and my father looked away, and so did I. That's all you can really do, look away, and try not to be ashamed of the tears.

I said, "Excuse me if you please," and went to my room. I turned on the Victrola, loud. *Wellington's Victory* was best at such times, although the *1812* would do well enough. I played both a good deal during the marriage. Dede could have claimed ear damage, but she didn't. She never claimed anything except that she loved me. *What a pity.*

It took me forever to start dressing. Of course I was terrified, and I had not yet learned that the wisest way to deal with such terrors was through a variety of pills, not like the ones I carried in France during the war. The ones I mean take a little while; the ones in France gave you instant relief, an instant out. The night of my first postwar concert in New York I took fifteen of the milder kind, fifteen bennies, and I got rave notices. Several of the critics were particularly impressed with my pianissimo.

Eventually I took a very long bath, using my mother's lavender bath salts, after which I examined all of me in the bathroom mirror, hoping there had been a miracle. Alas, no change at all except for more falling hair, and the thing near the end of my nose was angrier than ever, the result of a too vigorous scrubbing. I've always meant to ask F. how he got rid of that pimple.

The rest of my body was equally unsatisfactory, every nook and cranny of it misshapen, shadow-thin, and I was too short for my age. In school when they did *A Christmas Carol*, which I detested and which they acted out all year round, the way they played baseball, I was always Tiny Tim, that little faggot, that screaming, sanctimonious little faggot. I know where he ended up, hustling in Piccadilly underground, undercutting the other boys. "I'll show you a good time for tuppence, sir. God bless us every one."

Until I was sixteen or thereabouts, my voice didn't change like other boys'; I tell you, nothing happened like other boys. For eternities I was a squeaky soprano, surrounded by operatic baritones, and even when the change came, it was unsatisfactory. I was a sort of high alto, until I started my butch act, that is, and it never fooled anybody but me.

It wasn't that I hadn't worked hard to improve my body. By the time I was eight I had saved enough from my magazine route—*Liberty*, anyone? Read Viña Delmar's latest, "Kept Boy"—to buy all the dubious paraphernalia that a fraud named Charles Atlas sold to the gullible and undersized. It didn't help. I remained a sixty-eight-pound weakling. My chest was concave, concave and convex, " 'Twould fit either sex." One shoulder was higher than the other. My torso was too wide and too squat. My legs were thin and, I thought, longer than all the rest of me put together. (I never stretched; I was afraid stretching would cause my legs to grow longer.) As for the limp thing between my legs, it was preposterous.

One of the eyes beneath the glasses, which were always bent, was crossed; the nose would have served better as a sparrow's beak; the mouth was like a wilted rosebud, and my chin was transient.

Love? How could anybody possibly? How could anybody like me even? My father did, but everybody in town said he was odd. My mother talked about loving me, talked a lot, but I didn't believe it, not for a minute, and it has been my experience since that the more they talk about it, the less they mean it.

Altogether there was nothing about my body that I found tolerable, except for my hands. They were okay hands for a piano player. They were large, too large for the rest of me, but strong. My fingers were squat, and they didn't know their own strength sometimes. If I hadn't taken up the piano, I might have been a really good professional strangler. . . . Even Rosenberg approved of my hands. "I don't think they were meant for you. But perhaps. Since nothing else about you is right, your hands may be their way of apologizing, whoever *they* are, and in any case, since you have them, you'd better take care to make good use of them."

And there was this. I used Lifebuoy soap incessantly, two cakes or more a week, and the Lifebuoy people guaranteed that their soap made you *safe* night and day or double your money back. What's more, I had at least one of all the mouthwashes they sold at Elder's Drugs and Sundries, and I always rinsed my mouth out with several before going to school or anywhere.

I turned away from the mirror. There was nothing to be done about me, nothing. Praying would do no good. I had long since learned that you cannot count on God in a pinch. So I put on my goddamn BVDs, the white shirt my Aunt Karlene had bought me at Yonkers in Des Moines, the speckled blue tie from two Christmases ago, the silver-plated tie clasp with my initials from Herman's, the black socks, and the oxfords from Sears, Roebuck—$4.98 and guaranteed to take the roughest treatment from your huskiest boy. I was hardly anybody's huskiest boy, but there was a hole the size of a dime in the sole of my left oxford. That was the last straw, the final indignity.

I threw the shoe across the room, knocking over the goosenecked lamp on the worktable. The lamp fell to the floor, breaking the bulb, and a moment later my mother, looking more than ever like a bantam hen, scurried into the room.

"What in the world is going on here?" She snapped off the Victrola. "You keep this on so loud a person can't hear themselves think. And you broke your bulb. Do you have any idea how much a thirty-watt bulb costs? The way you break things and wear things out, we may find ourselves on the street without the clothes on our backs, and I don't care what President Roosevelt says."

"Have you finished? Because if you have, you ought to know there's a hole in the bottom of my shoe, and I'm not going."

"In times like these you are a very lucky young man to have any shoes at all. Half the time the Dedman boys go barefoot in the middle of winter with three feet of snow on the ground and never a word of complaint. Like that Spartan boy, the one with the fox. You know, what's-his-name."

I noticed then that she was wearing the long-sleeved black dress she'd worn only twice before, at my grandmother's funeral and at Aunt Grace's wedding.

"What are you all dolled up for?"

My mother, who would, I believe, have been a highly successful army tactical officer, said, "Did you put on clean underwear?"

"Yes, I put on clean underwear, but what's that got to do with the price of potatoes?"

"You should always dress from the skin out as if you were going to have an accident."

"If I had an accident, I'd be all blood and my brains spilling out, so who's going to notice if I have on clean underwear?"

"The same people who notice that you have a tiny little hole in the sole of your shoe."

"Okay. For once touché. But what are you all dolled up for?"

"Your mother's not as dumb as you think, you know. Tonight's five hundred club, but that's not until eight. So I thought I'd drop you at the Paynes' and maybe say hello to Mrs. Payne and then whip back to Esther Bryant's. She and I are cohostessing, and I'll bring you back some of her ladyfingers. Remember how you said they just melt in your mouth?"

"Ladyfingers, my ass. You can tell Esther Bryant what to do with her ladyfingers, and I'll bet they'd just about fit, too. And you are not going to drop me at the Paynes'; if you even so much as try . . ."

"I choose to ignore the vulgarity of the first part of your remark, though where you picked up that vernacular I choose not to think. Not, I presume, from the Jew, in which case, artist or not, we would be forced to dispense with his services forthwith. As for my not dropping you at the Paynes', what is that supposed to mean, that you are ashamed of your very own mother?"

"The point is that you weren't asked, and it would be embarrassing."

I guess she agreed with that, because she kissed me on the cheek and said, "You look nice, and if you keep your wits about you, there is no reason in the world why Horton Payne won't make a settlement on you. It happens all the time."

I have no idea what my mother thought she meant about the settlement. That was often the case. I do not know where she learned to talk the way she did or when it started. That is another of the mysteries about her that will now forever be unsolved. She didn't get it from reading. She read almost nothing, even in the *Times-Dispatch*. "Old Mrs. Sheeley died, and a blessing for all concerned, riddled with cancer the way . . ." "Esther, did you see where Myra Goddard is having a premature baby? Isn't that the limit? The Goddards must think other people can't count. Six months and four days, barring an hour here and there. You recall I said at the time of the nuptials, I said . . ." She read *True Story* magazine from cover to cover. "Will My Phantom Lover Return?" "How Shall I Explain to My Son

That I Am Unwed?" And *True Confessions*, also cover to cover. "At Fourteen I First Learned the Meaning of Love." "He Came, Wearing a Mask."

Some years later my mother visited me in New York, and since I had either hidden or given away or burned all but the softest-core pornography, I was surprised when she picked up Frank Harris's schoolgirlish *My Life and Loves*, flipped through it, then flung it in the fireplace. She said, "A thing like that makes me feel dirty all over, and did I tell you? I'm vice chairman of the committee to keep the filth off of the newsstands back home. Ever vigilant. That's our motto, and it would behoove you to remember it, George. Howsoever, when you're married and settled down, which I'm sure is already arranged and you're saving it for a surprise for me, your little wife will make you see . . ."

Perhaps she picked up the way she spoke at Coe College in Cedar Rapids; she spent a few uneasy months there before she met my father, and among the other nonsense she rubbed up against was a course in elocution. Almost everybody in town who had assembled in groups of ten or more had heard her rendition of "Over the Hills to the Poorhouse" at least once. The less fortunate and those not fleet of foot had heard it many times.

My mother had been at Coe because she had some thought of becoming a grade school teacher, but she went to a Pi Kappa Alpha dance in Iowa City one snowy February night, and she met my father, and it was whatever it was at first sight, on her part anyway. No, that's unfair; on both their parts.

"I often ask myself, Sonny, if I hadn't gone to that dance, where would you be at this very moment?"

I know less about my mother than I know about dozens of boys I've spent the night with, spent an hour with. . . . Dozens? Hundreds? Thousands. How many thousands?

Four or five years ago I made a list of all those I could remember. I refuse to repeat the number, and I hadn't even begun. . . . I met

a man in Rio once, a rich, dreadful man, a *deputado*, and he had
kept a record, he said, since he was sixteen. The number was 6,280.
And he had never seen anybody twice. . . . That was not the reason
he was dreadful. That was the reason he was sad.

I had a very bad time in Rio that trip, the last time I will ever go.

One night on the way back to the hotel after a concert . . . I gave
the boy all the money I had, but he wouldn't believe me. . . . They
thought I wouldn't live. I prayed I wouldn't.

It was in all the papers, but they were very discreet. The boy was
described as "an unknown assailant." When the police brought him
to the hospital, I said there had been a mistake. I said I'd never seen
him before. . . . He never told me his name. He had gray eyes.

After I got out of the hospital, I rented an apartment on the Ave-
nida Copacabana, and for four months or however long it was, I did
not speak aloud to anybody. I swam, and once I almost drowned.
When I got back to New York, everybody said I looked simply wonderful, and nobody mentioned the incident in Rio. . . . "You must
have had a wonderful rest, and I'll bet you can't wait to . . ." I was
very brown when I got back. It's becoming, but it can lead to skin
cancer.

I know that my mother was the eldest of six children, all girls, and
that when she met my father four of the younger sisters were already
married or engaged. She was twenty-nine. It was late. I know that
she always felt she had been denied something she deserved, but
then we all suffer from that to one degree or another. I know that
what she had in mind for my father was not what he had in mind for
himself, and neither got what he wanted. I know that not only did
Grandfather Lionel lose his money; her father, who had once owned
two entire sections of land, was, when my mother was growing up,
reduced to eighty acres, mostly dust and mortgage.

But what is any of that, except a few statistics? Did she love my
father? Did he love her? Ever? Always? . . . Those are things I'd
like to know. We'd all like to know, never do know. And I'd certainly

be curious to find out what she thought of the odd mutation who was her son. I'll never know how much she suspected, how much she knew, and how much she refused to know.

The night I played the concert at the high school, and it was a far bigger event in her life than it was in mine, after I was dressed and shined and . . . she swooped into my bedroom, much as she had the first night I went to the Paynes', inspected me, found me wanting, sighed, decided to overlook it, kissed me, said, "Good luck, not that you'll need it," said, "Don't ever be ashamed of being . . ." Hesitated, paused, swallowed.

Said, "If you're bathed and have on clean underwear and your fingernails are clean, you have nothing whatever to apologize for, ever."

That was not what she had in mind saying, but no matter. . . . She was never silent, and she never said anything essential.

"Now let me warn you about one thing. Do not mention the Jew in the presence of the Paynes. People like that simply ignore the existence of those of the Jewish persuasion."

"For Christ's sake, the way you talk you'd think the Paynes were royalty or something."

"They're as close to royalty as this town has ever known and most likely ever will, and now that you're a Presbyterian, I absolutely refuse to have you speak the Lord's name in vain."

Then she left the room, and I looked in the mirror again and started crying.

> He is a portion of the loneliness,
> Which once he made more lovely.

It's true that Percy married twice, but the second one, who was much more butch than he ever was, wrote *Frankenstein*. She had nothing else to do with her evenings.

But it was Thomas Hogg that Percy really loved; they left Oxford hand in hand, Percy mincing, his wrists limp, his voice high-pitched, his eyes, they say, gazellelike. Myself, I have never looked into the eyes of a gazelle, but Percy was a sissy all right, no good at all at baseball. And that boy he knew when he was only twelve: "The tones of his voice were so soft and winning that in listening to him the tears have involuntarily gushed from my eyes."

I fell in love for the first time when I was twelve; it may have been the last time, too. . . . Why couldn't I have drowned at thirty? Or died of exposure at thirty-six? In Missolonghi. It used to be easier to die, you know. Who needs this shit about keeping people alive for so long? Were you people asked? Not by me you weren't. . . . I'll tell you what I'm going to do. Next November in Saint Petersburg I shall drink a glass of unboiled water. "You can't help me. I shall not recover."

I can't find the tape recorder; I've looked everywhere.

21 /

Durable

I keep coming back to the day my father went to the bank to get the second mortgage on the house. It must mark some kind of turning point in my life. Turning point. My life is filled with them. I must always have turned the wrong way, right instead of left, east instead of west, north instead of south, gone down instead of up. . . .

Down, going down. Somebody once said to me, "You are the most spectacular failure of your generation." A girl it was. Dede? No, Dede never demeaned me. She thought I was more than I was, than I am.

Whoever it was said, "When I first knew you, you could have been . . . but you . . . I started to say you blew it." Har, har, har. Giggle, tittle, and baum. I could have been . . . The night of the most important concert of my life I was in one of those hotel rooms in the West Forties, Forty-fifth between Eighth and Ninth, and we were four. The room smelled of all the people who had been there before, thousands of them. I don't know why I was there. I wasn't enjoying it. I never enjoy it. I know before I start that I won't.

I can't stop, though, I could never, ever stop. And it was never any fun. I was remorseful before the curtain rose. And I was always gone before the curtain fell, saying my beads, asking forgiveness, trying to decide which punishment it would be this time.

❖

I've told you about the morning of the day.

I mentioned the silent breakfast; I described what happened at the railroad station; I told you all you needed to know about the ride with Lydell Griswald.

But I did not tell you how it must have been for my father going into the bank of which he was to have been president, his hands chapped, the hands of a common day laborer.

I did not describe how he must have felt when he stood in front of the desk that had once been his, humble, begging.

I can neither tell nor describe because I cannot imagine how it was. My imagination is not large enough. It was an act of great courage, though. It had to have been. I say that, and I put the thought aside. The thought is too painful. . . . Shouldn't there have been a medal? Dear father, now, too late, I say to your bones, you were a brave and good man, and I loved you.

No matter now, but I say it. I say it too late. Everything was always too late, for both of us, I'm afraid. Dear father . . .

It must have been after midnight when I woke up, and my father was standing at the window of my bedroom, looking out at the ominous poplar. I lay there for a while watching him, and then I said, "I'm awake." I said, "What were you thinking about?"

My father turned; he smiled, that sad, sweet smile, and he said, "I was thinking how lucky I am to be your father."

I said, "I'm not so much." I said, "Did you get the second mortgage?"

"Yes. Horton Payne was benevolently benevolent. He's weak, and I don't think he's very bright, but I got the mortgage. And the Paynes heard you at the high school; I guess you knew that, but what you didn't know is that they thought you were wonderful. And Mrs. Payne is a pianist herself."

"That's good." But was it?

"For some reason Horton Payne wants to see you at the bank in the morning at nine. How does that strike you?"

"It strikes me okay." At that moment it did. Maybe for once my mother was right; maybe Horton Payne did want to make a settlement on me. Was I not lord of all I surveyed? The heir apparent to everything there was? Crown prince of the universe? I would have been greatly surprised if Horton Payne had not wanted to see me. But let him come over to my table. Pearls before . . .

My father kissed me good night, and he said, "Just remember that I love you and am proud of you."

After he left, I turned off the light and tried to go back to sleep, but then the poplar started threatening again, hissing, hinting, disturbing, upsetting, plotting.

Within five minutes I was covered with cold sweat, trembling. I crept out of bed, dressed in the damp and terrifying darkness, tiptoed out of the room and the house, and walked the streets of the town as I have since walked the streets of a thousand others, searching for a nod of approval, a sympathetic smile. A disapproving smirk would do. Anybody, anything, anything at all to show that somebody, anybody knew I existed.

But nothing like that happened. It never does. I was without funds or visible means of support. And let me repeat. You have to buy love. A smile or a smirk. It doesn't really matter. You have to pay cash, cash on the line, and no matter how much you pay, all you ever get are remnants, discontinued models, slightly damaged goods.

And on the morning in question not even that. No one took notice of Oliver Twist in drag, the Poor Little Match Girl in knickers. . . . God, how I hated those knickers, ". . . made from an exceptionally strong, durable . . ." *Durable.* The goddamn things lasted forever. I was in eternal knickers and wool union suits until . . . I may even have had them on when I played the first concert at Town Hall. I don't remember. I told you. I was brilliant that night, and I waited until the next morning to arrange a suitable punishment. . . . *Durable* . . . "It is a crime and disgrace . . . still perfectly good, and you ought to get down on your knees, especially with the Armenians starving the way . . . and the Dedman boys would give . . ."

Knickers. Do you wonder that I liked to dress up in other people's clothes, even my mother's, although except for a rather moldy mink stole nothing of hers had any real style.

Whoever heard of wearing a moldy mink stole in late May? I wore the blue serge to the senior prom, and I didn't go inside at all. I told my mother I had had a marvelous time.

I never had a complete lady's wardrobe of my own. If I had, would it have made any difference? . . . I doubt it. I never wanted to be a girl. What I wanted was to be a regular little man. Big man. There's no operation for that. That I've heard of.

I wander. I digress. Back to the morning in question.

Since there was noplace else to go, no escape, not even a rabbit hole, I was standing in front of People's Savings at nine.

Just as the chimes of the courthouse clock started, Luther Prowley, who for as long as I could remember had been teller in the first cage on the left as you entered the bank, unlocked the door. He said I was certainly bright and early, wasn't I? I said that I had an appointment with Mr. Payne, and Luther said I guess you know where his office is, ha, ha, same place your father's and your grandfather's used to be. But it's not the same as it was when they were here. They wouldn't be doing all this foreclosing. You can take my word for that. They say Amos Lionel never met a stranger, and that's the God's truth.

Then, as if he were about to go on trial for heresy, Luther looked around to see if he had been overheard, and he quickly said, And how is your father. Just fine. Your father should still be in this bank, and there isn't a soul in this town don't know it, and some says it, too. And I read in the paper where your mother was in Des Moines last week for Eastern Star. I nodded. I did not ask about Luther's son, Jake, then a man in his thirties. One didn't ask because Jake had been hit on the head by a baseball when he was eleven and had ever since been strange. And one did not ask about Luther's wife, Lucille, who two years before had thrown herself in the Des Moines River and drowned. One did not ask about Lily Farrell's mother. Luther was said to drink a good deal of bootleg whiskey at Farrell's

Eats, and more often than not, it was said, Luther stayed the night.

Horton Payne had been detained at the courthouse, but Minna Gregory, who was an assistant treasurer of the bank as well as Horton Payne's secretary, said to make myself to home. She had been my grandfather's secretary, too, and the reason she hated me, one of the reasons, was that she knew that I knew that my grandfather had kept her out of the pokey, in which she had earned a nice, long stay for embezzlement. She only stole five thousand dollars, but in that town in those days that was all the money there was.

It was clear that when Minna invited me to make myself to home she didn't mean too much to home because her desk was just outside Horton Payne's office, and she left the door open, glancing in at me every few seconds, smiling from the nose down.

I sat very straight in the chair, directly in front of the huge table covered with green leather that Horton Payne used as a desk. On top was a manila folder in which there were half a dozen or so legal-looking papers. There was a darker green blotter on which nothing had ever been blotted, an inkwell, and an assortment of pens on a silver tray.

I have since learned that a desk that neat belongs either to a man who has an orderly mind and the soul of a certified public accountant or to somebody who doesn't have much to do.

Charley never said much about his father, and he said less about his mother. Where private matters were concerned, Charley was what people call close-mouthed. After all those years of our knowing each other, there were things about Charley that I never did know, crucial things, things that changed his whole life.

But then I suppose in Charley's case that was equally true of me. Maybe that is part of what friendship is, those private places, usually dark, private places that are left unexplored. Better left unexplored. Have I ever really *known* anybody? Is it possible to *know* anybody? . . . How could it be? At an official forty-nine I'm still coming up with surprises about me, most of them unpleasant.

❖

Horton Payne.

One afternoon, it must have been August, August again, had to be August because Charley and I were in Lydell Griswald's barn, and the threshers had been there the day before. The barn was filled with hay that smelled the way new-mown hay does. I miss that, but that's all I miss, ever.

Charley and I were looking at Lydell's cows. He had just got a loan from the bank to buy six Jerseys. . . . Why were Charley and I examining Jersey cows? I guess because there wasn't anything better to do.

Anyway, I remember Charley looked at me in that abrupt way he had, not too sure he ought to say what he was about to say. But he did; he almost always did. He said, "Do you and your father talk? To each other, I mean?"

"Sure. Sometimes." I was thinking, did my father and I *really* talk? Would you call the words, never many, that we sometimes exchanged *talking*? Actually conversation? "Oh, I don't know. I mean we're not exactly loquacious"—that was a period when I was trying to add one new word to my vocabulary every day—"loquacious, but we talk."

"What about?"

"Oh, I don't know. It sounds silly when you repeat it, but he says things like he's very proud of me and all and how I'm going to be this great pianist someday and how I mustn't pay any attention when . . . you know, when people call me names and how baseball isn't important and how when I used to get beat up that in the long run whoever beat me up was worse off because they were jealous of me. How they knew I had more on the ball than they did. That kind of stuff. It sounds sappy when you say it."

"It sounds marvelous. My father and I . . . I'm not blaming him. I'm sure it's as much my fault as his, but he . . . Well, he hardly says anything at all. It used to be he'd ask me what I'd learned in school that day. 'What did you learn today, Charles? Something of significance?' And Christ, I never had an answer to that because in the first place I practically never do learn anything because they're never teaching anything. But when I do, those rare times, you know, what the hell am I supposed to say? 'I learned that two and two are four and three times three are nine.' Crap like that?

"And we used to go for walks. Every Saturday morning after breakfast—we always have a big breakfast on Saturdays—he used to say, 'Are we ready for our weekly walk, Charles?' And I'd say, sure, and off we'd go, down West Main, out toward the high school and beyond, twenty paces a minute; he says that's the way they do it in the army."

"Walking is very good exercise, you know, Charles." No reply. "Did you hear me, Charles?" "Yes, sir. You said walking is very good exercise, and I don't doubt that it is." "I'm not like you, of course, Charles. I simply don't have the physique for any kind of athletics, but you do. You're very well coordinated." "Yes, sir; I know, but sports really don't interest me much." "Perhaps we ought to discuss things, Charles. I know you are a very apt student of current events. Miss Lowell when she was in at the bank the other day . . . Is it Miss Lowell?" "Yes, sir. Miss Lowell." "Miss Lowell said that you have a very real aptitude for current events. I am pleased that you are such a good student in school, Charles, without being what they used to call a greasy grind. You're certainly not that, are you, Charles?" "No, sir, I wouldn't say I was a greasy grind."

"It was really pathetic," said Charley. "It went on and on like that, and the fact is, was, we just didn't have a damn thing to say to each other. It wasn't his fault, and it wasn't mine. Would you say?"

"I certainly wouldn't say it was."

"Anyway, after a while we just stopped. One Saturday morning it was raining or snowing or something, and he looked out the window and said, 'I guess it's just too mean for us to go for our walk this morning. Isn't it?' I said that I guessed it was, and so he went down to the bank, and he never again mentioned our going for a walk. And now he goes to the bank every Saturday morning, and the trouble with *that* is that there isn't even much of anything for him to do during the week.

"Do you know what he does all week? I know you won't tell anybody because it's really rather sad. He does crossword puzzles all the time. He does the one in *The New York Times*, the *Times* my mother gets the day before, and then he buys crossword puzzle books, lots of them. They order them for him special at the Book Nook, and he keeps them locked up in the safe in his office. You won't . . . I know you won't."

"Of course I won't tell anybody. Who would I tell anyway? I don't have what you'd call a plethora of buddies."

"I know, and the only reason I mentioned it is because it's so sad. My father went to college in Chicago, and that's where he met my mother. They neither of them intended to come back here, but my grandfather—my father's old man; I guess he was a regular bastard— he made my father come back, and my father hates this town, and so does my mother, and so do I."

"I'm not exactly in love with it."

This must have been the August before we started our senior year in high school because Charley said, "Ten more months. It'll seem like forever, but I guess we can stand it that long because the minute school is over, it's going to be wham bam, thank you ma'am. We'll take our little diplomas in hand and good-bye forever. Only ten months from now. We can stand it for another ten months, can't we?"

"I guess so. We've stood it this long."

"When I get settled down, after law school and all, I'm going to get a place for my mother where she'll be happy. Probably in New York. And my father, too, if he wants to come."

I said, "Can you imagine anybody who wouldn't want to come?"

"Nobody in his right mind, no," said Charley.

That's the way I remember the conversation. I'm not sure it was that way, but that's the way it seems to me to have been, today. I'm not sure about tomorrow. I'm not sure what I had for breakfast this morning. If I had breakfast. Or lunch. I know I won't have dinner. I got out of the habit of dinner. By dinnertime I was always drunk. . . . Still, there's more of me left than I thought. I suppose you know that would happen, suspected that it would. That's why you gave me the typewriter. Ah, how bright you are. . . . It won't work, though. I have no plans to leave this place, ever, and please to remember that I want the ashes disposed of surreptitiously. Carelessly scattered over the south forty. And not a word must be said, before, during, or after. I want to go in silence. That's my last request, my only request.

Lydell Griswald came into the barn and, looking at Charley but not at me, he asked if you boys wouldn't like to stay to supper. We both said no, thanks. Lydell said that was too bad. The missus was a pretty good cook. That's *one* of the things she's good at, he said, especially not looking at me.

We'd hitchhiked out to the farm, but Lydell said he'd run us home in the pickup.

I don't remember what was said on the way into town; Lydell was not what you'd call talkative, but I do remember that as we got out of the truck in front of the Payne house on West Main, Lydell said, to me, "Any time you want another run down to Le Grand, give me a ring."

After Lydell drove off, Charley said, "What did he mean by that?"

I said, "Oh." I usually begin a lie with "Oh." It gives me time to think. "Oh, I was hitchhiking to Le Grand one day, and he gave me a lift. He's okay, really, for a farmer."

I don't know whether Charley believed what I said about Lydell or not. I never knew what he believed, what he thought, about me anyway. One day not long after we got to be friends, I said to Charley, "Do you mind that I'm . . . you know, peculiar?"

"Are you?" said Charley. "I hadn't noticed."

That night after I went to bed I thought about Horton Payne doing crossword puzzles at the bank because there wasn't anything else to do. And about his not knowing what to say to Charley and

Charley not knowing what to say back. And I thought about Sarah McCormick Payne saying, "I should have been born with a tattoo saying, 'Do Not Transplant in Iowa.'" And about my father and mother in the bedroom below, both snoring, and one, it could have been either, moaning from time to time. I thought, We're all in the same leaky boat, and it's sinking. Even Lydell Griswald, clean on Saturday, acceptable on Monday, smelly and stubbly on Friday, even old Lydell is up there in the stern, bailing out water but not bailing it out fast enough. And Lydell is just as scared as I am, scared that somebody will tell, scared that somebody saw us, scared that . . . And ashamed. . . . Who invented shame anyway? I know Paul is the one who came up with original sin. . . . I thought, Old Mabel Griswald is in the boat, too, bailing uselessly away. And the ugly Griswald boys, weighing the boat down with their fat asses. I thought, You bet we're all in the same boat.

For truth itself has not the privilege to be spoken at all times and in all sorts.

Montaigne should never have married. The only person he really loved was young Etienne de la Boetie, who was beautiful but not very bright. Bright enough to die when he was twenty-seven, though. That's how old he was when he ate a poisoned grape.

That's the best way, really . . . to die young. If I'd died after that first triumphal year, died of something romantic like hemophilia, I'd be immortal now. And they'd have made a movie of my life that would have all the brutal realism of the one they made about the Schumann girls, Roberta and Clara.

Horton Payne's office had thick beige wall-to-wall carpeting, and under the wide window that opened onto West Main were two knee-high shelves of books, most of them on banking. They had red leather bindings stamped in gold and had belonged to my grandfather, who had intended leaving them to my father, but my grandfather died before he made a will.

What my father got instead was a pair of military brushes backed in sterling silver. Beautiful brushes. When I went to New York for the first time, my father gave them to me as a going-away present. I forget which transient took them. . . . Several books on the cultivation of the azalea, the rhododendron, and the rose. Horton Payne spent a good deal of time in his garden. Cook books. Horton Payne fancied himself a gourmet. A popular life of Rembrandt, a two-volume history of the Middle Ages, *We* by Charles A. Lindbergh, and the autobiography of a foreign correspondent who'd been all the places I intended going.

I had never seen that office before, and I never went back. I suppose the reason I remember it so well is that I felt my father still belonged there. And I did, too. I certainly deserved to be a banker's son.

In the years since, I have often wondered if I felt any jealousy of Charley because of that. Because he was what I deserved to be. . . . I don't think so. I truly don't. I don't think I'm even envious. It seems to me I was born aware that nothing would ever work out quite the way I had in mind. Life is unjust, and although I knew nothing much could be done about it, I questioned it once in a while, in a quiet sort of way.

I remember an evening two, maybe three months after Charley and I met for the first time. I remember the lilacs were nearly gone. That would make it late May, thereabouts.

We were on our way to the Casino, and several people bowed, groveled, curtsied, said things like, "Good evening, Master Payne." "And how are you this fine evening, Master Payne?" "How well you're looking this evening, Master Payne." God, people are finks.

To me, if anything at all was said, it was, "Oh, hi there."

Somewhere a block or so from the Casino, not yet quite adjusted to the unfairness of life, I said, hoping I'd found a way to attack and possibly cause serious damage to my best friend in all the world, "You're sure sick a lot. I mean you sure miss school a lot."

"I guess you've decided to start helping out the truant officer," said Charley.

"Not at all. I was just making a simple, friendly observation. What's wrong with that?"

"Nothing, nothing at all, especially the friendly part, but it's true, I miss school a lot. I miss it as often as I possibly can, not willfully, you understand. It's just that I'm frail. And I have certain problems that can really only be understood by those who are as sensitive and as frail as I am. You're not one of those, but I'll try to explain anyway. Did I ever tell you about the time I had all that trouble with my eyes?"

"You're about to."

"It is only due to the miracles of modern medicine that I am here at all," said Charley. "I was in third grade when this calamity befell me. It was a time when most of my classmates were still trying to master the spelling of c-a-t. The teacher, one Polly Blizenheimer by name, wasn't much ahead of the class. 'C-a . . . Now don't help me, class. Let me guess.'

"Anyway, I remember one morning we were struggling through one of the classics, *Lear, Remembrance of Things Past, Chicken Little,* and we were taking turns reading it aloud. Well, when it came my turn to read, I looked down at the page, and my eyes simply couldn't focus any more. It was completely unexpected, rather like the way Saint Paul had that epileptic fit when he was trundling down the road to Damascus.

"Blizenheimer flew into a tizzy and wanted to know what was wrong, and I told her that while I could *see* perfectly well, I just couldn't focus my eyes on the printed page. She said, 'Oh, Master Payne, poor Master Payne, how awful.' And she rushed me off to the principal's office, and he loaded me into his Chevrolet and drove me home, saying inane things like, 'You're overworked, Master Payne, and I have only myself to blame for that, only myself. Too much homework. That's the nub of it, and being a straight A student like yourself, the pride and joy of Payne School, we have simply asked too much of you, and patient as you have been with us . . .' And similar bullshit.

"I wasn't quite sure what my mother's reaction to all this would ɔe, but she was upset, too. She called my father, and he rushed home from the bank, and they took me to Sam Caldwell's office, our friendly, moronic neighborhood optometrist. And Sammy bustled around and made all kinds of tests he didn't understand and couldn't interpret, and then he said to my parents, 'No question about it. There's a serious affliction here, and while I am more than competent in most cases of this kind, in the case of Master Payne I would not want to presume. . . .' So he suggested we go to a fool in Des Moines, and the Des Moines fool recommended a fool in Sioux City, and so on and so on, specialist after specialist, fool after fool, and would you like us to mail you the bill, Mr. Payne, or will you eat it here?

"Finally, we went to an eye doctor in Chicago who by some miracle was not a fool. He charged fifty dollars just to glance at me, and he also gave me an honest-to-God examination. It took half a day, and when he finished, he asked my parents to step outside, and he said to me, 'Now look here, young man, you're faking. There is nothing whatever wrong with your eyes. If there were, I'd know it, and I'd know what it was. I suggest you be back in school Monday morning with your eyes focusing properly. I'm going to tell your parents, throwing in a few words of Latin, that I have cleared up what was troubling you, but if I find you are not back in school on Monday, with twenty-twenty vision, I shall expose you as the little fraud that you are. All clear?'

"I said, 'You'd better be careful about the Latin, doctor. My mother understands Latin.'

" 'I'll manage that,' he said. 'Never fear. The only thing that bothers me is whether to charge five hundred dollars or seven fifty for this consultation. Which would you advise?' I said, 'Let your conscience be your guide, doctor,' and I guess he did, because he charged seven fifty. And I went back to school the following Monday with twenty-twenty vision, and we all lived happily ever after. It certainly gives you something to think about, doesn't it?"

"It proves you have to go all the way to Chicago to find an honest man with a conscience. I don't think Diogenes could have walked that far."

"The real question," said Charley, "is whether I was faking all along. Is it true I couldn't focus my eyes in class that day? Was it because I wanted to avoid reading those tedious words or . . . Which comes first, the chicken or the egg? Illusion or reality? When I get to Vienna, I'll ask."

Charley never got to Vienna, but the question is a good one.

And four months ago when I walked onstage in New Haven and couldn't hear a sound, thought I couldn't hear a sound, claimed I couldn't, was I faking? And is my restored hearing only temporary? . . .

I have asked myself that question over and over again. And I believe I've brought it up a time or two in talking to you. Neither of us seems to have come up with much of an answer. . . . Besides, what is there, here or anyplace else, that I want to hear?

On the off-white wall, behind the table that Horton Payne used as a desk, was an enormous portrait of his father. Matthew Payne was leaning forward slightly and glaring. He was wearing a black, formal-looking suit with a thick gold chain across his chest. He had on a white shirt with a high, stiff collar, and a black four-in-hand tie. His hands were folded on top of a cane with a silver head. He looked as if he might use the cane at any moment to eliminate the painter, who was clearly a menace. The old man was angry, no question about that. I told my father he looked as if he might be going to foreclose a mortgage.

"No," said my father. "In that case, he'd be smiling."

LEITMOTIV—The only time I actually remember talking to Matthew Payne was in the summer of 1929. We met on the street, in front of Penney's. My father must have hated the old man's guts, but my father was always courteous. He introduced us, and Matthew Payne said that he was pleased to know me. He did not use a this-is-the-way-I-talk-to-children voice. He did not say that I *took after* my father or my mother, that you could tell just by looking at me that I was a Lionel all right, a Winders all right. He did not say, sotto voce, as if I had suddenly disappeared, what a pity the poor child has to wear glasses; he'll never be able to get out and play like other boys, will he? He did not say he understood I was delicate, meaning queer; highly strung, meaning a sissy.

No, he said he was happy to know me and that I looked as if I'd been out in the sun a lot.

"I think he's going to be an amateur entomologist," said my father. "He's going to be a very famous concert pianist and composer as a profession, of course, but we got him a microscope last Christmas, and now he won't let his mother swat a fly or kill an ant. He won't even let her hang flypaper in the kitchen. He spends all his time when he's not practicing or taking lessons outdoors, examining bugs and butterflies and spiders, although I suppose spiders are insects, bugs, aren't they?"

Matthew Payne asked me if I had read the work of J. Henri Fabre. I said that I hadn't but that I'd read about him. There was no Fabre in the public library.

Matthew Payne once more shook my hand and my father's hand and said that it had been a pleasure indeed, and continued his walk, swinging his cane and whistling.

I said, "He seems like a nice man."

"Yes," said my father. "That is the way he seems."

Several weeks later Rod McCracken, the postman, brought a parcel post package from Marshall Field's. Inside was a handsome, illustrated copy of Fabre's *The Life of the Spider*. The card said, "With the Compliments of Matthew Payne, Esquire."

I grew to hate Matthew Payne, but I loved that book, and on those bleak dawns when I wonder how it would have been if I'd become an entomologist, I have an answer. I'd have fucked that up, too, but maybe more privately.

Me an entomologist. The poor bugs never did anything to deserve the likes of me. . . . But think of the fun the worms would have if I were to be put in the ground. The worms make a sound, you know, and on a still July night, if you listen carefully, you can sometimes hear them. It is the sound of a whispered invitation. They're really quite hospitable, the worms. Hungry, though. I wonder how long it takes. . . . Could you get all of me in the garbage disposal without chopping me up? Now that I'm losing all that weight? . . . If you love me, try. Funeral services were held in the kitchen of . . . and as the body . . . Those disposals make a lot of noise as they chop up the bones. . . . Put the giblets in first. If it hadn't been for the giblets, I'd have been a nice old eunuch, and they don't have sex with anybody. Do eunuchs?

Suggested epitaph: HE WAS DONE IN BY HIS GONADS.

I had the Fabre all through high school, through the time I was with The Clarinet Player, through the marriage, through love affairs that sometimes lasted for days. . . . I have sometimes fallen in love five times in a single day. . . . Before sunset.

I had the Fabre through numerous lifelong passions, uncounted momentary caprices, friendships. . . . Friendship must never be confused with love, which always begins and ends lustfully. . . . I had it through lifetimes of loneliness, not to mention the decades when I was lonesome. . . . But once when I fled some stranger's bed, I left the book behind.

My mother said, "It's very small type, and you'll ruin your eyes. When the time comes to get your glasses changed, I'm just going to send the bill to Matthew Payne, Esquire."

And she said, "But it's really nothing more than good business on his part. Matthew Payne knows good and well that one of these fine days you are going to be one of the biggest depositors at the bank. And not only that, he knows deep in his heart that your father ought to be in that bank at this very minute, as president."

"The scops made a habit of uttering his monotonous, piping note here, of an even, the Bird of Athena, the Owl, came hurrying along to hoot and hiss. . . ." Oh, on what stranger's bed did I leave my Fabre?

Aria—Below his grandfather's portrait and a little to the right was a large photograph of Charley, framed in gold. Charley was on horseback in Riverview Park. He had on a pair of white pants and a white shirt and was very tanned. I guessed that the photograph had been taken the summer before, after he and his mother got back from Cape Cod. Charley sat very straight in the saddle, straighter than Tom Mix or Buck Jones or William Boyd, and he had a crop in his hand and looked as if he would use it the way his grandfather would use the cane, offensively, defensively, whatever came to mind.

Altogether he looked handsome, lordly and loathsome, but I still loved him. The fact that someone is loathsome has never caused me to stop loving him. That's often *why*.

The shoes were the last thing in Horton Payne's office that I noticed, high-button shoes, a little worn, and they were under the table Horton Payne used as a desk.

I didn't know it at the time, but Matthew Payne's will had provided that those shoes remain there "for so long as my son and any of his progeny shall survive and the People's Savings Bank . . . continue to exist."

In a sense, you see, Matthew Payne never really left that office and that is the way he had wanted it. The shoes stayed there until the night Horton Payne killed himself.

Just before he put the revolver in his mouth, he took the shoes to the basement of the bank, put them in the furnace, and, although it was July, started a fire.

I don't know who was crazy and who wasn't. I leave that up to you people.

I was on my knees examining those puzzling shoes when I looked up. Horton Payne was standing in the doorway.

I stood up, my face beet red, and said—I was quicker in those days

—"I've got a hole in my pocket, and I lost a dime. I thought maybe . . . but I must have lost it outside."

Horton Payne cleared his throat, and he said, "The shoes, uh, the shoes, ah, the shoes, they belonged, uh, to my, uh, father."

I said, "Good morning, Mr. Payne," and he cleared his throat again, looking as if he weren't sure what I was doing there or that if he did remember that he'd invited me, he now realized it had been a mistake.

"Oh, yes," he said. "Yes, yes," throat-clearing, "yes," throat-clearing, period. "Sorry. You were early and I was, uh, de, uh, layed."

He did not shake my hand; he indicated for me to sit down, and he sat across from the shoes, beneath the portrait of his father and the photograph of his son. By contrast with either he looked drab. His skin was pale, and so were his eyes. His hair was in retreat and graying, and his less-than-determined chin was further weakened by the beginning of a second.

While he talked, he picked up a number of paper clips and bent each into the shape of a dollar sign. By the time I left the table was piled high with them.

He never looked directly at me; he never really looked directly at anybody. He always kept his eyes on the paper clip or whatever it was he had in his hand, and he always had something.

"I'm told that you are a very bright young man," he said. "Bright," he repeated.

He did not speak as quickly as that might indicate. There were the incessant "uhs," the constant throat-clearing, the swallowing.

"Bright," he said a third time. "I never know what that particular word means in that particular context. Do you? Do words fascinate you? They do me. They always have. I thought once, I was very young, I thought I might become a student of semantics. . . . But then."

Horton Payne often ended a sentence before what I often felt would have been the most interesting part. "But then what?" I never asked.

He glanced at the high-button shoes. He said, "A pot is bright if well polished. A morning is bright. 'They are all gone into the world of light,/ And I alone sit lingering here;/ Their very memory is fair and bright,/ And my sad thoughts doth clear.' One Henry Vaughan wrote that. Are you familiar with his work? A most neglected poet of the post-Elizabethan era. At least I have always felt that he, uh, was, uh, neglected. But I am sure that people who know something about post-Elizabethan poetry would not agree. In any case, in the patois of the natives around here, you are considered bright. We, my family and I . . . heard you play at the high school, and we, Mrs. Payne that is, uh, knows a great deal about music, and she thinks that you have . . . enormous talent."

I said nothing to that. Praise of even the mildest sort always renders me speechless. Censure. Ah, that is something I can understand. I couldn't agree with you more, sir, madame, as the case may be, and not only that, you probably don't know it, but only this morning I . . . And you know, the hell of it is I'm really quite a decent man. I am almost never deliberately unkind to anybody but myself.

"I was very fond of your grandfather," said Horton Payne, "and I was, uh, sorry about what happened. My father was . . ."

He looked quickly at the shoes, then away; he made another dollar sign with a paper clip.

"My father was a, uh, businessman."

Horton Payne paused, this time forever, and then he said, "I asked you here . . . because Mrs. Payne and I, uh, my family thought you might agree to come and see us. . . . We are, my wife in particular, is . . . quite lonely, and I believe Charles is, too. Charles is a very, an extraordinarily gifted boy. You have that in common."

He sighed again, and he said, "It is not easy to be gifted. Or so I have been told."

A knock on the door, and Minna Gregory stepped inside.

She said to Horton Payne, "Mr. Spaulding wants to see you."

"I'll be there," said Horton Payne. "Tell Mr. Spaulding that I'm occupied at the moment."

"He said it's important."

"Two minutes then, and, Minna, uh, if you don't, uh, mind terribly, close the door again. That's a good girl."

Minna slammed the door. Horton Payne had stood up when she came in, and he was shuffling the papers on his desk; his hands were trembling.

He said, "How would you like to come to the house this evening, say at seven-thirty? If you are not otherwise occupied."

I was not otherwise occupied. I said, "Yes, sir, that would be fine, and thank you."

"You are going to amount to something one of these days," said Horton Payne. And then he did shake my hand, and he said, "This evening at seven-thirty then."

And, a man headed for his own execution, he went across the hall to Titus Spaulding's office.

Minna Gregory looked at me and said, "I don't know what you two was talking about."

I said, "That is no doubt the reason Mr. Payne closed the door, so that you wouldn't know what we was talking about." I said, "Done any embezzling lately, Min?" I said, "My grandfather made a big mistake in keeping you out of the pokey."

I said nothing.

"Now look here, you little sis," said Minna. "Don't you be coming around here with your *Liberty* magazines no more. I talked to Titus Spaulding about it, and he don't want no more of your merchandising in this bank."

I said, "I take my orders from Horton Payne and not his underlings, thank you all the same." I said, "Has anybody ever told you that you look like a gangster's moll?"

I said nothing. I only managed not to sob until I got to the street. . . . The day after Horton Payne shot himself it was discovered that Titus Spaulding and Minna Gregory had embezzled half a million dollars from the bank. They both died in the penitentiary.

But I say again, where's the comfort in the fact that these people came to bad ends?

22 /

How Did He Do It?

I don't know that I can. I'm tired, you know. I don't think I can stand any more shock. Or any more of the drugs. . . . I looked in the mirror when I got back here, and I wouldn't have recognized me. What is left of the hair is all gone white. I must have lost at least thirty pounds, maybe forty. . . . How long have I been away from this room? The trees are bare, but is it the end of winter or the beginning?

I told you, feet first.

I thought about Shawn last night. I thought about the fact that the first question when the call came was "How did he do it?" I didn't ask, but that's what I thought. And I wondered again. If I had told Lily, would she have married him anyway? And if she hadn't, would she have been worse or better off? Would Shawn have been better or worse? Would he still be alive?

I keep going over those things in my mind, over and over, knowing there is never any answer. And does it matter one way or the other? And if so, to whom?

I was in the studio, working very hard. It was one of those rare periods when I was getting up at eight, was at the studio at nine, and at the piano until one, then lunch. And when the delivery boy brought lunch, it was a quarter tip and back to the delicatessen with you.

I was working on several songs. The music in each case was mine, with an occasional unacknowledged debt to this or that Bach chorale. All composers steal, with the possible exceptions of Johann Sebastian and Beethoven and Mozart and Dimitri Shostakovich. At least I doubt that Shostakovich does because nobody else writes music like his, and nobody ever has. No wonder he's always in trouble.

The words of one song I was working on—it turned out to be the best—were by Auden. "Lay your sleeping head, my love/ Human on my faithless arm." Some people whose opinions I respect liked the song, and the recording I made with Louise is still around, and I get an occasional royalty check.

Mr. Auden's poem is faultless. He's the best poet of this century. I think of Yeats as being of the nineteenth century. Dylan was a marvelous entertainer, and as for Saint Louis Tom, a man who wrote plays like that has to have a wide streak of fraud in him. Robert Frost? I am told, although I find it difficult to believe, that there are persons of intelligence who read Frost with pleasure. . . . Publicly he was a pleasant man, as pleasant as Shawn.

It was Monday after lunch. I played over what I had written that morning, making revisions. In me, not Auden. "Noons of dryness see you fed/ By the involuntary powers,/ Nights of insult let you pass/ Watched by every human love."

The call came about three, and the voice had that distant, official sound. It asked if I was George Lionel and was I the one by that name who was a friend of Shawn O'Hennessey. I said that I was. I already knew.

The voice said that my name and address and telephone number had been found on Mr. O'Hennessey's body. He had been knocked down and run over by a truck that was backing out of a garage on West Eighty-seventh Street, between Broadway and West End Avenue. The whole thing was most unfortunate, and it was nobody's fault. Nobody was to blame. The truck driver had sounded his horn continuously. All the proper precautions had been taken. There were witnesses to that. It was understood that Mr. Hennessey was a writer, and surely his mind had been occupied with other matters at the time. Possibly his writing. And he had been drinking. There was evidence of that, but this was not the time . . .

What had happened was one of those unfortunate accidents that occur in a large city. . . . And afterward, everything possible had been done. The truck driver, Joseph N. Riley, also an American of Irish descent, had been with the company for more than thirty years, and this was his first major accident. Mr. Riley himself had gone in the ambulance when the injured Mr. O'Hennessey was taken to Saint Luke's Hospital.

Everything had been legal, had been open and aboveboard. Mr. O'Hennessey had lived for nearly an hour after arriving at the hospital, but he had not regained consciousness. It was one of those unfortunate . . . And where could Mrs. O'Hennessey be reached? They had already called . . . And it was nobody's fault. Nobody was to blame.

I said, "Which whore lawyer representing the trucking firm am I listening to?"

The distant voice said, "This is Simon Liberman of Liberman, et cetera, and we do happen to represent . . . but there is no reason at all for such language."

"Go fuck yourself. Where's what's left of him?"

"The remains are at Saint Luke's, but since you, sir, are not related either by marriage or by blood, you have no right . . ."

I repeated myself, and then I hung up, and then I cried. The tears were not so much for Shawn O'Hennessey as they were for the way things are, the way things always have been and, I suppose, always will be. I cried because Simon Liberman of Liberman, et cetera, was walking around healthy and unctuous and awful, while Shawn, the boy-man who had meant no harm to anyone, was dead.

I thought, The good ones are going fast. I thought, But maybe I shouldn't cry. Maybe I should laugh. I thought, Shawn got out, and that is what he wanted, isn't it? He either wanted that or he wanted to be a good husband to Lily. A good husband and father. He wanted to go straight.

VARIATION—The day Lily first told me about Shawn I had just got back from the two years in Rome. I thought I had finished the "Lament for a Defeated Soldier," which was dedicated to Bernardo, the boy I met on the Spanish Steps, the only one who had lasted beyond the dawn.

I had a busy season ahead of me. That's what my agent called it. "And from here on in the future is limitless."

I was busy all right. Until I got to Houston. Stay out of Houston. They've got everything bugged, and the cowboys hanging around the bus station, even when they are not members of the vice squad, beat you up afterward. . . . I wonder how many bus stations I've been in, coast to coast, and never taken a bus.

It was in Houston that The Big Freeze began. When I started playing "Fugue for the Rich and Rude," they started hissing, and then they started walking out.

But that came later.

Lily was one of the first people I called when I got back from Rome. By that time she had her own listing in the Manhattan directory, Lily Ltd., on Madison Avenue in the upper Fifties. Lily was doing very well indeed; she wasn't rich yet, but she had come a long way from Farrell's Eats, and she was famous. She was a success. No room for failure in that part of town.

We agreed to have lunch at the best Italian restaurant in New York, maybe the world.

"It's on me," said Lily. "It's your welcome home present. Besides, it's deductible."

"Now I know I'm back in the land of the red, white, and blue."

"And I have a surprise for you. Wear your cheerleader suit."

We kissed, and we told each other how well we looked, and it was true. I was wearing my best Italian suntan, actually a Tangier suntan, and an Italian silk suit. I'd been off the booze for a week. I used to be able to do that. I didn't even have to go to a drying out place. . . . Lily was wearing an exquisite blue dress that did not quite match her eyes, a piece of costume jewelry, I forget what, and she had on a black cloth coat that was smart enough all right, but it looked a little sheer for January, to me anyway. I was always afraid Lily was going to catch cold. Get hurt. Hurt herself. . . . The coat looked expensive. No, *Expensive* isn't the word. It looked just right for her.

Lily ordered a Beefeater martini. It was the beginning of the Beefeater era. I explained about being on the wagon.

"I want to hear all about where you've been and what you've done," said Lily.

"I've been gone seven hundred and twenty-one days. Do you want it hour by hour or minute by minute? Besides, what's the surprise?"

"This," said Lily, and she showed me the ring, which clearly cost a great deal of money, too clearly, I thought. And surely Lily did, too. I looked at her closely. . . . No, no indication that Lily thought there was anything wrong with the ring. *Love*. One of the first things to go is common sense. And next comes taste. Goes taste.

I kissed Lily again. "Congratulations."

"I knew you'd be pleased."

"Isn't it rather a rash step to take without consulting your oldest, dearest . . . ?"

"As a matter of fact, I told him if you didn't approve, it was all off. But you will approve. You know him. You met him anyway. He was at a party at Harvey Lessing's, and he says you had a long talk. His name is Shawn O'Hennessey, the writer."

I said, I guess I said, "Oh, yes, of course."

"Did you like him? I mean didn't you like him?"

"We had a long talk, and I liked him very much."

Harvey Lessing's *annual*. "You've never been? Oh, my dear, you *mustn't* miss it. *Everybody* will be there."

Everybody is there, every fag in Christendom, every fag that's a Household Name anyway and their lovers and the hangers-on and the hustlers they bring.

Once a year, a hundred and fifty men in one overfurnished pent-

house overlooking Central Park. Harvey Lessing, diamond merchant, the world's richest, the world's most famous. . . . Once a year.
Just before Christmas. To introduce Harvey's newest Tunisian boy.
Always a Tunisian boy. I don't know why. You could ask him.
Tunisian and beautiful. . . . I wonder what happens to them when
the year is up. Back to Tunisia? I've been there, and you can't make
much of a living hustling, no matter how pretty you are, because
everybody hustles. Everybody.

Maybe Harvey gives last year's model a diamond.

A hundred to a hundred and fifty men in a single room. Not even
a tame dyke or two. Even the waiters are queer.

Can you imagine the sound of the voices, just to begin? . . . I tell
you. The detonation of one small nuclear device in that room . . .
The theater would be wiped out, the movie industry (this was
twenty years ago when there was a movie industry), advertising.
Television. Publishing would be in trouble. . . . Only a few design-
ers are invited, though. No interior decorators. One former cabinet
member always comes, the one with the mustache. A man who was
a member of Eisenhower's White House staff.

They can never seem to get J. Edgar Hoover to parties like that.
If they could, it might be more fun. . . . Lots of high-ranking members of our armed forces. And writers and musicians . . . and . . .
and.

I don't know why everybody came; I suppose they still come. I
know Harvey Lessing still gives them. I came once. I have never
gone back.

Shawn O'Hennessey was one of the few people there that I could
bear talking to. I had read his novel, and although I hadn't liked it
much, I said I had.

I thought he was attractive. He was then thirty, tall, six two, six
three, graceful. Dark hair combed down over his forehead in a way
that some years later a great many young men adopted, hoping
they'd be mistaken for a Kennedy. Large, innocent blue eyes, lo
lashes.

Somewhere along the way Shawn had broken his nose, and the doctor who put it back together had botched the job. The rebuilt nose sloped dangerously, drunkenly, and there was a bump in the middle. Still, the imperfection of the nose somehow added to his attractiveness. A cleft chin, a strong, good-looking mouth, good teeth. He laughed a lot, displaying the teeth. Very butch voice and manner.

We talked, about his book, about me. He liked "Fugue for the Rich and Rude." He'd been to a couple of my concerts. . . . He'd had quite a bit to drink, and he had quite a bit more. At one point he said, "Are you having an enchanting time here?"

"I don't like being in the same room with a hundred and fifty anythings, including fags."

"Let's get the hell out."

We went to my place. Shawn drank a good deal more, and he told me the story of his life. Naturally . . . His life story was pretty much the way it was in his novel. Except that there wasn't any queer stuff in the novel. In the novel the boy, I forget what Shawn called him, was simply a shy, sensitive boy who was misunderstood. In Kansas City. In real life and in the book. In the book the father was a manufacturer of ball bearings. In real life Shawn's father owned a chain of cut-rate drugstores. In the book the boy left the church because the priest drank, something like that. In real life the priest blew him when Shawn was fourteen. . . . That's enough. Nature imitating art again.

It was dawn when Shawn passed out on the sofa. So we did not go to bed together. I covered him up, kissed him on the forehead, and it was all quite a bit like a Metro-Goldwyn-Mayer movie in the thirties. Robert Montgomery was forever falling asleep on Norma Shearer's sofa, never any sex.

When Shawn woke up, it was the way it always is when people wake up on a stranger's sofa with a hangover. I gave him coffee and ice; he apologized for bending my ear. I said it had been . . . We promised to get together. He left his telephone number, and that had been the only time I saw him.

I was sure Shawn hadn't told Lily about passing out on my sofa, but did Lily know what kind of parties Harvey Lessing gave? Did she know about all the boys in Shawn's life? Did she care? Did she, like Dede, think she could straighten the poor boy out? . . . One thing about being a member of an underground. You never know how much the nonmember knows. Or suspects. You have to play it by ear. I suppose people in the Mafia have the same problem. And the early Christians.

"He liked you very much," said Lily. "He thinks you're very talented, too."

And then she told me about the colonial house, near Weston, and about the apartment on East Eighty-sixth Street, near Park, and about how she was going to sell the business and Shawn was already at work on another novel, and they were going to have acres and acres of yellow roses and millions of babies. . . .

And, "It's such a relief. I mean knowing I'm going to get out. Do you have any idea how tired I am? Really tired, bone tired? Shawn knows. He knows I'm not meant for this rat race, not any more. It wasn't really what I had in mind, ever. What I had in mind was getting out of Iowa. But now I want somebody to watch over me, just the way it is in the song. I'm weary of never having a decent meal, and . . ."

I wanted to say that if there was anything in the world that I understood, it was fatigue, but that fatigue and love, while often confused, are not . . . I didn't, though. For once I kept my big mouth shut.

"I'll be a very good wife," said Lily, "very loving. Really I will."

Shawn looked just the way I remembered him, attractive, sexy. We shook hands, a very butch handshake, and he'd lowered his voice an octave or so, basso profundo.

The blue eyes looked sharply at me. Looked at Lily. How much had I told her?

I congratulated him, and he said, his voice lower still, Ezio Pinza in *South Pacific,* "I was hoping you'd approve."

We talked. Nothing much. The weather in Rome. The weather in New York. What was I working on? The "Lament." Still. Again. Always. They couldn't wait. More about the colonial house in Connecticut, the apartment on East Eighty-sixth. We laughed. When Shawn was around, people seemed to laugh, although I could never later remember anything particularly witty he had said. Maybe it was just that he was nice, "pleasing, agreeable," perhaps a little less than "delightful," but one could with accuracy say that he was "modest, diffident, and reticent. *Lewd* is obsolete."

He kept touching Lily and looking at her as if he was afraid she might break. He looked as if he loved her, and maybe he did. He wanted to love her, and he tried to love her. No question about that. I tried with Dede, but it doesn't ever work. At least I've never seen it work.

Shawn, Lily, and I made a date to have dinner together a couple of nights later, and Shawn walked Lily back to her office. I went to my hotel and had been there for maybe twenty minutes when Shawn called. I'd been waiting for the call.

He sat on the edge of my bed, drinking a Coke. He said, "You didn't say anything to Lily?"

I said, "Lily told me you and I had met at a party at Harvey Lessing's and had had a long talk, and I said that we had, and that was about it."

"You didn't say anything about what kind of party it was?"

"No, Shawn. What would I have said? If in her line of work Lily hasn't heard about Harvey Lessing's annual queer fairs, she must be one of the few people on the island of Manhattan who hasn't."

"Look, in a lot of ways Lily never left Iowa, and that's fine. That's one of the things I like about her. She hasn't got all that phony sophistication. The way she and I met even. A guy in her office; a designer; we'd been lovers, but that was all over and we were just friends. I went there one afternoon to pick him up, and he introduced me to Lily. That's how we got started."

I said, "In the movies they're always talking about the boy and girl 'meeting cute,' but that's one they haven't used yet."

Shawn smiled, displaying all the teeth, and the eyes had never been bluer or more innocent. He said, "I fell in love with Lily right off. I've always been bisexual. You know. I told you that night. You remember?"

"I guess I was a little drunk that night, but I do know bisexuality is very big this year."

"Since meeting Lily I haven't even looked at another girl. Or another boy. I don't think I was ever really queer. I mean no offense, but I wasn't really ever homosexual. No offense."

"No offense."

"I'm in love with Lily, really in love, and I'm pretty sure she loves me, and we have the same tastes and want the same things. I *know* it will work."

"You've got to tell Lily, you know."

"There's nothing to tell her. The queer bit. That's all over. I've been going to a shrink, and he says every kid goes through—"

"How old are you, Shawn?"

"Look. He knows about these things."

"If the good doctor is speaking of being queer, it's a subject I know something about, too, and I have yet to meet anybody who gets to be thirty who stopped, much as he may have wanted to."

Shawn was no longer looking at me. He was looking at the electric log in the fireplace. "Look, I love Lily. I've never loved anybody before, never even come close, and we both want to get married and have children. I know it sounds corny, but we've really got everything in common."

"Shawn, if you really love her, that's all the more reason to tell her. It isn't fair. . . ."

Shawn threw the empty glass in the fireplace. It shattered nicely. He said, "Just because you fucked up your marriage. I suppose you told your wife. Well, the shrink says the less said about these things the better."

"Good luck, Shawn."

"Anyway, there is nothing to tell. I am not homosexual. I'm not even bisexual any more. I swear I'll make Lily happy, and if I don't, you can hire somebody to break my legs or something."

"Good luck, Shawn."

After he left, I decided I was no longer on the wagon. There's always something. . . . I didn't have to spend much time wondering if Shawn really believed what he was saying. I knew he did, every word of it.

Everybody else always seems to know. I mean about what's right and what's wrong. Everybody but me always has things all figured out. I never have.

What would you have done? By *you* I mean anybody. Lily was, after all, my best friend, my dearest friend, an older friend than Charley even. What was my duty, obligation? What was the right thing to do? . . . Things like that have always given me a lot of trouble.

Should I have said, "Look, Lil, this Shawn O'Hennessey that you've gone and got yourself engaged to. He's a nice guy, but he's as queer as a three-dollar bill. We met at a gay party, and then we went to my place, and if he hadn't passed out we probably would have hopped into bed. He's been to bed with lots and lots and lots of boys and men, but the night he told me the story of his life, if he'd bedded down with any girls, he failed to mention it. Maybe he swings both ways, but he's all mixed up. He drinks too much, and he's a fallen-away Catholic, and . . . It's none of my business, really, but I think you ought to . . ."

Anyway, I didn't. As Shawn said, just because I fucked up my marriage . . .

❖

They were married two weeks later in a civil ceremony in Stamford, and I stood there while a man with cigar ashes on his front slurred the solemn words, and I looked at the happy bride and groom, and they certainly did look like a magazine cover bride and groom, and they certainly acted like that, giggling and touching and kissing. And I thought, My trouble is, in addition to being a no-talent, fucked-up fag, my trouble is just because I can't seem to make anything work, I think everybody else is like that, too, and it isn't always the case. Some people do live happily ever after, and just because you personally don't know any doesn't mean that . . . You're always surrounded by neurotics and psychotics. Like attracts like, you know. But just because you couldn't go straight . . . Just because you couldn't make your bride happy . . . And I thought, "So the young porcelain people were left together, and they blessed the grandfather's rivet, and they loved each other till they broke in pieces."

It takes a fruitcake to write stories like that, and Hans Christian Andersen never found Miss Right either. "He shook his feathers, stretched his slender neck, and in the joy of his heart said, 'How little did I dream of so much happiness when I was the ugly, despised duckling!' "

After the ceremony, Shawn drove us back to New York, and we had dinner and a great deal of champagne at the Stanhope Hotel, which I have always thought is the kind of place everybody ought to live in. All the time. Shawn kissed Lily between each bite of filet and each sip of the champagne.

At one point a woman who said she was an Austrian contessa joined us. She could have been the lost Anastasia. She was wearing a bent tiara, and I remember the mascara being where the lipstick ought to have been, and her eyebrows as being painted under her eyes. I must be wrong.

She shared our champagne, and she persuaded Shawn to contribute fifty dollars to some charity or other, and half an hour and a magnum of champagne later, she borrowed ten dollars from me for a tip at what she called the "girlies'." After which she never returned, and we hadn't really expected her to or wanted her to.

It was all rather Scott Fitzgeraldish, except that our generation would never make the mistakes his generation did. . . . None of those people were queer, either. I then thought.

Eventually Lily and Shawn went upstairs, and all the rich, glossy people smiled, and since I didn't know any of them well enough actually to hate them, I smiled back and had too many whiskeys and got sick in front of the Metropolitan Museum. Too sick to pick anything up.

That night I'd have chosen a murderer.

The next morning, all three of us suffering from self-inflicted wounds, I saw Lily and Shawn off on the *Île de France*. It was one of those misty spring mornings with a pale sun, and the water was as blue as the sky, and everything would be like that forever.

They were both still beautiful, and there was a story about the marriage in the *Times*. And a photograph.

We had a magnum of the hair of the dog and laughed about the contessa, and it was still pretty Hans Christian Andersen. Until the steward came in anyway.

He was a blond boy with green eyes and very tanned skin, and I looked at him over the champagne. He refilled my glass and smiled, knowing. I saw that Shawn was looking at him, too, and then Shawn looked at me, and he blushed and kissed Lily.

The boy went out, looking back once, still smiling. French boys smile a lot. They're very reasonable, too, in all ways.

I wished Lily and Shawn all the . . . I kissed Lily, shook Shawn's hand, said they were both very lucky, and then I went ashore.

I did not look back. Just that once I didn't. It's the looking back that gets you in trouble. . . . I wondered when Shawn and the green-eyed boy would meet. And where. It's not too easy on shipboard, but it can be done. There are all those nooks and crannies. And the lifeboats. It's beautiful in the lifeboats, but be sure they haven't scheduled a drill.

23 /

Opus III Sonata

Stupid fool! Scribbler! Correct your own faults caused through ignorance, self-conceit, and stupidity. This is far better than to try to instruct me; for this would be just like a sow trying to teach Minerva. . . .

I saw Shawn and Lily together only twice during the two years they were married. I may have seen Shawn a third time. I'm not sure.

The first time I saw them together was at the apartment on Eighty-sixth, a little less than a year after they'd got married. Most of the time after I'd finished the tour that ended in Houston I'd been in Spain, Málaga and Torremolinos. I'd worked hard, "Rondo for a Bullfighter." Even Lennie recorded that one, but compared to George Szell . . . Or Eugene Ormandy . . . The bullfighter wasn't as handsome as El Cordobes, not as famous; magnificent, though. I've got dozens and dozens of ears and tails.

What does one do with things like that when it's over? ——is dead now. Of course. . . . But then everybody is dead. . . . Tomorrow?

The apartment was huge, too much furniture, decoratorish furniture, hotel furniture, nothing personal about any of it. Too many highboys and lowboys and too many Barcelona chairs and narrow sofas covered with black leather.

Too many people at the party. Drifters, wanderers. I can remember nobody's name, no memorable face, and I was sober during the entire first half of the evening. Nothing was said that I would wish to remember.

Lily and Shawn seemed okay. I mean they looked well. Shawn was on the wagon, and he said that, and he said that I'd have to stay after the others had left, and we'd have to have a good talk. He didn't seem any too anxious to talk, though, and once when we could have, his duties as host required his presence on the other side of the room.

I left at midnight, and Lily said she'd call me, but she didn't, and Shawn said we must, but we didn't. . . . I don't know how to tell how well a marriage is going. Lily and Shawn didn't scream at each other. No knife or plate throwing. They smiled at each other numerous times, maybe too numerous. Maybe they were trying too hard. . . . I was missing the bullfighter, and as I say, I left early.

The second time I saw Lily and Shawn was at the house in Connecticut, six months or so after the Eighty-sixth Street evening.

I didn't care much for the house either. Act I, Scene I: a handsome remodeled colonial house in Connecticut. . . . The house was painted too yellow a yellow; the shutters were too blue a blue. Too much furniture, too self-consciously antique. Decorator trouble again. . . . Shawn was still on the wagon, but I was not, and since they had forgot to order liquor or else it hadn't come, Shawn asked me to drive to Westport with him to get some.

I thought maybe he wanted to talk, but he didn't. Quite the opposite. He didn't look directly at me, not once during the entire evening (I thought of Horton Payne). . . . How had the tour been? What was Australia like, New Zealand, Hawaii, San Francisco? All fine, thanks, all the way they had been the last time I was there.

I did not mention having met K. in Los Angeles. Or the fact that I had brought him home with me. K., who'd been in more jails than Jean Genet. Who was as saintly. Who was going to write an epic poem greater than *Paradise Lost*. Of course I'd never heard of Genet at the time, and K. had never heard of *Paradise Lost*.

Shawn, looking hard at the uninspired Connecticut landscape, said that he was working on a new novel, said that he and Lily were happy. Very, very happy, he said. Said that he hardly ever went to the city any more.

We passed a gas station, and a boy in coveralls who was sitting in the front seat of a Porsche honked the horn and waved. I saw that the boy was dark and handsome, and I noticed that Shawn's return wave was not enthusiastic.

That's really all there is to say about the evening. Lily and I, separated by planets, had a couple of drinks before dinner, and there was wine with dinner, and the dinner was good. Lily had cooked it herself, and she had always been a good cook. She'd learned from her mother, Farrell's Eats. . . . We talked—the difficulty of getting a lawn mowed, the high price of, nothing talk. . . . Lily and Shawn were elaborately polite to each other. They seemed to be going through motions. Lily several times explained why she still went to the city four times a week and why she had not been able to find a buyer for Lily Ltd., why, why . . .

I yawned several times, and at eleven I said it's a long drive back, and it's been, and we must . . . And Shawn and Lily said that we must.

I stopped at the gas station. The boy must have been twenty, maybe twenty-one, and he had black hair and an advertising smile. Italian, I imagine. A lot of Italian boys in that part of Connecticut, willing, for a price.

He put in ten gallons of the regular. I said, "You're a friend of Shawn O'Hennessey."

He said, "Yah. We're friends, you might say. He tell you that?"

I said, no, that I'd been in the car when he honked at Shawn.

"Yah," said the boy, smiling in a way I detest. "Yah. He trades here. You know, trades. They got a nice place there. You know. I ain't never met the missus. You know. I service the car. I'm a mechanic. You know."

I gave him a five, and he brought me the change, and he said, "Yah. O'Hennessey's okay. Except you know he ought to watch his step. He tell you the trouble he got in that bar out near Norwalk?"

I didn't answer, and I didn't tip him.

"Of course it wasn't in the papers or nothing, but it's all over town. He really got beat up. I told him. I said, 'Why you out cruising the bars when I'm around?' Know what I mean?"

I drove away, feeling moral, feeling upright, how dare I, feeling pity.

One night in one of the bars in the city I thought I saw Shawn, but I wasn't sure. I left immediately. I knew that Shawn would not want me to have seen him. If it was he.

And then K. and I went to Europe, and a few weeks after we got back, the call came. Shawn was dead.

The afternoon of his death I went out and had however many drinks it was, and eventually, after I had done with the foolish tears, I called Lily at the Connaught in London. It was eleven o'clock there, and I told Lily what had happened in a voice almost as matter-of-fact as that of Simon Liberman of Liberman, et cetera. . . . Lily said nothing for a long time, and then she said, "I'll get the first flight. I'll let you know which flight."

The connection was perfect. Lily sounded as if she were in the next room. You know, perfect. She said, "Where's the body?"

I told her it was still at the hospital, and she said that Shawn hadn't wanted a service, nothing. He had just wanted to be cremated. It was an awful thing to ask, but could I possibly arrange that. I said that I would, and Lily said, "It's awful, but could you call his parents? It'll be better coming from you, a stranger. I know I should do it. . . . Oh, darling."

And finally, Lily said, "I'm glad it was you who told me. I'll cable which plane."

The rest of the night is a blank, but when I woke up the next morning, I appeared to be physically intact, no broken bones, no strange body in the bed next to me. "Oh, good morning there. I don't

believe we've met. My name is George Lionel." And nothing seemed
to be missing, except a few hours of memory that I could do without.

I had some black coffee and then arranged for the burning. It was
not simple. "You can't mean that you want a plain pine box for a
man of the distinction of . . ."

There had been stories about Shawn's death in the morning papers, and there was the welcome smell of loot.

I don't want to go into details, but the plain pine box cost $125,
and there were carting fees, and there was the certification of death.
As I recall, eight copies were necessary; eight palms had to be
crossed, and there was . . . I found myself using the word *fuck* almost as many times as I had in the OSS.

I had a little Irish coffee, which seemed appropriate under the
circumstances, and then I called Kansas City, thinking of the old
man and the old woman whose only child Shawn had been. His
father had been over fifty when he was born, his mother forty-four.
Three miscarriages before that, and the doctor had said . . .

Shawn had once told me, "Do you wonder that when I popped
out, physically intact and more or less mentally normal, they treated
me as if there'd never been anything quite like me in the history of
the race? I was spoiled rotten. I always had everything I wanted
and a great many things I was never imaginative enough to think
of wanting. . . . They were brokenhearted when I left the church,
but they always told themselves that I'd come to my senses, return
to the church, and marry in the faith. That's the way they think, and
that's the way they talk, and there's no changing it and never will
be. We're shanty Irish, as shanty as they come.

"True, my father made a lot of money in the drug business, and
we never kept pigs in the parlor, but they are both still obsessed
with crucifixes and blotchy reproductions of the Christ Child and
Our Blessed Virgin, by the smell of incense and Hail Marys and by
priests with pimply faces and many hands, wanting to talk about
the evils of masturbation."

❖

I talked, first, to the butler and then to the fragile old man who was Shawn's father. I told him what I had to, and he said, "I thank you very much, sir." And after a while he said, "I mean no offense, sir, but I knew at the time he married that woman that he was signing his own death warrant. If he had not married that woman, he would have returned to the church, and he would be alive and well and happy today. I mean no offense, sir, but I am a bitter man. My son was a boy of whom a woman like that could take advantage. . . . That woman . . ."

Finally, Shawn's father suppressed a dry, old man's sob, and he again thanked me for calling.

"It will not be easy to tell my wife," he said, "not easy at all, and it will not be easy to tell her that our son will not be buried in consecrated ground. Neither will be easy." There was the parched sound of another sob, and the old man hung up the phone, softly, slowly, as if breaking the connection meant the end of Shawn. Nothing left, not even a loving lie. And despite all that money, despite the unquestioned faith, despite what he and his wife had decided to believe about Lily, nothing would ever be easy again.

In the taxi from the airport to the apartment on East Eighty-sixth, Lily held my hand and said, "I haven't shed a single tear. Isn't that awful?" And she said, "It was an accident, wasn't it? I mean . . . there isn't any question about that, is there?"

I said that there wasn't; I said that nobody was to blame, that it was just one of those unfortunate accidents that occur in a large city.

Lily said, "Everybody always wanted to tell me—everybody except you, and I thank you for it—about the sex thing. And the thing was, the thing nobody understood was that I knew all about it, I mean I knew all I needed to know, and I didn't care. I suppose I'd rather it had been a different way but it was what it was, and I either loved all of him or I didn't love any of him."

"Did you ever tell him that?"

"How could I? It was a subject we never discussed. If Shawn

wanted to talk about it, fine. If he didn't, that was fine, too, and he never did."

"You were married two years, spent two years joined in holy matrimony, and you never once, either of you . . . ?"

"Never once. Either of us. I suppose getting married was really my idea. I was tired of the rat race, and I've always wanted to be married, and I liked Shawn, loved him I think, and I think as much as he could he loved me. I must say in all the time we were together he was never less than kind, never less than gentle, and never less than decent. I guess except for you he was the saddest man I've ever known or likely ever will."

Later, I sat on the bed in the apartment, and Lily said, "I used to think I was so rational about things. Everything *I* did was so beautifully thought out and planned, and *I* was so bright, and I pitied my poor, dumb, cloddish brothers and my poor, promiscuous mother, but Christ, my brothers are married, and they've got scads of kids, and every time I go back . . . they're happy. I mean they've got good marriages, and my mother . . . well, she never went to the university, and she never made Phi Beta Kappa the way her bright daughter did, but she's made . . . quite a few men happy."

She started sobbing, and she said, "I wasn't going to tell Shawn until I saw the doctor in London. I'm pregnant. Yes, Shawn's the father. There hasn't been anybody else."

I said, "I'm glad if you're glad. Are you?"

"Of course I'm glad and that's the hell of it. That's the biggest reason we got married in the first place. We both wanted children. If Shawn had just known I was pregnant, that would have made all the difference. That would have changed everything. Don't you think it would have?"

I said that I didn't know the answer to that one, and all I know now that I didn't know then is that nobody else knows, either. Nobody I've met anyway, nobody I've heard about, nobody I've read. None of it makes any sense. Things happen to people.

Lily knew that. I gave her two Seconals, and she said, "Who arranges these things? I mean they expect me to believe in God, but nothing makes any sense, does it?"

Peter was born the following May, and Lily worked right up to the day of delivery and got to the hospital just in time. He was a large baby, and Lily said he was beautiful. He had his father's eyes, large and blue and innocent.

Lily's lawyers wanted her to sue the truck company, but she never did, and when Shawn's parents made trouble about the will, Lily never fought back. She said let them keep the money, and they did. They built a grotto in Kansas City that is unequaled in ugliness anywhere, even in Kansas City.

It is almost as popular as Disneyland, though; people come from all over, and it costs a dollar to get in. Although the grotto was built to honor Shawn's memory, all of the money goes to the church he despised.

The night I left Lily asleep and alone in the apartment on East Eighty-sixth, I walked all the way home. I was then living, also alone, on West Eleventh, between Fifth and Sixth, a lovely part of the city. It was then anyway. Maybe it still is. I haven't been back. I told you I never return to places I've been happy.

As I said, I was working hard, the Auden song. I wasn't in love. Someplace Hemingway wrote that a writer writes best when he is in love. And that may be true for him. I must say I have never been able to compose anything much when I'm in love. I don't even find time to practice. And I become gross. Chomp, chomp, chomp. Getting fat is one way to get rid of them.

To me love has always been the most enervating, time-consuming pastime there is—the endless touching it involves, the inevitable exchanges of large chunks of unedited autobiography, the essential lies.

It's when it's over that you get the work done.

❖

When I got back to the apartment, I played Concerto for the Left Hand, Ravel's, not mine, until dawn. I thought how alone Lily would be, but would she? And I thought, They shouldn't have married, you know, and maybe I should have tried to stop it. And I thought, But I'm not God, and I'm really no good at all at playing God, and I thought, How can you ever know?

The kids will do better, won't they? Christopher won't hurt himself as much as I've hurt myself. Will he? Dissipate himself? Fritter himself away? . . . Please, God. Please, God? I'll take up Christianity if You promise. . . . Christopher and I. It's been three years now. Three years and we're still friends. Three years and we're still lovers. . . . To be truthful—and I know I'll eat a peck of dirt before I die and tell a thousand more lies, even if it's tomorrow—to be truthful, not at all any more, not for eighteen months, and it's better without sex. Maybe it always would have been. Friends; lovers no more. Sex is what causes all the trouble. If God had his wits about Him, He'd start making us without anything at all down there.

RONDO—And Peter. Shawn's son Peter. He'll be all right, won't he? Surely They'll leave him alone. Not that I know him, certainly not well. During the four years she was married to Bruno Hyerly I saw Lily three times, always in New York. If she had asked me to visit the Hyerly estate in Warren County, I would, of course, have refused, which Lily knew. She always sent me a telegram at Christmas, saying, with minor variations, that it was now possible, although not easy, to get through that particular day; and on my birthday, saying that she loved me.

Those were very creative years, and I was being what most people would no doubt consider a minor celebrity, famous for twenty-nine minutes, as Andy Warhol says.

I was for a while on the faculty of a pretty good school in northern California, and so far as I was concerned, each and every student retained his chastity, if any. I went on millions of tours, all of them the same tour, all of them terrifying.

The three times I saw Lily we had lunch at the Italian restaurant. Of her I knew what I had read in the newspapers, that she and Bruno Hyerly gave a lot of large parties. She and Bruno were at the Democratic convention in Los Angeles in 1960, and she was head of one of the women's committees during the campaign and often traveled on the plane with the candidate. There was gossip, but when isn't there. I remember only one picture showing her play touch football.

But Lily and I did not talk politics. We didn't agree. What was the point of talking? In those years, during our infrequent meetings, we never talked about anything much. I knew that Peter had got to Hotchkiss, which was what Lily had said she had in mind when she married Bruno Hyerly.

Lily said, "He's their star pupil, and everybody likes him, both the masters and the boys."

I asked the old question. "What's he going to be?"

"I don't know," said Lily, "but that's no problem. He's not only intelligent. He's smart, too."

Lily had developed one of those odd accents the fox-hunting people in Warren County use. "He's simply super. Bruno adores him, but he's very strict with him."

"Oh?"

"Bruno doesn't want to spoil Peter. He thinks that's the trouble with so many bright boys. He says that discipline is becoming a thing of the past in this country."

"Peter says that or the Honorable Mr. Hyerly?"

"Don't be funny. You're always making wisecracks. We are living in serious times, and the President says—"

"I'm not interested in what the President says."

"Oh, you and politics; I know you never vote, and while I think it's a disgrace, in some ways it's probably just as well; you'd be sure to pull the wrong lever or something. But the important thing is, I was right about Hotchkiss. I wonder what would have happened to us if we'd gone to a proper school when we were kids. Bruno says that a proper education . . . Well, he says that without one we all end up messes. That's why he's so insistent that Peter develop . . . well, the whole man, and now that the President has announced the physical fitness program—"

I said, "I can't believe that you've fallen for all this horseshit, Lily."

Lily touched my hand with hers, and she said, "Oh, darling." For a moment I thought she was going to cry, but she didn't. She said, "I've got to be running. I've got a dentist's appointment in ten minutes."

"You can't keep running all the time, Lily. At least I don't think you can, and I hope you don't try, and I hope Peter doesn't."

"So long, love," said Lily, running.

A year passed, maybe more, and Lily wrote me that Peter, who was sixteen, had got a perfect score in four college boards. "Please drop him a line congratulating him. He's very fond of you." I doubted that Peter was very fond of me, but I dropped him a note, and a month or so later, that's the way things go, I saw him at one of George Balanchine's better ballets, *Stars and Stripes.*

At first I wasn't sure the boy two rows in front of me was Peter. I'd seen him only twice since he was ten, and six years at that age . . . Lots of hair, not as much as Christopher, not as blond as Christopher.

Peter was passably handsome, rather like his father, not very special except, perhaps, the innocent blue eyes. He was painfully thin, hands and feet too large, his head a little too small. Everything would work out fine; he would emerge as a whole human being in a year or so, but not at sixteen. Christopher was the only wholly put together sixteen-year-old I have ever encountered. The colonel no doubt insisted.

Peter was alone, and at the intermission I went over to him and introduced myself. He was a shy boy, very withdrawn; perhaps he always had been. I didn't remember. But he had a smile that more than made up for his physical imperfections.

He said, "I recognized you, of course, but I wasn't sure you'd remember me."

We talked until the second bell rang. I again congratulated him on the college boards, and he said that he had decided on a small college in the Middle West. He was interested in the theater; he thought he might like to write plays.

He said, "I don't know if I have any talent, but I do have sense enough to know that there isn't really any relationship between what I did in those tests and creativity."

I asked, thinking of the Yale Drama School, why the Middle West, and he said, "It's a long way from Warren County, Virginia." And he said, "Of course what I really want to do is paint a picture, compose a symphony, write a novel and a play, have them all exposed to the critics on the same day, and they'll all get lousy reviews."

Afterward we went to the Russian Tea Room and talked until almost two. Peter had been to a number of my concerts, several times with classmates from Hotchkiss. "I did considerable bragging about knowing you," he said. I asked why he hadn't brought his friends backstage, and he said, "I'd have been too embarrassed, and besides, after a concert, I should think the last thing in the world you'd need is a bunch of inarticulate schoolboys hanging around."

"Do you like Hotchkiss?"

"Oh, it's a good school, maybe one of the best, but most of the boys don't seem to have many questions, about themselves or anything else. I was a lot happier at Riverdale. There all my best friends were either Jews or Negroes. Besides, it is quite clear I will never be the well-rounded man my father has in mind."

I said, "I have never known what well-rounded men were good for, except rolling."

Peter laughed and said, "I'd much rather have written *Childe Harold's Pilgrimage* than have swum the Hellespont, but it seems unlikely that I'll do either. 'I have not loved the world, nor the world me;/ I have not flattered its rank breath, nor bowed to its idolatries a patient knee.' At least I haven't so far, and I hope I never will. Does that sound pretentious?"

"It didn't to Byron, and it doesn't to me, but as you've perhaps observed, people with patient knees get more applause and make more money. And get elected things."

"Have you met the Kennedys?" asked Peter.

I said that I had not had the pleasure, not since Jack got to be President. What did he think of them?

"I don't think they have many questions, either. Besides, I don't care much for public personalities, of whom there are always a large number at the gracious estate in Warren County. I tend to go someplace and hide when they're around."

"Aren't you impressed with meeting a President?"

"No," said Peter. "Why should I be?"

I asked about Lily, and Peter said, "I guess her health is okay. By the way, if you see her and the subject comes up, I'd appreciate it if you didn't tell her what I said about dear old Hotchkiss. She keeps saying, 'It's very good for Peter.' I guess she actually thinks so, and I don't see any reason for disillusioning her."

I said that I agreed.

When we got outside, Peter looked down the disconsolate street and said, "And if you see my illustrious stepfather, New Frontier Hyerly, I'd appreciate it if you didn't mention that you saw me at the ballet. He has notions about people who go to the ballet."

I hailed a taxi, told Peter to take it, and as he got in I said, "I doubt very much that I'll ever see your stepfather again, but if I do, I'll keep your secret. And give my love to your mother."

The taxi drove off. Peter looked back and waved good-bye. I managed to return the wave.

SINGSPIEL—It was a gray afternoon in 195—; I don't remember the year. Those years were identical. I either was appearing before a committee or was not. I was either in a loony bin or was not. I paid for every sin I had ever committed during that age of revenge. I paid for every sin anybody had ever committed, ever. I prayed to God and cursed God, never for a minute believing that either mattered.

It was in the fifties that I stopped believing. I stopped caring. Boredom clung to me. I could never wash it off.

It was in the fifties that I stopped believing that the next one would be perfect, in or out of bed. I never stopped looking for the other, the better half of me. Plato told me not to.

A gray afternoon in 195—; Lily called and said, "I want you to be the first to know. I'm going to get married again."

"Congratulations. I want you to be happily married. To whom?"

"To a chap known as Bruno Hyerly."

I whistled and said, "I'm doubly pleased. I want you to be rich, too."

"Can you have dinner with us at the Pierre, at eight?"

"I've just got back from the heartland of America, and I've promised myself that beginning tonight I'm going to spend an entire week in bed, but I'll break that promise if you assure me that neither you nor Mr. Hyerly will ask if I practiced a lot as a child, ask if I was a prodigy, ask me to listen to the ivory tinkling of the local child genius, ask me, giggling, if I ever read *Confidential*, ask if I know Lennie and don't Lennie's broadcasts make up for all the dreck that's on television."

"I promise for both of us. I want to know what you think of Bruno."

"I'll see you at eight."

All I knew about Bruno Hyerly was what I had read, but it was impossible not to read about him. He had been born to a wealthy family that had an estate in Warren County, Virginia; I believe the money was originally tobacco. But Bruno had added greatly to the wealth, buying this, selling that; I know nothing about how people get rich. Obviously. . . . Bruno Hyerly was almost as rich as Howard Hughes and J. Paul Getty, but unlike those two reticent gentlemen,

Hyerly was forever giving out his opinions on one thing or another. The only thing he wouldn't talk about was how much money he had.

But he was a liberal, whatever that means, and he was a Democrat, and he said he was a democrat. . . . Democracy, son, is a system in which one has a choice between Richard M. Nixon and John F. Kennedy, between Lyndon Baines Johnson and Barry Goldwater, between Hubert Humphrey and Richard M. Nixon. You are allowed to choose between two evil men; you are asked to choose the lesser of the evils. . . . I didn't vote in the first two of those elections; in the last, although I didn't really think he had much of a chance, I voted for Eldridge Cleaver.

At the time I'm talking about here, Bruno Hyerly was (I think) already one of the people who thought that John F. Kennedy, who had then just been elected senator for either the first time or the second, ought to be President. I did not share that belief. I did not see any reason to believe that a bad senator would be a good President.

Bruno Hyerly looked exactly like the photograph that had appeared in *Newsweek* a month or so earlier. He had been in a stockholders' fight and had won.

He looked to me like a man who never lost a fight, physical or otherwise. He looked like a man who had never suffered a disappointment. His face was darker than I expected, but then he was always tanned. He probably had his own personal sun, and if he didn't want it to set . . . I knew that in addition to the estate in Warren County, he owned most of North Carolina, and he had that place in Brazil . . . and . . . and.

I know it sounds old-fashioned of me, but the night we met, my first thought was that his eyes were set too close together. That is probably because I used to read a great many Victorian novels.

Altogether, though, I suppose Bruno is handsome enough for any good purpose. A good body, looked as if he exercised a lot, bar bells, push-ups, chinning himself. He had a hearty handshake. Of course he did. He said that he felt as if we had known each other for years. I had no answer to that.

He heard every word he uttered, and he approved of every word he uttered. He spoke in an accent that was a combination of Oxford, where he'd been a Rhodes scholar, and Warren County, and that may be the reason that his most pedestrian remark was likely to sound more profound than it really was.

I said that it was a pleasure and kissed Lily on the forehead. Lily was looking well; she was wearing blue again, a vaguely mandarin dress, and her only ornament was a large gold sea lion. That and a ring which, unlike the ring Shawn had bought for her, was in perfect taste.

I thought that Lily was a quick study and that this time she'd make it. . . . At least that's what I thought at the beginning of the evening.

We had two drinks each. Bruno—he insisted that I call him that—said that we didn't want any more, did we, and before one had a chance to answer that always perplexing question, he was ordering the wine and the dinner. "I have eaten here a time or two before, and while everything is superb, the sweetbreads are out of this world."

I like to order my own meals in restaurants and have ever since I was about three years old and my mother started telling me, whenever we "ate out," that I was going to want the chopped sirloin. I must have been at least five before I realized that the chopped sirloin was always the cheapest thing on the menu. . . . I was sure nothing as crass as money would interest anybody as well heeled as my good buddy Bruno, but I did notice that the sweetbreads cost a lost less than the filet mignon Rossini.

I happen to hate sweetbreads, the reasons being partly psychological, but I ate them like a regular little man, masticating everything thoroughly. And otherwise keeping my big mouth shut. I did not break my vow of silence until we were well into our second demitasses.

Bruno Hyerly led the conversation, as he had been everywhere in the world; he said that himself, at least half a dozen times. "And I don't travel for the hell of it. I've got business interests in all the great capitals of the world. I was not born a poor boy, as you may know, but I have never felt that mere affluence excuses laziness. So I manage to keep busy, and I'll tell you this, and I know it's a cliché, but cliché or not, I go along with the late Will Rogers. I have yet to meet a man I didn't like, and the better I get to know him, the better I like him."

It was impossible for me to believe that the man was serious, but he was. I gather he was never less than serious, and solemn. The two, although they are not at all alike, are often confused. Your solemn man is your serious man.

It was also impossible for me to believe that Bruno Hyerly could make change let alone a fortune. But he had made several fortunes; the evidence was all there.

For what it's worth, I'll tell you what the solemn men who make fortunes and those they hire to run the government for them have in common. They are all cruel. . . . Power sucks; absolute power sucks absolutely.

The groom-to-be filled us in on many of the observations he had made during his travels. None of them made me want to leave home. He told several humorous anecdotes, and he was completely without a sense of humor. He told about a recent financial triumph in I believe Libya. He then launched into a complete account of his experiences in the Second World War.

Bruno had gone into the U.S. Army as a reserve major, and when he came out he was a brigadier general, and in relating his remarkable military career, not a promotion, not a staff conference, not a battle was omitted.

Bruno Hyerly had been one of Georgie Patton's boys. One might have guessed. He said, "We needed one of old Georgie, whatever his faults. In wartime it isn't always the people we want to have dinner with that win battles. Don't you agree?"

I moved my head in a way that could have been interpreted as a shake or a nod or both; I did not say that I considered George Patton a monster in 1945 and had not changed my mind. I said nothing. But I did look at Lily, and she was looking at Bruno Hyerly the way she had some years earlier looked at Shawn O'Hennessey. . . . What do you do? What do you ever do?

A little later Bruno started making telephone calls at the table. I believe he was buying the Roman Empire. I had the feeling that we were living in the fifth century A.D. and that the empire was going cheap.

After the phone was taken away from the table, Hyerly said, "I'm sorry, but in my line of work it's a twenty-four-hour-a-day proposition. I'm sorry to have to put you two to trouble."

I sipped a little of the coffee, and then I said, "It's always a pleasure to see a man of decision deciding things. I like being a front-row spectator at life in the raw."

Bruno Hyerly's eyes got even closer together, or so it seemed, and I thought he was going to say something, but he didn't. He excused himself and went to the men's.

Lily said, "You hate him."

I said, "Lily, I'm not marrying him."

"I know he comes across strong, but believe it or not, he's terribly shy, and he's been very nice to me, very thoughtful. Peter's fond of him, too, now that they've got to know each other."

"How is Peter?"

"He's okay. He's in his first year at Riverdale, but he's too good for Riverdale, really too good, too smart, too everything. I'd like to get him into Hotchkiss. I took him up there a couple of weeks ago, and we talked to the headmaster and several of the others, and he met some of the boys. He adored the place, and so did I. And I'm not being a snob when I say that boys who come from families of wealth . . . Well, as Fitzgerald said, they're different."

"They certainly are. They not only have more money than poor people, they smell better. They are forever rubbing themselves with sweet-smelling oils. But, Lily, you don't have to marry Goodbuddy Hyerly to send Peter to Hotchkiss. You're a rich and successful lady. You could do it yourself."

"I'm afraid not, dear heart. After the tax men are satisfied, and they are not easy to satisfy these days, there is the orthodontist, and there is the summer camp, and there is the trip to Europe, and there are the clothes, and so on and so on. After all of that, there isn't much left. Not that I'm complaining. It's just that I want so much for Peter. He's such a very special boy. You remember I once told you, the only original sin is being born poor, and I was and in most ways I still am. And I'm tired of it. If you think I was tired before I married Shawn . . . I sometimes look at the rest of us aging working ladies in the restaurants and in the lobbies of the hotels we frequent, and I wonder, Don't *they* ever get tired? I do. I'm tired all the time. I've become a four- and five-Dexedrine-a-day girl, and I can no longer lie to myself and say that the pills are to keep down my weight."

I said, "Lily, I'm not much of an authority on marriage, but fatigue doesn't seem to me to be a proper reason for getting entangled in any relationship."

"What I haven't said," said Lily, "is that I love Bruno." I guess she meant that, too.

I said, "It's very interesting about Peter and Hotchkiss, but are you sure it isn't you who wants to go to Hotchkiss?"

I believe that Lily might have slapped me then or cried, pushed one of those panic buttons that women are never without, but instead, she laughed and kissed me on the forehead and said, "I refuse to get angry with you because what you say is partly true. But they don't take girls up there, and even if they did, I'm a little long in the tooth for it."

"Long in the tooth for what?" said Bruno Hyerly, seating himself again.

"To go back to school," said Lily.

"You wouldn't have time for it," said Bruno, and he proceeded to fill us in on his plans for the honeymoon. They were flying around the world, six months of it, stopping off where they wanted as long as they wanted.

After the honeymoon, he said, they were going to spend most of the year at the town house in New York, his town house, overlooking the proper part of Central Park, which, I gathered, also belonged to him. . . . But of course they would have to spend some time in Warren County.

Bruno said, "Once you're born and raised in a place like Warren County, Virginia, it gets in your blood. You can never leave. Not for any length of time."

I said, "That's certainly something to think about."

He gave me a sharp look, an angry look, but he said, "Have you ever been down our way?"

I said that I had not, although I had been, several times, once for an extended period during the OSS training. One of the local gentry had turned his estate over for the duration; it was a beautiful house, but that is almost all that I remember. I was drunk a good deal of the time, that and terrified. Among my other fears was that when I was dropped into France, I wouldn't be able to remember a word of French, and that is more or less what happened.

I said, "I've been through. Nice country."

"The best," said Bruno, "and you must come down and see us, stay as long as you like. We've got scads of room."

I think he rightly assumed that I never would.

He said, "I've just been listening to the radio. The reds are still shooting them down in Budapest." And to me, "What do you think of what's going on over there?"

I said I thought that it was heartbreaking.

"I assume that means that you agree with me that we ought to get in there with a little more than just fancy speeches."

Lily said, "Bruno, please, let's not—"

"I'm interested in your friend's opinion," said Bruno Hyerly. "He's a very famous *man*. I want to know what he thinks."

I said, "I think what the Soviets are doing is evil. It's easy to say that, but I also think it was evil for our government to indicate that it would help a rebellion when it had no intention of doing so. Fancy speeches is all anybody had in mind, and that includes you."

Lily said, "Bruno, let's go."

"Evil," said Bruno Hyerly. "What an interesting choice of words. Your friend here is quite a well-known fellow, and if there is one thing he has studied up on, it's evil. I read all about it. You can in any barbershop."

Bruno was referring to the piece about me in a magazine called *Confidential*; we will come to that.

I said, "I hope you two will be very happy together," and then I said good night.

> Love seeketh only self to please,
> To bind another to its delight,
> Joys in another's loss of ease,
> And builds a Hell in Heaven's despite.

It's true what they said about poor William Blake, but his wife taught him how to read and write, and he loved her. . . . "And throughout all eternity/ I forgive you, you forgive me."

I forgive Bruno Hyerly; I forgive Cecily Broadmoor; I forgive each and every one of my trespassers. I forgive myself.

11 P.M. All right. I have done what you asked. I have gone to the movies. I have accompanied the other freaks in what you refer to as our weekly expedition into the outside world. . . . Never again, Frederika. I despised every second of it, and I despised all the other freaks and kooks and nuts, patients, paying guests, whatever you call them. . . . And as for that Swiss fag that works for you, whatever his name is, I'll kill him. Have him killed. Winking and leering. Making obscene suggestions. . . . Jesus, I hate sissies. Genocide for the queers. . . . I hear the trucks arrive at dawn, and those limp of wrist go first. . . . I used to try to pass, but it did no good at all, never fooled anybody. . . . Will they make soap out of us? Lavender? Scented?

I'll tell you one thing. I will not go quietly.

24 /

Geese

A note from K., along with a copy of his new book. He's been appearing on campuses, reading poems from the new book and from the older books. I never laid them in the aisles, but K. does, the aisles, on desks, Steinways, uprights, on lecterns. The surface doesn't even have to be horizontal. Or perpendicular. There doesn't even have to be a surface. Chandeliers. . . . I know you think I was promiscuous. But compared to K. . . . K., like Byron, uses every receptacle that is large enough. I once mentioned the matter of promiscuity and guilt to him, and he said, "As long as you've got time for it, what's wrong with it?"

Have you an answer to that one, maestro?

K. wants to come and see me, and the lady to whom he is married, a lady whose family owns all of Pittsburgh, wants to commission me to . . . Thanks, but no more commissions from rich ladies married to former lovers of mine. No more commissions of any kind. And sorry, K., no more visits, no more remembrance. . . . Where is Hollywood and Vine? . . . He was very beautiful then; in a way he still is. . . . That first night he said, "I'm not much of a hustler. I haven't got the patience for it, all that standing around. On the other hand, my rates are lower than most."

K. says that "Fugue for the Rich and Rude" is very popular with the kids. Everywhere, he says, on campuses all across the country. Adapted for the guitar, no doubt. . . . Anyway, it's nice to be popular again. It means lots of nice money, and of course I'll give it all to you. What's it costing now, dear heart, five hundred dollars a minute to be here, surrounded by the rich and rude and unbalanced, most of them fags and dykes? . . . I'll tell you one thing. If that bull dyke of a recreation director knocks on my door once more and asks in her dyke voice if I want to get into the Ping-Pong tournament, I shall see to it that all of her dildos are confiscated and turned over to the FBI. The director of the FBI.

Anyway, I'm sure K. exaggerates about the popularity of the fugue. Trying to cheer me up. K. is still fond of me. He's one of the few who's forgiven me for being kind to him.

INTERRUPTION—OPERA BOUFFE—Now that you've asked, I'll tell you how the fugue happened. . . . It was 1939, late August, hot, hazy, heavy. The day before Franklin Roosevelt had sent a note telling both Hitler and the Poles (to be sure the Poles) to behave themselves. And Pope Pius XI had made a speech asking everybody in the world, the Poles and Hitler included, to be more Christlike. And on the radio that Friday, during the endless drive from the city to East Hampton, H. V. Kaltenborn kept repeating the obvious, saying that there was a good possibility of war, but on the other hand . . . Over and over again. The usual bullshit.

Charley and I and an exquisite girl drove up from the city to spend the weekend at her father's place. L. V. Covington was in those days almost as big in the whiskey business as Joseph P. Kennedy. And his daughter Luna, who had red hair, was a member of something called the American Youth Congress and something called the American Student Union, and she was probably a member of the Young Communist League as well. She was fond of saying things like, "When the time comes, they will be dispensed with. They will be shot, like fascist dogs." She said that of almost anyone who disagreed with her.

There were a lot of girls who talked like Luna around that year. Up the barricade. . . . The Clarinet Player and I and two or three others went up to Vassar to play at a dance one quaint Saturday night. Between dances, all those girls talked about shooting fascist dogs. I know what happened to Luna, but I wonder what happened to all the rest of those crazy, pretty girls.

I remember they all wanted to dance with The Clarinet Player, not because he was beautiful, not because he played the clarinet magnificently; no, they wanted to dance with him because he was black. Except, of course, *black* was not an acceptable word in those days. . . . The language changes, but people do not.

The weekend in East Hampton was endless.

On Sunday morning Luna and Charley and I drove into the village to get the *Times*. I don't remember what the headlines were, but it was clear that due to the outrageous conduct of the Poles, the Germans were going to have to march in and tidy things up.

I remember that Luna said, "I don't care what a fascist, imperialist paper like the *Times* says, there won't be a war, thanks to the wisdom of the Soviet Union and the nonaggression pact. Also Hitler has cancer of the throat. My father knows that for a fact."

"You don't say," said Charley.

"I do say. My father's doctor knows a man who's also a doctor, and this other doctor has just got back from a big medical convention in Berlin, and while he was there he heard for a fact that Hitler has cancer. That's one of the reasons Stalin signed the nonaggression pact. It's not worth the paper it's written on. Let the fascist dogs eat each other."

"Speaking of eating," said Charley, "it isn't that your father doesn't set a good table, but it's been a long time since breakfast. Couldn't we stop and get a sandwich someplace?"

Luna said, "Let's pretend we don't know it's segregated. That's the best way, really. We'll pretend we don't know, and I'll take you both to lunch at the Maidstone."

"What's that?" said Charley. "A Coptic cathedral left over from the invasion of William the Conqueror?"

"It's a club, and it's awful, really awful. They don't allow Jews or anything."

"How about wops and spicks and niggers?"

"They won't even let *them* look at it."

"Good," said Charley. "I hate minority groups."

"It's decadent American capitalism at its most decadent," said Luna.

There were a few attractive people on the beach, young and brown and shining.

Nobody young in the dining room. There seemed to be scores of widows, though, all of them armed with the most modern weapons, including several tanks that I believe later turned up in the Louisiana maneuvers. One such tanklike lady, a Mrs. J. M. B. Woolf-Hauptmann, was an acquaintance of Luna's, and when she saw us, she said, "My dear Luna, why don't you and your friends join us?"

Mrs. J. M. B. W.-H. was the widow of a Wall Street lawyer, ". . . one of the nation's oldest firms, and the members are Anglo-Saxon. They always have been and always will be. Those of the Hebrew persuasion are simply not encouraged, not even as messengers."

"There's so little of that left," said Charley, and he smiled at Mrs. W.-H. in a way I knew. If I'd been Mrs. W.-H., I'd have excused myself then and there.

Instead she smiled back.

As I've said, an enormous woman, a good three hundred pounds on the hoof, her hair blatantly crimson. Her nose mottled and delicately veined in blue. Her protruding brown eyes were somewhat off center, and they seemed to pop and crackle and wink at you. At me anyway. Her lips, somewhat obscured by the vastness of her whitewashed cheeks, were the color of overripe strawberries.

She was wearing a tentlike maroon-colored dress, and her several rings were nearly hidden by the fat of her fingers. Her neck was encircled with a noose of pearls.

She ordered lunch with the air of someone founding a religion. The waiter-priest, an aging man with sad eyes and unliftable feet, repeated every word after Mrs. W.-H., as one properly does with a catechism.

"I want the double chicken broth, Carlo; I called about that. Chef knows."

"Chef knows," said Carlo.

"And be *sure* it's strained through linen. I can always tell."

"Always tell," said Carlo.

"I can feel a pea through thirty mattresses," said Charley.

"And the female lobster," said Mrs. W.-H., not hearing, never hearing. "The *baby* female, with the *beurre noisette*, and be absolutely sure it's the female, because we do not wish to have an altercation, do we, Carlo?"

"Do we, Carlo?" said Carlo.

"And now what are you children going to have?" said Mrs. W.-H.

Luna, after considerable thought, decided on a tuna fish on white and a glass of milk. I was perhaps too aware of Mrs. W.-H.'s figure, but I decided I wasn't up to meat and ordered eggs Florentine.

"And you, Mr. Payne?" said Mrs. W.-H., her maroon sleeves billowing like sails.

"I was considering the lobster," said Charley, "but how do you tell the sex of a lobster?"

"By the taste, my dear boy, and the female is more tender."

"That's unusual," said Charley.

"Have you two females, Carlo?"

"Two females, Carlo," said Carlo.

"Bring the young man one then."

"Young man one then," said Carlo, bowing his way out.

"Like every other red-blooded American, I'm fascinated by sex," said Charley, "but I seem to have neglected the lobster. How in the world *do* you tell? Do lobsters have genitalia?"

Mrs. W.-H. shook all over, causing the ice in all the glasses on the table to tinkle merrily. "Your young man has a droll sense of humor," she said to Luna. And to Charley, "You're a very handsome young man for a communist, and clean-shaven at that."

"The party doesn't actually require my wearing a beard," said Charley, "as long as I never bathe."

Mrs. W.-H. sniffed the air suspiciously, and Luna said, "Charley's not a communist. He doesn't even understand it. They wouldn't have him."

"That's right," said Charley. "Communism is way over my head. By the way, Mrs. Woolf-Hauptmann, how do you feel about the war?"

"There will be one," said Mrs. W.-H., sounding at the moment a little like H. V. Kaltenborn. "There will be one, and we will get into it, once again dragging British chestnuts out of the fire, but Hitler is perfectly right about the Jews, as will be proved in the long run."

"You don't say," said Charley.

Later, Charley looked over the sea of widows overlooking the sea and said, "I didn't realize there'd be so many of my Jewish friends here today."

Mrs. W.-H. laughed again, this time causing the coffee cups to rattle ominously.

"We have a very selective membership," she said. "Why, there are *white* people who have been waiting years, multimillionaires, breeding going back to the *Mayflower*, who have been found wanting where our standards are concerned. Selectivity, selectivity. That's our motto. That is what has made the Maidstone what it is today. We demand breeding in dogs, don't we?"

"We most certainly do," said Charley, "every time."

"We demand breeding in dogs and cats but, and I largely blame Franklin and Eleanor for this, we deprecate breeding in human beings. Which is one of the reasons we are turning into a mongrel race. Jews, kikes, whatever they choose to call themselves, have clubs of their own, and they prefer it that way. We can't have lunch with just anybody, can we?"

"We certainly cannot," said Charley, "and I want you to know that

I go along with every word you've said, and if my grandfather were alive, he would, too. He was a Rothschild, although we didn't know that until after my father was converted."

Luna started giggling, but Mrs. W.-H. took no notice. "You're a Catholic then," she said to Charley.

"No, Muslim. You see, my father was in Arabia with Lawrence, and when he decided to turn, they looked everything up."

"Of course," said Mrs. W.-H., nodding prodigiously.

"Not of course," said Charley. "In matters like this they take nothing for granted. The first thing they found out was that the Rothschilds, far from being Jewish, were of the Iberian persuasion."

"I beg your pardon?"

"There's nothing to beg my pardon about. The Spaniards have been misusing the word *Iberian* for centuries, and I don't want to get into the Portuguese. *They* didn't even have a Renaissance, you know, and while I have never personally believed that Beethoven was all black, his music certainly gives every evidence of being of mixed persuasions, and while we don't yet have the complete report on your late husband, we have found a good deal of Jewish, Negro and Iberian . . . And your own blood line is, to put it gently, certainly not without evidence that as late as a generation ago, an uncle you prefer to ignore was pure chink—"

"Carlo, the check if you please."

"Tell me, Mrs. Woolf-Hauptmann, if a Negro family of seven was drowning out there—"

"I'll sign it next time, Carlo," said Mrs. W.-H., rising quickly.

"By the way," said Charley, "are you absolutely sure those were female lobsters, because between what I suppose you might call the legs of mine there was the oddest—"

"It's been lovely seeing you, Luna, you and your lovely friends," said Mrs. W.-H., running.

"But we haven't even started to exchange views on selective breeding," Charley called after her.

I know I should remember more about that weekend, what Neville Chamberlain said. And Winston Churchill. And what was in Hitler's telegram to Mussolini. And what Mussolini wired back. But I don't, and I have no intention of looking it up. . . . The young know nothing of history. And why should they? My generation studied up on history, and look where it got us.

I remember that there was white furniture on the green lawn behind the Covington house. I remember that one of the guests was an Assistant Secretary of the Navy and that he never left the bar. I remember a pool shaped like a four-leaf clover. A lady named Lady Gordon-Smith Bennington; she had been one of the previous Mrs. Covingtons, and at one point she said to me, "I hear you're a prodigy, dearie. I've never encountered one before. So if I follow you around making notes, you must forgive me. I'm a student of the human animal." And an Air Corps brigadier general who seemed to be about nineteen, blond, a dimpled chin. Beautiful. He looked like many of the ensigns I later met at the Mayflower bar in Washington. Straight, though. At least I didn't make it with him. . . . He drank a great deal of bourbon and spoke with an accent of the deepest South. He said, "I've been meaning to resign my commission before the war starts. The only reason I went to the Point was to learn how to build bridges, and then they put me in the Air Corps, and now I'll be blowing up bridges instead of building them. . . ."

Toward dusk on Saturday he passed out; he narrowly avoided being sick on the white sofa.

The Assistant Secretary had a vague face and whiskers that made him look like a grieving otter. He had small, blank eyes, bloodshot and somewhat magnified by what are now known as granny glasses. He was drunk the whole time but didn't pass out. I don't remember his ever speaking, but he kept making little humming noises, and every so often he would laugh to himself.

And there was the dark woman from some vaguely Middle European country that either had been or was about to be taken over by the Germans. She said she had escaped with less than two million dollars and a great many jewels, most of which she appeared to be wearing. "Their worth is incalculable but they are of *no* monetary importance to me. All of my countrymen are like that. We place sentiment over money. That is one of the reasons the guttersnipe Hitler, who, by the way, has cancer of the throat—"

"You've heard that, too, have you?" said Luna's father.

". . . sentiment and the fact that our entire country was corroded by the Jews, as a result of which, cancer or not, we should have welcomed the entrance of the guttersnipe."

Charley said, "It's so interesting to get all your points of view. I feel in my bones that we will have many a lively discussion before our stay is over."

"You're fucking well right we will," said the fourth Mrs. Covington; she was a copper heiress from Montana.

That's what I remember and all I remember. Except that I remember thinking that the United States would get into the war. As Meg Taylor wrote later, Roosevelt had always struck me as a man who would be miserable if he didn't have a war.

But you know, it never occurred to me that the war would have anything to do with me. I was headed straight for the top. I would be immortal, just as my mother had predicted, and once I got to the top, I'd stay, and Toscanini would bow when I walked onstage to do the Rachmaninoff Concerto for Piano and Orchestra. No. 2 in C Minor, op. 18.

This. When I got back to the apartment, at about midnight on Sunday, I went at once to the piano. By dawn I had written almost all of the "Fugue for the Rich and Rude."

"To your knowledge, Miss Covington, was the Lionel fugue actually commissioned by the communist party?"

"To my certain knowledge it was. I was at a cell meeting with George Lionel, an agent of the Soviet Union named . . . and . . ."

"Was Charles Payne present at this meeting?"

"He was."

"Remember, Miss Covington, you are under oath. . . . Are you positive that . . . ?"

"In those years there was not a meeting of the communist party, large or small, that was not attended by Charles Payne and very often by his friend and lover, George Lionel, as well as . . ."

The last time I saw Luna Covington was in the late fifties, and it was on one of those streets in the West Forties that I know so well. Her eyes were vacant, her hair uncombed, her lips moving but no sound coming out. . . . Oh, they fell upon evil days, all of them. But, as I say, what good does it do?

25 /

Previews
of Coming
Attractions

I didn't get to the geese yesterday. Was it yesterday? I know I was telling you about K.

I believe it was in the late forties that we met. Before the black-lists began. Otherwise I wouldn't have been in southern California. The last movie for which I wrote a score was in 1951; the next year I was listed in a charming little volume called *Red Channels,* and after that I was blacklisted and never asked back. Except for the money I didn't mind much. I was never very happy out there, and I never stayed long. But I don't need to go into that. Too many people already have.

I met K. at Hollywood and Vine. You meet a different kind of hustler there than you do in the posh bars of Beverly Hills and Bel Air. The boys in the Hollywood and Vine area are cleaner, prettier, nicer. All they sell is their bodies. They tell you the price, and that's it, no haggling.

At the time we met, K. was twenty. He had spent what I presume one would call the formative years of his life in various West Coast orphanages, reformatories, jails, penitentiaries. Had K. been born in a different class in our classless society, he probably would have been handsomely rewarded for the things he did. Perhaps named to a high position in a motion picture studio or, say, the Bank of America. He had on occasion stolen money from people who had more than they knew what to do with. He had forged a few checks. He had from time to time rented out his body. He has a beautiful body.

K. had a good deal of spare time in those various institutions, and while he had read very little poetry, he tried writing some. He thought it was poetry anyway. But was it? . . . I read the poems the second night after we met. I thought that they were superb and ought to be published. When I came back East, as you know, I brought K. with me.

I don't know which interested me more, K.'s poetry or his body. As has so seldom happened in my life, I didn't have to choose.

Now, of course, K. is one of the half dozen best known and critically successful poets in the country. Auden's reputation is quite secure, but K. is good and is getting better.

His readings have become increasingly popular on the campuses. He doesn't drink as much as Dylan did, and his voice isn't as lyrical, but K. knows what to do with his voice and with his body. And he is much prettier than Dylan; he is even prettier than Shelley. . . . A thousand dollars a night is better than ten dollars a night, despite inflation.

I once asked K. if he ever goes back to the Hollywood and Vine area, and he said, "Where's that?"

I don't know if Mrs. K. knows about all the sex on K.'s tours; maybe she doesn't care. I never question the arrangements people have made to make it possible for them to get through the day. The night, actually. Until about 5 p.m., almost anybody can manage. If everything is turned off, you can.

I have no idea what K. has told the missus about our relationship, either. The night he introduced us he said, "George here defended me at a time when my luck had temporarily deserted me." True enough as far as it goes.

The main house in Pittsburgh has forty-five rooms, eight of which are baths. An electric fence, four armed guards. It's just as well K. married the lady; he'd never have been able to break in.

K. and I lived in the same house for eighteen months. Then his first book was published; he started the reading tours, and he started laying everything everywhere, and whatever had been between us was over. No recriminations. I told you. When both of you have trouble keeping awake in each other's presence, it's done with. Ennui, anyone?

K. got back from the city; he had just made his first appearance at the YMHA, and he was flushed with booze, success, and the look of a man well laid. A man who wanted out. A man who had made a new connection.

I said, "K., now that you're rich and famous, I think it might be just as well if we . . ."

He said, "You're not jealous or anything like that, are you?"

I said that I wasn't, that to the contrary I was glad, that his success was what we both had had in mind all along, wasn't it, and so on and so on, and it all sounded true. To my ears it did.

He said, "Well, now that I've got the Cadillac I might just as well start packing. Do you mind if I take the Mark Cross bag?"

"No, love, I bought it for you. Now if you don't mind terribly, I've got to . . ."

The other trouble hurt more.

The first danger signal was the piece in *Confidential*. Of course you're too young to remember *Confidential*. You weren't even in high school yet.

I don't mean to sound rude, but how could anybody who wasn't even in high school in the early 1950s understand my problems?

Confidential was a magazine that dealt exclusively with scandal, and it was scandalous. It was a magazine that nobody admitted buying, but everybody had read it—at her hairdresser's, at his barber's.

The editors of *Confidential* had fags on the brain, fags and reds, and you'd be surprised at how often they found that your fag and your red was the same person, gnawing away at the vitals of the nation. That last was their phrase, not mine. . . . Gnawing away at the vitals. Like me. They claimed that I was both.

It used to be that when awful things happened I'd turn everything off—the electricity, the clocks, the telephones, newspapers, milk, mail, everything. I'd close everything that could be closed and pull down everything that could be pulled down; I'd lock all the doors and windows, and then I'd pull a blanket over my head and stay submerged until the worst of the pain had subsided. A day, a week, a month, whatever.

Then I'd get up, turn on the juices again, and say, "George dear, fairest in the land, you're as good as new." I'd pound myself on the chest and say, "Me Jane. You Tarzan." I'd say, "You're as good as new, Georgette."

But you are never as good as new. I never was, never am. And it isn't only that fatigue becomes a permanent condition of life. It's that a piece of you goes every time. . . . "As George Lionel awoke one morning from uneasy dreams, he found that he had completely disappeared."

Isn't that the way it goes? Went? Not a trace. And when the last appendage goes, it hurts just as much as the first. I know all about disappearing appendages.

A good deal of me went in early August of that year, whatever year it was. We were saving the South Koreans from a fate worse than death. I remember that. And I remember that the week before I was scheduled to appear before The Committee, my phone rang every morning exactly at six, and when I would pick up the phone, there would be the sound of a single inhalation, then a click. Every morning for a week, and every midnight the same thing happened. And then at one and two and three and four and five. And then—it was on a cloudy Monday morning and light showers were predicted for the late afternoon—a man with dark glasses started following me everywhere; the glasses were tinted blue, and so, I think, were the man's eyes. He was young, and he wore a double-breasted suit. They all wear double-breasted suits. Auntie Edgar insists on it. She wears them herself, double-breasted suits and, after work, a Mother Hubbard.

I later asked the FBI man I knew if the telephone calls and the following were unusual. "Of course not," he said. "How else would they break you down for the inquisition? They wanted you nervous, baby. They wanted you jumpy, and you were."

"I'm not going to let you out of my sight until it's over," said Charley. And he didn't. We stayed up very late in the bar of the Willard Hotel, and I got very drunk. Charley took me upstairs and gave me a Seconal. I slept a little, but I don't think he went to bed at all. The next morning he took a couple bennies, but he only let me have one, and he wouldn't let me have a drink. He even kept the door to the bathroom open while I shaved.

And before we went he said, "Dear friend, don't get angry. Whatever you do, don't get angry."

". . . Esteemed colleagues, I am ashamed to say it, but in the little Iowa town where I had the privilege, the privilege and the honor, to be head coach . . . this *pervert* was already known and despised, yes, despised for what she [laughter], he, it, whatever you want to call her [laughter]—despised for what he was and always will be. . . . I don't need to tell you that this limp-wristed *pervert* wasn't exactly a star on the baseball team [laughter and applause]. And I tell you, a boy who doesn't know how to play the great Amer-cin—and I mean Amer-cin—game of baseball is *already* a foil for the commies and the anti-anticommies. . . . I tell you this. I was alert to the menace of communism and perversion, and they went hand in hand [laughter], even in those far-off days. I succeeded in keeping this *pervert* out of the shower when the other boys . . .

"And now the President of the United States wants to send . . . at your expense and my expense . . . And the Almighty alone knows

what *French* shower rooms she . . . he . . . it [laughter] might . . .
I am surprised that the President didn't propose sending one of the
limp-wristed cookie pushers who have taken over the once-glorious
State Department. There are *hundreds,* perchance thousands of perverts in that once-venerable institution, although I am not sure they
all play the piano [laughter]. . . . Mind you, gentlemen, lady, I have
no proof that this piano-playing pervert is a card-carrying . . . but
his conviction, his serving time for *perversion* is in the record and on
the record, and I cannot, I will not allow this day . . .

". . . As for his distinguished attorney, as for Charles McCormick
Payne, the piano player's friend, so-called *friend* [laughter], even
back in the green hills of Iowa, in that long-ago innocent place and
time, there were those among us who described their *friendship* in
a slightly different way [laughter, applause, cheers]. . . .

"Counselor Payne has attempted to make a point of his client's
. . . Yes, that's what she . . . I mean he is called. A *client.* Of his
client's devotion to duty, *so-called* devotion to duty in the Office of
Strategic Services during the Second World War, the Office of *Sub-
versive* Services more like, the Office of *Perverted* Services.

"It is a well-known fact that the OSS was an agency riddled with,
honeycombed with perverts and subverts and, as in the present instance, individuals who were, who are *both* subverts and perverts
[applause]. Counselor Payne makes a point of the alleged fact that
her . . . I mean his [laughter] hands were broken during said service,
an allegation that seems, even if true, and it is far from proven, of
little consequence when we are speaking of a period when hundreds
of thousands of boys who were *men* gave their lives so that . . . Of
course this so-called piano player was in the OSS so called. Who else
prepared the way for the sellout at Yalta, for the perfidy of Alger
Hiss, for the infamy of George Catlett Marshall? . . . And this, *this*
is the limp-wristed, time-serving, criminal-oriented pervert pianist
that the President of the United States wants to send to Paris, France,
as a piano-playing representative of the United States. Representative? Of the United States? Of this once great republic? I say no
[applause]. I say shame [applause]. I say *treason* [applause,
cheers]."

I said, "Yes, I was arrested in Miami, Florida, for a crime against nature. . . . Yes, I was arrested in Los Angeles, California, for sodomy. . . . Yes, I was. . . . Whatever you want me to say, I'll say. Now please excuse me. . . ."

"And you will further agree to withdraw your name . . ."

I said, "I already have."

I think I was the only one who was sick before he stepped down from the witness stand. A few papers printed pictures of that, but most of them didn't, due to the sensibilities of their readers. . . . Oh, I was a Household Word that day all right, and we all know what the word was. I was a Household Whisper. "Don't let Junior see the paper, Bertha. What that boy don't know won't hurt him."

My mother wept that day and many days thereafter, and then she conveniently and thankfully died. My father—there are small blessings—was already dead.

Charley said, "Now you're sure you're all right."

I said that of course I was, and I said . . . well, whatever I said about eternal gratitude. And when I got to New York, I went directly to the apartment, and as I say . . . As I said, my first appearance at Bellevue was on the front page of the *Daily News*; my wrists were already taped when they got the picture of me on the stretcher. And four days later I came here for the first time. Bad penny.

When I got out, my agent called. He said, "We're getting a few cancellations on the concerts, George. Nothing to worry about, though. With a genius of your caliber, we'll weather the storm."

I said, "What the fuck are you talking about? They've signed contracts. They can't cancel."

"Let's not get riled up over anything as of yet. This is not a time for making waves. This is a time for laying low and keeping our ears to the ground on all sides."

I hung up, and then I called him back, but for a week he wasn't in. He had had to go Out There all of a sudden, and the place he was Out There, they'd never heard of the telephone.

Your agent is never around when you're in trouble. All of a sudden it's the morals clause they're worrying about, and it's a girl with enlarged pores who's playing your concert in Cincinnati. She doesn't have to worry about the morals clause.

I'll tell you this. I didn't have a concert anywhere in this country for three years, and when the networks got up their own list, naturally my name was on it. And not only was I no longer asked to appear. For more than *five* years nothing I'd composed was played on radio or television anywhere in this country.

Yes, I cried some, and I still do when I remember. But do you know something? Most people have forgotten it ever happened. Or they deny it ever happened. Or they say, "I'm sure you're exaggerating."

It's like you couldn't find a Nazi anywhere in Germany in the late 1940s and early 1950s.

My agent said, "I think we will have to face the unhappy fact that your career has come to a temporary stalemate, George. It is a major misfortune, and I personally am heartsick, but I am very much afraid, things being what they are, I will have to dispense with you as a client. It is not an easy world, and myself, I am but a cog in the . . ."

They say I tried to kill him, but it is difficult to kill a cog. After which came the first straitjacket, the first state institution, the first shock treatment. They denied the shock treatment, but they lied. They did it all the time, and I lost everything. Even my name went.

I wouldn't describe the place if I could, if I remembered. There was one decent psychiatrist. I saw him fifty minutes a week. His name was Silver, and he was from San Francisco, and he said he had heard me. He said he thought I was good. Superb was the word he used, simply superb. . . . But you people will tell a patient anything to get a reaction.

I don't remember how long I was there; longer than six months, less than a year, I think.

I remember the common room had an out-of-tune piano, and Silver, his name could have been Gold, wanted to get it tuned for me, but I said, Fuck it.

My hands were arthritic, and I couldn't even remember the scales. A girl taught me "Chopsticks." . . . I also played Beethoven's Minuet in G. "Fleecy clouds are drifting by, drifting by, in the sky, in the sky."

There was a boy named Penelope, but we were not lovers. No love anywhere there, not as far as the eye could see, beyond the horizon. Under a queen's chair.

We played poker, I believe it was, and I lost; I was born losing because my label was mislaid, miss maid, and I was queen, night and day and dawning, always queen, never jack, never game. I was an ace in the hole but no love. Never, dove.

We played "Glow little glowworm, glimmer, glimmer." I once saw a Gypsy in an arch in the Alhambra. Can you imagine a Gypsy boy, darkly dusk, near an arch in the Alhambra? Fourteen he was, he said, and I said, You're too young to be fourteen, but he said Juliet was; Jesu is, he said.

His skin was translucent and softer than alabaster. Twelve lions watched me touch him. And the streets from below sound the heard as I touched him. The sky in Granada was blue, but there was no room at the inn for Jesu. I could not take him to my room at the inn. Dirty little alabaster, they told me, and so I left, and Jesu left, and we sat all night under the Gypsy star, loving without room. Waiting for the wise men and the shepherds and the dawn. And then Jesu kissed me, and I left Alhambra and Alabaster and Granada, without a star. *Adios*, said Jesu.

He would be twenty-five by now, dead by now.

I tell you, they are all dead. *Adios. Hola.*

Penelope came at night, called me Dora at night, unwove. Dora was my mother's name. My name was Minerva, but I never ever told. And someplace I knew a boy named Freckles and pubic, and he said, "What about the sissy here?"

We all laughed to see such sport.

Either they had a library or else some ladies came with a bookmobile. It is often ladies with a bookmobile, always gray, never gay. They had Kierkegaard. I'm sure of that. I'd never been much of a reader, my mother's last month's *True Story*, read under a blanket, by flashlight. After I jerked off I'd read. When I jerked off it was either Errol Flynn or there was a movie actor named Richard Cromwell; he was in *Lives of a Bengal Lancer*. He had also sent me an autographed picture, naked from the waist up. . . . My mother never did find that one. I kept it in my music roll. . . . Last month's *True Story*. I always identified with the unwed mother. . . . And there was a novel called *The Constant Nymph*. About a musical family, one of those. I read it over and over and over. The nymph was a pianist named Teresa. I mostly identified with her, although she died in the end, and nobody ever called me constant.

The other novel I read a good deal was about a boy pianist named Jean Christophe, and it was about twelve thousand pages long, and I thought Jean was almost as silly as Elsie Dinsmore. He was always getting into silly scrapes with girls. The girls made him unhappy, and he neglected the piano.

Which is the reason I have never allowed myself to make that mistake. Girls interfere with your practicing.

When I first came upon Kierkegaard—I think I began with the journals—I loved him from the first sentence on: "People understand me so little that they do not even understand when I complain of being misunderstood."

We had things in common, Sören and I; ugliness, glasses to hide behind, a receding chin, a high-pitched, rasping voice. . . . I don't think he was queer, though.

We had this in common, too, Sören and I: "From my earliest youth I was in the grip of a profound melancholy." And, "I have

just returned from a party of which I was the life and soul; wit
poured from my lips; everybody laughed and admired me; but I
went away—and the dash should be as long as the earth's orbit

----

and wanted to shoot myself."

Eventually I got out of the state place. I wasn't what you'd call
cured, but most of the time I was pretty sure what my name was.
. . . They denied it about shock, and I'd swear I was there before
1960. But decades don't change much, not really.

After I started remembering things, the first thing I remembered
was: "Which is harder, to be executed or to suffer that prolonged
agony which consists in being trampled to death by geese?"

I was born knowing the answer to that one.

K., the poet, not Kierkegaard, has, I see, written an inscription
on the flyleaf of the new book: "For G.L., without whom I'd still
be back there somewhere."

K. is a sweet man, boy-man, man-boy; they weren't all killers. . . .
Read the book? Not on your life. Not on my death. I've read my last
poem, especially by former lovers. He might be better than before,
and he might be worse. Either way, for better, for worse, they always end up with women. I'm the only one who . . . No, K.'s book
is my contribution to the library. You could use a good book of
poetry there. Not even any Auden. . . . I can hear them now: "It's
inscribed to G.L. Now who in the world was G.L.? A mistress, no
doubt. Which dark lady, did you say? . . . I understand he left his
second-best bed to his wife, but he had a mistress, too. Isn't *that*
sweet? I hear she was pretty as a picture."

> For I have sworn thee fair, and thought thee bright,
> Who art as black as hell, as dark as night.

No, K. did not write that. Look it up.

❖

I wonder if there was ever anything between Sören and his old buddy Hans. They called Hans "little girl" when he went to school, you know. That must have been just as bad as "sissy." I should think. And Hans liked to make dresses for his dolls. My mother would never let me have a doll. Baseball gloves, Christmas after Christmas after Christmas. And once a ball autographed by Robert Feller, who was whoever he was, and she said, "You could be another Bob Feller if you just put your mind to it, George." Hans liked to play "show." I always liked to play "show." The reason you play "show" is so you can be somebody else, anybody else. . . . Neither Hans nor I ever got to be a baritone.

Why didn't they tell us about all those fruitcakes? What's the big secret? . . . The big trouble is you think you're the only one. The only one who ever lusted after other boys, who couldn't throw or catch a baseball, who would have preferred to play jacks with the girls instead of kick the can with the boys, who hoped for a doll at Christmas instead of a teddy bear.

"How little did I dream of so much happiness when I was the ugly, despised duckling!" I wrote a ballet based on that one. A pretty good ballet, too. They still do it once in a while.

"For George." The skipper of a fishing smack knows his whole cruise before sailing, but a man-of-war gets his orders only on the high seas. "You are a man-of-war. Your old friend, Sören."

26 /

Capriccioso
and
Lamentation

I'm not sure why I'm so depressed today. Maybe the weather. The weather is even more Emily Brontë than it was yesterday. The leaves have deteriorated further. The Puerto Rican boy with green eyes, I swear they were green, is gone. And the prediction is for rain turning into snow. How could one not be depressed?

The letter from Christopher cheered me up for a while. He sent me the clips from the San Francisco newspapers. The reviews of his concert were all raves, and at the end of the Rachmaninoff Third, the audience stood and cheered.

As I am afraid Christopher would say, "Like wow." Christopher, like most members of his generation, is totally inarticulate. But if you can play the Rachmaninoff concerto the way he does, who gives a shit, man? Rachmaninoff said he wrote that concerto for elephants, and by God it takes hands like Christopher's to play it right, big, powerful hands, especially for the *finale alla breve.* . . . Oh, I once could, when I was twenty, before I, like the leaves, started to disintegrate.

There is an interview with Christopher, plus a huge photograph. It doesn't do him justice, but the giggly girl reporter says that Christopher looks more like a movie star than a pianist. And he says, . . .

well, he comes right out and says that he loves me, right there in print. He believes in letting it all hang out. Jesus, if I'd been able to say something like that when I was nineteen . . . Wow . . . How come the kids aren't all schlocked up, like us? No wonder we hate them. . . . Anyway, I'm sure the dear San Francisco ladies who mobbed him after the concert don't think he means he loves me *that* way. . . . But he does, ladies. . . . He also says he's going to make a record with me. He and the philanthropists at Angel Records want him and old George. Look, they want Christopher, and if they have to take old George for one record . . . It's cheap at half the price. Anyway, it's sweet of Christopher to have suggested it, but the answer is no. Not this time around, love.

As for happiness, it has hardly more than one useful quality, namely to make unhappiness possible.

It seemed like such a happy spring, for Charley and me anyway. I didn't see much of Lily. She was working very hard, in school and at Kresge's, studying hard and making enough money to get to Iowa City in the fall.

But for all of us, it was spring of the year we were going to get out; it was the spring Charley won the Extemporaneous Speaking Contest, the spring we went to Chicago. . . . It wasn't all that good, of course. Sweet and sour, gay and melancholy. I guess it's always that way if you know, can bear knowing.

It is bad today, and it will be worse tomorrow; and so on till the worst of all.

That old closet queen Arthur Schopenhauer knew.

In the town that year it was crisis after crisis, juncture upon juncture. First the dishonor of losing to Colo and then the Chicago crisis. . . . So what if Japan invaded China? What did it matter that Germany had taken over Austria? Who was upset when Hitler started cutting up Czechoslovakia? Who except Jews like Rosenberg, "And if he wants to stick that big nose of his into *their* business, he may just get it cut off and then some." I told you we'd get back to noses; everything goes full circle around here.

The spring of 1938 was the first time our high school had ever had an Extemporaneous Speaking Contest. We had a new speech teacher that year, and the contest was his idea.

All of our teachers weren't monsters. Loren Bainbridge was the noble exception. Perhaps there were others, although I doubt it.

Loren was singularly unqualified to survive in our public school system, and he didn't. Everything was wrong with him. Everything. . . . It was his first job. And his last. He had been graduated the previous June from Ohio State, and he was, as it said in the *Times-Dispatch*, laden with honors, scholastic and athletic. . . . Loren Bainbridge. An open-faced young man. Red hair, big, bristly. Ocean-blue eyes that reflected eternal surprise at the duplicity of which man was capable. . . . Loren refused to go to church. He refused to join Rotary. Or Kiwanis. Refused to become an Elk, a Lion, a Moose, an Odd Fellow. No wonder they were out to get him. No wonder he lasted exactly nine months in the town.

Charley and I liked him at once. Naturally. Coach Masterson naturally at once recognized him as a communist and a sissy (I doubt that the coach was familiar with the word *homosexual* or could have pronounced it if he had been) and a troublemaker.

Loren was not a sissy, it turned out. In fact, one of the counts against him was that he was seen coming out of the Tallcorn Hotel in the *morning*. He had bedded down for the night with a lady shoe salesman from Davenport. . . . If he had to be immoral, weren't our local girls good enough for him, for heaven's sake?

Charley and I spent as much time with him as we could, and that was another charge against him. Fraternizing with the students.

I don't remember all the charges against him. Smoking in the boys' was perhaps the most serious. Impudence to Gauleiter Easthook, the principal. Easthook said to Loren, "You don't have any respect for me, do you?" And Loren said back, "No, sir, only contempt." Of course his contract was not renewed, and of course Easthook refused to give him any kind of recommendation. In fact, Principal Easthook said that if he so much as heard of Loren's getting another job in the teaching profession, he would personally see to it that . . . Who calls those gentler times lies, sir.

I'll leave out the sentimental part, which has to do with Charley and me saying good-bye to Loren, loving him; both of us did. Noble. And my God, he was only twenty-three. Forever only twenty-three. No more. His fragile Oldsmobile crashed into a robust ten-ton on the Lincoln Highway somewhere between Independence and Dubuque. The day he left town. They said he died instantly. They said it was a blessing, going quick like that.

The death happened in June. The Extemporaneous Crisis began on an otherwise blue and even somewhat golden day in April.

I should perhaps explain how the contest worked. Each contestant was handed a piece of paper by Loren. On the paper was written a topic of current interest and importance. After which he or she, hopefully with a minimum of foot-shifting, arm-twisting, nose-blowing, throat-clearing, hemming and hawing, and with a maximum of logic and eloquence, was to speak on that topic for between twenty minutes and half an hour.

Eight contestants, and with seven we need bother only briefly. I remember one adenoidal boy whose topic was the recent Italian adventure in Ethiopia. He said, "It was nothing but a bunch of white guys cleaning up on a bunch of jigaboos that didn't even know how to build a nairplane."

In other words, seven of the contestants were mumblers of the inane, of ideas swallowed without being chewed, stomached but not digested. They knew that legs were visibly instituted to have breeches, and we have breeches. They were swellers of crowds, lovers of dogs and cats, haters of people. They were stupid. . . . Unfortunately, there is a limit to human intelligence, but, regrettably, there is no limit at all to human stupidity.

❖

Charley's topic was "Is Communism a Menace?" And it was apparent from the first sentence on that he was the clear winner. Charley was the most eloquent man I have ever heard, anywhere ever. And I am not prejudiced. Even *The New York Times*, July 8, 195–, page 1, column 6, paragraph 4: ". . . Attorney Charles Payne, a well-known civil libertarian, is widely regarded as one of Washington's most urbane, literate . . . Spectators applauded, cheered, and greeted with prolonged laughter Payne's thrusts against Senator . . . At one point, the entire audience in the hearing room rose and began to applaud, after which the hearing was quickly adjourned. . . . On the other hand, it is generally conceded here that despite Payne's eminence and skill, given the current atmosphere in Washington, pianist George Lionel, a lifelong friend of Payne as well as his client, is likely to have a long and arduous time . . . before he . . ."

The subtitle of Charley's speech was "The Unpaved Street," for which I took some credit. One day shortly after we met, I said to Charley about the one black boy in high school, "Do you know, he's cleaner than *anybody*, and I don't see how because they don't have any plumbing on McDowell Street where he lives, and there's only one outhouse for about every five of those shacks, and the street isn't paved, and most of the people, like Eldon Rickets' folks, don't even have electric lights."

Charley said, "Oh, come on now. There aren't any unpaved streets in this town, and you know it."

"Have you ever been on McDowell Street?" Charley hadn't, and we went.

I don't think Charley ever forgot the look of that street or the smell of it or the little boy, a beautiful little blond boy of twelve or thirteen, maybe a brother of Eldon's, who followed us asking for a dime.

Charley gave the boy a dollar bill, and the kid looked at it and said, "What's the matter? This a phony dollar bill? Give me a dime. I don't want no phony buck."

In the Extemporaneous Speaking Contest Charley's closing sentence was: "Wherever there are unpaved streets, wherever there is no electricity, wherever there are hungry children, wherever there are the sick without care, wherever the old are in need, there should and will be a demand for a different, a better society. And if communism is the only alternative, then communism it will be."

I applauded almost as loud and as long as I did the first night I heard Rosenberg play.

Q: Counselor Payne, you were a student at ——— High School in April 1938, were you not?

A: I was physically on the premises if that's what you mean. Under the prevailing circumstances being a student was an impossibility.

Q: Did you or did you not on the eighth day of April of that year say that . . . ?

A: I did not. In the first place, I spoke with some precision and in English; so I couldn't possibly have said that. Such garbled, preposterous misinformation undoubtedly came from the inevitably garbled, always misinformed files of the Federal Bureau of Investigation.

Q: Mr. Payne, are you aware that you are appearing before a subcommittee of the Senate of the United States?

A: To my sorrow, yes, I am aware of that.

Q: Did you or did you not say, "Dirt roads are more of a menace to this country than communism is or ever will be"?

A: I said, sir, among other things, "Wherever there are unpaved streets, wherever there is no electricity . . ." The sentence is somewhat rhetorical, but I was only seventeen at the time.

Q: Mr. Payne, are you now or have you ever been a member of . . . ?

A: Good God, no. I was never that young.

Charley won the contest, but the way the *Times-Dispatch* carried on, you'd have thought Charley had tried to blow up the courthouse, which then and now is a defensible idea. The American Legion demanded an investigation of the local school system. How could Charley ever have *learned* such things? And the other seven extemporaneous speakers extemporaneously said, "You betcha he won. Didn't have nothing to do with what he was talking about, neither. Him and Bainbridge, who if you ask me is half sis himself and may be . . . not to mention Sister Sue herself. . . . You ask me . . ."

And somebody, perhaps Coach Masterson, perhaps Easthook, Tweedledee or Tweedledum, telephoned the nearest office of the FBI, which in those days was in Des Moines. Nowadays, the town having grown as it has, and subversion and perversion exploding faster than the population the way they are, an FBI agent is stationed in the courthouse, in an office behind the malicious larch. The SS man is next door, shaded by a beech. The Gestapo, fifty or a hundred strong, is in the town hall.

Later that long ago April Charley went to Des Moines. I don't remember, if in fact I ever knew, what he talked about there, but he won. . . . Was the town delighted at the honor, pleased with his success? Was he considered the conquering hero? . . . "Naturally he won. Anybody could of if they'd just had Master Payne's advantages, and who knows what money greased whose . . . ? And anyway, all he had to do was *talk*. I been talking all my life, and nobody writ me up in the *Register* or the *Gazette* or anything like that."

Shakespeare, Madam, is obscene, and, thank God, we are sufficiently advanced to have found it out! If we must have the abomination of stage plays, let them at least be marked by the refinement of the age in which we live.

The next crisis had to do with whether or not Charley should go to the National Extemporaneous Speaking Contest in Chicago, and the whole thing took up a lot more space in the *Times-Dispatch* than Germany taking over Austria. . . . Earlier that year the state legislature had increased the appropriation for pig research at the college in Ames. At the same time the legislature decided that no more of the taxpayers' money was to be wasted ". . . for the participation in nonathletic events taking place outside the sovereign state . . . this specifically excludes the use of moneys for . . ." among other things, the National Extemporaneous Speaking Contest. The *Times-Dispatch* couldn't have been happier. ". . . while, despite his radical, not to say communistic . . . young Payne's victory in Des Moines was, nevertheless, and . . . in more prosperous times the state could quite possibly and with justice afford to support such fringe activities as extemporaneous . . ."

"I cannot speculate, and I cannot reason, but I can see and hear."

Finally Charley decided to pay his own way to the contest, and one exuberant Thursday afternoon in late May he said to me, "Why don't you come along? You might as well be there to witness my sure defeat, and for short periods, Chicago is quite bearable. Besides, we're going to graduate in a few weeks, after which anything may happen, so let's have a weekend in the windy city."

I said that I'd love to but couldn't possibly afford it; thanks anyway.

"I'll pick up the tab. They've finally settled my grandfather's estate, and I'm rolling in money. Billions. Trillions. Come on. I need your moral support."

My mother said, "In many ways, I'm against it; your eyes have always been bigger than your stomach, George, which is one of your many troubles. And it's never a good idea to live beyond your means no matter who is paying for it, which if Franklin Roosevelt would only bear in mind, we would not at this very moment be spending our way down the reckless road to national bankruptcy. . . . On the other hand, a journey to Chicago could turn out to have certain educational advantages, not to mention the opportunity to further your friendship with . . ."

"Why don't you start packing?" said my father.

Forty-eight speakers in Chicago, and Charley, whose topic was "Is Socialism Inevitable?" ("Yes, if capitalism doesn't work, and at the moment it doesn't seem to be") won second place. The first-place winner was a rotund boy from Portland, Oregon, whose blank eyes were almost hidden behind enormous, thick-lensed glasses; he spoke about the Ruhr Valley. I cannot remember what he said about it, what there was or is to say about it, but he said it solemnly and slowly and without enthusiasm. Two of the judges, both full professors from the University of Chicago, split their votes. The third judge, a lawyer who was on some kind of New Deal board or commission in Washington, cast the deciding vote for the Oregon boy. Later, he said to Charley, "Your speech had a good deal of wit and bite and originality in it, and as pure rhetoric was . . . much superior, and the logic was . . . However, these are serious times, and . . ."
The rotund boy, still wearing glasses, once made the keystone speech at a national convention of a political party. I never know which is which. . . . It could have been the same speech, slow and solemn, so slow and solemn that he was nominated for the Vice Presidency, and for all I know he was elected. . . .

That night Charley and I went to a play, my first play ever, unless you counted the nonsense that went on in the high school auditorium Back There, and I never did. The play was A Doll's House, and Ruth Gordon was the lady, and I loved it and her almost as much as I loved Errol Flynn. Differently, I suppose, but is it? Love is love, and there's so little of it around, it doesn't really matter whether it's a man, a woman, or a goat. It's the ones who can't love who worry me, particularly since they're in charge of it all. Have they always been? Don't the lovers ever win?

Charley and I had adjoining rooms at the Palmer House, which I thought was surely the most elegant hotel in the world, and at breakfast, eggs Benedict, also for the first time, and I thought that if

I could just stay in a grand hotel and have eggs Benedict for breakfast every morning, I would . . . But I did, and I didn't.

Later, we went to the Art Institute and, as I had at the play, I made up my mind not to forget anything; I had to remember it all, every detail, so that I could tell my father.

I did remember most of it and described it for him, and what he said was beautiful. I thought so then and still do. He said, "There are so many beautiful and exciting and wonderful things in the world, and you must see all of them. Being bored ought to be against the law."

Well, there you are. I've seen most of the wonders of the world, and I was bored most of the time. Kept yawning . . . Nothing ever lived up to expectations. Especially me, I guess.

After lunch, I forget where but remember it as being elegant, Charley said, "You want to go out to —— with me?" I said, "Sure." I didn't ask why. I never asked Charley why about anything.

I'm not sure if I knew then that the campus we visited was where Charley's mother had spent the early years of her life. We walked around for a while, pretty girls and beautiful boys, looking secure, looking nearly serene, looking confident. Suffering no visible pain.

I looked at Charley, and he shook his head and shrugged. I think what he meant was that he and I weren't like that and never would be, and it would seem that we certainly were not, but then one wonders. Did anything in *their* lives live up to expectations? Even come close? Is anybody ever what he had in mind being?

Some of those secure-looking kids are still around, in their mid-fifties now, those who have survived the killings public and private, the debasements, the disappointments.

Still around, and if they haven't seen The Joke by now, I'm afraid it's too late. If you had a choice, would you want to be born? Would anybody? Why?

It was a small campus, neat, the requisite wide sidewalks and green grass and the ugly pink brick buildings. We went to the house that somebody told us was where the college president lived. A

pleasant enough white clapboard house with green shutters. A neat
front lawn on which some years before there had been those vagrant
ashes, the fleeting remains of dreams and paintings and music. As
I say, I don't think I knew about that then. . . . I do remember that
as we stood at the edge of the lawn I looked up and saw that Charley had tears in his eyes. I had never seen him cry before, and it
happened only once again that I saw.

He was crying, and he said, "My mother is a very sad lady," and
he said, "Let's go."

I did not yet know that his mother had begun, as they said in the
town, to "act funny." Or that his father seemed always to be seized
by melancholy. Or that his father and mother went for days, weeks
sometimes, without speaking to each other.

I don't think they hated each other or even blamed each other for
what had happened. I think it was that they were unable to share
their despair. Does that make any sense? It's as close as I can come
to explaining, but I doubt that it's very close.

I used to think some people were luckier than others, but I'm
not even sure of that any more. . . . As old Herodotus said, no matter what baubles they hand out along the way, no matter what
trinkets we knee our way to and grab, in the end we all utterly
perish. Nobody goes out whistling. No matter what they say. Nobody I ever knew has, and I'm an old party, baby, old, old, old.
Been to bed with every Tom and every Dick and every Harry.
Loved them all for at least a few seconds, and everybody was the
same body. I realized that ten or fifteen years ago. I noticed then
that this was where I came in, and unless it was Errol Flynn, I
never sat through a feature more than once.

He's dead, too.

On the train going back to the town I said to Charley, "You're going to be head of it all, president of everything."

And Charley said, "If that's the case, why did I place second?"

"For God's sake, Charley, you were better than that knucklehead from Oregon, and you know it. Even the lawyer from Washington admitted it."

"Yes," said Charley, "I was better, but I didn't win, and maybe that's what it's all about."

"What what's all about?"

"Everything."

"I don't know what you're talking about."

"You will," said Charley.

I'll tell you what else he said, Herodotus, not Charley. He said, "Nothing in human life is more to be lamented than that a wise man should have so little influence."

27 /

Farewells

Did I mention what Renoir said? Two hours before he died he said, "I think I am beginning to understand."

They wouldn't let him live after that. He might tell. . . . It took Buddha a lifetime to find out, and he said, "Seek refuge only in the truth; seek refuge only in yourself." Of course. I always knew you couldn't trust anybody, not anybody. What I didn't know is that it's not whom shall I love that you should ask yourself. It's whom shall I not love? . . . Whom shall I not love? Think of the pain I'd have been spared, we'd be spared. It's not the people who reach out to embrace you that you have to watch out for. It's that in you that makes you want it that causes the trouble. It's the seeking in others what can only be found in yourself that mucks us all up. I guess that's what old Buddha was getting at. . . . I was always dependent, incomplete. Plato knows. . . . But is everybody?

Explain this.

Trish was the one Charley should have loved. Cecily the one whom he should not have. Cecily is the killer shark. I think it's husband number five now, five or six. Cecily, supercunt. And bright Charley. Shining Charley. Golden Charley. I guess. . . . The professor in law school, I forget his name, the one who was later on the Supreme Court, said that Charley had the best brain, I guess *mind* was the word he used, that the professor had ever encoun-

258

tered. . . . Oh, Charley was a very smart fellow. A sure winner. All three of us were smart enough. Lily, too, I mean. . . . Apparently being bright has nothing much to do with it.

Charley and Trish met at a dance while he was going to law school. She was secretary to one of the deans, if they have deans at Yale. A very nice girl. Tall, long-legged, that New England well-bred look, glistening, except that Trish was from San Francisco. Not a raving beauty, not a raving anything; Cecily raved. Trish was pretty, nice and pretty. Kind. A suggestion in her voice of an actress I used to like, Margaret Sullavan; not as throaty.

Trish. She and Charley went together, dated, had a romance, whatever, for about ten months, until just before he finished law school, until just after he met Cecily Broadmoor. . . . They'd come to the city, dance at the Plaza, go to the theater, ride in Central Park, what you do, did when you're young and in love. I thought they were in love. I thought they'd get married and have lots of long-legged children who'd look like the best of both of them, which would be very fine-looking indeed. And I'd be this distinguished older man; nobody would ever talk about *that,* and I'd come to dinner on Sunday and on Thanksgiving and Christmas, always with presents, and they'd call me Uncle George, and we would all . . .

Trish called from Grand Central, and I knew at once that something was wrong. Something had happened to her voice. Her voice had died. She asked if she could meet me, and I said sure, and we met at a ticky-tack bar near the studio, and she wanted a double Scotch. . . . Her eyes were puffy; her lipstick was streaked, and her hair looked as if it had not been combed. She said, "Forgive the way I look. I've been . . . oh, hell, I've been crying my eyes out." She said, "I don't usually do that. To use one of my mother's most quoted but least practiced expressions, I don't approve of people who wear their hearts on their sleeves. She, poor dear, never wore hers anyplace else."

She finished the first Scotch, said she'd have a second, a single this time. Said, "I'm going back to San Francisco. Maybe I never should have left. Maybe the climate here is wrong for me." Said, "It's all off between Charley and me. Maybe it was never on, but now it's off. Over and out." Said, "You've heard about Cecily Broadmoor."

"Heard what about Cecily Broadmoor?"

"She and our boy are engaged to be wed."

I said that Charley didn't even know Cecily Broadmoor, assuming she meant *the* Cecily Broadmoor. "Is it *the* Cecily Broadmoor?"

"The one and only, and he only met her Friday week. Her father came to New Haven to set up a chair, whatever you do about a chair of higher learning. Anyway, he brought along Cecily, and Charley met her and fell in love. Head over heels. It was all very whirlwind, and now they are to be wed. She's a very fast worker. Except that isn't fair. I haven't even met her; she may be the dearest, sweetest . . . She's always doing good. She is a doer of good. It's in all the papers all the time."

Close to tears, "Anyway, since the martyr's role is not for me, having spent a lifetime watching my mother give a star performance of it, I am going back to San Francisco and marry my orthodontist. Don't ask. I'm sure you were about to. Ask if I love him. Well, the answer is I love Charley, but I like the orthodontist. He's a good sort, and he's bonny, and we'll have many bonny children and live . . . peacefully ever after. It won't be exciting, though. He knows nothing of Immanuel Kant or Oliver Cromwell or Oliver Wendell Holmes the younger or Cato, and while he will suffer, it will not be in the Grecian manner. He will tell me jokes, but with him I shall never laugh at the sadness of life. But there. I am going on."

I took Trish's hand and kissed it, and I said, because what else is there to say, ever, said, "I'm sorry." Said, "This head lady I'm seeing now, and it isn't going to work, and we both know it; we both know we're just pretending. She said of recent date, 'Seek out the dull people; avoid the neurotics. It's not as exciting, perhaps, but in the long run . . .' She didn't crack a smile when she said it, either."

"How true. And now write me five hundred words on how to tell your friends from the vegetables. Or, if you prefer, 'How I spent my summer vacation.'" Said, crying, "Oh, goddamn everything to hell anyway and goddamn that rich bitch. Except maybe she isn't a bitch. And the real question is, do I want her to be or don't I? I mean, since I'm not going to have Charley, do I want him to be happy or miserable? I hope the former, but I'm not at all sure, and I never will be." Said, "Now kiss me on both cheeks so my face won't get lopsided, and I will say fare-thee-well, and I'm glad I knew Charley, and I'm glad I knew you. You, too, are a good sort, very good really, better than you know, better than you want to know." Said, "Nothing ever works out, does it?"

Trish's bags were at the station; she was going home, going to San Francisco by train; she said she needed those long days on the train to sort herself out.

She wouldn't let me walk her to the station, though. She hated good-byes, just as Charley did, just as I do. She kissed me. She said, "Beware of the executioners, Dimitri." Trish thought the "Lament" sounded like Shostakovich, which was sweet of her but was wrong. "Beware of the executioners. They are everywhere among us."

I said, "Your children will have beautiful teeth; the orthodontist will see to that, and these days that's a lot. Maybe that's everything." I said, "He'd better be nice to you. I'll know if he isn't."

Trish said, "Finish the 'Lament,' love. It's important."

Then she got in a taxi, and she waved good-bye to me, and the taxi drove off.

Years later, maybe ten, maybe twelve, Trish and the orthodontist came to see me after a concert in San Francisco, and he was bonny enough, red hair and one of those ageless, impish faces, very clean, competent-looking hands, orthodontist's hands, and it all seemed fine. He was tender with Trish, and I felt sure tender with the four children with perfect teeth. It looked like a storybook romance, but how can you tell in an evening? A month? A year? A lifetime?

When Trish and I were alone for a moment, I said, "Do you ever think of Charley?" And Trish said, "Sometimes; no more than is healthy, I think. But sometimes. And I read about him and am proud." She did not ask about Cecily, and I was grateful for that, because what would I have said? I did say, "Are you happy?" And she said, "Happy enough for any good purpose."

And then the orthodontist came back, and I could see that he probably knew nothing at all about Cato.

I'll get to Cecily tomorrow, if there is one, have one. Someone is knocking at the door, but I have it double-locked. Everything is going downhill. You've taken away the Puerto Rican boy with his green lies and filled the yard with fruitcakes and dykes, and some of them are screaming their heads out, lungs in, and I hope they do both. . . . I once tried to cut my wrists with the jagged edge of a broken piano key; it didn't work, of course. Is it because I didn't really want to get out? You keep saying that. . . . Every morning Pablo Casals plays two Bach fugues and preludes. Every mourning. If only my grandfather had left us a straight cello. I'd be immortal by now. . . . Except the last time I was here there were bells. The bells rang, and you knew it was time for dinner, and it was five minutes before the lights would go out, and a bell rang before they shocked you. Dr. Gold rang a silver bell, and you went to him. And it was like the Kingdom of Hell. . . . But without bells, how do you ever know?

You are certainly aware that I do not allow clocks in this room. That is the way it has been in every room since I murdered my aunt's cuckoo. . . . I was never allowed a cock when I was in the Office of Sissy Subversion. Or a watch. No ticking, no tocking. And for years after I was allowed out I couldn't sit in front of a door that was open, closed, locked, unlocked. They broke open the door before they broke open my hands. . . . And in France that day a large, brave American soldier observed my then tattered beret, and he said, "Parlez-vous français?"

I said, "A little, but I'm a lot better at English."

❖

I don't remember when I died. Days ago, weeks ago, months, hours. I died, and sooner or later the body starts to putrefy, but you have a hard on when you die. We all do, sissies and cowards, too, every single penis owner among us does, and then the putrefaction begins. . . . But I don't know if it's day or night. Since you've painted all the windows black, it is impossible to tell. . . . And why, if I'm dead, can't I die? Why must I breathe through a broken piano key for all of eternity?

Charley never said good-bye, you know. He said, "I'll see you," which he had never said before, but I didn't notice. I said, "Sure," and then Charley hung up, and he went out to the three-car garage, and he took out the Porsche, and he drove out to Rock Creek Park and put the .45 in his mouth. . . . Maybe it would have turned out that way no matter what. You never know, never ever know, and I doubt that it does much good to waste time trying to figure it out, because if you do begin to understand, you die in two hours, with or without a clock or a cock or a watch. You go either way, any way. People said of Charley's life, death and breath, what a waste, they said, and maybe it was, and maybe it wasn't. It's sad, though. . . . A woman I once loved said, "We must not mistake a disappointment for a tragedy." Maybe Charley was a little of both. Maybe we all are. . . . If everything had . . . If his mother hadn't . . . If his father hadn't . . . If he hadn't married Cecily . . . If Sandra hadn't . . . But where does that kind of thinking get you? . . . I wish you hadn't painted the windows black. I wish it would be spring again, but I've had my last spring. Winter, summer, fall . . . I never stopped falling, couldn't stop falling.

28 /

Toccata for Brass

We live at the mercy of a malevolent word. A sound, a mere disturbance of the air, sinks into the very soul sometimes.

Charley called a few days after Trish went back to San Francisco, and he told me that he had met Cecily Broadmoor and that they were engaged. He asked me to come to a party in New Haven to meet her. She'd taken a house there. I said congratulations, and . . . I said I'd come to New Haven.

What I knew about Cecily Broadmoor was this. Her father was Victor Broadmoor, and Victor Broadmoor, who had been on Wall Street, whatever that means, had a good deal of money, not a lot, not rich rich but rich enough so that there was a big place near Pawling, a town house in the East Eighties, and when Cecily got that age, she would have come out. Instead she gave the money that would have been spent to some charity. There was a lot in the papers about that, and a few years later when she and her father started the Broadmoor ballet, a good deal was written about that.

It's a good ballet company, too, not as good as George Balanchine's company, nobody's is; first rate, though. I give her that.

It was said that all of the male dancers had to sleep with her father before they were hired. Maybe, maybe not. He had seemed to me to be a voracious man. Voracious, wanting to absorb, obtain, consume, possess everything, including boys, maybe girls, too. I really don't know. Or care. . . . I had met him briefly before the war, my generation's war. A man who then had what I thought was the most beautiful town house in New York used to entertain a group every Sunday afternoon, all men. I was often one of the group. Because the host liked me and because I sometimes played for them.

Victor Broadmoor came twice, a heavy man, I thought, heavy in all ways, and both times he brought a Spanish boy named Rodriguez who came from Seville and was exquisite-looking. . . . In those days Victor Broadmoor had a subcabinet post in the Roosevelt administration, and during one campaign, I think 1940, maybe '44, he was a treasurer of the Democratic party. He was considered a liberal, a word that has always eluded me, was a member of the board of directors of the American Civil Liberties Union, something or other in the Ethical Culture Society, a director of the Urban League, the Metropolitan Museum. And so on.

As I say, he came twice to the Sunday afternoons, and in addition to the heaviness I thought he was ridiculous. The first afternoon when he was introduced to me he said to our host, "Is he safe?" I thought he meant was I contagious. The host said, yes, I was perfectly safe, and I was allowed to shake Victor Broadmoor's hand, which was damp. I am allergic to moist palms. Broadmoor said, "I have to be careful. A man in my position has to watch his step. You must not mention meeting me here, under these circumstances, not to anyone."

I said, "Mr. Broadmoor, I've spent my whole life not mentioning you, and I see no reason at all to change."

He said, "You are an impertinent young man, and I shall . . ."

I walked away.

Later I was talking to Rodriguez, whose English was limited, and Victor Broadmoor came over, glaring and perspiring. To the boy he said, "We're leaving." And to me, "I advise you to keep your hands off him." I said, "Broadmoor, you are a damn fool and an oaf. Or am I being redundant?"

He didn't hit me; he got very red, and he put that plump, damp hand on Rodriguez's slim shoulder, and I felt sorry for Rodriguez, and they left. . . . The next time, maybe it was two more times, Rodriguez smiled at me, but he didn't speak. Broadmoor did neither. . . . Rodriguez had a very sweet smile.

> The power of one fair face makes
> my love sublime, for it has weaned
> my heart from low desires.

So much for what I knew about Victor Broadmoor, still big in the Democratic party, still on all those worthwhile boards and commissions, still a speaker at bleeding-heart dinners.

As for Cecily, I'd seen her picture in the papers from time to time, at this museum, that opening, the other concert, and she always made an appearance when the ballet opened at City Center, made a speech. Like her father, Cecily was, as Trish said, a doer of good, comfortable good, the kind of good that would never get her in any trouble with the committees in Washington, and it seemed to me that she was always sure to have a photographer around. But there. I was prejudging, and if Charley liked her, loved her, she must be okay. I wanted very much for Charley to have a good marriage. Truly I did. . . . I knew that Cecily had been married twice before, but I didn't consider that a count against her. In that area I judge not.

In any case, that's the way I remember feeling on the way to New Haven. I didn't know whether or not Victor Broadmoor would be at the party. I hoped not. Had he mentioned meeting me to his daughter? And anyway, how much did she know about what I suppose you'd call the dark side of her father's life? . . . I never told Charley that Cec's father and I had known each other, not before or after the evening I'm talking about now. It wouldn't have made any difference, though. At least I don't think it would have. But you can never be sure. . . . I don't think my silence was because of the threat, but I can't be sure of that, either.

❧

Cecily's house was in an alley, a small house, no more than twelve by twenty, I'd say, four stories high. Cecily herself met me at the door, and she kissed me on the lips. There are strangers who do that. She stepped back to examine me, the way, I felt, she might have examined a dubious stallion or a black Angus of uncertain ancestry that had, uninvited and unwelcomed, arrived at the place near Pawling. She said, "I'm not at all surprised." I said, "Neither am I." And I hadn't then and haven't now the slightest notion what either of us meant.

I'd seen all those photographs of Cecily, but photographs never really help me much. For me it's the face and the body in action, the way people handle themselves, and the voice. I believe I've already said that I couldn't possibly love anybody who didn't have a pleasant voice, or wasn't shy. . . . A small woman, short, no more than five four. Hair cut short, mouse brown, defiantly so, I felt, as if to tell the world that she could, of course, have exotic and wonderful things done to her hair, but being Cecily Broadmoor, she had chosen not to do so. She had large brown eyes, too large for the rest of her face. The eyes suggested, though only faintly, a hyperthyroid condition. They suggested that she was forever on the verge of hysteria and something more dangerous than that. To me they did. But that is probably hindsight. . . . A slight cast in the left eye that might for some have been attractive. Small, straight nose. High cheekbones. A dimpled chin that she always kept tilted upward, I believe with the mistaken impression that when viewed from above the angle of the chin added to her height. Fashionably thin, but it was not a boy's body. Her thighs were a bit thick, perhaps from all that walking; she did a lot of walking. And riding. And hunting. Blood sports. . . . Her mouth was unfortunate, too long and too thin. She wore no makeup; never.

It was the voice that upset me most, too high-pitched, too contained. It was the voice of a peevish little girl. I thought, think. . . . Her movements were slow, and they were always studied. Nothing casual about Cecily, nothing relaxed. No spontaneity. As I've said, we all make ourselves up, but Cecily Broadmoor had done the making up early on, once and for all. She had constructed around her a total, intricate structure, and I always felt that if so much as one brick were removed, one nail, total disaster would result for Cecily and for all those who had ever been around her, who had ever once passed in front of her or behind her, however briefly. I have seldom, perhaps never, been so right.

I said congratulations, and she said, "Charles has told me all about you, and there needn't be any secrets between us. I believe in the defense of all minority groups. My father was one of the founders of the American Civil Liberties Union." Already it was time to go; it was past time; but I stayed. I never learned when to leave the party.

Cecily introduced me to the other guests. The kind of people you meet in such places at such times, the Household Names from New York and Washington, and those who were still working on it. Some faculty members and students from Yale, a few of whom I'd met when I was in New Haven for a concert, and we said that we were glad to see each other again. A few anxious young men and women, the kind one always encounters at the gatherings of the rich, the guests of wealth. And the aging, who had long ago given up all hope of any of it rubbing off, but their names were still on a list, and the Broadmoor liquor and food were plentiful and what better way to fill up an otherwise empty afternoon and an empty stomach?

Charley was talking to a senator with a large body, white hair worn long. Dressed the way senators dressed in those days. A morning coat and striped trousers. He had on his public voice. There was a spot of egg yolk on the front of his pleated shirt and a coffee stain shaped, or so I convinced myself, like an American eagle.

I didn't hear what the senator said, but Charley said, "I'm afraid that's nonsense, sir, and dangerous nonsense at that."

The senator, who looked as if he had high blood pressure, said, "Young man, it has taken me thirty years to reach certain fundamental conclusions, of which that is one."

Charley smiled and said, "Sir, the length of time it took you to come to a wrong decision is interesting but unimportant. I've never been one of those who felt that experience is a great teacher."

Cecily said, "Isn't Charles wonderful?" and I said, "I'm fond of Charley, but I guess I must not be much of a political animal because I have never understood why saying what you think is anything more than should be expected."

Cecily smiled in a way that reminded me of her father when he frowned, and she said, "Would you like to look at the house?"

I have already said that the house was small, and I didn't think it was attractive. Cecily said it was the oldest, maybe she said one of the oldest houses in New Haven, and she told me the names and gave me the full biographies of several people who had lived there. Cec was, I imagine still is, a compulsive talker. Words oozed from her, poured from her, spilled from her. They never stopped, and they could not be curbed or dammed. They could only be endured. And of course Cec never listened. . . . I've known one or two other people like that, one a man, so it isn't totally a female complaint, unending talkers. There is simply no explaining it. Useless even to try. . . . Do they know it, do you suppose? Do bores ever know they are bores? . . . Am I?

I remember that the house had a museum feel about it, a museum smell, too, and for some reason I was reminded of the joyless few hours I once spent in the Adams house in Quincy. I thought on that day not of John Adams or of John Quincy but of poor Henry, that narrow, hating man whose only real talent was for fawning on the rich and corrupt. I thought of the woman he had helped drive insane, and I thought of the autobiography and of Henry at three holding onto his grandfather's hand, already knowing that he had on him the mark of Cain and a disturbing lack of distinction. I thought, That's too young to know.

After we had finished with the third floor of the house, Cecily told me my opinion of it, favorable, and then she said, "My father is very anxious to meet you. He's heard you play, and he thinks you're wonderful, and so do I."

Okay. That solved one problem. Officially, Victor Broadmoor and I had never met.

He was standing at the window of a small, overfurnished room on the fourth floor. The window was open, and in the alley below some boys were shouting obscenities at each other. Victor Broadmoor was smiling. I wasn't sure whether he was smiling at the sight of the boys —I couldn't see how they looked—or at what they were saying.

Cecily introduced me, and Victor Broadmoor shook my hand; no change there, still damp, damper if anything. "We'll excuse you," he said to his daughter.

"But he hasn't even had a drink yet."

"I'll give him a drink," said her father, and after Cecily had excused herself, he said to me, "I understand you're a vodka man." Had I drunk vodka in 1940? I couldn't remember for sure, but I don't believe I drank much of anything in those days. I wanted to keep a clear head, unlike now, when the more muddled I am, the better. In those days I'd done certain exercises every morning when I got out of bed, usually at five-thirty, and there were the finger exercises, and I was practicing as many as ten hours a day, in addition to the lessons. What's more, I tried never to look in a mirror. I had heard that Toscanini never did, presumably for different reasons.

Dozens of bottles of liquor and ice and glasses on the round table in the small, round room. Delicate glasses, green. Beautiful. Victor Broadmoor made me a very strong vodka tonic, and he did not speak while he worked. He had always struck me as someone whose mind focused on one subject at a time, only one, and so far as I know, the only subjects that interested him much were his daughter—he loved his daughter, no question of that—his daughter, money, politics, and boys.

Victor Broadmoor had not physically improved with the years. He was now monstrous, and his beard and mustache, which he had worn when I first met him, had turned from brown to dirty gray, and they were larger and more untidy than I remembered. He had a great many chins that decreased in size as they cascaded down his oily neck. Several stomachs seemed to be competing for the same space, one reaching almost to his knees.

The pudgy hand pushed the drink in my direction, and I took it without touching Victor Broadmoor. He looked at me from behind the small, dismal eyes, and he said, "You remind me of someone I knew briefly a long time ago." I said, "How's Rodriguez, Mr. Broadmoor? Or have there been so many boys since him that you've forgotten him?" He said, "I assume this is a matter you have discussed with Charles Payne." I drank, said nothing at all. Broadmoor said, "Is Charles bisexual? I have had him thoroughly investigated, and the agency found no evidence of it, but you of all people would know."

I finished the vodka and put down the glass. I said, "Go fuck yourself, Mr. Broadmoor."

"I have plans for Charles," he said, "and if you do anything at all to interfere with them, I'll have you killed."

I closed the door behind me, softly closed the door behind me. I didn't for a moment doubt that Victor Broadmoor meant what he said or that, if he wished, he could have me killed. I'd be an easy victim. ". . . well-known . . . found stabbed this morning in a Times Square hotel. Police said . . ."

The cost would be remarkably low, and it might even be deductible.

I walked downstairs, trembling. You'd think I'd have gained a certain immunity to fear during all those months, often alone, in occupied France. But I didn't. I was terrified from the day I went to the place near Washington where I met The Colonel until the dubious afternoon I left. I was terrified the first time I jumped out of a plane and the last time and every time in between, was terrified the night I jumped into the darkness near —— in France, until the morning the immaculate blond lieutenant ordered them to start in on my hands. The lieutenant asked if I knew Horowitz. He spoke perfect English, and he had quite a large collection of records. He'd heard of me. . . . How did he know my name? He asked, and I told him. Nobody else's, but I told him my own. . . . And all the nurses terrified me during all the months in all the hospitals, and all the doctors, and the more I found out about how little they'd found out about the human interior, the more terrified I got. All surgeons should be put to death, slowly and painfully.

There must have been seventy people in the room on the second floor when I got back. A boy named Federico was playing the piano. I knew him, and I knew how bad a pianist he was. There were, however, compensations. Federico was very tall and very brown and very handsome. He was studying pharmacy, paid for by an older man interested in pharmaceutical science and in Federico. . . . In this case, this single case, the story does have a happy ending, did the last time I knew. Federico was manager of a very popular drugstore in the Murray Hill district. Aging ladies from the few remaining brownstones in the area and sissies from miles around. They come because Federico is still good to look at and because he supplies them with a variety of pills without bothering about such nonsense as a prescription. . . . I walked over to the piano. "They haven't yet arrested you for disturbing the peace?" Federico said, "I have been busted only once, and not on that charge." I said, "How did you bamboozle your way into this circus?" "The master thinks I am good." "As a musician? He may be rich, but he is without taste." "I believe he has other things in mind for later," said Federico, "but I have brought my track shoes, and in high school I did well in the fifty yard dash." "How much is he paying you?"

"Fifty dollars," said Federico, "and I have made it clear it is only for playing the piano. He is not to my taste as a person. You know what tune he likes best? I have already played it six times."

I knew; I remembered. That first afternoon Victor Broadmoor had made a request of me, and I had said, "Under no circumstances." I said to Federico, "The master's favorite song is the immortal 'Why Do I Love You?'"

"You have been cheating," said Federico, and as punishment, he started playing the loathsome song again, loud and clear and off key. By this time the senator and several other people were in a mood and condition to sing.

Federico said, "I play loud, and as you can see, that is better than being good."

"Only among gringos."

Federico laughed, and Cecily Broadmoor, who had been standing behind us, said, "Do you two know each other?" I said, "From time to time." She said, "I'm not at all surprised." And I said, wishing I hadn't, "Have you ever been surprised, dear heart, in all your whole life through?"

Cecily started to say . . . but instead she said, "How did you and Papa get along? Did you have a splendid little chat?"

"Splendid. We're practically asshole buddies."

And she said, "You people always have a vicious tongue, don't you, that and a certain surface flashiness."

I said, "I've had a simply splendid time at your wake, Miss Foxcroft of whatever year it was. It gives me renewed faith in the American Civil Liberties Union."

"I was so hoping we could be friends."

"No, you weren't, honeybee, not ever."

I went to where Charley was being admired, and said, "Don't let me interrupt you, but hello and good-bye. I've got to get back to the city."

Charley said, "But you just got here."

"I know, and I'm sorry I can't stay, but this thing came up at the last minute, and I've got to get back."

"I'll drive you to the station," said Charley.

Cecily, who oddly enough was standing nearby, said, "Do you really think you ought to, darling? You are the guest of honor, and I could call a taxi." Said it softly, soft as silk; the voice-raising didn't come until later. To me, softly, silkily, "Robert, the driver, is picking up some other people. Otherwise he'd take you."

"Of course. I'll take a cab." Of course, of course, of course, nodding, nodding, nodding.

"I won't be long," said Charley. "Why don't you come with us? It'll only take a minute."

"And abandon our guests?" still softly, like little cat's feet.

"Most of them are too blind drunk to notice."

"Darling, that's not very kind."

"I'm sorry." A forehead kiss. "I'll be right back."

Cecily adjusted a shroud and put on a smile of martyrdom, both of which she was to wear constantly, although it was years before Charley noticed.

"The senator in particular. He's rather important, and he came all the way from Washington just to meet you."

"He's a corrupt horse's ass, and he's drunk, and his coming all the way from Washington was a waste of both our times, and if that's rude, it happens also to be true." And then Charley, who was a sensitive man, kissed Cecily again and said, "I'm terribly sorry, and I'm grateful to you, but I don't like these aging liberals."

And Cecily said, "Darling, the senator was one of Franklin Roosevelt's earliest and closest advisers. If it hadn't been for him and *aging* Bob Wagner, we wouldn't have a wages-and-hours law."

"We'll talk about it later," said Charley. "You sure you won't come?"

The bride gave him a Judas kiss and said she would not. She said, "Do hurry then." And to me, with the smile of an undertaker's assistant, "I'm so glad you could come. Next time we'll have a long, long talk."

As Charley and I left, Federico smiled at me and because of that and because I was leaving anyway, I forgave him for what he was doing to the piano. Victor Broadmoor had his hand on Federico's shoulder, and he, too, was smiling.

The next time I saw him I asked Federico what had happened later that night, and he said, "I had never seen a hundred-dollar bill before, but also I had never seen so ugly a man, and so I put on my track shoes."

On the way to the station Charley said, "Well?"

I said that it certainly was a charming house.

"What did you think of Cec?"

"We hardly had a chance to talk."

"She likes you very much; she said the minute you met she knew that the two of you were going to be friends."

I said, "Good." And when we were in front of the station Charley said, "They want me to join . . ." mentioning the name of New York's and Washington's most distinguished law firms. "Victor and Cecily know them all, and they've done a lot of talking about me."

"Of course they want you to join the firm. I'd guess you could join any firm you want to. But I thought you were going to work for Justice —— for a year or so."

"On account of the war and a few other delays along the way, I'm afraid I'm a little long in the tooth for that kind of thing, especially if I'm going into politics."

"Politics, is it? I didn't know about that. This fellow I once knew, this one-time friend of mine, he hated politicians, good ones, bad ones, reactionary ones, liberal ones. He disliked all politicians. He used to talk about lonely voices. He used to say a man could speak only for himself, and when he tried to trim his sail to get elected, even dogcatcher . . ."

"I didn't say I was going to. I just might. That's all. I might take up residence in New York State, and who knows? I'm not that much younger than Jack Kennedy."

I said, "Charley, what is this? Jack Kennedy, the glamorous new liberal congressman from Boston, is, I believe, the same Jack Kennedy who said that people like members of the American Veterans Committee made him nervous and uncomfortable. The implication being that they smelled, and since you are a member of the ruling body of the AVC . . ."

"Jack denies he ever said that."

I put on my own smile of martyrdom, and I said, "Charles, that house tonight was filled with a number of people you, when in full control of your faculties, despise. All those moldy liberals. You used to say that the trouble with moldy liberals like that is that they don't get laid properly. Is that your problem, not getting properly laid?"

Charley said, "You're tired. I hope you haven't been hitting the pills."

"Charley, old friend, all I really want for you is for you to be happy, be what you're capable of being."

Charley smiled, and he gave me a quick pat on the shoulder, and I thought of the day . . . and the days . . . and then he drove away, and it was years before he ever really drove back. If he ever really drove back. . . .

LEITMOTIV—Cecily said, "He may be your oldest friend, but that is not what people are going to say. They are going to say that you two were lovers. Maybe still are lovers."

Charley said, "I have never been overly concerned with what people said about me, and I thought that you never had been, either."

"Charles, it's regrettable, but you simply cannot defend people like that. Believe me. I know."

"I can't defend *people like that?* What a very odd thing for anyone, especially you, to say."

"If you do, if you defend that faggot, it will not only be the end of your career, it will be the end of our marriage."

"That," said Charles, "is a chance I will have to take."

I know about that particular exchange because Cecily told me about it. And I didn't doubt a word of what she said. Cecily is cruel, selfish, uncaring. Except for the baby. She did care for Sandra. But she is not stupid. I wish she had been, because then perhaps . . . Charley always liked smart ladies, and he used to say, "Cec is a very intelligent woman." And say, and say.

I never denied that she was bright.

So Charley did defend me. In the end, nobody else would, nobody anywhere. I know you don't believe it, but it's true, lambkins. Cross my heart and hope to . . . In Washington that season it was weeks before they could find a lawyer with enough guts to defend one Henry A. Wallace, a former Vice President of the United States. The one they threw rotten eggs at, the one who said, "Am I not an American?" So who was going to stand up for a fag piano player?

You've forgotten that about the Vice President, you say, or else you never knew.

Well, it's true, baby, and don't ever forget it. That is the way it was, and that is the way it no doubt will soon be again. Only this time I won't be around to see it. Or hear it. You can only take one of those in a lifetime, if that.

SECOND MOVEMENT: INTERMEZZO; ADAGIO—Charley called on a merciless February afternoon and said, "If you're working on something just say so, but otherwise, how would you like two visitors on Sunday?"

"I'm not working on anything. I've given up work forever, and I'll be glad to see you and Cecily anytime."

"I hear you two didn't hit it off the night of the party. Cecily's very upset. And you two have to be friends. You will be, too. I absolutely guarantee it."

I said, I'm sure of it. Of course I said, I'm sure of it, but I didn't for a moment think we ever would be friends. And I was sure Cecily didn't think so, either. We were natural-born enemies, and we both knew it.

I said, "How about two o'clock on Sunday? I'll try and get up a little food to go with the booze."

Sunday was even gloomier than the day Charley called.

I was then living in a lavish apartment in the East Seventies, sharing it from time to time with other transients.

There was a huge window in the sunken living room and beyond that a terrace and a small solarium in which were a few tropical plants that should have been more cheerful, but their bright colors somehow seemed only to emphasize the gloom. The view of the river must have been spectacular on a calm summer day, and there were still some of those in 194—, but I was long gone by summer, and on that Sunday in February the river was as black and angry as the sky. A north wind and a fog and no hope for any alms from the sun, none.

Still, as nearly as was possible, the apartment was bearable. The maid had built a fire and lighted candles. Fresh flowers in all the vases, and all the lights were on. A few years before I had started buying a few paintings, all abstract and all by young artists. The paintings were also well lighted, and I thought they were good paintings.

Altogether, I thought, a pleasant apartment. Better than Cecily's mausoleum in New Haven.

Charley was usually a punctual man, but he and Cecily were two and a half hours late that Sunday afternoon. By which time I had had three hefty drinks. Charley, who was also not usually a mumbler, mumbled an apology. The lady said, "We were at . . ." mentioning the name of the Big Liberal Law Firm that was surely going to honor Charles by letting him in. . . . That happened, and later the head of the firm was one of the first to spill his guts before The Committee, and he was one of the first to back Coach Masterson's and Joe McCarthy's work in Washington. "Their tactics are a little . . . but as a former member of the party I know the real danger . . . and you can't make an omelet without . . ." The bastard was a noted gourmet.

"And he was so impressed with Charles that we just lost all track of time. Do forgive us."

Her lips reached for mine, but I avoided them. She wanted a Scotch, light on the Scotch and heavy on the rocks. While I carried out her orders and also made another drink for myself and one for Charley, Cecily made a quick but thorough appraisal of the apartment and everything in it. She said, "How gay, how very gay. Isn't that the word?" Charley didn't know what she meant; this was more than twenty years ago, and that curiously inappropriate word was not yet part of the vocabulary of most people. . . . Cecily looked at the paintings. "Are they yours?" She stood a little away from one, the way people do when they want you to think they're queer for painting, the way other people and very often the same people close their eyes and sway their heads ever so slightly at concerts. . . . Not at my concerts, though. When I see that happening, I pass among them with a baseball bat. The only good use I've ever found for the endless supply of baseball bats I always got for Christmas and on my birthday.

Cecily said, "The doodles I mean. Did you paint them?"
"I bought them; I know most of the artists."
"They're nifty," said Cecily Broadmoor. "But I'm afraid when it comes to art, I'm an old stick-in-the-mud. I'm a classicist. Gay art just simply eludes me."

I might add, I will add that when I sold my collection, shortly before one of my visits here, I got a quarter of a million dollars for it, about ten times what I'd paid when the artists were hungry.

A good deal more followed, talk and talk and talk. I did, however, manage one question. I asked Charley how the exams were going. He said they were going well enough.

And Cecily said, "Well enough? Charles is not only editor of the *Law Review*. He is going to take all the prizes there are."

Having said that, Cecily listed the prizes; she named all of the previous winners; she gave a lengthy history of each of their illustrious careers. . . . Oh, Cecily was terrified of silence and repose, always, always, always.

She was saying, "Fred Rahlson. Do you know who Fred Rahlson is and what he said about Charles?"

I nodded. I knew who Fred Rahlson was and what he had said about Charley. But Cecily was not one to be stopped by a nod. "Of course Freddy's an old friend of Papa, but that isn't the reason he said what he said about Charles. He says that Charles has the most brilliant . . . and considering who Freddy is . . ." She gave me a run-down on Rahlson's career. Said, ". . . and I certainly agree about Charles. Our Charles is a genius, and . . ." She turned to Charley and in the too large, flawed eyes there was something that was, I suppose, akin to love. Maybe it was love.

She was saying, ". . . and one of these days, our boy here is going to be President, and not only that, he will . . ."

I looked at Charley, who was looking at some distant object on the river, and I thought of something his mother once said. She was talking about how much the people in the town hated her. She said, "I should have taken up five hundred and needlepoint. I should have learned to talk endlessly on the price of a pound of spareribs. I should have pretended I consider it one of the true glories of life to exchange recipes for meat loaf. I should have had an ordinary son." I thought of Charley saying, "If I don't stop telling the truth, they're not going to let me live." I thought, Cecily Broadmoor is going to try to make Charley seem ordinary; she will want him to avoid the truth. She is going to want to cut him down to size, I thought. And maybe that's the best thing. Prove it isn't.

For a time after dinner Cecily and I were alone. We were sitting on the large red sofa; I had, reluctantly, turned on the record player, Segovia. I like listening to records alone. Or if there has to be somebody else, he must understand the uses of silence. . . . The Segovia was Cecily's idea. Segovia is very good at what he does, but I do not believe that Johann Sebastian, saintly man that he was, would have cared for it. . . . But Johann Sebastian knew the uses of silence; he knew when to keep his peace. He must have wanted to talk back to Prince Leopold now and again, and as for his second wife, pill or not, he must at one time or another have been tempted to shout, "Stop."

The river looked calmer in the darkness, and a brightly lighted white boat was passing. Cecily, well into her third snifter of brandy, said, "I talked too much the other night in New Haven." I said, "We all do sometimes." "All is forgiven and forgotten then?"

I said, "I'm glad to see the fog has lifted. It's going to be a long drive."

"Try to forgive me for being rich."

"I don't mind your being rich. I don't choose my friends on the basis of how much money they've got or haven't got. I don't choose my enemies that way, either." All right. That did it. From there on in it was all my fault, mostly my fault; but it didn't really matter. It would have turned out the same way in the end. It's all written down.

Cecily's entire face changed. The distorted eyes darkened; a spot of red appeared on each of her naked cheeks, and the mouth became a pale pink line of disapproval. The little girl's voice rose at least half an octave, and she said, "You just plain don't like me. Is that it?"

I said of the virgin ship not yet quite out of sight, "I always wonder where they're going, and wherever it is, I always wish I were going, too." And she said, "Okay, Lucy, I'll level with you. Your trouble is that you've never really liked any of Charles's women except that pale-faced, breastless boy who calls herself Trish. You've never liked any of his women because you've always wanted to hop into bed with him yourself, and he says you've just never had the guts to try." And I said, "Leaving Trish aside, there are two things wrong with what you've just said: Number one, you couldn't possibly level with me because you're not tall enough. And number two, Charley would never say such a thing to you. I know Charley too well to believe that."

Cec then shouted several things that I felt she could not have picked up at the fancy schools she had attended. And I said, "There's something about me that makes you acutely uncomfortable, and I don't think it has anything to do with me. Or with Charley. I think it has to do with your father."

She dropped her snifter glass on the carpet, and in her mama doll's voice said, "Oh, dear. Have I made a messy-wessy?"

When Charley came back he said, "I thought if I left you two alone for a while, you'd get to be friends. I'm always right about things like that, always. . . ." Poor Charley, so sensitive to most moods, so aware of the heart of most matters, so understanding of most people. . . . I got the lady's coat and helped her on with it, but we did not see each other. We saw each other only once in all the years that followed. After Sandra's funeral she said, "I wish it had been you; I wish he had run over you, and then I'd like to see him get the electric chair, and I want to watch. . . ."

We saw each other that afternoon all right, and a little later Charley did die. But Cecily and I go on. . . . Do you still think there isn't a pattern? . . . Our junior class play in high school was *Death Takes a Holiday*. Guess who played death.

Charley took Cec's arm and tenderly guided her to the door. And he said something about how he'd call, and maybe the three of us . . . Said it had been a wonderful . . . Said again that he had known that the people he loved most in the world would . . . Then they went into the gloom to start the long, treacherous drive that was to lead to New Haven and beyond, endlessly beyond. Endlessly until the night after Charley appeared before The Committee, the night he had however many drinks he had, the night Sandra heard the car and ran out of the house and ran under the wheels of the car and ran no more.

The jury acquitted Charley of the manslaughter charge, but Cecily did not acquit, would not forgive. Laughed when she heard that Charley was dead, not with hysteria, with joy. Would not identify the . . . Said, "My only regret is that he didn't suffer more." Poor Cec? After that you still say, Poor Cec? . . . Oh, I suppose. Poor Cec.

After Charley and Cecily left, I made myself the largest and strongest drink in the world, and I sat at the Steinway for a time, thinking of the unfinished "Lament," wondering how soon arthritis would set in permanently in my hands. . . . The Segovia record ended, and there was no sound from the bleak river. Only the useless silence.

I thought of calling Trish in San Francisco, but what would I have said?

Psalm for Chorus
and Orchestra

Urah, haneval, v' chinor!
A-irah shahar!

The recreation director, and I no longer think it's a bull dyke, I think it's a man, and you know how I feel about drag queens. I wouldn't even wash with a cake of soap made out of a drag queen. I'd feel dirty all over if I did. . . . After I left your office, he accosted me in the ball, arrested me in the hall, call, and they turned off all the lights and painted the windows black. When do they do that, the blacking? Sacking. I wait and I watch. I never sleep, never ever sleep, but I never see them paint or pant, hard or soft, on or off, up or down, go or cum. I never see them paint, but they put black crepe on my door, near the floor. . . . The recreation director would not let me pass. No passing, lass, he said, and he began preying and praying and groping and importuning. Said, next summer, as if I'd be here next summer, any summer, anywhere, said that every summer some of the lunatics, the safe ones, he said, as if any of them are safe, us. Come to a camp for, and I was talking to the doctor, said he, and he said the doctor and I think that you . . . He would not let me go, go me. So I bit his hand, drawing blood, leaving marks, sharks, and I ran. See the fag run. Run, fag, run. . . . But the chorus followed me, through the lock, double-locked, rocked and clocked. Followed me, singing. I hear the ringing voices from the camp, damp.

The Lord is my shepherd.

THE WOMAN. Restless, complaining, lamenting, wheedling, coaxing, threatening, saying, singing. Accompanied by two harps and a large percussion section. *Recitative.* "I've just had a very, very long and very, very nice chat with Mr. Doan, the new man down to the Y, the one they brought in special from Ottumwa after the previous director, and I will not even allow his name . . . should have been tarred and feathered . . . with a twelve-year-old boy. . . . Doan, the new one, told me to call him Tom, and he is just the nicest man ever, and he can't wait to meet you, George. He's heard all about you, all good, he said, and he said he likes to take on challenges, and he considers you a challenge, George, and they're having this special camp up at Pine Lake in October, and he wants you to come, especially, he said. You won't have to go to school all week. It'll be just like having another summer vacation in the fall."

I shall not want.

BOY SOPRANO, accompanied by the harp. "Well, I'm not going."

THE WOMAN. "You listen to me, young man; you are going. I insist on it, and for once I am going to have my way."

BOY SOPRANO, harp plaintive. "When the hell didn't you?"

THE WOMAN. "I am just going to ignore that remark, and I told Tom, I says, 'Sonny's always afraid they're going to tease him because he's not as athletically inclined as some of the boys,' and Tom says, 'Mrs. Lionel, there will be no taunting in my camp. You can take my personal word for that.'"

BOY SOPRANO. "I'm still not going, and you can't make me. You can tar and feather me and cut off my tongue and everything, but I still am not going."

THE WOMAN. "George, please do not force me to . . ."

He maketh me to lie down in green pastures.

FIRST MAN. "Dora, you are not going to force this boy to do anything he doesn't want to do. He's nervous enough as it is."

THE WOMAN. "Monte, do not interfere with me, because this time . . . Just do not interfere if you know when your bread is well buttered. . . . Now, Sonny, do you know what else Tom said?"

Boy Soprano. "If you'll wait just a minute, I'll run and get a pencil. I'm sure it's something worth remembering."

The Woman. "He says, 'Mrs. Lionel, you send us a boy, and we'll send you back a man.'"

First Man. "The man is clearly a fool and probably ought to be locked up. George here is twelve years old, and he can hardly . . ."

The Woman. "Monte, *I* am making the money that keeps this house going, out in the public all day, on my feet, and until you are able . . ."

First Man. "Dora, I do not believe in God, but I do believe that someday you are going to be punished. . . ."

The Woman. "Speaking of which, they are going to have daily Bible readings and prayers twice daily, and your religion could use a little brushing up, George, no two ways about it. Now I see that look on your face, but this is one time when your mother absolutely puts her foot down, and for your own good, I might add. That's all I'm thinking of, your own good."

Boy Soprano. "There is nothing you can say to make me go."

The Woman, pianissimo. "I should not like to force you to stop taking lessons from the Jew."

First Man, accompanied by flute, plaintive, off-key. "Dora, please don't threaten the boy. I warn you, if you . . ."

The Woman. "*You* warn *me?* Are *you* making the money that makes the lessons possible? No, you are not. Have you ever in your life been a good provider? No, you have not. You are not worth the powder and shot it would take to blow you up, and I refuse to listen any longer to the failure I made the mistake of marrying."

Boy Soprano. "Okay. I'll go. Just stop shouting. I can't stand the shouting, and let's not talk about it any more."

The Woman. "You'll go, and you'll have the time of your life. You'll hike, and you'll hunt, and at night you'll sit around the fire with the other boys and talk and sing and roast wienies and marshmallows, and it will be an experience you'll look back on for the rest of your life, and I hope you'll remember who you have to thank for it. And not only that, Tom says they've got a nice piano in the recreation hall, and when there isn't anything else to do, although they'll keep you very, very busy, you can practice to your heart's content."

FIRST MAN. "Dora, take one look at George's face, and if you still think . . ."

THE WOMAN. "I say again, when you are making the money to pay for the lessons and keep this household afloat, I shall listen to you, but until then, I advise you to keep your silence. . . . Now, Sonny, I'm going to start packing. Tom gave me a little list of what you'll need."

BOY SOPRANO. "But it's not until October, for Christ's sake. . . ."

THE WOMAN. "A stitch in nine saves time."

FIRST MAN. "God forgive you."

He leadeth me beside the still waters.

On Saturday it snowed. I told you that some years it started snowing around Labor Day. . . . Snowed hard, deep, drifted. And they called from the town and said that the girls, who'd been coming up by chartered bus for a dance, wouldn't be able to make it.

CHORUS. "Je-sus. How do you like them meat and potatoes. I haven't had my ashes hauled since . . ." "Man, I ain't knocked off a piece of ass since . . ." "Poon-tang. That's what the boy here needs, a little old poon-tang." "I'd got myself all horny just thinking about it, and not only that, I was in town the other day and got myself two whole packs of rubbers, and . . ."

SECOND MAN. "All right, men, I want you to take a hike in the woods. There won't be much snow in the woods, and you pick up some wood for the fireplace and hike around for a while. Mrs. Doan and I are going into town for a few hours, and I want you boys . . . No, George, you cannot practice. You are up here to develop your body, and so you go with the other boys, and tonight you can lead us all in prayer."

He restoreth my soul.

In the woods, fine, pine, line, only the brown and ground, hard round, and the lakes of the water were not frozen, but there were no ripples in the wakes. Not a ripple in the take. . . .

CHORUS. "Give me another swig of that beer." "A man can't get along without a little piece a ass now and then, and we been cooped up here, and . . ." "That's right; you don't get a little fuckin' ever so often, you forgit how, and your thing falls off, and . . ."

THIRD MAN, Irish, Irish McKennon. "Who needs girls? We've got the sissy here."

They started laughing, all of them, all again, and I was laughing, too; I always laughed, afraid if I didn't laugh, so laughed. And then I saw that I was laughing alone; the others were not laughing; they were looking at each other, and I saw that it was no laughing matter, scatter, and I got up, glid up, and was to start to run, stun. They always laughed when I ran, everybody laughed. See the sissy run, they said. Run, fag, run, they read. . . . But this time I didn't start, couldn't start, had no feet to start. Irish, McKennon he was, reached out and tripped me, hipped me. Sang, "You've got a nice little ass there, lass, crass." In the lake were bass. And he sang, "Ass, and you don't even need a rubber." "Mass," he sang, "grass." Only there was no grass, only needles on the brown grown. Sang, "I'm first. I thought of it." Sang, "You hold his head and shoulders." Sang, "You hold her feet." Sang, "And you just lay there nice and quiet and don't make a move. Because if you do, you little sissy you, I'll beat you so hard you are going to wish . . ."

He leadeth me in the paths of
righteousness for his name's sake.

The boy never knew how many; he went blank and back and never felt how many. Was any, and the blood and the small snow through the fine pine made a mud, mud and blood, and that white that wasn't snow was some, come. No tripples in the lake, no take. No scream. Never any scream. Never any tears.

Yeah, though I walk through the valley
of the shadow of death.

DOCTOR, vibrato. "No permanent damage, son, not at all, at all. A few slight abrasions, but they'll clear up in no time. You get yourself a good night's sleep. I'm going to give Mr. Doan here a pill that'll put you right to sleep, and by tomorrow morning you'll be up and around, good as new and twice as sassy."

I will fear no evil, for thou art
with me; thy rod and thy staff they
comfort me.

SECOND MAN. "You can go ahead and cry if you want to, George." Sang, "Those boys have done a terrible thing, a terrible thing, but I am not going to punish them for it. God will punish them, and they know that, and they know what they have done, and they are sorry. Their consciences hurt each and every one of them more than you hurt. You can take my word for that. I know it hurts, but you're a regular little man, and . . ." Sang, "We are all Christians, and Jesus said we must forgive seventy-seven times seven, didn't He? Forgive and forget is what Jesus said." Sang, "We are never going to tell a soul what happened, are we? We are just going to wipe this whole thing out of our minds and . . . Those boys had a little too much beer, although I don't know where they got it, and ninety-nine chances out of a hundred, with all that beer, they didn't even know what they were doing." Sang, "And if you told anybody, even your mother and father . . . I don't believe in *lying* to your parents, but we don't tell them everything we know, do we? We all have our little secrets, don't we?" Sang, "And if any of us was to say anything at all to anybody, why, the disgrace would . . . And I'm thinking of you when I say that, George." Sang, "You'll stay up at the big house with Mrs. Doan and me from now on, and you don't have to do a thing you don't want to, and we're just going to forget the whole thing, aren't we, George?" Sang, ". . . in a month or six weeks, you'll forget all about this, all." Sang, "Shall we shake on it?"

Thou preparest a table before me
in the presence of mine enemies.

SECOND MAN. "A most unpleasant incident took place here this afternoon, men, and we all know what it was, but none of us are ever going to mention what it was, not to anybody, not even to each other, because if it is ever mentioned, I would personally see to it that any of those responsible for this unpleasantness would go to the state pen for life and then some, and I never go back on my word. Is that clear? Raise your hands if that . . . Now we will pray. 'Our Father who art . . .' And now we shall sing a hymn, 'Jesus, Wash Us from Our Sins,' and after the hymn, the unpleasant incident will be gone from all our minds. God will see to that."

Thou anointest my head with oil.

THE WOMAN. "You've gained weight. I'll bet you've put on ten pounds, hasn't he, Monte? And those roses in your cheeks. I've never seen you look better. For once wasn't your mother right when she said . . . And now you can return to school and to your music lessons with renewed vigor. . . . Tom Doan says you kept right up and then some with the boys in the hikes and everything, and he says they wanted to name you best camper and everything, but due to the generosity of your heart . . ."

FIRST MAN. "Son, you look tired. Why don't you go upstairs and take a nap?"

My cup runneth over.

The boys, the Christian boys, would cross the street when they saw me coming, and when they didn't see me in time to cross, they wouldn't look at me, never looked at me. Even when we were in the same class, they never looked my way. . . . Do they ever think of it now, do you suppose? I want them to. I want them to lie and die thinking about it. Forgive? Not once. Not then. Not ever. Would Jesus? I'll bet he wouldn't, couldn't. There are things you can never forgive. Or forget. I wish there were pieces of memory they could extract, like a tooth, a benign tumor, but this. This malignancy will never go. Oh, how I wish it would! That's the nightmare that causes me to be dawned upon, all dawns, every dawn that has been, will be. . . . No more dawns, please. I'll go quietly. I won't shed a single tear. I didn't then. Why should I now?

Surely goodness and mercy shall
follow me all the days of my life.

The boy they called Irish now has the Ford agency in town. And the last time I was there, ever there, he put out his hand, and he said, "You sure have made a name for yourself back East there, haven't you, George? How about shaking your old buddy's hand here, George, because I'm mighty proud that you . . ."

> *And I will dwell in the house*
> *of the Lord for ever.*

Doan didn't stay; he left town the following spring, but he has stayed with the Young Men's Christian Association. Of course he has. You can read the name of that Christian gentleman, see his name in the newspapers. Oh, all the time. See his name, never his shame. . . . I never shook their hands or granted them absolution, but a man with an unshaken hand without absolution can go a great distance these days, can go to any lengths.

CHORUS. "They said Amos Lionel's word was his bond; they said Amos Lionel never met a stranger. When Amos Lionel was at the bank, you never had to sign a note or anything. He'd get you the money, and all you did, you shook on it."

> *Hineh mah tov,*
> *Umah nayim,*
> *Shevel ahim*
> *Gam yahad.*

30 /

Brilliantine

I wrote nothing yesterday. I stayed in bed all day. I wasn't really sick. Just tireder than usual, just wondering how I've been able to pick them up and lay them down for so long. . . . Wondering why I never had a garden to cultivate. I mean a garden like Candide's. Dummy. Have you read nothing but Havelock Ellis's *Sexual Inversion?* And you've only read that since I've been here.

> . . . of cureless ills thou art
> The one physician. Pain lays not its touch
> Upon a corpse.

Oh, you know who wrote that, do you? . . . There may be some hope for you after all, despite your nose. . . . No, I do not think I've been avoiding it, telling you about the night I went to the Paynes' for the first time, the night I sometimes think it all began for me. I know one thing: if Sarah McCormick Payne hadn't given me the money, I'd never have got to New York. . . . What if I hadn't? Oh, I'd probably be at the state place in Iowa. The loony bin at Cherokee.

It was an important night all right. The most important of my life up to then. And what important has happened since? You've read it all. Tell me.

So. It was thus. Or thus I remember it.

The gamin gave himself a final, hopeful look in the magic mirror, then turned away, ignoring the tears. His mother brushed him, kissed him, wished him luck, said, lying, that he looked like a regular little man. . . . And when at last, and the journey took years, the poor little poor little poor boy, sometimes known as Elsie Dinsmore, got to his destination, he walked up and down in front of it for an ice age or so. He thought, The Payne manse is bound to be a house of mirth, a bushel of giggles, a barrelful of monkeys. "Happy families," et cetera. I had not yet come across those words, but I was convinced ours was the only totally unhappy family anywhere except maybe for a few starving Armenians.

We were miserable. Of course we were, and a year is a series of three hundred and sixty-five disappointments, and leap year gives it twenty-nine. We would have been happy, though, if (a) my father had been a good provider ("Monte has never been a good provider; that's our only trouble"), (b) my mother hadn't aimed at being the first lady president of the Parliament of Man and fallen somewhat short of that goal, and (c) I hadn't been a sissy.

Take, for instance, the only other family I knew anything about, the Goldsteins. I'd been to supper at their house a few times, and while it is true they didn't eat until six-thirty, by which time a person could starve to death, when they did get around to it the food was good. Kosher, but despite what my mother said, not lethal ("Who ever knows what that rabbi is up to, with all that hair on his face, and it might be poisoned; that's part of the conspiracy, to poison those of other persuasions"). Circumcision was never mentioned, and the Goldsteins had a good time while they ate, too. They talked. Talked about what had happened at school that day. At the store. At home. Talked about letters and telephone calls and visits from an endless number of adorable aunts and uncles and cousins. . . . We never said anything at meals except my father reading things at breakfast. We certainly never mentioned any of our relatives, who were certainly not adorable.

Once I remember the Goldsteins laughed, every single one of them, at the same time and not at each other. I had never heard anybody laugh before, except once in a great while at the Casino. . . . But there's a fly in every ointment, a rotten apple in every barrel, a mote in every eye, a nigger in every woodpile. The Goldsteins were Jewish and, thus, could not be completely happy, as happy as larks, which is what all us *goyim*, circumcised or not, have a right to be. It says so in the Constitution. Or did before they rewrote it. . . . This time you won't have to be Jewish to go to the ovens. You won't even have to be queer. All you have to be is in line, and you go either way, pushing or not, with gum or without.

But the Paynes, for Christ's sake, they were bound to be happy, had to be. They didn't have any money problems. Matthew Payne had been a good provider, and he'd left it all to his son, Horton. Horton may have been a disappointment to the old man, but Horton got the money anyway. And Sarah McCormick Payne, so it seemed to me that night, didn't want to be anything she wasn't. Or want anything she didn't have. What could that possibly be? And Charley wasn't a sissy, not if Elaine Jacobs was to be believed. "Although, as I've told you girls, Charles has never gone the whole way, not even half, he's all man. . . . I've never seen it, but it's . . . it is of more than adequate dimensions."

All right. So, as Horton Payne had told me, maybe the Paynes got a little lonely now and again. Who didn't? But at least they weren't lonesome. And that's what separates the men and boys from the sissies. Sissies are never anything else. . . . And who really needed me, a sis going bald, his granny glasses held together with adhesive tape and hope, orally underprivileged. Nobody wants a sis around, not with a real boy in the house.

And if I played the piano for the Paynes, it was more than likely that they'd hit my hands, the way Elsie Dinsmore's father did, although I personally always felt that that little crybaby deserved all she got, that she was about as adept at tinkling the ivories as Elaine Jacobs, probably up to her ass in her very own rendition of the "Barcarolle" from *Tales of Hoffmann.*

Okay, Elsie, Elizabeth, Eliza, Betsy, Betty, Bessie, Bess, Beth, Bettina, mother of John the Baptist, cousin to the Virgin Mary, ring the fucking bell.

The bell was the first disappointment of the evening. It just rang.

It did not play a lively little tune the way some doorbells did. The Jacobses, for instance, had a bell that played the notes to "How Dry I Am." So already at the Jacobs house, you had something to talk about and had had yourself a good chuckle, the first of many.

After a long time Jerome, wearing a butler's uniform and a much-used frown, opened the door. Jerome drove the Cadillac, and he helped Mrs. Fearly in the kitchen and served the meals.

Knowing who was calling, Jerome asked who was calling, and I told him and told him I was expected. The frown deepened. Jerome was a large, unwholesome-looking man with a flat head, small, bitter eyes, a flabby mouth that gave the impression that its owner had just bit into a large chunk of overripe Camembert, and a more than ample nose that always seemed to be smelling it. Jerome's face had a look of perpetual suspicion, no, more than suspicion. The look was that of a hanging judge. And all the defendants were guilty, always. And the judge personally performed every execution, with love.

The entrance hall was very long, very gloomy. Gloomy portraits on both sides. Not family portraits. I had been told by somebody or other that Matthew Payne had bought them years before at an auction in Des Moines. Bought them cheap. Ill-drawn, villainous faces said to have belonged to a pioneer family of wealth. One sure mass murderer, a girl of nine or so. A somber umbrella rack against one wall. A discouraged coat rack. Three sorrowing chairs in need of recaning. A smoky mirror that gave forth distorted, always malevolent images. . . . An awful hall, and I wondered why Mrs. Payne hadn't bothered to brighten it. Mrs. Payne. Sarah. She asked me to call her that a hundred times or more, but I never did. Except for Dede I was probably fonder of her than of any woman I've ever known. I must say I never thought of her as Horton Payne's wife. They were even more separate than most married people. . . . I just never called her Sarah. It didn't seem right.

When we got to the living room, Jerome disappeared. Horton Payne, who was wearing the first smoking jacket I ever saw outside the movies, shook my hand, rather too heartily I felt, and at the same time I felt, as I had at the bank, that he had, perhaps, forgot entirely who I was. *What* was I doing there? How soon, pray, could I, would I leave?

He said, "I don't uh believe uh that you know uh my son."

Charley put down his book and shook my hand. His hand was cool and dry and brown, and he had very long fingers. And he had a man's voice, compared to mine anyway. He said, "We heard you play at the high school. You were great. I mean I liked it, but my mother, who knows all about music, said you were 'very remarkable.' She said, 'For one so young I don't think I have ever heard anyone so talented.'"

I shuffled and shrugged and said thanks, getting red.

Charley smiled. It was the smile of someone who had always had everything and always would. A smile that said, "There will be a great deal of me, perhaps the most of me, that you will never see, that no one will ever see, and you might just as well make up your mind to that right here and now. Nothing against you personally. That's just the way it is with me." And it said, "While most of me will, as I say, remain submerged, like an iceberg, I already know all there is to know about you, and frankly, beyond the fact that my mother thinks you're an okay piano player, you aren't that interesting."

Close up Charley looked just as arrogant and forbidding as he had when I saw him in church, as he did in the photographs in his father's office. He looked as if none of the concerns of ordinary human beings ever had or ever would trouble him. Other boys might have acne, pimples, and other disturbances of the skin and of the flesh. Not Charles McCormick Payne. Other boys might sweat. Not Charles McCormick Payne. He wouldn't even perspire. Other boys might grow too tall or not grow tall enough, might be too fat or too thin, might suffer from too much love or too little. Might laugh too loud, or cry. Charles McCormick Payne never would.

Others might want for food, for money, for the moon. Charles McCormick Payne would never have to worry about money or food, and if he should decide he wanted the moon, he would arrange to

get it without any help from anyone, but thank you all the same for
your kind offer of assistance.

He had heard that most men were not islands, but Charles Mc-
Cormick Payne was, and he had every intention of becoming a con-
tinent, and with a minimum of effort he would arrange that, too,
the minute he got around to it.

"Have you always lived in this town?"

I confessed, with the blush of a hopeless provincial, that I always
had, and Charley said, "I can't wait to get to college, can you?"

I said that I couldn't, not feeling it necessary to add that the way
things looked, college was not very likely for me, not unless I went
to the state university and worked my way through.

Horton Payne, looking at nobody anywhere, said, "Uh, how would
you boys like a Coke? And then it'll be about time for dinner."

Dinner. It didn't seem possible. It was already seven-thirty. The
Paynes hadn't had dinner *yet*? Maybe it was some kind of joke. . . .
I started to say I'd already eaten, but for once I kept my mouth
shut. I said a Coke would be fine, thanks.

"Charles?"

Charles, who was always polite to his father, said, "No, thank
you," and he added, "sir." To me he said, "Bring your Coke along.
I'll show you the house. Even if you don't want to see it, I'll show
you the house."

"But I do. Thanks very much." And I did want to see the house.
Who in town didn't? "Of course she's absolutely ruined one of this
town's fine old mansions; nevertheless, I'd like to see . . ."

Charley's father said that seeing the house was a fine idea, and
by the time we got back, Mrs. Payne would be down. "You won't
forget what time dinner is, will you, Charles?"

"No, sir. I'll keep that firmly in mind."

As we started upstairs Charley said, "You've already had dinner,
haven't you? Only you call it supper."

"Okay. So I've already eaten and we call it supper. Big deal, and

it's not very gentlemanly to say things like that. You're supposed
to be this big gentleman."

"Who said that? I never did. The only thing I've ever claimed
to be is a scoundrel."

"Elaine Jacobs says you're a gentleman."

"Does she indeed? What else does she say?"

"She says you're engaged to be married."

"I doubt very much if it's a good idea to repeat every idiot remark Elaine Jacobs makes, since most of it couldn't be of the
slightest interest to anyone, including her birdbrained mother, but
I assure you, and her if she wants to know, that I have no intention
of ever marrying her. I have no intention of marrying a complete
moron."

I said, "It seems to me you ought to be congratulated on that
decision."

Charley smiled and said, "This is the library, but it's quite possible you'd have guessed that without my telling you."

I had never seen a real library before, except, of course, for the
Carnegie on North Center. I had been in rooms that people called
libraries, but there were never more than a few dozen books in
them, and the books were always behind glass. "We just love our
Shakespeare. We have the bard's collected works, you know, and
every evening after supper [*sic*], Sam takes it down and . . . There's
nothing we enjoy more than reading aloud to each other. . . . The
bard and the Bible. With them books on hand, we have never felt
the need for more frivolous . . ."

Books. *The Little Shepherd of Kingdom Come, Pollyanna, Anne
of Green Gables, Black Beauty, The Scarlet Letter*, its pages uncut, *The Marble Faun*, its pages uncut, *Five Little Peppers and
How They Grew, Tales from Shakespeare* by Charles and Mary
Lamb, always the same books, always bound in bile green. An in-
dentured book salesman must have wandered through town and
then, wisely, wandered out again. . . . The things I remember, the
things I wish I could forget.

I don't know how many books were in Sarah McCormick Payne's library, maybe two thousand, all on open shelves of polished mahogany, all looking as if they'd been read again and again, books I'd have bought if I could have afforded them and if I'd known enough about books, and they were not in any particular order. . . . Beware of orderly bookshelves. They bespeak a disorderly mind.

I said, "How do you ever find what you want?"

"My mother can. She never even has to look. She always remembers where everything is. She has an IQ of 156, and I take after her. What's your IQ?"

"I don't have one," I said, feeling as if I was missing some vital member.

"You've got one. Everybody has. You just don't know what yours is. It's probably high enough. You seem bright."

"Thank you," I said, feeling nearly complete again.

"Have you read *War and Peace*, all of it, I mean?"

"Of course. Years ago."

"How did you like the part where they sell Natasha into white slavery?"

"I didn't like that part nearly as much as the part where she's crossing the icy river, being chased by bloodhounds."

"You're not so dumb. I haven't read all of it, either, but my mother has. I think I'll die in a war. I can see myself dead and bloated and with a hard on. Did you know that when you die, you get a hard on?"

"No, but it's certainly something I'll try to work into a conversation the first chance I get."

Charley laughed, which pleased me. Plenty of people had laughed at me, but this was the first time I'd made anybody except my father laugh at something I'd meant to be funny.

"I guess we're both stuck in this town for the time being," said Charley, "and while it's probably no worse than Devil's Island, it certainly isn't much better. Learning anything in school is, of course, out of the question, but my mother tutors me. I told you. She's awfully smart."

"Which college are you going to?"

"Yale, I think, maybe Princeton or Harvard. It's simply a matter of choosing. I'm not stupid."

"I can see that. My God, who ever thought so?"

"Me, sometimes."

Charley looked closely at me, and I detected an inner sigh. He said, his tone suggesting rue and regret, "If everything works out, we might even be friends. I mean who else is there?" He touched me on the shoulder. He said, "You're okay."

It was nothing much. It was a good deal less than nothing much, but I wouldn't have traded it for a dukedom, for a four-year, all-expense scholarship to Juilliard, for a rave in the *Times*, for a year's contract to play first base for the Yankees. Oh, yes, things being the way things were, I'd have chosen the Yankees over the Philharmonic. I still would. Name one thing that's improved.

"I'd like it fine, our being friends," I said, coming out from behind a cloud. . . . Of course I would. This was an evening of firsts. It was the first time anybody had ever looked at me and confined himself to an inner sigh. Usually the sigh could be heard all over town. It was the first time that anybody had said that despite my blemishes I would do. I was okay.

I said, "I have to warn you I'm not much good at sports and things like that, and I'm told my personality leaves a good deal to be desired. In fact, I'm an anathema to most people in this town. And I think you ought to be aware of the probable loss of prestige on your part as the result of any intensive association with me socially."

I thought Charley was going to laugh again, this time *at*, not *with*, but he didn't. He said, "An anathema. I don't believe I've ever met one before. It'll be something new." He touched me on the shoulder again. "Now look here. My mother's going to ask you to play something, and I hope you won't get all giggly about it and go on about

how you left your music at home. That's what Elaine Jacobs did
the first time she was here, which was also the last time, and nobody
even asked her to play. She kept saying, 'I just know you want me
to play, but I can't. I left my music at home.' Then she started giggling. God."

"Elaine Jacobs and I have nothing whatever in common, plus, as
I remarked in a somewhat similar context earlier this evening, I
have memorized a thing or two."

Charley laughed again; what a beautiful sound. Of course I loved
him. He said, "My mother thinks you have a chance to become a
great musician, and those are her exact words. She said . . . Well,
I'll let her tell you, but she says you ought to go to New York to
study."

"That's what Rosenberg says; he's my teacher. But at the moment
it doesn't look as if that's going to happen."

"You never can tell," said Charley. "You like to see my mother's
workroom?"

I said that I would.

"I assume you're not a gossip. I'm told there are people in this
town who'd give anything to know what goes on here. I think they
think we have orgies."

"I could tell you a thing or two about the people in this town."

"I'll bet. Look, I hate mentioning it, but if we're going to be
friends, I might as well tell you, that tie clasp has to go."

"Gee—gee, thanks. The crown prince is already telling the com-
moner how to dress, and I've only been here a few minutes. Gee,
thanks."

"If you like it, by all means continue wearing it."

"What's wrong with it?"

"For one thing, it has your initials on it."

"That's bad?"

"Not if you're the type of fellow whose idea of a good time is
leading the singing at Rotary Club meetings, it isn't. Otherwise, it's
the worst."

I put the tie clasp in the pocket of my jacket. It weighed in heavy, like an albatross. I said, "I guess I have a lot to learn. I mean even more than I thought."

"Things like that aren't all that important, but if you're as bright as you are, you might as well do the little things right, too." A moment, then, "Nobody else does, I don't allow it, but you can call me Charley if you want to."

Several weeks later, I don't remember just when, but it was warm enough for Charley to go swimming in the river, and I waded and ducked my head in the water a couple of times, like an apprentice Girl Scout about to bake her first cookie. It was late May, say early June. We were dressing in Charley's room, and I said, "Have you got any brilliantine?"

"Brilliantine? What's that?"

"Stuff to put on your hair to slick it down. Everybody knows what brilliantine is."

"I've been meaning to speak to you about that."

"The brilliantine has to go?"

"It has to go. It makes you look like an unemployed Italian waiter."

"Gee, thanks. That certainly helps build up the old ego."

"You asked me. I told you. Keep on using it. It's no skin off mine."

"All right already. What else is wrong with the way I dress? I mean we might as well get it all over with at once." I combed my hair dry; it looked awful.

"Well, that tie. It's too insistent."

"Insistent on what?"

"On being noticed."

"It just so happens this tie is from Marshall Field's in Chicago and cost a dollar and a half."

"I'm not interested in the price or where it came from. It's a terrible tie. Here."

The tie he handed me was also from Marshall Field's, but it had thin regimental stripes and didn't insist on anything. I could see the difference at once. Handing it back, I said, "It's a nice tie."

"Idiot," he said, "I'm giving it to you." "Thanks. Look, Charley, is there anything right about me?"

"You're a brilliant pianist. That's just to begin. You'll probably be very famous one of these days. Play before the crowned heads of Europe and that sort of thing."

"My mother saw Queen Marie of Rumania in Des Moines. She said the queen was just as common as an old shoe."

"I wouldn't doubt it a bit. But we were talking about you. So you're going to be rich and famous. And it looks like you've got a high IQ, even though you act like a jerk a good deal of the time. And if you'd just stop resenting everything I tell you, always on my part with the unselfish motive of trying to improve you, you might learn a thing or two from me, and I might even learn a thing or two from you."

"I doubt that last. Socially I am most maladroit. Miss Eisley, the guidance counselor at the high school—they sent me to see her even though I'm not in high school yet. Anyway, she said that my problem isn't only that I'm . . . well, she called it eccentric. She said that I was always arguing with people, like teachers, for instance, telling them they were wrong when I thought so. She said even if they were wrong, I ought to keep . . . well, you know, quiet. She said that would probably improve my social standing."

"I have never met Miss Eisley, and I sincerely trust I never will, but she is obviously an asshole. You keep on being an anathema. I'm one myself and plan to be even more of one as the years go on."

Sometime during the sweet summer that followed, I said to Charley, "What are you going to be when you grow up? I mean have you decided?"

And Charley said, "Oh, I don't know. I'll probably be a lawyer. The ones around here are all fools, but then the anythings around here are mostly fools. I want to be a lawyer like Clarence Darrow, not a mortgage forecloser or some stupid shit who spends all his time searching out titles at the courthouse. A real lawyer. You know what old Plato said: 'Let the speaker speak truly and the judge decide justly.' That's what I have in mind. Or maybe I'll be a famous surgeon. A real one, not like the killers in this town. Or a writer. My mother says I have some talent in that line. But really, what I choose as a profession isn't too important. I can be pretty much what I decide to be, and not too many people can say that."

Charley believed that then, and so did I, every word of it. I always looked on Charley with awe and complete faith and love, even at the end.

Even after the death of the girl, even when Charley at times seemed . . . well, befuddled, as befuddled some days as old Joe McCarthy himself, as befuddled as the lawyer, a half-senile old man, who defended Charley at the trial.

But Charley wasn't befuddled with alcohol or age. It was as if some part of his mind had withdrawn from the carnage that was everywhere around him. But even then I had faith that Charley would somehow pull out of it and be all golden and shiny again. What happened to Charley? Somebody said, "Life happened to Charley." And that will have to do, I guess. Life happened to all of us.

The evening I'm remembering now, though. My God, not only was everything possible for us; everything was possible for the world, too. It could be remade, perfected, and while it might take somewhat longer than six days, it would not take very much longer.

I suppose that that is part of what being young is. For everybody? I don't know, but I hope so. I hope everybody in the world has a time, even if it's only a day or an hour, when absolutely everything seems possible.

You know the songs I wrote, based, ever so loosely, on Arthur Rimbaud's *Illuminations.* Christopher says those songs are still being played, sung.

I alone have the key to this savage side show.

I was thinking about Arthur this morning, that dirty, beautiful little sissy arriving in Paris with those lovely poems in his oversized peasant's hands. It must have been like that for him, too, the dreams all glittering, all reachable. All he had to do was stretch out his hand and . . .

And then he met Verlaine, who was then also without the wounds of defeat, and they fell in love, or else one fell in love and the other allowed himself to be so treated. However it was, ever is. . . . And after a while, after almost no time at all, everything started to be bad, worse than bad, awful, sordid, ugly, rotten. And it wasn't because they were queers, not just because of that anyway. I don't know what it was because of.

When did they outlaw happy endings?

I know one thing. It wasn't in the *Times*. I looked.

The day they put Charley in the ground, in addition to the reporters, seven people showed up, one of them the justice of the Supreme Court who'd known Charley at Yale, another a man who'd worked with him when Charley was a consultant to George Marshall's State Department, and a man Charley had defended before The Committee. A clerk-typist, something like that, not an important man, but the day Charley defended him, you'd have thought the future of the republic depended on that man's keeping his job, and, by God, he did. Charley won that one. And Charley kept me out of jail. And then the defeats began.

Charley hadn't wanted a service; he hadn't wanted to be put in the ground. Cecily knew that. You couldn't know the least thing about Charley without knowing that. And yet Cecily, knowing that and knowing how Charley felt about fraudulent men of the cloth, chose one of the most fraudulent to say the sanctimonious words. And she did not herself come to the service.

How can you explain that? How in one million years? I know she's a hating woman, a psychotic woman. *Know?* Do I? For sure?

Charley once said, "Remember when you and I, when any two people look at a third person, we never see the same person." Another time he said, "Cec is frightened of just about everything, including you." I said, "Me? I've never hurt a . . ." Charley said, "Don't ask me to explain it, but you even used to frighten me a little. The last thing in the world you seemed to need or want was friendship."

After the service that morning Lily and I had coffee, and I said, "Were you ever in love with him, Lily?"

Lily said, "As a kid I always hated him. He was such a snob, and I always thought he was the one who had made up that phrase about me being a pushy little peasant. But I found out he wasn't like that. He was a snob, but when he passed me on the street he always smiled and spoke. His mind always seemed worlds away, and I was always sure that my stockings were crooked. And whenever I met him in later years I still felt that way. Did he ever make you feel that way?"

"I never got over the feeling that he was putting up with me, that fond as he might be of me, I would never ever be quite up to the standards he had in mind for a friend."

And that is true. I used to frighten Charley, and I wanted his friendship and love more than anything else in the world. But I never thought I had ever earned either. . . . Is there no explaining anything, ever?

Lily said, "That lunch you arranged a couple of years ago was the only meal I ever had with Charles McCormick Payne, and it was lovely."

I had already arranged to have lunch with Lily, and when Charley came to the city on unexpected business, I suggested that it be the three of us instead.

I remember Charley said, "I never really knew Lily back home, and now she's married to one of the summer patriots. I don't care much for him, but you can't blame Lily for the man she married, can you?"

We had lunch at "21." Charley liked such places. I suppose he *was* something of a snob, but maybe I say that because I don't like such places. Charley liked being around fancy people, what are now called the beautiful people, as much as he liked being around anybody. Which wasn't much. Charley was forever defending the great unwashed, but he never had much of anything to do with them outside the court or hearing room. . . . Sure Charley was a snob, but is that a sin against the Holy Ghost?

On the morning of the funeral, over coffee, Lily said, "And my God, everybody at '21' knew him, and he was being patted on the back by all those nice, safe liberal types that eat and drink at '21.' And people came over, including the movie star who asked for his autograph. And then Adlai Stevenson came over and said he wanted to shake Charles's hand, and he said to Charles, 'I agree with almost everything you're saying these days, but it just isn't possible at the moment for me to join you.' And Charles said, 'If not now, when?' I was watching Adlai, and he looked at Charles as if he thought . . . well, thought there sits a better man than I am, and at the time I thought old Adlai was right, and I still do. It doesn't sound like so much now, but at the time . . . Well, you know more about the time than I do.

"And I remember when we sat down at lunch that day Charles looked at me and said, 'George speaks highly of you; he always has, and in such matters George is always right.' Well, there you are. That's all. That's it. Nothing very great, but I went around glowing for days, weeks. I don't know that I ever really loved Charles, but I certainly did admire him, and that's a kind of love, isn't it?"

Maybe Lily and I cried then. Maybe we didn't. We did what we did, felt what we felt, which was sorry. We sorrowed. What a pity.

After which Lily got in a taxi and, I suppose, went to the house in which Bruno Hyerly was also in residence. And I went wherever I went, and that is the way it was the day they put what was left of poor Charley in the ground.

That first night Charley said, "Well, let's go look at the room where my mother has her orgies."

Sarah McCormick Payne's workroom had one wall that was

largely glass. It was that wall, looking into the gardens and the infinite brown hills, that had desecrated one of the town's fine old mansions. The *Times-Dispatch* said so, the ladies' garden club, the DAR, the Optimists, the Moose, the Elks. . . . They passed resolutions; they wrote letters; they nagged; they pouted. . . . My Grandfather Lionel's house, also on West Main, was a much better house; he had taste, but his house had been hideously remodeled into a funeral parlor, and nobody said a word against that.

Matthew Payne's will had specified that a great many things in the house had to remain as they were. Exactly as they were. Thus the chairs in the entrance hall could not be recaned; the smoky mirror could not be replaced; the umbrella rack had to be kept where it was. But fortunately, he had not had the imagination to forbid tearing out a wall and replacing it with glass.

In the middle of the room was what Charley said was a Louis XV table, covered with books, many of them contemporary artbooks imported from Europe. And I remember Thornton Wilder's novel *Heaven's My Destination*, which had recently been published. I remember because Sarah McCormick Payne lent it to me sometime later. She said, "I don't like it much, but see what you think." I said, "I don't know anything about books, Mrs. Payne." "You're intelligent. That's what counts. I read in the *Times* that the Wilder book was at the bedside of Justice Oliver Wendell Holmes when he died, but I don't think Holmes thought heaven was his destination, do you?"

Mrs. Payne was the only person in town who got the *Times*. Mrs. Look-Down-Her-Nose-at-You was too good for the *Times-Dispatch*, too good for the *Des Moines Register*, even, incredible, too good for the *Cedar Rapids Gazette*. . . . Besides, who wanted to read news that was four days old? In a newspaper that had come by train all the way from New York. And anyway, if you read *The New York Times*, how did you ever find out who had spent the day shopping in Ames?

❖

The other three walls of Mrs. Payne's workroom were white and almost completely covered with paintings. Maybe as many as fifty, all sizes. The smallest was no more than six inches square. The largest was almost seven feet across and six feet deep.

I had never seen anything even remotely like those paintings. I didn't know anything like them existed—blobs of the most blatant colors, reds, yellows, oranges, greens, blacks, all without identifiable shapes, all of them suggesting anger and danger and despair.

The paintings disturbed me, and they later became part of my daytime delirium, the large one in particular. It was all black except for a single swab of red. And what I saw was a huge bird, probably a roc, in what could have been a cage but was probably a coffin. The bird's neck had been broken, and it was dying, but with its last breath it was, like Sarah McCormick Payne, like me, like all of us, crying out for help, for a kind word, for recognition of its existence. But I knew that the bird would die unheard and unseen.

I don't mean that I saw or thought any of those things that first night. I mean only that the paintings, strange, foreign, puzzling, impressed me, and I knew that they would haunt me, particularly the large one. Sarah McCormick Payne called it *The Captive.*

The last time I saw her was when I was in town on my way to the concert in Omaha. I was twenty years old; I was filled with the conceits of my New York success. I was in love. It was 1939, the best of all possible years.

I wasn't sure I should call Mrs. Payne. My mother had said that people in town had said she was acting funny. But then people in town had always said strange and unkind things about Mrs. Payne. So I called the Payne house. Mrs. Payne answered after one short ring. Her voice sounded odd, although of course it had been a long time since I'd heard it.

She said, "Yes, yes. This is Sarah Payne. Is it you, Charles? I've been waiting for your call."

I told her who I was, and she said, yes, of course, and how nice and please come to see her. "Right away," she said. "Do hurry. That dreadful woman, the one who was Matthew Payne's mistress. Mrs. Fearly. She's out at the moment, and so is Jerome. So hurry and bring Charles with you." I said, "Charley isn't with me, Mrs. Payne, but I'd like to come anyway." And she said, "I know that's what they say, but I also know where Charles is and that he will come. You must promise to bring him along."

I said I'd be right over, but I didn't go immediately. I hesitated, partly because I wasn't sure it was right to go. Sarah McCormick Payne had certainly sounded peculiar, and maybe I shouldn't invade her unsettled privacy. That was the noble reason for not going. But ignobly, I was scared. What if Mrs. Payne got violent? I did have a concert in Omaha to think about, and suppose something happened to my hands? Even at that early age I was aware of certain self-destructive tendencies in me, and Lester Brockhurst, a fairly observant man as well as a good piano teacher, had said before I left New York, "If you allow anything to happen to your hands, and what does happen will be of your doing, you had better start looking for another teacher."

Anyway, I went to see Mrs. Payne, and it was either that I was being kind, or I was being foolish, or both. They are almost impossible to tell apart anyway.

She was sitting in her workroom, looking out at the bleak hills. The Louis XV table was piled high with unopened packages of books and records and magazines still in their wrappers. There was a feel of disorder in the room, of withdrawal, of some final defeat.

When the woman turned toward me, I felt that it wasn't really Mrs. Payne, that Sarah McCormick Payne had gone to some distant place and left behind this distortion of herself. The hair was now a dirty gray, and the face was heavy. There was something lopsided about it, and the eyes I had loved were unfocused, unable to focus. The woman in the chair was old, the oldest woman I had ever seen. . . . I remembered the time Mrs. Payne had said to me, "I made the most important decision of my life, to get married, when

I was seventeen years old and in panic." And the time she had said,
"When we got to this dark, hideous house with its haunted rooms,
even before we got out of the car I said to Horton, 'Let's turn
around and go right back or head west or north or south or up or
down, but let's get away, anywhere.' And Horton said, 'We all have
to face reality, Sarah.' I didn't ask why, although the question has
since occurred to me now and again. I should think, things being
the way they are, we ought to go out of our way to avoid facing
reality. Wouldn't you? And then Mrs. Fearly came to the door, and
first she looked at me, and then she turned to Horton and said, 'I
would have guessed that you would marry a plain woman.' And I
saw that Horton was scared of her, scared of the housekeeper. I also
saw that the man I thought I had married had disappeared on West
Main before we got to the house."

I believe it was then that Mrs. Payne said, "I've never talked to
anyone like this before, and maybe I shouldn't be now. I keep for-
getting you're only a child, but then you're not really a child. Some
people are born knowing about pain and melancholy."

The old woman did something with her mouth that I believe was
meant as a smile, and she said, "Kiss me."

I kissed her on the forehead; she smelled of stale and sour things.
She said, "Charles, I am so glad you are back. The winter has
been endless, and my tattoo has throbbed daily, twenty-four hours
a day. But now that you're back . . . I've missed you."

"It's not Charley, Mrs. Payne. It's me, George Lionel."

"Sit down, Charles. Have they recognized your brilliance in New
Haven? You are doing well, aren't you? I needn't ask. Of course
you're doing well. Would you like some lemonade? It has been so
inordinately hot."

I said, no, thank you, and how have you been, Mrs. Payne?

She indicated the painting on the easel. The paint was mostly
red, and it wasn't quite dry. She said, "I've painted another bird. I
just finished it. What do you think?"

What had been the bird was black, like the one in the earlier, larger painting. But this was only part of a bird, a broken wing, a beak that seemed still to be seeking a final breath, eyes on an ocean of blood, and there were bloody feathers everywhere. Finally, surrounding the broken, scattered parts of the body, was a silver cage that seemed to be hung with emeralds and rubies and diamonds.

I said, "I'm not sure I understand it, Mrs. Payne, but I like it."

She hadn't heard. She said, "I've just been looking at you, Charles. You're going to be a very handsome man. One of my silly aunts once had the family tree traced all the way back to Charlemagne. You remind me—and isn't it silly of me to say such a thing—of Charlemagne, only handsomer and, I trust, more humane."

I said again, "I'm not Charley, Mrs. Payne. I'm George Lionel." And she said, "Of course you're not Charles. I could see that at once, Eric. You're too blond, and you have such deep blue eyes. I have never seen eyes as blue as yours, Eric." She looked again at the empty hills. She said, "My father will never approve, of course, but then he needn't ever really know. We could rent a boat, and we could take a picnic lunch and row across the lake. I've never been, but I'm told it's very peaceful and quiet over there. If it's really that way, maybe we could just stay. Forever, I mean. I've always wanted to live in a place where there's never any turmoil. And where it's always summer. My father would never approve, of course, but we could change our names, and they might never find us. Don't you think that's possible?"

I managed to say that I thought it was.

She stood up, kissed me on the forehead, and said, "I suppose I should take a nap. They all say that I need plenty of rest, but now that we're here in Minnesota, I feel ever so much stronger. I haven't told my father about meeting you, and I see no need to, ever. I'm sure Minnesota is perfectly awful in winter, worse than Illinois, I'm told, although that seems hardly possible. But in summer, like now, when it's June, it's really the nicest place in all the world, and in the fall we can go someplace where it's always summer."

I said, "Have a good nap, Mrs. Payne." And she said, "There's really no need for us to feel so alone, Charles. We have friends, but we have sometimes hesitated to call them, afraid we'd be imposing, but come to find out, whoever it is, they are usually just waiting for us to call them. It's they who've been afraid of imposing on us by calling. Educated people often feel that way. Is it snobbish of me to speak of educated people? Am I being what they call stuck-up? What an ugly phrase. They're always accusing me of being stuck-up, but I try not to be. It's just that I feel at home with certain people. There isn't anything wrong with wanting to spend time with people who read books and listen to music and have something interesting to say, is there?"

I said, no, that there wasn't, and Mrs. Payne said, "Next summer we'll have to go away. Maybe to Europe if there's money for it. Of course you'll be so educated and sophisticated by then that maybe . . . No, you'll never be like that, Charles, ashamed of your provincial mother. We'll see Europe together, the first time for both of us, after which I won't mind if I die. Life has never seemed all that precious to me. . . . And, Charles, you must promise me one thing. No matter what happens, you are not to blame your father. He didn't want it to turn out this way."

I said, "Good-bye, Mrs. Payne," and she went to her room.

I went outside and was sick in the snow on West Main. On West Main I lost all of the breakfast that would have fed an army. It was all there, the vomit and the salt from the tears and the black snow.

I never saw Sarah McCormick Payne again. Three months later they took her away in a straitjacket, strapped to a stretcher from Joiner's Funeral Parlor.

That was the only thing she ever did that the town approved of. For hours after it happened there was not a private or a party line in town that wasn't busy. "They took her East, you know, someplace in the state of Connecticut. Just like everything else. Our loony bin wasn't good enough for her. . . . Mrs. Fearly says she never lifted a finger to help out with the work. Too high and mighty to get some good, clean dirt on her hands, and she had Mrs. Mc-Lean, Fred Martin's widow, that is; he's the one took down with pneumonia, telephone lineman; they had that place on South King. Fred Martin's red zinnias used to be the talk of the community. The insurance he left, though—and you know how stingy the telephone company is—the insurance he left didn't hardly pay for getting him in the ground even, and that's why his widow come to the Paynes' two days a week to help out with the washing and ironing. And Mrs. Fearly kept house, and that fellow from Chicago, Jerome they called him, drove the car and served the meals and all. So she never had to lift a finger even, and if you ask me, that was her big trouble. If she'd of kept busy, none of this craziness would of happened."

I think I knew that winter afternoon that I'd never see Mrs. Payne again, that except for an hour now and again her mind would never return from the far place it had gone.

And I wondered who the blue-eyed Eric was. And I wondered where it was always summer. I know now that there is no such place. It isn't always summer even in Africa. I've been in Tangier in December, and the wind blows cold and drear, and there are no blue-eyed people. Nobody named Eric, and you cannot escape. You never get across the lake. You are found and stopped and punished, usually forever. Everything ends but punishment.

31 /

Con Brio

Once, if I remember well, my life was a feast where all hearts opened and all wines flowed.

That first night, again, still. Charley said, "What do you think of my mother's paintings?"

I said, "I don't know really, but they make me nervous. I'm sure that sounds silly, but I've never actually looked at any paintings before except, you know, on postcards my father buys and crap my mother clips out of *Pictorial Review*. But these are real and . . . well, I know it's silly, but I have a feeling they're good, and also they make me nervous."

Charley said, "It doesn't sound silly at all. It sounds very perceptive."

We both looked away from the paintings and out the wall of glass, and I saw that under the oak, half hidden by a patch of remaindered snow, was a single, tentative crocus, looking as forlorn and alien as the dying bird in the painting.

"God, how I hate this town," said Charley. "I go to sleep at night hating it, and I wake up in the morning hating it. I know that's probably very neurotic, but that's the way I feel. There's nobody in this town who even *thinks*. Present company excepted, of course. How do you—I mean being born here—how do you feel about it?"

I said, "Intense loathing," and Charley laughed again. He said, "As soon as I finish college, I'm going to live in Paris most of the time, maybe all the time. My mother says that Paris is really the only cosmopolitan city in the world. She says that other cities are metropolitan, but Paris is cosmopolitan. I can't wait."

I said that I couldn't either, wondering what *metropolitan* meant, what *cosmopolitan* meant.

"My mother was going to study painting in Paris," said Charley, "but then . . . she didn't."

"Why didn't she?"

"It's of no importance. Anyway, I'm going to live everywhere, in Paris and London and Hong Kong and Rangoon. But especially Paris. Elaine Jacobs' father has been there, and he calls it 'gay Paree.' My God, there must be more fools in this town than anyplace else in the world."

"Than in all the rest of the world put together."

Charley said, " 'Paris is well worth a mass.' Henry IV said that. I mentioned it and him in school the other day, in modern European history class, and do you know what Miss Drizzlebrain said? You won't believe it. She said, 'What country was he king of?' "

We both laughed, and Charley said, "Someday I'll meet you in Paris, and we'll walk down the Champs Élysées when the chestnut trees are in bloom, and we may even pick up a prostitute or two. The prostitutes in Paris are said to be very intellectual."

I said, "I've heard that myself," wondering what in the world I'd do with a prostitute. I didn't know then that boys did it.

I was in Paris the spring and summer the war ended. They were as nearly perfect as springs and summers can be, and it never happened like that again. . . . True, my hand was still in a cast, and I was technically still in the hospital, but discipline was admirably loose at the hospital. All I had to do was sleep there the night I collected my pay, and I had to check in for an hour or so every other day to have my hand looked at by a doctor who looked and talked very much like Lew Ayres in the Dr. Kildare movies I remembered with love.

Kildare looked at my hand and said soothing things like I'd be playing concerts in no time at all, and he kept saying he wanted a free ticket for my first postwar concert at Carnegie Hall. First row center, he said.

He was an almost handsome, boring, incompetent doctor. It turned out he was an anti-Semite, too. Until I met Rick and until Kildare said what he said about him, I thought I was mildly in love with the doctor. But I could never love an anti-Semite, not for more than an hour or so. Arab boys are more interested in money than politics.

Anyway, nights that were not Friday, I slept around, happily and haphazardly, with civilians and soldiers and sailors and marines and personnel of almost all of the not yet United Nations.

I did that until late July, when I met Rick Bankhead. That was not his real name, but a few days before we met he had seen a movie with Tallulah, and he fell in love with her, as persons of our gender often did in those days, and since his own name was, so he said, Polish and unpronounceable, he became Rick Bankhead.

We met on a moonless night, in a *pissoir*, if you must know. When I've talked about Rick, I've always tried to make our meeting more socially acceptable—if such meetings ever can be. I have said that we met at the Café Flore, violins in the background, crinoline. I've always yearned for a hooped skirt. And to dance a gavotte. . . . I even sometimes pretended the Café Flore fantasy with Rick, but he, unburdened by groping Methodism, not to mention the galloping Presbyterians, always said, "The point is not where we met. It is that we met."

Who said the Poles were stupid?

I never knew how old Rick was. He said he was seventeen, but he lied about things. He looked about twelve, and his first words to me were, "I am in need of Inca love, and you are an Inca, are you not?" He meant Yank, not Inca, but he was certainly in need of love, and of food, and a bath. Mostly love, though. You can go for years without the other two.

Rick claimed to be the son of a Polish prince, and he described the estate on which he said he had been born and spent the first eleven years of his life so persuasively that I most of the time believed him. I tried to anyway; I desperately wanted to.

He talked of the great rooms of the great house, of the endless lawns, of the gardens and gardeners, of the great balls that were held. Of the royal ladies in gowns of lace. Of the gallant titled gentlemen who danced with them. Of the blind grandfather who told him stories about his royal ancestors. Of the butler who seduced him when he was nine. Of the maid who did what she did when he was ten. Of the governess who . . . He described his handsome, princely father. His dark princess of a mother. . . . And it all sounded so beautiful, and his eyes glowed so exuberantly when he told it, that I wanted it all to be true.

And then, Rick would say, his stately father went off to war, and the Nazis came and took away and no doubt raped his gentle mother, after which the young prince ". . . wandered, alone and afraid, all across the face of Europe, until I came to Paris and met . . ."

Met me. At the Café Flore.

Rick was so skeleton thin, his bones so delicate, so breakable, that he could have been a prince, I thought, with perhaps a blending of some errant Gypsy blood. He had startled dark eyes that, remembering them now, seem to have taken up half his face, with the longest lashes ever.

Rick moaned in his sleep, screamed in his sleep, shouted in his sleep, and begged in his sleep in a language that could have been Polish. And I held the screaming skeleton in my arms, and he slept on.

He had black hair that never really got untangled, although he often shampooed it as many as half a dozen times a day. And it seems to me he washed every hour on the hour; but he always looked dirty, appealingly, sweetly dirty. And when we were not sleeping or having sex or talking, Rick ate, eight, ten, twelve meals a day. He ate greedily and gratefully, but he never gained an ounce of weight; he was still and always a skeleton.

And we walked. It seems to me now there was not a street in Paris that was not known to us, not an art gallery, not a museum, not a concert hall, not a theater.

Sometimes I would practice with my left hand for a while, and princely Rick would sit beside me, asking nothing; he was always grateful to be there, where he was, I was, we were.

I wrote the first Concerto for the Left Hand that summer and dedicated it to Rick.

One day I took Rick to the hospital with me, and Kildare did not like him. He said—and this was the summer of 1945, mind you, just after the concentration camps, after Buchenwald and Auschwitz and . . . after the deaths of six million—Kildare said, "If you ask me, with eyes like that and a nose like that, the kid's a kike. A kike trying to pass. A Polish prince, my ass; all you have to do is take one look at that nose. . . ."

I told you that Rick had great, frightened eyes, and he had a straight nose, not too large, with a slight bump on the end. . . . Here we are, noses again. Anyway, it seemed like any kind of nose to me, and I loved all of Rick, bumps and humps and warts and all. To me he was always a Polish prince who would never get enough to eat. Or gain a pound. Who screamed in the night, and Jews, passing or not, and princes scream the same way.

Then one Saturday morning toward the end of August, Rick disappeared. As we often did, we had spent the previous night in a small hotel near the hospital. The sheets were always damp. I remember that. We had breakfast nearby, and then, it being Friday, I went to the hospital and collected my pay. Kildare looked at my hand, and I had to sign a piece of paper and spend the night at the hospital.

The next morning I went back to the hotel, and Rick was gone. The clothes that I had bought him were still there. He had gone in the rags he was wearing the night we met.

I think I knew then that I would never see him again, and I never did. No one had seen him go, and he left no good-byes. No, we had not quarreled; we never quarreled.

I went to the police, but in that year the Paris police didn't have much interest in a boy who, princely or not, called himself, pre-posterous, Rick Bankhead, a boy who, despite all the loving and eating, was still skeletal.

That's the end of it, all of it. Life never ends neatly; it is all loose ends. . . . When I think of Rick now, and sometimes I do, I think of the huge eyes, the thick, long lashes, and I think of him sleeping, not screaming, still looking like an orphan of twelve. Or a prince of eight. When I think of him now, I sometimes cry.

I hope he found someone strong and loving and rich. I hope that he, like Nicky Pondorus, owns a yacht. I hope that he is pleasingly plump and rich and adored. I hope. . . . As I say, it is ever so much better when you don't know what happens to people.

When asked what wine he liked to drink, he replied, "That which belongs to another."

Charley came to Paris not long after Rick disappeared. I hadn't seen him since the gray November morning four years before when he came to New York from New Haven and told me that his mother had managed to jump out of a window at the place in Connecticut and had, fortunately, died at once. On that morning Charley's face was as gray as the day. In so short a time his father had killed him-self; the bank had closed; the money was all gone; and now his mother was gone, too.

Beyond the grayness I cannot remember much about that morn-ing. We had a drink at the men's bar in the Biltmore, and we agreed that that was the first time either of us had ever had a drink in the morning.

I walked Charley to the train, and he went back to New Haven. A few days after Pearl Harbor he enlisted in the army, and then he went to officer candidate school, and by that time I was in the OSS. And then Charley was in a tank outfit. . . . He was never much for writing, and neither was I. . . . A card from North Africa . . . and then one from Sicily, and after that Italy, and then from the hospital in Rome where they took the arm. . . . So went those years, so quickly went those years.

Charley and I never talked about the arm. I don't know how it happened. Charley said, "Two arms are redundant anyway." And he said, "I'll miss skiing, but think of all the sympathy I'll get from all the judges and the juries."

Charley came down to Paris from a place in Normandy called Camp Lucky Strike, where he was waiting to be sent home. He had all the plans all of us had at the time, except that, to me anyway, Charley's plans seemed grander.

He had five thousand dollars saved from his army pay and his winnings at poker, and he was going back to Yale, getting his B.A., then his law degree. "And then," he said, "we shall together remake the world, not necessarily in our own image, but judging by what we've seen in the last few years, we could do a lot worse, don't you think?"

Naturally I said yes; I always said yes to Charley. . . . But you know something? For a while it looked as if it might work that way. And then one morning the phone rang, and I picked it up, and there was a silence, and I put the phone down, and it rang again. The same thing happened, time after time after time, week after week. And then I realized I was being followed. . . . But that must wait.

In Paris that night Charley and I sat in a tiny bar in Pigalle. The cognac was bad but cheap, and madame sat behind the bar and smiled at me. She had lost a son in the war, and she said that I reminded her of him. Madame was kind. It seems in my memory that everyone was kind that summer and even in the early fall.

I remember Charley, who was a major, saying that he had carried a copy of Herodotus all through the war, from Benning on to the night his tank exploded just outside whatever town it was in Italy.

Charley said, " 'They joined battle, and the Phocaeans won, yet it was but a Cadmean victory.' " He said, "I would like to kill the man who broke your hand." He said, "No, no more killing. I have had enough killing to last me. To last all of us." He said, "It's going to be okay. We are going to be okay. Things are not going to be perfect, but they are going to be ever so much better. I've spent the last four years telling myself that. I had to tell myself that or I wouldn't have gone on." And he said, "How sad we are, the two of us. I didn't know we were going to be so sad. Did you? But that's all over, the sadness. From here on in, everybody will be free in four different ways." He said, "I don't really believe that, not all of it, but I have had to believe some of it. Otherwise . . . Shall we have another cognac?"

We sat in the small, immaculate bar all night, drinking madame's bad cognac, remembering what we allowed ourselves to remember. And just before dawn we walked to the Champs Élysées and then up to the Arc de Triomphe. It was that bleak hour before dawn when even the whores had retired for the night. We stood for a time in front of the tomb of the Unknown, and it seems eternal, Soldier, and I think we both prayed to the promising sunrise. I don't believe either of us thought we had made the world safe for anything at all, but we had bought ourselves a little peace, hadn't we, a time of quiet?

Later that morning Charley started back to Camp Lucky Strike, waving good-bye with the arm he still had, looking lordly and arrogant again, and I loved him again. . . . I thought a good deal about that missing arm, but in those days there was so much publicity about how marvelous artificial arms were that you sometimes wondered why people didn't cut off their real arms just to get an artificial one.

Charley never wore an artificial arm; he never wore an artificial anything, except once in a while in the early days of his marriage to Cec. In those days he tried on a few artificial opinions; he wanted very much to please Cec, but he never ever did. And he took off the fraudulent opinions, and then there was the night the little girl ran out of the house when she heard Charley's car, and Charley didn't see her.

At the trial Charley said he wasn't drunk, and I believe that. I never saw Charley drunk, never. The bartender said he had had eight drinks, maybe nine, but he said he would not have considered Charley drunk. . . . The little girl died, though, and not so very much later so did Charley, and he was the last of the Paynes, the very last. Maybe the Paynes were cursed. That's what people said, but it never made any sense to me.

Wandering Jews

Perhaps some day it will be pleasant to remember these things.

Rick, of course. That preposterous boy with the unpronounce-able name. Yes, I knew he was a Jew. I knew it all along. Yes, I lie. I hold things back. I distort, conceal. You will never get to the bottom of me. I should think it best that you not try. . . . There will always be another surprise. I'm a magician, with tricks up my sleeves and concealed elsewhere on me and in me. . . . As a child, I had a magic set. I could produce rabbits out of hats and take coins from people's ears. And I transformed things, yellow water into blue, gold into dross. I was the only thing I could never transform. And I'd have settled for anything, you understand, anybody else, any-thing else. . . . I'm coming back as a bumblebee. Guess.

I knew Rick was a Jew because late one night he screamed for mercy for his father. His father was a rabbi, and his father burned in a bake oven. I think at Auschwitz. . . . No, I never mentioned the screams to poor Rick. It is my theory that we are all entitled to our secrets. . . . No, I never mentioned the screams. I took Rick in my arms and comforted him. That's really all you can ever do. Comfort them, calm them, care for them. Keep their secrets.

It is enough to have perished once.

Rosenberg. I never did finish telling you about Rosenberg. About

323

the last time I saw him. Saturday, the second Saturday in September, and that year it did not snow on Labor Day. In September, 1938, the year our eighteen-year-old hero went to New York, expecting to find the streets paved with gold. Instead I met The Clarinet Player, and that was all pure gold, beginning to end. Maybe it's better if they die. You die.

The September day I'm remembering was searingly hot, and Rosenberg's nose was more than ordinarily forbidding, his eyes more than usually bloodshot. His hands were steady enough, though, and shortly after I got to the stifling room on East Main, he sat down at the piano and played Mozart's Sonata in A Major. More than thirty years passed before I heard it played that well again. In Royal Festival Hall in London. A stocky redheaded man walked onstage with a glass in his hand; he placed the glass on the piano, and I assumed it was filled with vodka, though most likely it was water.

In any case, whatever it was, Emil Gilels did not touch it until the concert was over; then he drank half of it at once and acknowledged the applause and cheers. I cheered.

I wished that night that Rosenberg could have heard Emil. He would have approved. Mozart would have approved, too, and he was not an easy man to please. . . . "That kind of sight reading and shitting are all one to me." . . . "Instead of sitting in the middle of the clavier, she sits right up opposite the treble, as it gives her more chance of flopping about and making grimaces. . . . She rolls her eyes and smirks."

When Rosenberg got up from the piano, Chicken Little was crying and said, in a sorrowing soprano voice, "That was beautiful, Rosenberg. As you can see, it even made me cry."

Rosenberg said, "Please. Spare me your bourgeois sentimentality, and I in turn will try not to wince with pain while you, as usual, bungle it."

I didn't bungle it. As a matter of fact, I'd never played it better. Not in a class with Gilels. Not even close to being as good as Rosenberg, but for the time and place and considering the handicaps, not at all bad. . . . Of course the Russians turn out the best pianists. I don't know why. They just do. Richter is not as good as Gilels, but he is better than any of us. Except maybe for Christopher. Ten years from now, if Christopher doesn't . . . doesn't do any of the ten thousand things he likely will do to diminish himself, he could be the best there ever was. . . . I don't know why it's so hazardous. Obviously.

I got up from the piano, and Rosenberg, who was standing at the window, said, "There have been worse." "Worse what, Rosenberg?" "You know what I mean," he said, and I said, "As a matter of fact, I don't. So why don't you come right out and say it?"

And Rosenberg said, "Through some fluke, and I really don't understand it, you weren't too bad today."

"Do you think I'll ever be really good?"

Rosenberg said, "I couldn't possibly know that, and besides, it's of no interest to me." I said, "Well, I guess that settles that." And I put the ten dollars on top of the piano and said, "It's a hell of a way to say good-bye. You know damn well I'm going to New York in the morning. So good-bye, you bastard."

Rosenberg turned then, and there were tears in his eyes. I wouldn't have thought Rosenberg could cry. Or ever did cry. . . . For one thing, I couldn't imagine Rosenberg as a child. A thirteen-year-old with that nose? Don't be silly. A child of nine, his slender shoulders laden with that much dandruff? Of course not.

Moreover, it was my particular conceit at the time that I was the only person anywhere who was so sensitive to pain and, thus, entitled to cry. And who else could feel a pea through thirty mattresses?

I'll tell you this. If I'd known that at—oh, hell, honey, honesty pays, but what does honesty pay?—if I'd known that at fifty-two, everything would hurt just as much as it did when I was eighteen, when I was eight, if I'd known that the sores never really scab over, except for the minor ones . . . Petulia, if I'd known that, I'd never have got out of the crib. I'd still be sucking away at that shriveled titty.

❖

Rosenberg said, "Lester Brockhurst is a very good teacher. Within a month you won't even remember my name."

"I'll never forget you, and you know it. I'll never be able to thank you enough, either. I wouldn't even know how to start."

"Then I suggest you don't try."

"I'll see you around Christmas time then. I'm coming home for Christmas. My mother made me promise I would."

"Do you really think you'll see me? Do you think I'll stay in this forlorn spa after you've gone? All these years and you know me no better than that? Do you think I like the malicious weather here? I have stayed because much against my better judgment I have dared hope that you might become a competent musician someday. Not a *success*. Artur Rubenstein is a *success*, and he should instead be locked up. No, competent. That is the most I can hope. Go now. Go quickly."

I started toward Rosenberg, my hand outstretched, but at the sight of his stoplight of a nose and the look in his despondent eyes, I stopped. I said, "If you do leave town, Rosenberg, please let me know where you go. So that we can keep in touch."

"I doubt that where I'm going that will be possible," said Rosenberg.

And those were the last words he ever said to me. I walked out the door, closed it, went down the steps with the neglected carpeting, and was still crying when I got to the house on South Third Avenue. I went directly to my room, for the last time locking the door behind me.

Rosenberg died in November, leaving behind nothing much more than the portrait of Beethoven in the silver frame, which he wanted me to have and which I have now passed on to Christopher. I don't know what happened to the quotation about the jealous gods.

Do you know what I will always regret? Oh, not the boys and men I've bedded down with, however many there were; not the people I've loved for an hour or so, and it was love no matter how transient.

It's the people I haven't touched that I regret. I regret that I never

once told Rosenberg that I loved him. I never once touched him. . . .
That's the kind of rue and regret any decent god would understand. . . . A tender toucher. Don't you see? It's good, not evil; it's
life, not death; it's joyous, not sad. Go thou forth and touch.

Zeus, who has always been my idea of the kind of god we ought
to have more of, never stopped drinking wine and touching Ganymede. And why should he? Ganymede was the most beautiful youth
alove. I've touched thousands of them. . . . Thou shalt not commit
unloving.

When I was home at Christmas time Florence Canady gave me
the Beethoven portrait, and she said, "When you was still here, he
used to stay sober until after he give you your lesson, but after you
up and left, I don't think he drew a sober breath, and he never slept.
Pretty soon he didn't have no pupils; they all quit him. I let him
stay, though, even if he didn't have no money left except for the
booze. If they're boozers, they can always find money for their drink.
I learned that from Canady himself, poor man. The mister was a
boozer, too, you know.

"And anyway, to make a long story short, Rosenberg was at the
place where he bought the booze, and I have no intention of naming
that house of infamy, and when he was about half a block or so
away, he slipped on the ice and broke I don't know what all, and cut
himself on the glass. The booze went, too.

"He was laying out there in the cold and the blood for hours before they found him, and when they got him to the hospital, I says
to your mother, I says, 'Dora, he'll never get out.' I says, 'That's the
end of poor Rosenberg.' And it was. He died a week later. Double
pneumonia, not to mention his liver and other injuries too numerous
to mention.

"And buried way out there in the country. I and the undertaker
was the only two there. I says to him, I says, 'Rosenberg, you're going to want a service when you go, and I'll get Rabbi Krantman. . . .'
And you know what he says, his very words, he says, 'You let a rabbi
near me, and I'll get right up out of the pine box and kick you and
him right square in the ass. Is that clear?' Oh, he talked dirty some-

times, but he was a good man, one of the best. . . . And he liked you,
young sir. Why, to hear him tell it, there wasn't nothing in the world
you couldn't do. He said, 'That boy is a genius, and the day will
come when this town will be putting up statues of George Lionel.'

" 'And, Florence'—he called me Florence—'Florence,' he said, 'I
want no monument of any kind when I go. No marker, nothing.
George Lionel will be my monument, and he is more than monument
enough. Someday that boy will be the best of them all.' "

I am glad poor Rosenberg died still thinking that.

The day before Christmas I got in the car, a very old Packard,
ten years old, maybe more. My father had bought it secondhand, and
it was the last car he ever did buy. The undertaker drove it to my
father's funeral, and then the undertaker bought the car from my
mother. By then it must have been at least twelve years old. Packards
were built to last, but my father was not.

I drove down West Main very slowly. Some people nodded and
beeped their horns at me. There had been a long story about me in
that morning's *Register*, and a photograph: ". . . local boy wins . . ."
And there was another story and photograph in the *Times-Dispatch*
that afternoon: ". . . one of music's most honored awards goes to
local . . ."

Five or six miles out in the country I turned off what was then
called the Lincoln Highway onto a dirt road that was a dead end.
Now it is part of the superhighway. All concrete, coast to coast,
border to border. Grass was outlawed years ago, and the last of the
trees will go in August. Except for those in the Malevolent Forest.
That has become a national shrine.

But in those days the road I'm talking about was a rutted, single-
lane dirt road. I stopped at the edge of the tiny graveyard, at the
foot of a giant oak.

There were maybe twenty headstones. I used to be able to remember the name and inscription on each. "*Jacob Ritner, 1806–1853. He
passed on far from home. Beloved Wife Anna Ritner, 1810–1863. She*

suffered much but complained not at all. Dale Ritner, 1901–1907. He did not linger long.

Those are the only ones I remember now, and I remember the slight mound in the snow, unmarked save for a bouquet of artificial flowers. The flowers were no doubt from Florence Canady, and under them were the bones of Rosenberg. All of that wandering Jew that was left anywhere, except in my mind. In the mind of the unstable monument he had left behind, a monument that creaked in the slightest breeze, that shuddered and shivered and shook on the clearest days. A monument frightened of moving shadows and shadows that do not move. I have screamed at the sight of the web of the smallest spider. I have shuddered at the imprint of the footstep of a unicorn. Rabbits threaten me. I have been deafened by the sound of the wings of a gypsy moth. . . . What an insubstantial monument. Poor Rosenberg.

I remember the day I took Rosenberg to the graveyard. It was summer, and after the lesson I said, "Come on, Rosenberg. I'll take you for a drive in the Packard. It'll do you good to get out in the country."

"What possible good would it do me? What it will do is cut into my drinking time, and I never allow anything to do that."

"Please. As a favor to your favorite pupil."

"*That* is hardly a distinction, but I'll go for half an hour, half an hour only, and I pray that you are a better driver than you are a pianist."

I said, "I am. I had a better teacher. My father."

Rosenberg laughed, and do you know, in all those years that is the only time I remember him laughing. I cannot remember the sound of it, only the fact of it. Who was it who said of someone that he seemed always to be stepping out of a sadness to meet one? I don't remember who, but that is a perfect description of Rosenberg.

I took Rosenberg to the tiny graveyard because as a child I had liked going there myself. The graveyard was within walking distance of the place we lived before moving to town. We lived on a sixty-acre farm where the only crop was dust, where the barn burned the week after my father let the insurance lapse, where the cows got tuberculosis and died, where the only horse broke his leg in a post-hole, where . . . The last summer we lived there the corn was filled with rust and was unsalable. And that same summer the stream in which I used to go wading dried up completely. We were not a family noted for winning.

I used to walk barefoot to the graveyard when, as my father said, "Things get too much for you." Things got too much for me two or three times a week, sometimes every day, and I'd go there and sit on one of the headstones, probably Jacob's, it being the largest. . . .

Rosenberg said, "Do you suppose they could put my body here instead of that garish public burial ground on East Linn?"

I said I'd find out. I didn't have to ask why Rosenberg wanted to be there. I knew that even in death he wanted to be as far away from most people as possible. . . . I think Rosenberg paid the farmer who then owned the land fifty dollars for his plot, and that is where they put the shell of him.

That summer afternoon I said, "It's silly of you to talk about dying; you're a young man, for heaven's sake, but if something should happen to you, somebody has to be notified. You'd better give me the name—"

"Nobody has to be notified," said Rosenberg.

And that was the end of that. The mystery remains, will always remain. But even wandering Jews, touched or untouched, someday die.

I have always looked at the obituary page of any newspaper first, but during the last few years I have approached it with caution, afraid my own closing notice would be there. . . . I've read what they'll say about me in the *Times*. Three-quarters of a column, more than I deserve, and most of it true, which is unusual, considering the fact that they have left out all the most interesting things about me.

I've seen my FBI dossier, too, two full drawers of it, the most damaging evidence imaginable, imaginative. I don't know why they didn't keep me in for life.

The reason there's so much of it, all my enemies, and I appear to have had nothing but enemies, talked. Also it turns out that two of the people with whom or of whom I had carnal knowledge were undercover FBI agents. They claimed I raped them. . . . I forget how they were in bed. Ask Auntie Edgar. I doubt if they were much good, though. People who take notes during almost never are.

How did I get to see my dossier? That's a good question. I'm glad you asked that question, Antigone. . . . The third FBI man I knew and loved, though not for long, did not kiss and tell. He resigned and brought his dossier and mine with him. And we read them aloud to each other and laughed and loved and groaned and moaned. And then he went into some other line of work. I believe he became a shepherd.

No, not all FBI agents are fruitcakes; only about ninety percent, I'd say, has been my experience. . . . But I'll tell you this. They've got enough on all of us for burning. The stage will be littered with corpses, all burned to a wisp.

33 /

She Saw
the Water Lily
Bloom

A note from Lily. She is back in London.

Of course it has rained every day since I've been here, and of course it is chilling a good deal of the time; I haven't really been warm once in the last three weeks. However, everything is very green, and next week the rhododendron and the crocuses will be blooming in the circle in front of my hotel. So I may survive. Besides, Peter is joining me the last week in May. I don't know whether we'll do the Grand Tour or just mosey around England. Whatever Peter wants. He is not a frivolous boy and does not make frivolous decisions. So says his doting but, hopefully, not too doting mother.

I have thought about Shawn a good deal since I've been here, remembering him with great affection. He was such a sweet man, and I don't think I appreciated sweetness enough of the time. I didn't know how rare it is. . . . I've been thinking about you, too, of course, and about Charles. Thinking about us and crying some but only in the privacy of my room. Thinking how far we all came and how none of us ever left home. I now don't think that we did.

I have not given much thought to Bruno Hyerly. That is really all blocked out or blacked out. I'm not sure which, or if it can truly be gone, but it's not in the front of my mind these days. I don't think it is anyway.

Observe how uncertain I am If I recall my youth correctly, I did not allow for uncertainties of any kind. How ignorant I was. . . . But my question now is this: Does everyone make such wounding, crippling, suicidal mistakes as we do? Did? Have? Every day on the streets I pass people my age and more who seem to be all in one piece, collected, calm, unscarred, happy even. I have heard them laugh.

And I ask myself, myself because there is almost never anyone else to ask: How can that be? Is it because I don't know these people that they seem content? Is it because they are English? The climate? And, the darkest question of all, do I look that way to them?

In any case, I was today thinking, gratefully, of you and how twice you comforted me. At very crucial times I mean. . . . You may not know it, but you are really a very good person. I have decided to tell people things like that now. Not wait until after reading the obituary and then regret not having told them.

There are never many to tell, but we don't do it anyway, and so beginning right now I am telling you. You are a good person and a good comforter. I give you A plus in comforting. The day Shawn died, for instance, and the day I left the man who shall remain nameless because he has all the other attributes of a bastard. If it hadn't been for you . . .

If it hadn't been for me, it wouldn't have been all that different, Lil. Believe me. You are a stalwart lady. You are not as strong as steel, and your skin is not of brass, but you are well put together at the seams; you do not come apart easily, and, Lily love, from where I sit that is a very great deal.

And I didn't really do anything. All I did was be there. But then maybe that's enough. I was there, and I listened, and I sorrowed for you. I wished the best for you. . . . I guess we all have to settle for that.

When my father so lengthily and painfully died, much as I loved him I couldn't wait to escape from that deathly room. I remember once he said in the diminished voice that came from so far inside of him, "It wouldn't have made any difference."

And, wishing I felt more sorrow than I did, that I loved him more than I did, I said, "What wouldn't have, Pop?"

He said, "Oh, I don't know. I keep thinking if I'd turned right someplace instead of left, if I'd finished college, and I could have, I suppose, if I'd just worked a little harder. If I'd—and I know you won't tell your mother I said this—if I'd married someone else. If I'd, if we'd had more money and lived in grander houses, seen all the things we planned seeing, if . . . But then I really know that no matter what, it still would have ended up pretty much like this. Just in a different room. Don't you think?"

That was the longest speech I ever heard him make, and it exhausted him, and he soon fell asleep. I managed to say, "I don't know, Pop. I don't guess anybody ever does." That was the only time ever I guess that I called him Pop. . . .

Oh, yes, I remember the day Lily left Bruno Hyerly. I hadn't seen her for more than a year. I didn't even know she was in New York. She spent a good deal of time in Washington, and as I've said, she and Bruno always seemed to be having dinner at Camelot.

The phone rang, and Lily said, "Could I come to see you? Right away? It's important."

I was working hard on a concerto that was to be played at Tanglewood in less than a month, but of course I said of course. What a welcome excuse to stop work and at the same time play Florence Nightingale. I could tell from the sound of her voice that Lily was in trouble.

She looked as if she hadn't slept for weeks, and for the first time in all the years I'd known her she looked disheveled; even her stockings were baggy. She came into the apartment—this time it was on Riverside Drive—and said, "Could I please have a drink? Make it a double and don't get all moral about my drinking in the morning."

I said, "Alcohol is one of the many, many things about which I have never been moral."

When I got back from the kitchen with the drinks, two of them, blow the day, Lily was looking at what I was writing, and she said, "I can't read a note of music any more, but I'll bet it is going to be wonderful."

"Mildly wonderful."

Lily's hands were trembling, and when I handed her the drink, I also gave her some Kleenex. She drank half the drink and said, "I'm leaving Bruno. And I'm scared. Isn't that silly? No, it isn't silly. He could and would have a person killed. Maybe he already has, hundreds for all I know. I know a lot about him. Don't I just? I've got a lot on him but not that. But it probably would be hundreds. Because as he so often and so wittily says, he never does anything by halves. He's *capable* of having somebody killed. I know that. And I know that he doesn't want me to divorce him. Oh, not because he loves me or likes me even; he gave up that pretense some time ago. He doesn't like or love himself or anybody else in the entire wide and shining world. He says that if I divorced him, it would be a reflection on *him*. Besides, he thinks I'll talk."

"Talk about what?"

"All the rotten, ugly things he does every day and every night. What I know about him would make the front page of the *Times* for days and days, not to mention sending him to jail for life. But I am not going to do anything about it. Nothing at all. All I want is to be put in one of those boxes that psychiatrist had. Was it Reik? I'd like to be put in one of those for life. And could I have another drink?"

During our second doubles Lily said, "I don't think I've ever really hated anybody before, not totally. Bruno is crazy. I mean it. He is dangerously insane. He is a certifiable paranoid, and he has a room full of guns, and someday he is going to use them for something other than blood sports. Blood sports and sex. The latter practically a full-time occupation with him. When he isn't taking over something or consolidating something—and he can't keep occupied twenty-four hours a day just with business—it's sex. Girls, boys, everything, everybody. He beats them and makes them say they adore him. And more. And more. And more."

"I hope you're going to take him for plenty."

"All I want is out. He won't believe that. He knows I know enough to take it all if I wanted to, but I don't. If I did, if I took anything, it would give him a hold over me. That's what he thinks anyway, and I think he may be right. But I want nothing. I've got enough to get Peter through college, and that is really all I care about."

"You could use another drink."

"Don't worry," said Lily. "I won't become a lush. After today, I'll turn teetotal and become a virgin."

Later Lily said, "It was such a really beautiful day. It is still a very beautiful day. Just look . . . I got up and looked out the window, and I said to myself—I talk to myself a good deal these days—'On such a day as this I am going to have a good time; I am going to enjoy myself, and nothing and nobody can stop me.' I started getting dressed. I was going to start out this good day with a long walk in the park. And then he came in. He'd been up all night. Three boys and three girls. I'd heard all of it. He always wanted me to hear all of it. Every grunt, every scream.

"He came in, looked at me, and said, 'I'd take my clothes off if I were you. It's somewhat more comfortable with your clothes off.'

"When it was over, I got dressed again, and he was on the bed. He said, 'I expect you back in two hours, and we'll have another go at it.' I told him I was leaving him, but I still don't think he believes me."

"It can't be all that sudden, just what happened this morning."

"Oh, no. In fact, this was what might be called one of our better mornings. I've been thinking about it for months, for years, but I thought I'd wait until Peter finished at Hotchkiss, and now he is, and—"

"Does Peter know?"

"He knows it was coming. We had dinner last night; maybe that's why I decided what I decided this morning. I mean because Peter and I had had dinner. He is such a nice boy. I know you think *nice* is a silly word, but he is simply nice. And to use my final silly phrase of the morning—what a cliché dropper I've become—Peter seems to know who he is. Which is more than can be said for his aging mother."

"You're tolerable, Lily, really quite tolerable."

"Well, I'm not responsible for all or even any of the wonderful things Peter is. The headmaster at Hotchkiss said, 'He's the kind of boy we most appreciate, and there are never many like him.' I think Peter is going to make it. Have a good life, I mean."

"I hope you're right. I've never been quite sure what a good life is, but I hope Peter has one."

I offered Lily another drink, but she said, "No, I'd better pull myself together and then go see my lawyer and renew my passport. I'll go to Mexico, I suppose, and—"

"Not today you're not. You have another drink, and I am going to get all dolled up and take you to *our* Italian restaurant, and then I'm going to take you to the Frick or the Whitney, you choose, *and* the Metropolitan, and then we will have tea at the Stanhope, after which we will see. It will be just like the afternoon shortly after you first got to New York, and we both played hooky and did just that. And that night I took you to Eddie Condon's, and we stayed up until all hours, and somebody saw us, and we were written up as what I believe is called 'an item' in Walter Winchell's column."

"I'm afraid it won't be just like that, but it will be beautiful," said Lily, and she kissed me and said, "You're my oldest friend, and I think I love you more than anybody."

"It is most unfortunate that I am not the marrying kind. You and I might have made sweet music together, Lil."

"But if you were the marrying kind, you wouldn't be you. And I for one don't want you to change. Okay, Arturo?"

During lunch I said, "Lil, my love, why the hell did you marry Bruno Hyerly in the first place? It wasn't really because you wanted Peter to go to Hotchkiss, was it?"

It took Lily quite a while to answer, but she has always been fairly good at answering questions, even the hard ones. She said, "I did think that. Often for as long as fifteen minutes at a time I thought that, and I did want Peter to go to Hotchkiss, but I could have managed that without Bruno, with some squeezing I could have. But mostly, I'm this commendably honest person with myself. Wouldn't you say?"

"For years when people asked me about you and often when they didn't I have said, 'Lily is this commendably honest—' "

"The first time I married for love, or what I thought was love. The second time I thought, Well, why not? I have never been one of your big believers in love. To me it has always been highly overrated, and I thought . . . Well, you remember I once told you that being born poor was the only original sin. And I wanted to get as far away from Farrell's Eats as possible. And from the girls at the sorority when I was in college. When I came into a room, they'd sniff the air and say, 'Does it smell like hamburger in here? Oh, hello there, Lily dear.' Things like that, the dears."

"God, the lengths we go to to get the favorable opinion of people we don't give a damn about. Is it worth it, do you think?"

"I can answer that one," said Lily. "It's not, but try and stop us from trying. So there was Bruno with all that money, and I thought he wasn't a bad fellow. Indeed, before the nuptials he was kindly to me, and he is comely enough, and he makes all those liberal and humanitarian noises, and he knew the man who was going to be President, and we all want to be Cinderella, and midnight will never come, besides which I have always hankered after a glass slipper."

"Isn't it a pity. Things never work out the way it is in fairy stories, not even for fairies."

"I'm afraid not. I did not like any of those people. Even when we were having dinner with the king and queen at Buckingham Palace, I'd listen to them, and I'd think, 'These are not nice people. These are unkind people and cruel and cynical people. They are monstrous people, and why is it that nobody ever writes or tells the truth about things as they are?' "

"I have wondered that myself," I said.

And that's the way it was the day Lily left Bruno Hyerly, and now she is in London and writes,

I am alone, and I think now that I always will be, except once in a rare while when I am with Peter. But then I was alone during all of one marriage and a good part of the time during another. And as I believe you once pointed out to me, there are worse things. It is better to be in a room in which there is nobody than it is to be alone in a room in which there is somebody else.

I get through the day, and, dear friend, maybe that is all there ever was or ever will be. I love Peter, and I believe he is fond of me. Isn't it odd? Even with the ones closest to us we always have to say, I *believe* he is, she is fond of me. I love you, and I believe you are fond of me. . . . I tried to see you before I left, but the jailers said . . . Why don't you get sprung and get on a plane? We could have such a good time, and you know how much Peter likes you. Come on. You are the only one I love, or ever did.

A very good letter from Lily. Yes, I guess I love her, too. That's possible, you know, for me to love a woman. I still love Dede. It's just the going to bed part that . . .

No, I do not want to see the doctor. It isn't my time to see the doctor. I don't have to see him again until . . . Oh, Jesus. All right. I'll go, but nothing he has to tell me will . . . Look, if it's so goddamn important why doesn't he . . . All right. Stop shouting. I hate scenes. I hate loud voices, in particular yours, Miss Benson. I am not fond of your voice even when . . . I knew something like this would happen. No wonder I hate Thursdays. It is? All right. I hate Fridays, too. How many days in a week are there now?

34 /

I'll Be There

The limousine will be here in fifteen minutes; so this is written hurriedly, on the run, but then what in my life has not been? No, I did not know. I knew about the pot, but I did not know about the other. . . . For God's sake, why? Why did he have to? The boy who has everything. Somebody said that, wrote that, thought that. Perhaps it was I. . . . The boy who has everything has taken an overdose of . . .

The doctor said he was reasonably sure it was accidental.

"But not totally sure?"

"Of course not. He hasn't completely regained consciousness, but there was no note, nothing to indicate that he was despondent, and last night he was simply magnificent. A standing ovation. I was there myself, and before he played the Grieg concerto he said, 'And I dedicate this to my great and beloved teacher, George Lionel.'"

A little later I said, "He'll be all right, won't he?"

The doctor said, "It will be a long, difficult fight, but I think so. He's going to need your help, though. He keeps asking for you. Those are the only words we've been able to make out. He keeps saying, 'Is George here yet? When will George get here?'"

"I'll be there," I said, instantly regretting it. And then I said, "Is he a regular user . . . an addict?"

"I'm afraid so," said the doctor.

I said, "I'll be there by midnight."

But, Christopher, my love, I can't. Really I can't. What would be the use of it anyway? I'm not an M.D., and I am certainly not a psychiatrist. What I am is an emotionally crippled, aging, cowardly faggot, and what possible good could a person like that do? Harm is what a person like that will do, has done, everywhere, always.

And anyway, baby, I'm crazy as a bedbug, and if I leave here I'll probably hack away at my wrists again. And I'll get on the sauce again. I was up to a quart and a half a day just before I came here, and I'd surely try to better that record. I have to be champion of something. I could never play baseball, not in pink tights I couldn't.

Besides, I'm highly contagious. Thousands of boys have caught it from me.

No, I should not be allowed out, will not allow myself out. I have not been farther from this room than the doctor's office for . . . several lifetimes at least. And you want me to go *outdoors*. And after that sit in the back seat of a car driven by a convicted murderer. And if I should survive that, and there isn't one chance in a thousand that I will, I would have to get into a flying coffin that is certain to crash. . . . No, I can't, love. Sorry.

Baby, why did you? Why must you? Especially today. Today is the day they convict me. The jury is still out, but I'm told they'll bring in a guilty verdict by sundown, and the execution is at dawn tomorrow. I must be here for my own execution. That is the one thing you can't get a substitute for.

"It's going to be a long, hard pull," said the doctor. "He's going to need somebody with him constantly."

I said, "I can't come. I'd like to, but I can't."

"I'm sorry," said the doctor. "He keeps asking for you. How about his mother? Is she still in Louisville?"

"For God's sake don't call his mother," I said. "He hates his mother. I'll be there by midnight."

❖

Goddamn you anyway, my love. Why did you have to . . . ? Please, God. Oh, please, God. I don't give a good goddamn about me. I never have. But please protect that fragile boy. That sweet, breakable, beautiful genius. Why is it that those who have the most, are the most . . . ?

God, please make him well again. Look, I won't make any cheap promises. I'd despise myself if I did, and You'd despise me. But Christopher is important, God; he matters. . . . Love, this is the only time I haven't asked for something for myself. Doesn't that count for something?

"Those are the only words we can make out," said the doctor. "He keeps asking for you."

I said, "I'll be there at midnight."

All right, Bensy. So the limousine is here. Good for the limousine. I could change my mind about going, and anyway there's no hurry. All right then. We'll miss that flight. There'll be other flights. . . . No, don't call Gunther. I'm coming. . . . Look, Bensy, call Los Angeles. Tell the doctor I'm going to make it. Have a limousine meet me at the airport at midnight. And be sure he understands about Christopher's mother. She is not to know. She is under no circumstances to be told. I'll deal with her later. . . . And emphasize that it must be kept out of the papers. After I get there I will make a statement to the press. Christopher has been working too hard, and he is in the hospital for a few days of much-needed rest. . . . I'll talk to his manager after I get there, the goddamn crook. No, I do not want him allowed in the hospital. Make that clear. Have him arrested if necessary. They don't need a charge. There is no crime of which the sonofabitch has not been guilty. Arrest him but do not allow him in the hospital. . . . Christopher's hands are all right. That's the important thing. Christopher's hands are the most important hands in the world. . . . It won't be easy, the doctor said. Okay, it won't be easy. A long, difficult fight, he said. All right. Long and difficult, but I'll be there the whole way. We're in this thing together, Christopher, the two of us. . . . Coming, love.